'*Greater Sins* is a glimmering debut. A muddy, pastoral fable written with an equal measure of beauty and morbidity...

Lucy Ro

'A striking

'Beguiling and eleg... ...unravels a tale of mystery and longing in captivating, unfurling prose that completely absorbs you. A book to sink into.'
Lucy Steeds, author of *The Artist*

'With her subtle use of dialect and plain yet evocative prose, Griffiths builds a haunting picture of a small, intense environment where isolation can breed solidarity and warmth as easily as superstition and exclusion.'
Financial Times

'The unearthing of a woman's body in a peat bog during the first world war is the catalyst for a gritty tale of secrets, guilt and desire . . . What begins as a rural mystery becomes, instead, an affecting love story . . . Griffiths' use of the vernacular vividly conveys the period . . . She writes well about forbidden desire, guilt and shame.'
Observer

'*Greater Sins* has an extraordinary sense of place and time, written by an exciting new voice from Scotland.'
Radio Times

www.penguin.co.uk

'An atmospheric and assured debut.'
Daily Mail

'A striking debut, filled with folkloric mystery and yearning. Griffiths' prose is as elegant as it is perceptive. Read it, then read it again.'
Amy Twigg, author of *Spoilt Creatures*

'I absolutely raced through it! What a beautiful book. The prose is so lyrical and the structure so cleverly pulls the reader along.'
Hanna Thomas Uose, author of *Who Wants to Live Forever*

'A haunting and extraordinary debut, which will stay with me for a long time . . . told in tender, sinuous prose, this is a simmering tale of outcasts and buried secrets, love and redemption. An incisive look at power and gender, Griffiths explores not just the darker impulses we share, but how we can find connection in unexpected places. This novel had me feeling silt between my toes and looking for ghosts in every shadow.'
Danielle Giles, author of *Mere*

'Stunning; every phrase, every sentence is like poetry. And the characters – they're complex, fascinating, and oh so relatable. A truly unforgettable read.'
Fiza Saeed McLynn, author of *The Midnight Carousel*

'Beautifully written. As the mystery of a woman's body found preserved in the peat bog unravels, we follow a darkly lyrical tale packed with secrets, intertwined relationships and a smattering of folklore . . . so compelling, I could almost feel the chill, and taste the drams.'
Emma Cowing, author of *The Show Woman*

GREATER SINS

Gabrielle Griffiths

PENGUIN BOOKS

TRANSWORLD PUBLISHERS

UK | USA | Canada | Ireland | Australia
India | New Zealand | South Africa

Transworld is part of the Penguin Random House group of companies
whose addresses can be found at global.penguinrandomhouse.com

Penguin Random House UK, One Embassy Gardens,
8 Viaduct Gardens, London SW11 7BW

penguin.co.uk

First published in Great Britain in 2025 by Doubleday
an imprint of Transworld Publishers
Penguin paperback edition published 2026

001

Copyright © Gabrielle Griffiths 2025

The moral right of the author has been asserted

This book is a work of fiction and, except in the case of historical fact, any
resemblance to actual persons, living or dead, is purely coincidental.

Every effort has been made to obtain the necessary permissions with
reference to copyright material, both illustrative and quoted. We apologize
for any omissions in this respect and will be pleased to make the
appropriate acknowledgments in any future edition.

No part of this book may be used or reproduced in any manner for the purpose of
training artificial intelligence technologies or systems. In accordance with Article 4(3)
of the DSM Directive 2019/790, Penguin Random House expressly
reserves this work from the text and data mining exception.

Typeset in Minion Pro by Falcon Oast Graphic Art Ltd.
Printed and bound in Great Britain by Clays Ltd, Elcograf S.p.A.

The authorized representative in the EEA is Penguin Random House Ireland,
Morrison Chambers, 32 Nassau Street, Dublin D02 YH68.

A CIP catalogue record for this book is available from the British Library.

ISBN: 9781804994214

Penguin Random House is committed to a sustainable
future for our business, our readers and our planet. This book is
made from Forest Stewardship Council® certified paper.

So when they continued asking him, he lifted up himself, and said unto them, He that is without sin among you, let him first cast a stone at her.

John 8:7

PART ONE

ROUND WHITSUNTIDE

May 1915

JOHNNY

A toast to himself for getting by unseen. Outside are the folks who'll want things from him – so first, alone, a drink. Johnny has his ritual: slip a hand round a cool glass, feel the weight as it rises heavenward. Agnes has lit the paraffin lamps despite the bright day and so he holds the dram before the light to admire its syruped beauty. He brings the whisky to his lips and pauses, lets the scent beguile him – peat-sweet, a sigh in the nose. But as Johnny opens his mouth to drink, something disturbs him. A noise slips under the door – a plaintive keening that starts low then swells like the river in spate. It is not a babby's cry but something wilder, the lavish wail of a woman. Johnny lowers his dram and waits – if there is trouble, it'll surely come strutting in. The cry rises higher, until the chatter outside ceases and it hovers in the air above the inn then stops, clipped.

'A sad day for someone,' Agnes says.

Johnny shrugs. The Cabrach is not a place for great displays of emotion – its people know hardship and they know loss, and it's expected they won't fall down weeping about either.

Outside, talk resumes. Johnny begins his routine again: the grasp, the lift, the tilt, then the first mouthful. A sharpness on the tip of the tongue; the land made liquid – the heather and the hay and the cold, clear water, the tang of the midden that gets into everything.

No trouble has found him.

Johnny takes his second sip quickly. A moment, and he will feel it in his shoulders. On the third, he realizes his fist is clenched. He waggles his fingers and tips his head back, a knot cutting into the soft flesh of his throat. He could forgo the neckerchief on such a fine day, but it is how folks know him – today a twist of sanguine. Could just as easily have been violet or ochre or turquoise – Johnny likes the way those words sound, the imagination in them. His kin round here like to tease him about the colours at his throat, but he pays no heed to loons with shirts like sheep, filthier the closer you get to them. He rolls his head, runs the pad of his thumb over the worn-smooth bar and the years of drink embedded there – beer from jubilant tankards, whisky from glasses smashed over wages or women. Johnny could lick it and fall down pished, probably.

Outside, engines start up. Some folks will surely be there more to witness the spectacle of two polished motor cars than to wish Godspeed to their soldiers – little excitement to be had here, the arse-end of nowhere, an hour's walk between every croft. That, and they'll be glad of a break from their labours – today, the Cabrach's pastures will go unsown, the peat half-cut. The cars move off, raking up the track, and must only have got as far as the bridge over the Black Water when the door clatters open. Sunlight sloshes across the floorboards and here they come, proud as provosts and replete with drink. The landlord tops up glasses as they pile in – not his best stuff, mind, but a free dram is always a fine thing.

'A toast!' someone cries. 'A toast to our good men!'

Johnny takes in the lie of the land: a rabble of farm lads, bellies jangling with ale – they'll want his wit and a song or three. Then the auld men, who'll settle at the hearth and beckon him with hooked fingers, whispering for ghost stories. The men fill the air with pipe smoke, and Johnny pretends not to notice someone hollering his name. Rab is here, a head above the others, and it pleases Johnny to see a smile on his friend's face. He rolls his shirtsleeves up and necks his last mouthful.

'I should have known he'd be here.' Johnny's earlobe is pinched hard and he whips round to a faceful of Dougie's spittle. 'Where were you this afternoon, then?'

Johnny stays quiet, for that is their game. Jock Campbell is here for a turn too, his neepie head emerging from behind Dougie's shoulder. 'I thought he'd be halfway tae Dufftown, off singing for his supper.'

'I'll bet he was lying wretched in his bed. Heavy night last night, eh, Johnny?'

Neither accusation is true, but that is not what matters. Johnny reaches out and twists Dougie's red nose. 'You ought tae stay out of my business.' He turns to Jock. 'And you and all.'

'It's nae like you to miss such a thing as this.'

'But it is like him tae pass the time of day at the inn while the rest of us get on.'

The two farmers splutter their mirth, and Johnny regards them in affectionate irritation – it has all been said before. He lays a hand to Jock's shoulder. 'Come on then, tell me what happened.'

They take their usual chairs at the hearth, the cushions so knackered they bear the shape of the farmers' arses: Jock's, hefty off his good land and his wife's good suppers; Dougie's so narrow his breeks drop off him, for the main reason he opens his lips is to wrap them round a bottle. Sinclair, who scrapes a living from a stony plot of land near the kirk, is here too. He's allowed himself a sensible wee nip and a few minutes of leisure, though he'll no doubt rise at four in the morn to atone for it. When he sees the others he folds his paper carefully and sets it down square at the edge of the table. The news is days old, of course, by the time it reaches them, the latest from the front at a remove that makes the war seem to Johnny to be distant, unreal.

'Right,' says Jock, settling himself. 'This is how it went. The men came down and gathered outside – six of them, though you surely know that. The wee one tried the first speech, God love him—'

'—No, Mysie came darting round with flowers first.'

Sinclair tuts. 'That woman.' He eyes Johnny, as though she is somehow his fault. There is quiet for a moment, each man absorbed in discontent – whether they rue the inheritance of Mac's hundred acres by *that woman*, or picture with dread the single audacious hair that sprouts from her chin, is not for Johnny to know.

'Fair enough – white heather for luck, speedwell tae haste the journey.' Jock holds his hand up, a concession to Mysie's charms.

Sinclair looks askance. 'Prayer is what they need. And luckily our good Reverend was there to give it to them.'

Johnny slips a finger behind his neckerchief, loosens it a touch. The air is close, a fug of muck and stodge, the heat of the day in a hundred armpits. 'That's all well and good,' he says, 'but I want tae know what that scream was about.' Across the room, Johnny signals to Agnes for an ale. He will give the men a moment to assemble the story.

Jock leans forward. 'That was William Calder's wife. Folks were saying their goodbyes and she opened her mouth and howled like a banshee. It was as if someone had stood on a cat's tail – I've never heard the like.'

'And they say the wealthy have more dignity.'

'I wouldnae have expected that of her,' Sinclair says. 'What I've seen of her at kirk – she seems a quiet wee thing.'

'Och, but would you nae be hysterical if you were her? Her husband off tae fight.'

'And as good a man as that.'

Johnny hasn't properly seen or spoken to the man Calder, but understands he comes from some high-born line, lives in the stoic granite house by the Black Water. He owns the inn, but doesn't lower himself to drink in it. Johnny has peered at him in his motor car, flitting from business in Huntly or Elgin, and has doffed his cap at the roadside, but Mr Calder always speeds by, his face a blur.

'No one made him go,' says Dougie.

Jock wags a finger. 'Soon enough they'll call up the married men, you mark me on that.'

'Maybe nae you though, they'll nae get a helmet the right shape for your head.' Johnny looks to the others for a laugh, but they're strangely sober for now. He meets Sinclair's eye and the farmer takes a tight sip of his bitter.

'Disnae seem right tae me, married men feeling they need to go. They should round up all the rest of them first.'

Agnes has left Johnny's drink on the table and he picks up the tankard and studies himself closely in its side. The scuffed surface warps him, makes him dull and edgeless. From the corner of his eye, he sees Sinclair's pursed lips twitching under his moustache. Can always tell the state of that man by what his mouth's doing, and it's seldom smiling.

'You ought tae join up, Johnny, though I cannae see you in army gear.' Sinclair eyes Johnny's neckerchief, his good white shirt, as though he considers it a vanity to try to keep yourself clean in this place of filth and labour. Johnny ignores him; it seems inevitable he will end up knee-deep in mud eventually, whether it be toiling on the land or shuddering in a trench somewhere. This lot talk as though the only place a man might find his honour is in the ground.

'Aye, no excuse if you're young and single,' says Dougie, nudging Johnny's shin with the toe of his boot.

'I'm nae so much a whippersnapper as I look, gents.'

'You're nae yet thirty.'

'Nae too far off it. And only a bachelor as long as I want to be.' Johnny keeps his voice light, as though it has floated away from the weight in his chest. He casts about again for a smirk to be returned, then shrugs at their stony indifference and shifts position in the lumpy chair. Sinclair carries on staring his reproach but Johnny looks pointedly beyond him towards the back of the room where the farm loons rove, loose-limbed, jostling about as laddies do. He wants his fun while it's going. Johnny catches sight of the resplendent red beard of Alex, Rab's first ploughman, and watches him for a moment until their eyes meet. Alex grins and it is all Johnny needs. He excuses himself, touching a hand to Sinclair's shoulder. 'Have nae fear, my man. They winnae call you.'

Shoving his way through the crowd, Johnny picks over the young faces. He knows most of them. Most have agreed to bide this Whitsuntide term, which is not surprising – with so many off to fight, those who have stayed can name their price. There are a few newcomers, edgy lads who posture half in shadow. They are watching, getting the measure of the rest: who can be trusted, who is a cheat, who can be relied on for a dram and a fine time. They get the odd rogue in the Cabrach – in such a faraway place, either you're here because you were born so, or because you came to get away.

Alex slings a friendly arm round Johnny's shoulders. 'Didnae see you there when they left.'

Johnny gives the lads an angel's smile. 'I was otherwise engaged.' Knowing his audience, he leaves it at that and shoots the new loons a final glance, satisfied that he recognizes none of them.

'Here,' Alex calls, 'anyone see what lassie was missing this afternoon?'

There are sniggers: this is the type of banter they come for.

'That should be your first story, Johnny.'

'There's no story there lads, I'm sorry tae say. I've a good one about a horse trader at Tomintoul, but there's time for all that. I want tae know what happened at the market.'

Lads wet their lips and get the facts straight in their heads, or whichever facts will give the best tale. In the niches and neuks of The Pheasant, gossip tends along common lines – money made and lost, seed scattered where it shouldn't be. As they ready themselves for their tattling, Johnny turns to Alex. 'Rab get his second ploughman?'

'Arrived this morning.'

'Where is he then?'

'Back at the farm. Knackered fae the journey, supposedly. Said he was still suffering on account of his send-off the night before.'

Johnny snorts, for a wicked headache and green stomach are no excuse not to show your face at the inn. 'How far's he come from, like?'

'Up Nairn way.'

'Oh aye? He's always been up there? How old is he?' Johnny takes a sup of his ale, too much, so it slops over his lip and makes quick progress through his beard.

Alex shrugs. 'No idea, a few years younger than you?' He is distracted by a whoop from beyond them, where another gang has pushed back tables and formed a circle, making drums of their breeks.

Johnny calls over the caper. 'Did he say which farms?'

The tempo is established, quick and jittery, a thud of boots on the boards. Alex opens his mouth but only to yell some goading words at the dancers.

'Alex – did he say which farms?'

Before he gets his answer, Johnny's wrist is seized from behind and a calloused thumb presses to the smooth place where his pulse beats. 'Come and do us a tune, Johnny.'

*

He has done six or seven songs and his throat hurts. Johnny's voice starts supple as good leather, but after a few, bellowing over the rabble, he gets hoarse. He has sung the usual ballads of bastard grieves and snide farmers, bonny lasses with golden hair, though the lads scoffed at that. *Tell us about her tits!* one of them called, and Johnny laughed but thought – use your imagination, boy. He sinks now beside the fire, weighted by booze and exertion. As the sky outside slipped past gloaming-pink the auld men had dragged themselves off home, then the gangs had gone too, down the tracks to drink ropey whisky in their scattered crofts.

At the inn, the party is over. Johnny is with Rab, ending the evening as they always do – Johnny and Rab at the hearth, melting into companionable silence. Rab is what anyone would call a decent man. He works hard and treats his men and beasts well, provides for his family, is sensible with his coin but will stand any man a drink. He dons his Sabbath best each week at kirk. Rab Stuart bounces his bairns on his lap, plays the fiddle with passable competency and, Johnny imagines, at the end of a long day he might take his wife's work-worn hands in his own and rub the ache from them.

'I hear your new second's come a long way – strange for lads to travel all that distance,' says Johnny. 'What farm was he at before?'

'Och, one of those that sounds like the grimmest of places on God's earth.'

Course, they all do up there, names made of words like cold and bleak and windy. Johnny considers. 'Has he references?' He looks at his friend, who frowns at the dwindling fire.

'There wisnae much choice. If you'd turned up this afternoon you could have sussed him out yourself. He went away soon after the cars left – tired fae the journey, he said. And he said he would forgo his liquor tonight in order to make a good impression at kirk.'

'Is that so?'

Rab manages a smirk. 'Aye, I know. It was a case of take what you could get. You couldnae move for khaki jackets trying tae make farmhands into soldiers. But the lad seems fine enough. A bit timid, maybe. You'll meet him at kirk anyway.'

Johnny lifts his head and goes to speak, but Rab does it for him. 'You're nae coming tae kirk, aye, I know fine well. Monday then, come up and help with that fence?'

Already Johnny has lightly disappointed Rab with his reluctance to rise for Sunday service and it seems easiest not to refuse him anything else. When he agrees, something slackens around his friend's eyes.

'I worry, Johnny. What if I cannae get the labour? What if Alex joins up? I cannae do much more myself.'

'It'll be fine. There's plenty dinnae want tae go.'

'It winnae be a case of want, at this rate.'

'Aye, but even if they start calling men up, they cannae take everyone – we still need workers.'

'They'll get the lassies in tae the fields then. There's already been a meeting in Keith about it.' Rab sighs. 'You're off wandering this year then?'

It has been playing on Johnny's mind. The last trip, war just declared – it hadn't been the same. Before, it seemed noble enough to make his living through music and laughter, shaking folks loose. But the last time there had been a futility to having nothing in his hand but a dram. Johnny realizes that Rab is watching closely for his answer and is unsure what to say – instead he drinks, as the final clod of peat in the hearth cleaves and drops, taking the moment with it.

The friends stand, Rab mumbling about work to do in the morn. They do their usual routine – the reach to shake hands, but then there is the ah-go-on-then grin and their arms clamping round each other. When Rab pulls back there is a delicate set to his lips, a seriousness not usually there at this time of night, and in Johnny's chest something clenches. It is aching, strange – surely just the acid swill of whisky making pain at his heart.

LIZZIE

She'd thought it a nice touch, that howl. It had unspooled quite naturally from her mouth, volume increasing in direct correlation to the alarm seeping across her husband's face. Folks paused mid-sentence, shuffled their feet, accepting Lizzie's performance as touchingly heartfelt. Jane, though, was clearly unconvinced and, when it came down to it, neither woman had cried as William Calder ducked into the car and, with a curt raise of his palm, slammed the door closed.

Despite Lizzie's dry cheeks, one of the farmer's wives had broken rank and come to lay a tentative hand on her shoulder as the motors started up. *So brave, so noble*, this woman whispered. Folks had cupped their hands over their eyes and watched until the cars crossed over the Black Water and slipped from sight. William drove, being one of the few who could, and Lizzie wondered if he would slow to let the lads toss an offering over the bridge. Before the burn reaches its namesake – the Calders' house – it diverges around a small island, unremarkable aside from the superstition some folks hold over it. They lavish the island with coins, silvers glinting under bent brown grass, and ask for prosperity or protection. William doesn't believe in such things, and some might call that a shame, for he has cash enough to be richly blessed with both. Lizzie had swatted an errant fly from her arm and closed her eyes against the sun. It was a fine and bright day, when her husband went to war.

The men had soon grown eager to retreat to the inn, away from the sniffling women, and pressed their way through the door, gruff with pride for their soldiers. The Reverend Bruce then appeared like an apparition beside Lizzie and Jane, a flush in his neck; he'd taken a nip. 'Godly women. How courageous you are to let him go.' He had touched Lizzie's wrist with fingers cold despite the mild day.

'It was what he wanted.'

'Then you are faithful to obey him.' Reverend Bruce bestowed a peaceable smile. 'An excellent wife is the crown of her husband.'

Jane leaned in. 'Proverbs 12:4, Reverend.' Her voice was tinged with something that could have been pride, were that not a sin.

'Indeed, you know your scriptures. But I would expect nothing less of a sister of William Calder. A most excellent man, a credit to his community.' The Reverend looked expectantly at Lizzie.

'Truly,' she said.

'I will pray for him every night – and for you both,' he added, before making off to get round the rest of his flock. Lizzie wondered idly if the man ever slept, with the great list of prayers he had to work through: goodness, salvation, deliverance from temptation, along with the more bodily concerns of his congregation – rheumatism, chilblains, hoary coughs – and all the woes of land and labour.

'Come on,' said Jane. 'We'll go away home.'

In truth, Lizzie had wanted to stay awhile longer in the sunshine, amongst the chatter. But folks were already drifting away, women headed down the track in twos and threes; those women she knew little of beyond nods at kirk, the good mornings they'd say before she took her seat in the Calder pew.

'Come.' Jane took Lizzie by the arm. To an onlooker, perhaps the motion might have appeared tender, sisterly. But Lizzie felt the strength of Jane's grip, the fingers that pressed into her flesh as they started in the direction of the house.

'We stand for three things.' Jane pauses to check her sister-in-law is listening. 'Prayer, purity and temperance.'

Miss Gow declares a decisive amen. The housekeeper and Jane sit on either side of the parlour fireplace, the latter in Lizzie's usual chair. In their plain dark skirts with their feet neatly crossed, they remind Lizzie of the snooty pair of porcelain dogs that had sat on her mother's mantelpiece.

'Now then,' says Jane, 'if you want to make yourself useful while William is away, why not help me set up a Women's League here? It'll be good company, and a support for those with sons gone – sheep need a shepherd, as these farmers' wives should know. I've already had some interest from Mistress Sinclair.'

Lizzie sits with her feet up on the chaise, dabbing at a crumb of scone on her tea plate. 'What were the three things, remind me?'

Jane repeats them slowly, as though speaking to a child of low wit, and Lizzie considers how well such virtues might be upheld by the women of the Cabrach. They certainly pray with zeal each Sabbath, a chorus to the men's pleas for clement weather and strong crops. Purity, she cannot be sure – Miss Gow gripes often of maids who allow themselves to be wooed by handsome ploughmen, who fee for six months then leave them with a swelling belly. Temperance, well – not here, where the river runs half whisky.

'Actually, I—'

Jane raises an eyebrow.

'I have other plans.' Lizzie has not rehearsed this. 'I've heard they're looking for volunteers for the moss-gathering. They use it in bandages, supposedly – something special about it that helps absorb the blood.'

The other eyebrow lifts to meet its fellow. 'Hardly a place where one ought to find a woman of your standing, Elizabeth, delving about in a bog.'

'The war affects all of us. We all must pitch in.'

'You'll be covered in muck.'

Jane has clearly forgotten, having not visited the Cabrach in a long while, that being covered in muck is a frequent occurrence, when the rain turns the tracks to loose slugs of mud, and Blackwater House's lawn to marshland. Dirt hardly troubles Lizzie any more – it is a long time since she arrived in soft town shoes, dithering by the puddles as William strode to the front door in his stout boots.

'It is good work,' she replies. 'It will gratify me, knowing that it helps the men.'

'Stuffing moss into bandages seems an odd idea to me.' Jane sighs with a deep strength of feeling; she is suspicious of nature encroaching upon civilized society. 'You'd be better off doing something a bit less . . . physical.'

Lizzie looks down at her lap. 'Fine. It was only an idea.'

'No, you carry on. It sounds as though you'd made up your mind long before you told me. You always were strong-willed.' It is not a compliment, but has an air of concession at least.

Lizzie resists a smile, for in truth her name is already on the volunteer list. 'I just feel I ought to do something.'

Miss Gow agrees. 'Aye, better that than nothing. I saw that man by the burn again earlier, wandering around, writing in a notebook. Havering,' she spits, as though it is a deplorable sin.

'Making the most of a fine day, I expect,' Lizzie says.

The housekeeper rolls her eyes. 'Havering. He ought tae join up, if he's got time on his hands.'

'Some men just aren't much into fighting, I suppose.'

'Tough! He was trussed up with a red ribbon round his neck and all. Where he gets the coin for that nonsense is beyond me.'

'He's the singer, isn't he?' Lizzie has heard him mentioned by the pious folks who sit in the kirk's front pews. He is said, begrudgingly, to have a fine voice and feet slick at the two-step, but otherwise to be of a worldly nature, with the soft palms of an idler.

'Aye, dreadful philanderer, so I hear.'

Jane twists in her chair and looks out of the window, as though the rogue may yet be loitering. Chance would be a fine thing – no one ever comes to Blackwater House. It is too much of a traipse, even by Cabrach standards, down a track of its own and elevated so the dormers in the roof look like haughty eyes peering down the valley. Lizzie is used to sitting in the parlour of an evening with only the hiss of the gas for company. There are no visitors and she has no friends – facts she can baldly acknowledge because they have been true a long time. She had tried, when they'd arrived here, but what must folks have thought – Lizzie only eighteen, a newly-wed better off than men who'd toiled until their knees gave out.

Jane turns back round. 'Well, not to worry about that. I'll be here to guard against any ruffians who might turn up.' She smiles at her own joke and it makes her look younger, barely altered from the family wedding photo on the occasional table. It is William who has changed in the decade since: spreading further, shedding his hair. He has grown a beard, a dark thing that masses on his face and makes him nearly unrecognizable from when Lizzie married him.

Jane stands. 'Right. I'll go up and get unpacked.' She straightens the cushion on her chair, brushes something from the arm. 'Miss Gow, we'll eat in the dining room at seven, please.'

'The meal's usually ready for six, but—'

'Yes,' says Lizzie, 'I've always preferred it earlier.'

'Seven, please.'

Miss Gow nods. 'I'll come and take your bags upstairs.'

'Oh no, don't trouble yourself. I'll manage.'

*

After dinner, Lizzie is summoned to Jane's bedroom. She waits in the doorway while Jane finishes hanging her clothes in the wardrobe, smoothing the wrinkles from her blouses. 'Did you need something, Jane? I was going to have an early night.'

Jane turns. 'Are you unwell? A sore throat? All that shrieking earlier.' She gives a pinched smile.

'A bit of a stomach ache,' Lizzie says. 'Eating late doesn't agree with me.'

'Well, you'll get used to it.' Jane looks around, surveying her new kingdom. She has mostly unpacked – her Bible on the bedside table, the shelf above the washbasin arranged with the small vanities of a comb and a jar of cold cream.

'Are you settled in?' Lizzie asks.

'Aye, I'll be comfortable. This is the room I used to stay in when I was wee.'

'Of course – I always forget you used to come here.' It seems strange to Lizzie that the young Calders ran around this house; she cannot envision Blackwater as a place filled with children, gaiety. Her husband told her when they'd arrived as newlyweds that her bedroom was where he used to sleep when he came on hunting trips as a young man. She has imagined him there, the sweat dried on his back and trousers flecked with blood, ears ringing with the sound of shot and the whimpering of some unfortunate animal, chased to exhaustion. Lizzie had once asked William for stories of his summers in the Cabrach, but he had wiped the breakfast crumbs from his lips and stood, declaring there was nothing to tell.

'Listen, I hope you don't mind me coming to stay?' Jane barely waits for the shake of Lizzie's head. 'Of course, I might need to go back if there's any urgent business, but in the meantime . . . well, I'm happy to be able to do this for you.'

'It's good of you.'

'It'll keep you out of trouble, anyway.' Jane gives her breathy little laugh. It is not clear why she decided to come. In recent years Jane has seldom visited the Cabrach, akin to her brother in preferring the comforts of town. William had simply announced it one day, said that he and Jane felt Lizzie ought not to be left alone.

'Not much of that out here.'

'I daresay. Anyway, I wanted to give you something, wait while I find it.' Jane picks up a leather document case and produces an envelope, which she holds out to Lizzie. 'William's will, God forbid it be needed. I thought, as his wife, that you should keep it.'

'Oh.' Lizzie finds it oddly inauspicious to hold such a thing, when her husband is not splayed on some battlefield but has only gone as far as the Keith Drill Hall. When the woman touched her shoulder at the inn and asked her how it felt to see William march off to war, Lizzie had hesitated. She has grown used to her husband's absence. Over the years, his trips to town have become more frequent, William returning with a smugness to him, and perhaps for a day or two he'll be talkative – comments at the breakfast table that he positions as inconsequential, off-the-cuff: *I daresay, Elizabeth, you'd like some of the fashions the women in Elgin are sporting.* Or: *I always feel invigorated after a trip to town, it is so dull here.* She does not ask him to take her – he would refuse – and besides, there is little in Elgin for Lizzie now that some other family live in the big house her father once bought.

'Thank you, Jane – let us hope it is not needed soon.'

'Let us *pray* not,' says Jane. 'Now, I'll let you get off to bed. It has been a big day for you.'

In her bedroom, Lizzie turns the will over in her hands. The envelope is weighty, the paper thick and finely textured, sealed with the Calder crest – a buck's head mounted on a shield, regarded from above by a proud crowned swan and a knight hidden beneath his helmet. Underneath, in minuscule calligraphy, the family motto: *vigilans non cadit*, the vigilant man falls not. Lizzie can picture her husband preparing all this – removing his signet ring and pressing it hard into the oozing wax. She edges a fingernail round the seal, finds it stuck firm at first, but she works her way underneath and once one side has lifted the rest follows easily. Lizzie peels up the flap of the envelope, careful to make no sound, for Jane's ears will surely prick up at any sign of transgression. The paper yields, then tears, and Lizzie flinches – she will not be able to hide her tampering now. She can imagine William's expression, how it might snap from blithe amusement to anger – *wishing me dead were you, darling?* But she carries on, sliding the paper from its envelope:

The Last Will and Testament of William Hugh Calder

I, William Hugh Calder, of Blackwater House, Cabrach, Moray, hereby revoke all former wills made by me and declare this will be my last will.

1. I appoint my sister, Jane Mary Calder, of Cramond House, Elgin, Moray, to be the executor and trustee of my will. Should she have pre-deceased me or be unable or unwilling to act, I appoint, in the following order of priority, one of the persons hereinafter: my father, Hugh Calder, of Cramond House, Elgin, Moray, and my cousin, Douglas Mackenzie Calder, of The Manse, St Michaels, Elgin, Moray.

2. I give my residence, Blackwater House, to my sister, Jane Mary Calder, with the instruction that the property be held in perpetuity in the Calder family.

3. The remainder of my monetary and physical assets I give to my sister, Jane Mary Calder.

4. I direct my executors to organize the management of the business affairs for which I am responsible on behalf of the Calder family, namely:

> i. *The Pheasant public house, Cabrach, Moray*
> ii. *The farms and estates of Cauldbraes, Nairn, Moray; Mains of Burnhead, Nairn, Moray; Greenloan, Nairn, Moray; and Boghead, Nairn, Moray*
> iii. *Those tenants as reside at the above properties*
> 5. *I request that from my monetary assets a suitable sum be provided as a pension in support of my spouse, Elizabeth Christina Calder. I request my executors to determine a sum that is sufficient to keep her until her decease.*

Lizzie hastily scans the rest: a fussy inventory of crofts and houses and fixtures, carefully listed in case anyone should try to claim something that belongs to a Calder. The fifth point perturbs her, of course – Jane's presence at Blackwater is clearly less an act of sisterly kindness than a watchful eye. Perhaps Jane will record misdemeanours in an exercise book, noting down slipped blasphemies, uncharitable comments, not singing loudly enough at kirk – things that will count against Lizzie, feathers plucked from a nest.

Lizzie throws the papers across the room. The will flutters to the carpet while its envelope – weighted by the broken seal – smacks against the wall. Immediately, she gets up. It was an impulsive move, and her hands shake as she gathers up the pages and slips them back into the envelope. She presses the split wax together and holds the nub of a candle to it, cursing as the heat reaches her fingers. The wax melts; the Calder crest is indistinct. Lizzie's eyes sting, but she isn't going to cry about it.

JOHNNY

Johnny dawdles his way to Brawlands. The day is close, sticky heat like a caul on his skin, and he tells himself this is why he's slow – that, or the lingering effects of his night at the inn. It is another fine spring day, the braes a green blanket, torn here and there to show the dark peat underneath. His shadow is thrown long on the track behind him, following him to the farm.

Johnny lets himself into the yard. Rab's farm is an assembly of blue-doored buildings, with the stables facing south so the sun might seep in and warm the horses, the midden positioned so the wind snatches the stink of manure and carries it away over the pastures. At the centre of it all is the honest wee farmhouse, solid granite with small square windows hung with gingham curtains. Johnny peers through one, past a jug of yarrow that Maggie has set out. It pleases him that she has found time in the cycle of washing and cooking, darning and mending and churning – the lot of the farmer's wife – to pick the frothy plumes and put them there as greeting.

Johnny lingers a moment to watch the gang at work in the top pasture – the broad back of Stephen the orra-man, Alex's red beard. And there is another figure: the new second ploughman, must be. Johnny squints against the sun; he's wondered what type of lad would sooner traipse from Nairn to the back of beyond rather than go off to fight. The newcomer is a lanky thing, though he moves with a certain determination in the rhythmic turning of his hoe, hauling up creeping thistle. That tenacious stuff grew in the front yard of Johnny's ma's old house, and he thinks of her standing with her feet set wide, yanking at it and cursing when the stalk snapped but the roots remained in the ground. *That'll be back*, she'd say, eyeing the thistle as though it might already be plotting its return.

Johnny goes to the barn and sticks his head round the open door. 'Rab?'

The farmer calls a greeting before emerging from the gloom. 'Ah, Johnny, thanks for coming up. As it happens we've sorted that fence – it was only a couple of loose posts in the end, praise the Lord.'

'You're lucky. That was an ill wind blew in the other night.' Brawlands is an exposed place: high ground, few trees. Most of the Cabrach's farms have their afflictions. Dougie's land is boggy, prone to sudden floods when the rain comes on strong or the Deveron goes over, and Sinclair works a tract of land so stony and undernourished that even kail can barely be arsed to take root there. For Rab it's the hoolies that blow in off the braes, so that fences and saplings and tottering calves will fall clean over.

'Long may my good fortune continue,' the farmer says. 'I think I've made a decent pick with my new second and all. He's tougher than he looks, and if there's one thing I need it's good hard workers.'

Johnny toes at the dust on the barn floor. 'Have you anything else that needs doing, then?' He has been considering his own profession, such as it is – the jigging and singing and stamping his feet, and his rewards after, when the bar is lined with nips and tankards and maybe some soft fingers come to graze his shirtsleeves.

Rab laughs. 'Always something tae be done.'

'I just mean . . .' Johnny's mouth is dry, and again he will blame the whisky, but he's made up his mind, he thinks. 'I was thinking I'd stay this summer. You could do with the extra hands.'

'Och, dinnae stay on account of me.' Rab shifts, looks behind him as though for a task needing his attention.

'It'd be a pleasure, my man.'

'Well then.' Rab takes Johnny's hand, then thinks the better of it, pulls him into a brusque embrace. 'Thank you.' He steps back, a brightness in his eyes that Johnny hadn't noticed before. 'Now, come away in. Maggie does a fine dinner for the workers.'

Johnny follows behind, thinking how absurd it is that he'd tussled half the night with the decision, reluctant to stick a stake in the ground instead of letting himself be carried wherever the wind sees fit. Maybe it'll be satisfying to work to some common aim with the lads he can see toiling up the slope, bathed in strident sunlight. The new ploughman is caught in profile and for a moment there is a familiarity to him, the angles of his cheeks, but it's hard to tell. Johnny looks away; he'll meet the loon soon enough.

In the kitchen, Johnny greets Maggie with a bow, deep and flamboyant enough that she tuts and tells him to get up. Rab's wife's a good woman who welcomed Johnny when he arrived in the Cabrach those few years back, knowing no one. He likes to joke that it was her stovies that convinced him to stay, and she'll admonish him, blushing. Maggie stirs her broth and bustles from sink to side, chopping kail and spreading yellow butter on their bannocks, pausing once to let her husband press a kiss to the nape of her neck. It must be nice to have that uncomplicated comfort with someone, Johnny thinks, sure he's never seen it come as easy as it does between Rab Stuart and his wife.

'I've tae feed one more, do I?' Maggie asks.

'Aye, if you dinnae mind.'

'Course nae. You're always welcome, Johnny – especially if you're putting yourself tae some use.'

Maggie begins to ladle out the broth, while Rab goes to the door to call the gang. Johnny can see them coming down the pasture, Alex first and then the orra-man, and the newcomer last. He hurries behind the other two with a strange gait – his stride long, chin jutting first, then body following. Johnny feels another jab of recognition, but isn't this just last night's drink and all – his world not quite tipped back the right way up. Alex comes in, grins at Johnny, then Stephen fills the doorway with his great barrel chest, bellowing his hello. Then finally, the second. Rab claps a hand on this shoulder. 'Come in, come in. Come and meet Johnny.'

The man lifts the cap from his head as he steps in, but before Johnny can get a look he's turned to close the door behind him. The back of his neck is to the room, hair shaved closed to the skin, a tarnished chain fastened round. Johnny follows the line of it as the man turns – a sick old gold, hung with a crucifix that rests in the pit of a clavicle. Not often you'd see such a thing on a ploughman. Johnny looks up at his face.

And it is Johnny who loses his colour first. He blinks hard and looks again, feeling suddenly as though his lips are numb and his blood's stilled and someone's playing a devious fucking trick on him, because this is a man he recognizes. Those searching eyes, set deep in a face that has squared and tightened, but still, Johnny knows it. In his mind he gives a yelping prayer to whoever that he's wrong, and gets up to offer his hand. 'Johnny.'

'Johnny,' the man repeats.

For a moment, Johnny thinks he might have got away with it – that time has scrubbed his memory, the lad meeting so many men on the farms that their faces have overwritten each other, merged into something foggy and formless. Johnny is different now, too – he has grown a beard, grown up; he is older, better.

But he sees the very second that recognition hooks the cheek of the other man. The newcomer mutters his name and of course it is him: Henry.

They shake hands: an artless jerk, quick withdrawal, but their eyes linger. All the things Johnny might remember if he cared to think of them – the loon's egg-freckled skin, the thick bottom lip that always looked like it had not long been punched. Henry still bites his nails – they are ragged, down to the quick – and it strikes Johnny that people never change as much as you think they might.

Rab sits down at the table, gives a vague gesture for the others to join him. 'Where is it you were fee'd again, Henry? Johnny was asking the other day when I said you were from up Nairn way.'

'Oh, well, a few places up there.' Henry sits carefully at the table, clasps his hands in his lap. 'Most recently I was at Weariefauld and Cauldbraes. I started as an orra-loon at a farm called Windyhillock, though it's nae running any more, far as I know.' He glances at Johnny, and for a moment it seems like he might slip a question, but mercifully Alex speaks.

'You didnae bide long at any, then?'

Henry looks unsure, for he'll know as well as any of them the things said of a ploughman with too many fees. 'I . . . well, I like the freedom I suppose.'

'I should hope you'll be taking it in mind tae settle a bit now, lad your age,' says Rab. 'What are you, twenty-two?'

The loon looks down. 'Twenty-five, Mr Stuart. And aye, settling down is what I'd thought.'

The men lapse into silence as Maggie sets their bowls down and they dig in, ravenous from their labour. Johnny tries to suss out the loon, surreptitiously, through the steam coming up from the broth. Henry is taller now but still has that same leanness, all rope and knuckle, like the unsteady legs of a lamb. It's a mystery how the lad's got to second ploughman without laying on any bulk, but maybe there's strength in him somewhere. Rab wipes his mouth with the back of his hand and gestures at Johnny with a torn piece of bannock. 'Johnny's helping over the summer, though it's nae his usual thing, so you'll have tae show him the way.'

Henry, bowed over his dish as though he's at prayer, looks up. 'What do you normally do then, Johnny?'

'In the winter I pick up odd bits of labouring, if I can find them, and in the summer I make my living from music, travelling round the inns, doing the dances and that.'

'A singer?'

'Good guess,' says Rab. 'You'll no doubt hear one soon enough.' Stephen smirks. 'He's got all sorts, writes them himself.'

'What type of songs?' Henry watches him steadily, looks down to where Johnny's left hand is resting on the table. He takes in the twisted skin, ham-pink, and Johnny moves it away.

'Just the old ballads. You like music?'

'Only the hymns at kirk. I dinnae have much of a voice.'

Johnny doesn't think it needs replying to, instead prods at a lump of tattie in his broth and regrets the stupid grasp at decency that compelled him to come to Brawlands and offer to stay. He realizes, after a moment, that Henry is still looking at him.

'Have you been fee'd before, then?' the loon asks.

It is too much. Johnny sets the spoon down on the table and stands. 'I'm sorry, Rab. I've, ah . . . I've an errand I'd forgotten about.'

The farmer frowns. 'Eh? You'll finish your dinner first?'

Johnny concedes to a final mouthful, bending awkwardly over the bowl so that the broth slops off the spoon and on to his shirt. 'Sorry, Maggie – delicious.'

'You'll come again in the morn though?' Rab asks.

Johnny nods, pulling his cap down over his brow and promising, despite the screaming urge not to, that he'll return.

*

Mysie looks up from her knitting as Johnny comes in. 'You look like you've seen a ghost, loon. And you're home early? Was Rab pleased tae have you staying for the summer?'

Johnny hangs up his coat and pretends not to have heard, keen to retreat upstairs to his room. He had stood in the kitchen doorway that morning with a dopey grin on his face, telling Mysie his plan, and she'd looked pleased and all, told him it was the right thing to do.

'Well?'

Johnny sighs. 'I was thinking I'd maybe go travelling after all.' He still has his back to Mysie, but can practically hear the rolling of her eyes.

'Sit down, loon.'

His landlady is formidable; has had to be, with the things folks say about her – though maybe they'd simmer down if only the woman had ever learned to still her salted tongue and show up to kirk once in a while. As she hasn't, she's a fertile seam for local claik – Mysie, who'd turned up twenty years ago as auld Mac's new wife, three grown daughters at her heel and somehow one fair, one dark and one a redhead. She surely knows what it is to have a past, though Johnny's not about to talk to her of his. He slumps in the armchair by the range, burying his feet in the rag rug. Mysie sets down a half-made sock and eyes him.

'Now, I'm nae having you flitting. You've said you'll stay, and stay you will – you've a duty to Rab now.'

Johnny flinches; he hates words like that, weighted with expectation. Duty has always struck him as having little to distinguish it from burden. 'Och, he'll manage – the loons he has are fine enough. I'm nae sure I've got it in me.'

'Where are you going, then – off tae fight?' Mysie's eyebrow is raised just so.

Johnny reaches down the side of the chair for his pipe and tobacco. He rarely smokes, not liking the way the stench gets into his clothes and hair, but sometimes he needs it. He plucks a fat clump of tobacco between thumb and forefinger, presses it into the bowl. He'll let Mysie say her piece.

'Come on, you might nae be as strong as the others now, but you'll soon get going. You know fine well, Johnny, that if you go off jigging round the inns, you'll have a wretched time because you'll be thinking of Rab, out at the hairst and needing the extra hands. Even I'll be heaving my bones uphill for the moss-gathering, so maybe you ought tae stick around and make yourself useful. You dinnae want folks accusing you of idleness.' She chuckles at this.

Johnny takes a hefty first draw of the pipe, fills his lungs to bursting, then exhales. The taste of the smoke reminds him of being a much younger man – how he'd take pipe after pipe with the other farm lads until his mouth watered with the need to cough. The rank black phlegm he'd spit into a handkerchief as soon as the lamp went out. 'I can do what I like.' It comes out more vehement than he'd intended.

'Well, dinnae come crying tae me when folks speak ill of you for flitting.' Mysie takes up her knitting again.

Johnny's ma would have told him to do what made him happy, and he's quite sure toiling through the summer with Henry Boyle won't do that. But the last time he'd been off roving he'd struggled to enjoy it; there had been something seedy about his midday bedsheets, the dingy places he'd sung in as folks muttered of war. The inns were either lifeless with fusty auld men, too knackered to dance, or lined with thick-necked brutes who'd eye Johnny for a scrap. Johnny had found himself skulking up to bed each night with a bottle in hand, to drink until his eyes gave out.

His da would tell him to put duty over personal contentment, that if you'd made a vow you ought to stick with it. His da might have been on to something, Johnny reluctantly concedes, although when he'd made his decision last night, he hadn't reckoned on turning up at Brawlands to find Henry there. But it was a long time ago, and the loon had been at enough farms that they must have all melded together now – the wheres and what-fors, who said this, did that. Besides, it would do the loon no favours to turn up in a new place and start dredging up the past, telling tales on a man like Johnny Nicol.

'You're right, Mysie.'

'Seldom's a time I'm nae, loon. Now, there's tatties on the side.'

Johnny gets up, finds the pipe has worked its wonders, and maybe things aren't so bad after all. He'll go back to Brawlands in the morn, take Henry aside and make a joke of it, them both washing up here. The loon always did like to follow him around.

PART TWO

THE HAIRST

September–October 1915

JOHNNY

They have built up a rhythm over the long summer. Today, the others are labouring in the top pasture, while Johnny and Henry work the lower, tying sheaves together into their stooks. The harvest is almost done, and thank the Lord for that, for it is the type of work that sets an ache in the small of their backs before the sky has even lost its pinkness.

'I'll be glad when we're finished,' says Johnny, pausing to survey the stooks set out across the field, fat golden figures standing in clusters, heads together like they're scheming. 'I go tae my bed every night and sleep like the dead.'

'Aye, it's tiring work,' says Henry.

'Funny how you dinnae forget it, though. I've nae done hairst work since—' Johnny stops. Theirs is an unspoken agreement, to let Windyhillock lie, and they've muddled along all right, trampling the past under their shared purpose. They make light conversation, though Henry's not much of a talker nor one to complain, has borne his vicious sunburn with a martyr's grace, even when folks have whistled between their teeth and said how it must hurt. The weather has held for weeks and they've worked with bone-dry lips and thrumming heads, the dust gritting their skin – but no one gripes about fine weather.

To fill the silence, Johnny starts up whistling. Henry ignores it, which seems an encouragement of sorts, so Johnny opens his mouth and sings a line, a good wholesome song: 'O I met a bonny lassie, last Whitsun at the fair, with eyes so blue and smile so sweet and curls of chestnut hair—'

'You'll be slowing down, if you're capering.'

Johnny looks over, half expecting Henry to be grinning, but the loon is sombre. 'I can surely sing and work at the same time. I'm a man of many talents.'

'You know some of the other farms have finished?'

Johnny's well aware. Jock Campbell first as usual, for he somehow managed to wangle a couple of furloughed soldiers to make up his numbers, but most farms are at least a man down. Johnny's seen Rab's resolve harden – it's difficult to rest until your crop's safe in – and he doesn't appreciate the loon's implication that he might have worked harder; this is harder than Johnny's worked in years. 'We'll be done in the next day or two.'

'Aye, though only if we keep a pace up.'

'We will, loon, we're doing all right.'

'You're just standing there.'

For a moment Johnny is bemused at Henry's manner, how he's as serious as the grieve at Windyhillock, that savage foreman who used to bark orders in the loon's face until he was blinking back tears. But Henry is right – Johnny's talk is distracting him from his labour – so he shuts his mouth and the pair of them carry on.

An hour or so passes, the heat shimmering over the pasture. Johnny is beginning to think about dinner, and how fine it'll be to gulp a cold beer, and is relieved when Henry stops and looks back at the farmhouse.

'What on earth?'

Johnny follows Henry's gaze. Someone is approaching along the track – a woman in flapping green rubber boots, her skirt bunched in her hands. She isn't quite running, but she's quick, single-minded in her march up to Brawlands.

'Looks like that wifie fae the big house.'

As William Calder's wife reaches the yard, the farmhouse door opens and Maggie bustles out, taken unawares in her apron. She stops. From this distance, Johnny can just make out the rapid movement of the visitor's lips, the dove-white of her sleeve as she swings an arm up to point towards the braes. Maggie calls for Rab once, then again, sharply.

Johnny's always game for someone else's drama. 'Come on, we'll see what's happening. If Maggie's troubling Rab in the final days of the hairst . . .'

Henry shakes his head. 'I'll carry on.'

'Suit yourself.'

The loon gestures to Johnny's chest. 'You'd better . . .'

'What?' Johnny looks down. 'Oh.' His shirt is open nearly to the waist, and he supposes he ought to do it up; the sensibilities of a woman like Mistress Calder are surely different to those of Maggie, who spends her days amongst sweating, stinking men.

He is barely out of the field when Mistress Calder calls out to him. 'You're Johnny Nicol, aye?'

He's taken aback by her directness and folds his arms. 'Aye. Who's looking for me?'

'Mysie said to come and get you.'

'Och, what's happened to her?' Johnny says it lightly, as though she's some frail wee biddy who needs a hand tugging her boot from the mud, but worry nudges at him; his battleaxe of a landlady seldom asks for help.

'We were gathering moss up at the peats and, well, there's something up there.'

'Something . . . like?'

Mistress Calder hesitates. 'It looks like a body.'

Johnny chuckles, sure it's some prank of Mysie's and she'll

let rip with her dirty cackle when she hears he's fallen for it. 'Is Mysie having me on?'

'I was the one who saw it.' There's an edge of defiance in her tone, and Johnny finds himself wanting to respond in kind.

'And how do I know *you're* nae having me on?' he says, surveying the visitor. 'I dinnae know you from Adam.'

Maggie tuts. 'Less of your cheek, Johnny. You know who Mistress Calder is.'

'Maybe, but I've never had the pleasure of making her acquaintance.' Johnny sticks out his hand, keen to see if the wifie from the big house will recoil, since it's mucky and dried to cracking. She barely looks at it as she offers hers, which is likewise dirty, her nails rimed with peat. Her handshake is firm, and Johnny decides he'll take her seriously.

'So then, a body?' He tries for levity, but Maggie's gone pale and he's well aware that if they've lost someone, even just some solitary old sheep farmer who's keeled over up the braes, it'll be sorely felt. 'And you're sure it's nae just some animal bones or something?'

'It's not an animal,' says Mistress Calder. 'And it's not bones. There's a box in the bog. We couldn't get it out, but there's a hole in the corner and I saw something in there.'

Rab comes in through the gate, a fair pace on him because he doesn't like stopping when the hairst's on. 'Can I help you?'

The farmer listens, thumbing his moustache, as the visitor fills him in on the discovery, how she needs someone to come and bring the box down. But Rab Stuart is not a man to lose his head in high drama. 'I've never heard the like but, Mistress Calder, I cannae spare one of my men to go running up tae the peats today. It'll surely nae be a body, anyway, nae in water – the skin would be off its bones in a matter of days.'

'I assure you, Mr Stuart – there was something. There was . . . hair. It looked like red hair.'

Rab chews his lip. 'All right, I'm nae saying I dinnae believe you, just we've work tae do here.'

'We can't just leave it there.'

'She's probably right,' murmurs Maggie.

Softened by his wife's opinion, Rab relents, though not without a sigh. 'Johnny, away up and get a look, will you? Whatever it is, bring it down here.' He turns back to the pasture and gestures at Alex and Stephen to carry on. 'And Maggie . . .' Rab pauses, for a moment uncertain. 'Send for the Reverend.'

Johnny follows Mistress Calder out of the yard and on to the track, enjoying the breeze on his arms and the break from his toil. He tries to whistle a wee tune, but the woman looks over her shoulder at him.

'We should hurry.'

'You're very keen, Mistress Calder, but I've been at work the whole morn and I'm tired. I dinnae know how you're so fast in those boots, anyway – they look about five sizes too big for you.' The boots emerge from under a fine skirt spattered with mud, and the combined effect is of some vagrant gone thieving clothes from the laird's manor.

'They're my husband's. He's not getting much use out of them so I thought I would. If I can walk fast in these, you can speed up too.'

It is a fair point, and Johnny quickens his pace though stays behind, for it's good to finally get a look at the wifie from the big house. She's probably around his age, with dark hair unfurling from its style and a mole on the back of her neck. Bonny, as a few men down at The Pheasant have remarked after seeing her at kirk, though Johnny's not in the business of admiring another man's wife these days. 'Is he a fisherman then, your husband?'

'Something like that. He's been known to wade out into the

burn and make a grab at the salmon, though I think he expects them to come to him.'

'Is that right? I've never met him.'

'Not much community spirit in him, I'm afraid.'

'No, I've never seen him in The Pheasant. What does he do of an evening then – and you, come to think of it?'

Folks call Johnny idle, but he fills his days. There's always kail to be lifted from the garden for supper, and peat to be cut, logs chopped, odd bits of work so he has coin for a dram down the inn. He can barely imagine a life where all that's done for you – *that* ought to be called idle.

'Oh,' she says, 'walking, drawing. I've probably got a thousand sketches of my left hand, though they never get any better. Anyway, we should hurry up.'

Johnny concedes, hastens his step to walk beside her. 'I apologize, by the way, for my tone back at the farm. It was insolent to talk like that tae someone like you.' He's not sure himself if he's in earnest, says it more out of curiosity for her reaction.

Mistress Calder looks at him as though she knows his game. 'I wasn't offended. Though if you've a taste for insolence you may as well call me Lizzie.' She turns and carries on.

They make their way uphill. The track is narrow and crumbly from the weeks of drought, and Johnny watches as Lizzie pitches herself up the brae with a certain tenacity. When they reach the top the whole of the Cabrach opens up before them – the bare peak of the Buck presiding over lesser hills, clusters of Scots pine in the valley. The land is carved up by fences and dykes – the boundaries of each man's livelihood – and down the middle the Deveron flows, joined here and there by the Black Water and any number of dribbly wee burns. Johnny likes to walk by the river, chuck in a feather or blade of grass and imagine its journey down to the Firth to be spat out into the cold North Sea.

'We're nearly there.' Lizzie waves to a figure up ahead – the dot of Mysie, sitting in Mac's old waxed jacket. She gets to her feet as they approach.

'It's given me the creeps, sitting here alone with that thing.' Mysie looks at Johnny with an expression that unsettles him; he has never known fear to dare live in her. 'Thank you for coming, loon.'

Johnny shrugs, though in truth he's pleased to be the one called. He surveys the scene, the baskets of moss sitting by the stacks of cut peat that have been left out to dry. Johnny has been out at the cut before, knows the flex and grunt and blistered thumbs from shoving a flauchter through the clag. The stuff stained his hands, black lines in the palms even after he'd scrubbed them raw with turpentine. In all honesty, it's a job he'll make excuses to avoid. He's never liked it up here; even on a fine day the place is bleak. That, and Johnny can never shake his ma's old tales of strange silver lights rising vaporous from bogs, luring travellers from the straight path. Portents and omens, all ill – and all a nonsense, he's well aware.

Johnny goes to where the uncut peat makes a steep, dank wall. 'Just down here, is it?'

'Aye,' Lizzie says, appearing next to him. 'Look over the bank – there's a box sticking out.'

Johnny crouches down to peer into the bog, sees first the reflection of his own searching eyes and then the clumps of sphagnum moss just beneath the surface. He realizes what Lizzie's on about – a corner of the box protrudes above the waterline, too far for him to reach from the bank. 'Christ, how am I meant tae get that out? I cannae just wade in there like this.' He looks down at his clothes as though he is wearing a finely cut suit and not a dusty pair of breeks and a shirt with yellow armpits.

But Lizzie is already slipping out of the rubber boots. She tosses one across the scrub. 'Here.'

With no further excuses readily available to him, Johnny unlaces his boots and swaps them for Mr Calder's, cringing at the weird intimacy of wearing another man's shoes. The two women watch from the bank as Johnny throws a leg over the side and grapples for purchase in the peat wall. He suppresses a shudder at its sticky density, then clambers down until he can drop into the water. As he breaks the surface, Johnny's foot sinks too far, and there's a stab of panic because he remembers those stories too; of the bog getting men in its mouth, dragging them clean under. He struggles a minute against the sucking mud, but then his feet meet solid ground and he tosses his hair back from his face and looks up at his audience. 'I'll want double my farm rate for this, you know.'

But the women don't laugh, and above them the sun has disappeared. A wall of cloud has knitted together, glowering and steely like in the old seascape Johnny's ma had hanging in the hall – the type of weather working up the nerve to topple a galleon. Keen to get it over with, Johnny yanks his feet up and plunges through the water to where he can see the corner of the box. He bends, trying to get a grip on its sides, gummy coils of weed slipping between his fingers. Johnny crouches lower, the water threatening to inundate his boots, and finally he gets his hands round the thing. The box is longer than it is wide, and the first thing that strikes Johnny, as he hauls it from the bog, is that he could fit in it, probably; that it is something akin in shape and dimension to a coffin.

He manages to lean the box against the peat wall, brown water pouring from the crack in its lid. 'Go on then,' says Lizzie, 'have a look through the gap.'

And Johnny thinks again of his ma. How she'd have him quivering under the covers with her ghost stories, then she'd kiss him on the brow and tell him it wasn't the dead he ought to be frightened of. He takes a deep breath and peers into the box.

Nothing there, and he's about to tell Lizzie so – until his eyes adjust to the darkness.

'Christ!' Johnny steps back so abruptly that the water leaps up, soaking his breeks. 'I think you're right.'

LIZZIE

They lay the box on the kitchen table. It is perhaps five feet long, the lid crushed inwards. Maggie eyes it as she clears space.

'Was it heavy to carry down?' She asks it lightly, as though enquiring as to the wellbeing of a friend, but there is an uneasy bloom in her cheek.

Lizzie watches the bob in Johnny's throat as he drinks a pint of water in one go. He sets the glass down and wipes his lips with the back of his hand.

'Heavy enough.'

Lizzie finds herself surprised at his honesty, for he'd shunted the box on to his shoulder with a certain bravado and trudged off like a pallbearer, even though his face told a different story. She followed behind, thinking intermittently to ask if he'd take help and deciding against it – he was muscled enough, if not much taller than her, though had at least not succumbed to the stubby stout-bottle build of other men not bestowed with height.

'I'll make us some tea,' Maggie says, prodding the range which glowers with half-spent peat. 'Mistress Calder, do take a seat. And you, Reverend. I've scones, if you'd like?'

'Oh, no thank you. I'm much too intrigued to eat.' Reverend Bruce's eyebrow is a little raised, and Lizzie wonders what the

Lord might have to say about the derisive edge in the voice of His representative. They had seen him as they approached Brawlands and Mysie had stopped abruptly, said she'd head on home and hear about it later. Johnny had made a joke then, something about his landlady going up in flames if she got too close to a holy man.

'Tea, then? I'll just get the kettle back on.'

But Rab holds up a hand. 'Let's just get a look at this thing, then we can get back tae work.' He eyes his gang, the older two fizzy with excitement and the lad standing a little back, wide-eyed as a heifer. Everyone looks at Johnny and he sighs, like he is a man used to labouring under expectation.

'I suppose I'll do it, then.'

From what she has heard about him, Lizzie half expects Johnny to open the box with a bow and a flourish, but he is tentative, smooths a thumb along its lid, touching for an opening. The lid sits flush with the sides, with no easy entry other than the hole in the corner. Johnny slips a finger through the splintered crack, wincing at whatever it meets.

'What is it?' Lizzie asks.

When he withdraws his finger, there is something hooked on it – a shaggy form, little starbursts of green. Johnny drops the moss on to the table.

Rab glances at the clock. 'Henry, run out and get a crowbar, will you.'

The lad is corn-yellow, but he swallows hard and nods, does as he's told. The rest of them stand watching the slow spread of water across the tabletop, the dark veins that emerge in the grain.

'Can you see anything through the corner?' Lizzie asks.

'Aye, have a look through that gap,' says Alex.

Johnny crouches, brings his face to the box, closing one eye as he peers inside. From somewhere comes a clamour of nails scratching on wood and he leaps up, looks around to see if anyone noticed. Maggie is distracted by her bairns, who started scrabbling at the door at the crucial moment – but Lizzie saw.

'Too dark to see,' Johnny says.

Rab takes a paraffin lamp off its hook and strikes a match, which snaps in his fingers; he tuts as another one follows. Henry comes back with the crowbar and Johnny takes it off him, tests its weight with a loose grip.

'That should do.'

They watch as he sets to it, deliberating over the right angle to position the tool, a fussiness to his movements as though he is playing for time. Johnny wedges the crowbar in the broken corner and levers upwards, his knuckles white, and with a crack of splintering wood the lid peels open. He lifts it off and steps aside, arm extended in invitation.

The room is still. Windows fogged, plaster sweating. Some moments are thresholds, and this is one. Lizzie knows it as she steps forward, almost as if the box – its contents – is urging her on. It seems as if the room shrinks away from her, the others becoming distant – Rab with his arms crossed, the lad Henry biting down on his lip.

Lizzie looks inside.

In the box is a slack sack of mud. It is a thing made of hide, the creased discards of a bootmaker. She struggles to make out what it is at first, her throat closing in fear that she has been fooled; that she has disturbed the men at hairst for the sake of some old scraps of leather. But Johnny appears on the other side of the box, reaches in to brush away loose clods of peat, and the thing begins to take form beneath his hands: the kick of a hipbone, an arm wizened as a spent match.

Henry's mouth opens. 'What on earth is it?'

The thing is naked, skin stretched over the jut of ancient bones like a piece of cloth caught in a tree, the empty suggestion of breasts. 'It is a woman,' Lizzie says.

They gasp when they see her. Curses slip out, are hastily recanted. 'I've never seen the like—' Rab lifts the lamp, spilling light further into the box. Lizzie sees her face then, burnished black, like a gold statue that has been touched too many times. Jutting chin, nub of nose, eyes closed only softly, as though their lashes might flutter. Lizzie finds her fingers are on the edge of the box, though she doesn't remember putting them there, watches as they creep in, beguiled. Her thumb skirts the back of the woman's hand, the skin rucked and twisted, then moves upwards over the taut forearm, a shoulder hard and apple-round. She touches something cold and leans closer to see a curve of metal resting round the woman's neck – half a ring, a semicircle, like a mouth in a smile or frown. The metal is twisted along its length, stoppered at the end with a ball that rests in a sunken clavicle.

Lizzie is jolted back as the talk starts up – the men are done with their reverence.

'That thing's long since dead,' says Alex. 'I've seen a dead body, a recent one.'

'When?' asks Stephen.

'Auld hermit who lived out on the Rhynie road. I was sent tae check on him and when I turned up he must've been gone a few days, all bloated up like a haggis . . .'

'That's enough of that. There's ladies here.' But Rab looks not at Lizzie but at Henry, who steadies himself with a hand on the back of a chair. He is curd-faced, quivering.

'You all right, loon?'

Henry snaps upright. 'Aye, course.' He glances at his colleagues, who are contorting themselves into approximations of this bog woman, joints at odd angles.

Rab raises the lamp once more, catching the hair bunched in a corner, curled as though just pulled from its plait. It is violently, wondrously orange. When he sees it, the Reverend blasphemes, begs forgiveness in the same breath. Then he looks Lizzie dead in the eye. 'We'll need to bury it.'

'Her,' Lizzie murmurs.

Reverend Bruce turns to Rab. 'You'll spare Johnny to dig?'

'Christ,' Johnny says, and is given a sharp look. 'I'm knackered. I'm nae digging a grave and all.'

'You're still in your working hours, are you not?' says the Reverend.

Johnny snorts, ready to argue, but Lizzie stops him.

'Hold on.'

Under their gaze, she peers back inside the box and is startled by how much it feels like tenderness to look at the little clasped hands, the sharp ridge of bone in the woman's nose. Eyes so gentle, but there, at her curled black lip, what could be a sneer. Resolution coats Lizzie's throat. 'We can't just put her back in the ground.'

'I will bless her. And then we will lay her down.' Reverend Bruce is like a schoolteacher or a father, inviting no disagreement.

'But she might be . . . we need to find someone to look at her. She could be important, scientifically.'

The Reverend displays a thin smile. 'It is a corpse, Mistress Calder.'

'Aye, but not an ordinary one. Look how well she's preserved. Have you ever seen anything like it?'

'Mistress Calder, I really think it best that we just bury it.'

'Her. She is a woman, Reverend.'

'Her, then.' His voice drips a bland benevolence, as though he only need keep his patience and the facetious child will be placated. 'Listen, you've had a shock. I'm sure Maggie will accompany you home while we make the burial arrangements.'

Of course – settle the woman with smelling salts and a tiny sherry. Lizzie's temper rises like steam. 'I'm sorry, but we need to get someone to look at her. We should have the constabulary come. There might have been a crime.'

'We can't call on the Constable, he won't come all the way out here for this.' Reverend Bruce seems almost entertained now.

'Didn't you once say that your brother's a doctor, Johnny?' asks Alex.

Johnny seems surprised to have been spoken to; he has been watching the scene with his arms folded over his chest. 'I should think he's more concerned with the living.'

'I know someone,' says Lizzie. 'He's an officer in Elgin, an old friend. I'll write to him tonight.' The words have slipped out before she can consider their implications.

'There's a war on,' the Reverend says. 'Folks have more important things to be doing.'

'This *is* important.'

'I'll put her in the hayloft,' Johnny says. 'Mistress Calder's friend can look at her there. Maggie, you've some sackcloth or something?'

Maggie hesitates, looking to the men for a consensus. Rab just shrugs and defers to Reverend Bruce, whose mouth opens and closes, colour seeping up his neck. 'No good will come of keeping it unburied, mark me on that.'

But Johnny is already searching the dresser for something to wrap the body in. 'I hauled her out, Reverend,' he calls over his shoulder, 'and Mistress Calder found her. Surely it's up to us what to do with her now?'

Reverend Bruce purses his lips and rolls his eyes upwards, as though seeking the Lord's counsel. And perhaps the Lord is a softer shepherd, or else is keen to set a caper going in the Cabrach, for when the Reverend looks down again his manner has calmed. 'Very well. I will pray over the body. But first, cover her head.'

Johnny has found a length of sackcloth and unfurls it, releasing the scent of camphor. It must rouse Henry, who suddenly looks bewildered.

'The hayloft? We cannae – we should do as the Reverend says.'

'You scared?' asks one of the other lads, scuttling his fingers along Henry's shoulders. The lad jumps, then worms away.

'Course I'm nae scared.'

'Good, because it's decided.' Johnny tears a strip off the cloth, then reaches into the box to lift the woman's head into his palm. Her skull fits neatly there, and Johnny is delicate in the way he wraps the fabric round, tucking her hair inside the shroud. The effect is unpleasant, though – suddenly, head covered, she brings to mind some criminal being led to the gallows, blind to the judging crowd around her.

'Come,' says Reverend Bruce, 'let us pray.'

They stand in a circle, heads bowed. The Stuarts hold hands, and Henry clasps his tightly together, nodding vigorously as the Reverend asks his favours of the Lord. Lizzie watches Johnny as he steps a little away from the group, rubbing his fingers together as though some damp trace of the bog woman lingers there. She watches until he notices, and their eyes meet, and she mouths a silent thanks.

At Blackwater, Lizzie smooths a sheet of paper under her palm and searches for the words. She had promised herself she would never write to him. It has become a matter of pride, actually – holding back all the times she has wanted to – so it troubles Lizzie how easily James came to mind in the kitchen at Brawlands, as though all this time he has lingered at some periphery, smirking over a brandy glass. But these are extenuating circumstances; Lizzie thinks of the bog woman and her shrunken body, curled and boxed, her spine pressed against the wood. The feeling, she supposes, is something akin to duty – a responsibility towards a stranger left abandoned on a lonely brae. Lizzie dips her pen in the inkwell and begins to write:

Blackwater House, Cabrach
28th September, 1915

Dear James,
   It has been a long time, and I write under strange circumstances. From what I have heard you are an Inspector now, and I beg your assistance with the discovery of a woman's body in a peat bog here in the Cabrach. She is like nothing I have ever seen before – somehow perfectly preserved. If you are able, I ask that you might visit to appraise her, so we can try to find out who she was. If you can help, please return a note to advise when you might come.
   I hope you are well, and regards to your family.
   Yours,
   Lizzie Calder (Brodie)

She licks the envelope carefully and presses the flap down, addresses it to the house on Fore Street where she hopes James still lives – that solid granite place, huge and airy with wedding-cake ceilings. She had imagined, once, gliding through the glossed front door, hanging her coat beside his black wool jacket. He would come hurrying to wrap her in his arms, smelling of tobacco and oranges, would kiss her jaw under the stained-glass roses. She tuts at herself because she is here instead: no roses. No roses, only this parlour which is cool now, and the brittle grass on the lawn, and miles of nothing. Still, she allows a moment more for silly fantasy before opening her eyes to find Jane standing next to her.

'Ah, you're writing to William?'

Lizzie cannot be sure if Jane has already seen the envelope, sitting on the table with its blatant black ink, the flourish she put in James's name. Jane's face hardens as she reads.

'Now, there's a man I've not thought of in a long while.'

Lizzie has not prepared an excuse. 'Nor have I, but . . . I've an errand for him.'

'And there's no one else who can do it?'

'Jane, let me explain—'

'And did you write to him before, when William was here, or only now he's gone?'

'Never before.' Lizzie hates the cowed tone in her voice.

'Well thank goodness for that.' Jane sits, crossing her ankles. 'Go on then, enlighten me with what this errand is.'

There is no choice. Lizzie knew she would have to tell Jane soon enough, and surely the tale of their discovery has already grown legs and started trotting through the valley, but still it feels like a relinquishment of something that is hers. Jane listens and, when Lizzie has finished, she raises an eyebrow and asks whether James Esslemont is really the right man to call on.

'Well, he's the only person I can think of who might be able to help,' Lizzie says.

Jane's expression is one of concern – sincere, possibly.

'But is that wise, sister? Surely you've no wish to see him again?'

Surely not. But Lizzie is committed to her responsibility, finds it clasps hands nicely with something else, a curiosity that has gnawed for so long that she has learned to ignore its dull ache. She has wondered if James is the same, stoked hopes that he might have grown portly, balding, unhappy. She has wondered if he has any regrets. But Jane is probably wise, and that particular wound ought to remain closed.

'You're right, Jane. I'll throw the letter in the range once Miss Gow has lit it.'

'Do as you like, Elizabeth, it makes no odds to me.' Jane rises, smooths her skirt. She stoops to peer out the window where the light is strange, borne by jaundiced clouds. 'Ah, here's the rain come on.'

And sure enough, on the glass, a first decisive drop.

JOHNNY

A bead of liquid drops from his brow to his hand, and Johnny lifts it and presses it to his tongue, expecting the hot salt of sweat. But this is tasteless, and then there is another drop, and one on his neck. There is a moment when he looks at Henry and the loon looks back, and Johnny opens his palms to the heavens. Before he can say anything, there is Rab. He paces across the yard, fingers outstretched to gauge how bad it is.

'Fuck.' The farmer's voice is clotted with panic. 'Fuck. Fuck!' He cricks his neck back, face to the sky as the thunder groans and the deluge comes. Alex and Stephen come running from the top pasture and Johnny heads to the yard too – the rain, warmed up to its business, now pelting in spears across the ground. For a moment, he can't take it in – how only a few hours ago it was hot and bright, the sky clear, and now Rab is kicking a pail and crying out in despair. 'The weather couldnae have held for one day more? Fuck it, Johnny, it's all going tae be ruined.'

'Go inside, it's just a shower.' Even as Johnny says it, he's dubious – the clouds are dense and filthy, seem to smother the whole of the Cabrach.

Rab spits on the ground. 'We should have had it all in the stacks by now. It's never taken us so long before.'

Maggie has rushed out from the farmhouse to stroke her

husband's back, cooing her consolation, but Rab pulls loose and stalks off away from the gang. 'Go home, Johnny,' he calls over his shoulder, 'the rest of you go in. We're done.'

'I'll come up in the morn, we'll finish then,' Johnny says.

'Hardly matters now.'

And Johnny knows how it is, that destructiveness that holds its arms open once one thing has gone to shit. Easy then, a relief, to shrug your shoulders and let everything you were carrying tumble to the ground; easy like it is to keep running once your legs get a few strides in, to keep doing wrong when you've a few decisive sins inked in the Lord's ledger. He turns and walks towards the farmhouse to get his things and go, pausing on the way to lay a hand on Henry's shoulder. The loon is standing in the middle of the yard, letting the rain clear tracts through the muck on his cheeks.

'Go in, my friend,' Johnny says. 'No sense in getting drenched and catching a cold.'

But Henry jerks away. 'We should have been faster. We could have had it all brought in today.'

'Come on, we weren't tae know it'd rain.'

'It's been threatening it all afternoon.' Incredulity in Henry's tone, as though all of this would have been obvious if only Johnny had been paying attention. 'We shouldnae have stopped.'

'What, you're telling me when that wifie came tramping down the path we should have turned her away?'

Henry shrugs and squints through the rain at the field, where the huddled stooks are already sagging, their gold turning dark.

'You're obviously nae so gallant as me, loon.'

'No, I know what's important. You've nae changed, Johnny.'

And Henry turns and walks away, his shirt soaked to a second skin across his hard back.

*

Johnny pulls his chair closer to the fire in Mysie's parlour, hoping to draw the damp from his bones. He's barefoot, the skin wrinkled where the rain soaked through sock and boot-leather.

Mysie knits. 'What a day, eh? Nae been rain like this in months.'

'I just wish we'd finished.'

'It's hard luck.'

'Or my fault, according to the new loon.' It bothers Johnny – less the judgement of Henry himself, but more in case Rab agrees.

'But if you'd gone off wandering Rab would have been a whole pair of hands down anyway. You've done what you can.' It's rare for Mysie, a staunch believer in responsibility, to placate Johnny like this, and he appreciates the gesture, but somehow also finds it unbearable. Not that he doesn't want to be comforted – he imagines Maggie kissing the tears away from Rab's cheeks, and the gang tucked in the chaumer, a kinship in their despair – but he isn't sure he deserves it.

'I'll tell you one thing, though,' Mysie says, 'I'll nae be back to the peats for a while, rain or shine. Spooked me, that body.'

From her choice position on the hearth rug, the cat peels an eye open. Johnny watches the creature, unsettled by the timing of her curiosity. She gives him the creeps – the sleekit black body and the way she stands to yawn, shuddering with her back curled round.

'Aye, I've never seen the like.'

'What was it like, when you took it out?'

Johnny considers; ever the raconteur, inclined to embellish and exaggerate, up the drama. But he thinks it's important, probably, to describe the bog woman only as she was. 'She was like . . . a wee imp. Or, well, just a lassie. Shrivelled up small, and her skin was all blackened, but she had this bright-red hair. Alex reckons she must have been buried a good many years.'

'And now she's picked her time to come to light.'

Johnny eyes his landlady; does not like the way she's phrased it, as though the woman's been waiting, sentient and choosy. 'I'm sure there's a logical explanation, something in the water that's preserved her. Lizzie Calder's sending for some chap from town. She says he'll know.'

'And was Lizzie all right? She was awfully excited, but sometimes when that's died down you find yourself shaken.'

'She seemed fine to me.'

'Good.'

'You're friendly with her, then? She ought to be careful, she'll be getting a reputation if she's seen tae be chums with Mysie MacDonald. Lord knows it's afflicted me.'

Mysie tuts. 'As a matter of fact, I am. I used to think she must be a bit high and mighty, up at the big house, her husband shooting round in that motor car and never taking a minute to wave as he goes by. But she's nae like that – she's got a good head on her shoulders.'

'You know,' Johnny rests his head on the back of his chair, 'they say that her husband hasnae written to her since he left to fight.'

'Is that right?' Mysie's tone is flat, unquestioning – she'll not show if she's intrigued. But Johnny carries on, needing the succour of mindless claik.

'Aye. Postie told someone he's nae delivered a single letter to Blackwater in months, except addressed to the other wifie – the sister.'

'Always someone watching, eh, in the Cabrach?'

Johnny shrugs. 'It's only what I've heard.'

Later, Johnny slouches in his chair in the last of the firelight, the rain still beating on the windows. He's lit a pipe and sups it slowly, turning over the day. It's troubled him, truth be told. He's seen a dead body before, or as good as, but this is something else – something long dead, warped and shrunken and strangely beautiful. But still, maybe she ought to have stayed buried. Johnny is sure he's misremembering, bothered by Mysie's words, but it seems to him now that the bog woman had a look on her face, like she'd been expecting all this.

Johnny puts the thought from his mind, runs his finger over the crumpled skin on the back of his left hand. It is a habit, a small comfort, though he can barely feel anything, there where the nerves had never quite knitted back together. Still, at least it had healed – the morning after he'd got the wound, he hadn't been sure it would. He remembers Henry's concern – the loon back then was sensitive, too much so, and it made him a target for the other men. The farms were fucking brutal – everyone wanted to be top dog, and if you couldn't be that, then you'd do anything to be part of the pack. The Henry back then was not the same as the one in the yard today, his shoulders tight with resentment. But he'll be all right in the morn, surely. The rain will stop.

It is nearly midnight. Johnny necks the rest of his dram, sets his pipe on the dresser. The cat lifts her head and regards him with her usual light contempt, but is placid enough as he reaches to hook a finger under her chin. But then she swats at him, her claws showing. 'All right,' Johnny mutters, 'I dinnae like you either.'

LIZZIE

Her umbrella sags with the weight of the water, rain streaming off the spokes. James had said three o'clock in his letter, and at some time past Maggie had stuck her head out of the farmhouse door and invited Lizzie to wait inside, but she had refused – she would rather wait in the yard than be surprised by a knock at the door.

Eventually, two yellow lights appear through the murk, and a car turns up the farm track. It drives into the yard fast enough to disturb a puddle, and Lizzie jumps back to avoid the water spattering her skirt. The engine dies. Motion behind the smeared windscreen, features smudged, the dark rectangle of a constabulary jacket with its row of silver buttons like new coins. The door opens and James gets out, wrapping himself in an overcoat with a deliberate grace that suggests he is well aware of Lizzie watching him.

'I must say, I don't have the clothes for this,' he calls out. 'I've never seen such rain! If we had it like this in town it would make the newspaper.'

Lizzie raises the umbrella high enough for James to duck underneath. 'Then town has grown dull since I was last there.' She offers him her cheek, lets him kiss it, pulls swiftly away.

'It's good to see you again.' James's eyes move over her face, and then he steps back to regard her wholly. Lizzie stands, uncomfortable in his appraisal, and tells him brusquely that she is likewise pleased by his visit. Her own subtler assessment finds James much the same – the colour in his cheek that was always there, whether flushed by candlelight or roused by dancing. He is still in possession of the same thick hair, the good physique. Lizzie notes all this with disappointment and a sudden, startling pleasure. James is holding her gaze; she looks at her feet.

'Thank you for coming out.'

'Not at all, Lizzie.' His voice is soft and there is a moment, brief, before he claps his hands together. 'Now, where is she? I'm desperate to get a look at her.'

They move through the dim barn – James first, glancing at the crop gathered in two humped stacks that fur the air with a dank smell.

'She's up in the hayloft,' says Lizzie, and James goes to the ladder, tests the first rung with his foot, then begins to climb. When he reaches the shelf, he leans over and extends his hand; Lizzie resists taking it until she is nearly at the top of the ladder and looks down, vertigo shifting the ground beneath.

'James.' She grabs his hand, finds it warm and firm and familiar.

He looks at her with concern. 'Are you all right?'

'Aye, I'm all right.' Lizzie climbs on to the shelf, irritated by how quickly her composure has dissipated. 'Now, are you ready?'

'I'm very ready.'

They crouch in the hay. There is a timeless smell up here, dry and summer-sweet, of country fairs and rolling lovers. The parcelled body lies between them – after their prayers in the kitchen Johnny had wrapped the rest of her, securing the sackcloth with twine around her waist, her wrists and ankles. James's fingers work at one of the knots.

'How did you find this, then?'

'I was gathering moss for bandages. She was up in the peats in a box.'

'Lizzie Brodie, knee-deep in a bog – somehow I can well imagine it.' James grins. 'You always were . . .' He tails off and regards her, waiting to be asked. She won't. 'You always were game.'

It is not the first time she has been called this. Bridget, their old housekeeper in town, would mutter of Lizzie being too game for her own good when she would sicken herself on too much sponge cake, or the time she pressed a razor blade to the soft pad of her thumb to see what it felt like. *Surely you knew it would hurt*, Bridget had said when young Lizzie set to crying.

James begins to pull away the body's wrapping. 'Incredible . . .'

Lizzie watches the way his eyes widen. It is a tender intimacy, witnessing another person's wonder, and her instinct is to look away as James touches a fingertip to the woman's wrist, then strokes the length of her arm. He pulls back the shroud, revealing the soft hollow at her collarbone, her throat, her face. 'I can't believe this.' He gently touches her mouth – those curling lips that could be smiling, coy; or set hard in refusal of tears.

There is a clatter from below. The door opens and Rab and Johnny Nicol come in, the farmer peeling back the tarpaulin on one of the stacks and leaning in to sniff the crop. Johnny stands back, watching. He's soaked through, twisted brown cotton round his neck, the colour of a dubious bottle of whisky. 'Still wet?'

'Soaking,' Rab says. They turn to go, but James leans over the edge of the hayloft and raises his palm.

'Hello! I do apologize – ever so rude – in my excitement to see this woman I came straight up here without greeting her hosts.' He climbs down the ladder and strides towards the men with an outstretched hand. 'A fascinating thing you've got up there.'

'Aye,' says Johnny, shaking James's hand with one quick jerk, 'it was me who took her out the bog.'

'Then you'll be well acquainted. I've some theories about her if you'd like to hear them, though . . . perhaps inside. The cold out here!'

Rab hesitates. 'Aye, well, if it doesn't take too long. Come on, I'll have my wife boil up a kettle.'

James touches Rab's shoulder. 'Kind of you.' He turns to Johnny. 'We'll need to re-wrap the body, stop the air getting to her. Would you mind?'

Johnny mutters agreement and stands by the ladder, averting his eyes as Lizzie clambers down.

In the kitchen, Lizzie wrestles her arms out of her damp coat while James hangs his on a hook and settles himself into a chair by the fire, a man apt at finding his ease. Rab and the gang stand, though Johnny has pulled up a dining chair and sits with one ankle crossed over the other knee so the clotted muck on his boot presents itself to the room. He is wearing a holey pullover, giving off the stink of wet wool, and watches with something like disdain as James gets out his pipe, fills it at his leisure, tamps it, sparks a flame from his silver lighter.

'So,' the Inspector says, 'I think it's the water. There's something in the acidity of bogs that can keep things preserved. I've heard of peat cutters finding old scraps of fabric and the like, but never anything like this.'

'You're saying it's some kind of magic water?' asks Johnny.

James laughs. 'Not magic, no. It'll be a mix of things – the composition, perhaps something to do with oxygen levels. Do you know much about chemistry?'

'That was more my wee brother's thing.'

'Right. Well look, I'll make no promises, but I know someone at the university in Aberdeen. He's a geologist, really, but he'll likely have colleagues who'll be interested in this sort of thing.'

'When might he come?' Lizzie asks.

'I couldn't say. They'll have had their own share of men joining up. But I'll write to him.'

'All right. But who do you think she was?' she asks.

Johnny jumps in with his theory. 'She probably had an accident up there, fell down and was never found.'

'Wouldn't have thought so,' says James. 'Lizzie said she was found in a box – seems unlikely she'd have fallen into that.'

'Duh,' says Stephen.

Johnny shrugs. 'Aye, well, whatever.'

'*I* think,' James takes another pull on his pipe, lets the blue smoke disperse before continuing, 'well, it could be foul play, but more likely it was some outbreak of disease – measles, or worse. They might have decided to bury her far from the living.'

Lizzie hadn't thought of this but it makes sense, and James sounds confident in his assertion. He always was that way, back in town, presenting theories as facts with such assurance that he was rarely challenged. 'But what about that metal round her neck?'

'Ceremonial, perhaps? Part of some sort of funeral ritual? Lord knows what folks got up to around here many moons ago. Whoever she was, she's some find.' James looks at Lizzie and there is something knowing in his gaze, as though he suspects her of devising it all to draw him back to her. 'I'll try to find out more – dig out some files from the area, see if there are any reports of a missing woman, things like that. I think I'll bring a couple of my colleagues over in a few days and have a look at where you found her, if you'd be able to take us up there?'

Lizzie agrees – it seems essential to the investigation.

'Marvellous!' says James, rising from his chair. 'I'll leave these men to their work then, I've taken up enough of everyone's afternoon.'

Rab waves a hand. 'Nae bother at all. In fact, it's past four. You go, Johnny, there's nae much more we can do today.'

'Oh, I'll easy stay.'

'No, away home, we dinnae need you.' He means nothing ill with his words, surely, but Johnny's face drops and he gets up, crams his soggy cap on his head.

'Which one's yours?' James asks, rummaging amongst the coats on the hook before holding up the tatty jacket Johnny had been wearing in the barn. The Inspector fingers a sleeve, a shadow of distaste in his expression. 'It's damp, still, I'm afraid. How about I run you home in the car? I'll be dropping Lizzie off, so it's no bother.'

Johnny shakes his head. 'Dinnae worry about it, I'll gladly walk.' He has been surly all afternoon, scowling in a way that doesn't flatter him.

'Come on, you'd be foolish to walk in this rain when James will be nigh on passing your front door,' Lizzie says.

The Inspector nods. 'It's really no trouble – your wife will give you a scolding if you turn up dripping all over the kitchen.'

'He disnae have a wife,' says Henry.

'Really,' Johnny says, shooting him a look. 'I wouldnae dirty this good man's car.'

'All right, well, you take care.' James stands for a moment, surveying the gang as they get up, ready to finish the day's tasks. His mouth twitches in the manner of a man who has formed a joke and finds himself greatly pleased with it. 'I must say, I haven't seen so many young men in one room for some time!'

Johnny, at the door, pauses with a hand on the latch. He turns his head, looks at the policeman in his sharply fitted wool. 'Aye, well, you've tae eat, don't you?' And he opens the door and steps back into the rain.

In the parlour at Blackwater, James peruses the art. Lizzie hadn't intended to invite him in, but could hardly let him make the long journey home without rest or refreshment. She watches as he leans in closer to the portraits, perusing them like a critic.

'Long dead Calders,' says Lizzie. 'I don't know who most of them are.'

'Your husband, which one is he? I can barely remember the great William's face.'

They were never really friends, James and William – would encounter each other on the same town circuit, but William was older, too serious, unmoved by James's easy charm. James liked to spar, ideally with a partner who would meet his banter with similar good humour, but William was never a man who appreciated being laughed at. Lizzie finds she does not particularly want to show James the wedding photograph, but gestures to where it sits on the side table.

'Ah well, you've not got to rely on the eye of an artist for that.'

She watches James's face as he scrutinizes the image – she, stiff in the chill of a Cabrach February, smiling though her hands shook in her lap. William is sombre, dressed in black that is harsh beside the off-white of his wife's high-necked lace.

'You all look very serious,' James says.

'Serious business, a wedding.'

'Aye, but your father – that's not how I remember him. He'd a big sturdy grin on his face most of the time.' James sets down the frame. 'How are your parents anyway? I heard they moved south.'

Lizzie doesn't want this interrogation. James always was good at deflection, flattering people with interest so they might only realize later that he'd told them nothing about himself.

'Edinburgh. My father was offered a role at the bank's head office, quite high up. I don't often see them.'

It is easier, Lizzie supposes, for her parents' genteel city friends to know only that they have a daughter up north who has married well – if well means into money. Her parents hadn't visited much before the move in any case; a few awkward evenings at the dinner table, her mother rabbiting on about the paintings and rugs and silverware, William responding in syllables. The last time, when Lizzie's father took her aside and asked, earnestly, if she was happy, she could have wrapped her hands round his neck and squeezed.

'Will you have a drink?' she asks now, to stave off further questions.

'Oh, go on. A small one.'

Lizzie goes to the cabinet and roots through the bottles for William's good whisky. Her hands tremble and she scolds herself as the lip of the decanter knocks against the tumbler – she is being ridiculous.

'I must say, it came as a surprise when I heard you were marrying William Calder. I didn't realize you two knew each other very well.' James paces in front of the fire as he makes his enquiries, employing the detached, neutral tone that he might use with anyone – victim or perpetrator. Lizzie runs a finger along the rim of the glass, presses down on the fine crack that now splits the crystal, lets it hurt her for a second. She takes the two drams and it seems diminishing, somehow, to go to his side and give him something.

'We didn't, really.' She raises the ruined glass she has taken for herself. 'Slainte.'

'Slainte.' James drinks, and for a moment he meets her eye before looking up at the ceiling. 'It's some place you've got here. I'm surprised they didn't sell it.'

'It's been in the family for centuries.'

'Aye, but that was a hefty sum William and his da were trying to get together.'

'When?'

'Oh, ten or so years back?'

Lizzie frowns – that was when they married. Back then, James's father had looked after the Calder account at the bank.

'There was a farm they were trying to buy, but it didn't work out. William and his father fell out over it. I'd imagine the money was for that,' Lizzie says.

'Maybe. Though I could have sworn the funds were all drawn down. I seem to remember my father being called out of his bed on a Saturday morning. Perhaps that was someone else.'

'Can you ask him?'

James smiles at her indulgently, as if she were a child playing detective. 'If you like.' He swallows another mouthful of his whisky. 'Anyway, I'm glad they held on to this place, it's a fine old house. Though . . . it must be awfully lonely out here?'

Lizzie has answered all his questions, but she will not give him this. 'I'm not alone. I probably should have said – Jane's come to stay for a while. Just to keep me company.'

James stops, his glass half raised to his mouth. 'Oh, I didn't know.'

'No, well. You wouldn't.'

'Is she well?'

'I suspect . . .' Lizzie says, pausing at what sounds like footsteps in the hall, 'you'll be able to ask her yourself.'

When Jane comes in, she looks at their drinks and the clock and then at Lizzie. 'You posted the letter, then?'

'Clearly,' says Lizzie.

'Your prerogative, I suppose. Anyway, Mr Esslemont.' She endures his kiss on the cheek.

'It's been a long time, but a pleasure as ever, Miss Calder – or, so I still presume?'

Jane looks at him as if he is stupid to suggest she might have cuffed herself to a man. 'I won't haver long, I've things to be getting on with. Are you well, James? How's your wife?'

'She's well, as am I.'

'A shame not to have met her properly,' Jane goes on, 'we didn't get to speak much at the wedding. And your bairns – how many are there now?'

'Three, all girls.'

'How lovely!' Jane's voice is cloying, and she looks at Lizzie for a reaction, but if she thinks these simple facts will pain her she is mistaken. Lizzie knows the circumstances of James's life – what she has wondered is if he is content with them. And James looks uncomfortable all of a sudden, caught in a net of questioning he's rather more used to casting himself.

'They must keep you busy,' Lizzie says.

'Ah, well, they're in Forres most of the time, we've a place there. Charlotte prefers the school and it's close to her mother, so ...' He drains his glass and sets it loudly on the side table.

'That must be a lot for you, going between Forres and town for work?' Lizzie says.

He runs a palm over the crown of his head, disturbing the elegant wave in his hair. 'No, I stay in town, mostly. With this job it's ... easier.'

Though she has forced it, Lizzie finds herself alarmed at this slippage – the fluttering of a curtain that has revealed something untoward. Part of her wants to cover it back over, but she is also well aware of her own capacity for cruelty. 'Well, you ought to bring the family out for a visit one day. I'd love to meet the girls.'

'Perhaps, when the weather's finer. Anyway, I'd better be off. I'll come back in a couple of days with the others to continue the investigation.' He has fallen back into the easy authority of his profession. Lizzie watches him as he goes out to the hall to put on his coat – the familiar slant of his shoulders, a pattern of freckles on the back of his neck. It is a small consolation that if Lizzie is unhappy, at least James is too. And yet the realization doesn't bring her any satisfaction, as she'd always thought it might. She tilts her cheek to him and he places a kiss there, withdrawing too slowly for her not to hear his sigh.

JOHNNY

Johnny shoves the door open. Rain hurls in behind him, the wind nudging him over the threshold as though he might have it in mind to turn back round again. The inn is full – a low simmer of perturbed men, the wet clearing of throats. He wants to get a dram in before he is accosted. At the bar, Agnes gives him a hard-luck look and reaches for a bottle of her better stuff. 'No peace here tonight, loon, though you'll give them something to talk about that's nae the new liquor restrictions, and for that,' she slides the dram across the bar, 'you can have this on me.'

'You, my darling, are an angel and a saint.'

Agnes gives him a steady look, flattered despite herself. 'Go on then, they've all been waiting for you.'

Round the hearth, the men have drawn their chairs into a circle – democratic in their misery, all tales of woe equal to the rest. They will be ired mostly by the weather, but once they get going other grievances soon spill out. Dougie sits rubbing his swollen knuckles, though manages a grin when he sees Johnny.

'Now we'll hear it fae the horse's mouth.' The farmer slaps the cushion of an empty chair and Johnny sits, notes the sullen expressions of the other men – Sinclair's got a face like cream on the turn and Jock looks tetchy. Johnny pats his head.

'What's the matter with you, Jock? Only a chop for your supper tonight? A hole in your fine feather quilt?'

Jock tuts. 'Shut your gob.'

'What've you heard already, then?' Johnny asks. It has been several days since the body was found and the rumours and speculation will be well under way.

'Well, you tell us the facts,' says Dougie. 'You hauled it down.'

'You could have asked the loon.' Johnny nods towards Henry, who sits with a tankard that looks too heavy for his wrist. They've scarcely exchanged two words since the rain came, bringing in the drooping stooks with barely a look in the other's direction. Johnny gets it: the loon at a new fee, eager to impress, and he'd let his disappointment get the better of him. But still, Johnny had thought he might hear an apology.

Dougie narrows his eyes. 'He's new, how are we tae know he's honest?'

'I'm honest as a judge,' says Henry, but the men ignore him and continue to badger Johnny for his story. Johnny removes his coat, takes his time to get comfortable – his audience will wait. He takes a sip of Agnes's good whisky and regards them. 'It's a body. A lassie. And she's been in there a good long time.'

'And? What did she look like?'

'I hear she's six foot tall?'

'And she's got just the one eye – is that right?'

'Someone told me she's got bright-red hair . . .'

'Aye,' Johnny says, 'You're right about the hair. But the rest . . . as I said, she's just a lassie. Normal-sized, two eyes, nose, mouth, and the rest of it.'

Dougie raises both hands and squeezes the air like he's milking a heifer. 'Aye, I heard she has the rest of it!'

'Gads, man, it's a corpse.'

The farmer huffs. 'So she's just a normal lassie – where's the story in that?'

'I dinnae know, but I can do you a song about it.' Johnny looks expectantly at the group, thinks it might cheer them to get a bit of music going, stamp the mud from their boots. But Jock puts up a hand.

'Nae in the mood, man.'

Johnny shrugs. In truth he can't really be arsed either – he's irritable, had wanted to get out of the house for a drink and a blether, but he sees there's no cheer to be found here tonight. He closes his eyes, detaching himself from the men as they take up other lines of talk: flaring gout and boggy pastures, sheep growing scabby with rain-rot; and, to insult them further, a dwindling supply of ale with which to drown their sorrows, for the brewery over in Dufftown has lost its men to war.

'I've barely slept,' says Dougie. 'The burn's nearly in spate again at the foot of my land. I'm nae sure how much longer the banks will hold.'

'Aye, there's lads out with sandbags, though they'll not keep the Deveron back if it goes and all.' Jock shakes his head. 'I'd a bad night as well. Could have sworn I heard something moving about the yard.'

Henry joins in too, muttering to Sinclair about bad dreams. Johnny looks around for better company, but finds the same dreariness is afflicting them all. The men turn as the door opens, and Johnny peels his head off the back of the chair to see who's come in – three figures in black, standing in the doorway. They step in, these men in well-fitting worsted, hatted, not from round here. As lamplight glances off a silver button, Johnny realizes it's the constabulary men. He watches as the officers shake rain from their coats and Inspector Esslemont turns to speak to someone outside. He is inclining his head, beckoning, trying to entice them in. Johnny can take a good guess who. As Lizzie Calder enters she looks about, not with trepidation but curiosity, and Johnny supposes it must be novel for a woman like her to peer through the billows of pipe smoke into a man's domain. He is not sure there is much to recommend it tonight.

The group goes to the bar. The youngest man is short and lithe, with too much pomade in his hair, and he doesn't impress the barmaid as he dumps a handful of coins on the counter for her to pick through. Agnes brings out the good bottle, pours four ungenerous measures. The men lift up their drams and begin an ostentatious show of swirling and sniffing, as if the stuff's fine wine, and the youngest takes a tiny sip and gives a theatrical grimace. Lizzie stands a little outside their group, a silk scarf covering her hair, and Johnny watches as she pulls it off, sliding it over the curve of her scalp in one liquid motion. He realizes then that the room has gone quiet.

Dougie lowers his glass. 'What's this? A lassie in here . . .' He is wifeless, maidless, with only a knackered grey mare for female company, though perhaps he is less troubled than Sinclair, who eyes Lizzie with open suspicion. Jock, himself replete with the good Anne Campbell and their five bonny daughters, shakes his head.

'Unbecoming for a wifie like that.'

Typical of them, Johnny thinks, to be more perturbed by a woman in their midst than by the three strangers. The constabulary men take in The Pheasant's comforts, such as they are – the mucky floor and scruffy parade of chairs, the old dartboard with a hole clean through the triple twenty. James Esslemont's gaze falls over the group at the hearth. He raises a hand when he sees Johnny and strides over.

'John – good to see you again.'

'Inspector.'

'Let me introduce my colleagues.' James gestures at the two young officers who are wending their way through the crowd, careful not to let their uniforms touch a farmer. 'Peter Dawson and George Emslie – both detective constables.' He says their title proudly, and Johnny thinks of his brother – when he stopped being Charlie and became Dr Charles Nicol, with a bunch of letters after. 'And you'll all know Lizzie Calder, of course.' The men at the hearth offer her their good evenings, muttered in strained deference.

'Are you well, Lizzie?' Johnny asks. 'Find anything useful?'

She must have done, he thinks, because there's an energy coming off her, something that's put a brightness in her eyes. 'We found the other half of that ring she had round her neck.' Lizzie rummages in her bag and holds it up to the room.

'Just looked like an old bit of metal to me,' says James, 'but I'm told it might be important.' He winks at Lizzie, and it strikes Johnny that the officer's motives for coming back to the Cabrach may have little to do with curiosity over the bog woman. He nudges James on the arm with the dirtier of his two hands.

'Are you nae supposed tae take all the evidence seriously? Being a policeman, and all.'

James smiles. 'Oh, of course. I'm teasing. We didn't find anything else, I'm afraid, and got tremendously wet for our troubles.'

'Terrible rain, this,' says Jock. 'If it carries on much longer . . .' He tails off, leaving each man to ruminate on his own worst fears, those things fretted over when the light's gone and there's nothing to do but bargain with the Lord for dry. And perhaps James Esslemont is unsure what to say, or is not a man adept at empathy, for instead he laughs.

'Weather!'

And isn't it only weather to James – only rain, an inconvenience, muddy boots for his maid to scrub. But the farmers fall silent. Damp men, aching men, beleaguered. Johnny decides he will speak for all of them. 'It's ruined a fair heap of the crop.'

'Aye, I'd say nigh on a quarter of my yield.'

'Nearly half mine.'

'Awful,' says James.

'It is when it's your livelihood.' It is Lizzie, her hand cupped round a dram as if she's one of them. The weather has got to her too, a damp lick of hair stuck to her forehead. 'Rain means something different here, James.'

'Oh, of course.' The Inspector looks at his colleagues. 'Right, we'd better head back, it's a fair old journey back to town.' He is about to go when Dougie leans forward.

'Hang on, have you seen her though? This wifie out the bog?'

'I have,' says James. 'I went to see her at Mr Stuart's farm.'

'Right, you can settle this, then,' Dougie smirks, whatever mystery that's been fermenting between his ears clearly of great amusement. 'Some loon told me she's got a pair of tits saggy as an auld hag – is that right?'

Sinclair tuts. 'Mind your mouth, man. We've a lady here.'

'And it's no place for one. Come on, tell us.'

Johnny knocks the old farmer's knee with his foot. 'Leave it. I told you already, she's just a normal lassie. Sorry, Lizzie.'

She finishes her drink. 'It's fine. I'll be off, though, leave you men to your conversation.'

'I'll take you home,' James says, and Johnny sets eyes on the policeman; knows what he means, but it sounds like something else.

'I'll easily walk,' says Lizzie.

'Not in this weather, surely?'

'I'd like the fresh air.'

'You were glad of the lift the other day.'

'I'm much obliged, but I'll let you get back to town. Come on, I'll see you off.' Lizzie is tying the knot of the headscarf under her chin. 'Have you written to the man at the university yet?'

'It's on my list,' says James.

'Can you shunt it to the top?' Her directness bothers Johnny, because it hints at some past between Lizzie and the Inspector that transcends the careful politeness of mere acquaintances.

When James puts his hand to the small of her back as they go to leave, Johnny finds himself calling out to her.

'I'll see you soon, Lizzie, aye?'

She turns. 'Aye, surely.'

The door has barely closed before the men are on him, snapping like hounds. 'I bet you're bloody hoping so!' Dougie's leg is bouncing with excitement.

'What you on about?' says Johnny.

'Och, come on, we all saw the way you looked at her. I'd usually warn against a fancy lassie like that, but now I've seen her up close, maybe nae – she's got a glint in her eye. Might be good for a—'

Jock holds up a hand. 'Enough with that.' He likes banter but he's got no stomach for bawdy talk, for it surely reminds him of the base nature of men – the same ones who'll eye his five comely daughters, get ideas.

'Well,' says Sinclair, 'if a quine'll come in tae the inn with some man who's nae her husband, she can hardly expect folks nae to talk. William Calder's got influence, she ought tae remember that. He's an impressive man. I remember the day when he shot that great big stag at Aldivalloch. Carried the thing all the way back tae Blackwater, head bouncing up and down on his shoulder . . .' Sinclair seems lost for a moment in manly admiration.

'Own up,' says Dougie, 'you've an eye on her?'

Johnny doesn't like the way they look at him, Henry with his tankard half raised, listening.

'As Sinclair says, she's got a husband.'

'That's nae stopped you before!'

It hardly seems worth defending himself. The best Johnny could offer is that he's done nothing like that in a good long time, and he won't do it again, especially not with a woman whose husband has gone off to fight.

'Behave, you lot,' says Jock. 'Anyway, this body. Dougie mentioned her ... parts ... but I heard she'd another. On her hand.'

'Another what?' Dougie asks, knowing full well.

'A tit. A third tit. That or some other sort of mark on her.'

Johnny rubs his temples – the evening has worn on. 'Jock, she's just a normal lassie. Preserved in some way, aye, but she's nae a monster. And she'd no extra tit.'

'You probably just didnae see it.'

'There was nothing tae see!'

'He'd have been too busy goggling that Calder lassie,' says Dougie. 'I've heard a few people say it was there.'

Johnny rolls his eyes. 'And you'll listen to folks who've nae seen her over those who have?' He gestures at Henry with his empty glass. 'Loon, you were there, will you tell them?'

The men turn their attention to the ploughman. He is edgy under their gaze, glances at Johnny, who offers a nod of encouragement, glad to find the loon on side.

'I didnae see anything like that.'

'See?'

'Though ... I didnae see all of her, really. Maybe ask Alex or Stephen, they got a better look.'

Jock must see the crack of doubt, just wide enough to edge a finger in. 'So what you're saying is you couldnae confirm with certainty, yes or no, whether or not she'd the tit?'

Henry bites his lip. 'Well ... I suppose no.'

'You suppose you couldnae say for sure?'

'No. In fact, now you mention it ...'

Jock leans forward in his chair, glances at Dougie. He pats Henry's knee in encouragement. 'Go on, son.'

'I might have seen something – I cannae quite mind.'

Jock sits back. 'That's more like it. Now, let's get you another drink, help you loosen up the memory.' The farmer digs in his pocket, proffers a penny. 'Away and get yourself a wee glass of mild and we'll have a chat, get to know you a bit better and all.'

Henry takes the coin and Johnny leaps up. 'I'll join you at the bar.' When they are out of earshot of the group, he cuffs the loon round the wrist. 'Come away outside a minute, will you?'

'What? It's pouring with rain.'

'Please.'

Henry looks at him; a man's look, not the easy acquiescence Johnny could once have expected. But when he sees Johnny is in earnest, Henry agrees.

Johnny knows a spot. There is a sheltered niche tucked round the back of the inn – he'd used it once with some quine from a travelling band, though he doesn't like to think of that now – degrading even for him. He steps inside and Henry follows. 'Look,' Johnny says, 'dinnae encourage them, all right?'

There is only a little light – spill from the oil lamps, fug of moon – but he can see Henry's quizzical expression. 'What do you mean?'

'All this talk of third tits and strange marks – it might seem harmless, but once that lot get going, they come up with all sorts of funny ideas.'

'Like what?'

'You know – superstitious stuff.'

Henry's fiddling in the pocket of his breeks, takes out a bashed old tin which he balances in his palm. He opens it and takes out a paper, then gathers a scant clump of tobacco. Johnny hadn't realized the loon had taken to smoking – back at Windyhillock he would cover his head with his blankets while the others took their pipes, throat bulging in an effort not to cough.

'Seems harmless enough tae me.' Henry arranges the baccy, long fingers moving deftly. He pauses before licking the paper. 'I thought you liked stories?'

Johnny doesn't want to argue with the loon, stoke ill-feeling between them – but he's been in the Cabrach long enough to know what happens when folks take on queer ideas. The winters spent muttering about cloven-hoofed footprints up croft walls, snow-blind farmers swearing they saw a quine up on the braes, tinted blue with cold. Then after the melt, after weeks of being pressed in by thoughts and snowdrifts, they might find a wifie with two black eyes, or a man in an armchair soaked in piss and liquor, or a farmer round the back of his barn with a shotgun in his mouth. It was best to nip in the bud anything that sounded like superstition – it served no purpose other than to let folks content themselves that there was an explanation for life's cruelties and misfortunes, something they might control.

His ma would chide him for this opinion – she was a devotee of magical thinking. Johnny remembers the day he came home from school and told her he could write, and as he began that tentative first letter she snatched the pencil from his left hand and shoved it in his right. If his ma had seen the bog woman, hauled from the peat with hair like fire, she'd have pressed the glassy surface of her hagstone to her lips and hung rowan from the lintel to protect them from the devil.

The ploughman lights his cigarette and takes a short, hard draw. 'Are you jealous?'

'Of what?'

'Well, back in there, it seemed like folks were keen tae listen tae me.'

'I told you, loon – they're forming their own stupid theories, and they want you tae help them. It's got nothing tae do with jealousy.'

'But what I mean is, they were keener tae listen tae me than you – and I know that might upset you.'

The men are close, the niche only size enough for lust or conspiracy. Henry takes a deeper pull on his cigarette, then rolls his eyes back in pleasure as he exhales. He fancies himself as some kind of hero, probably, lauded for as long as he tells the farmers what they want to hear. Johnny knows all about that, and maybe he ought to allow the loon one sad evening of glory. He's about to go, leave it for tonight, when Henry takes him by the wrist. 'I know you, Jack.'

'What did you call me?' It is a whisper, Johnny's mouth suddenly dry; he's unsure if the loon even heard him under the ceaseless pounding of the rain.

'Jack was a nice name, why did you change it?'

Johnny winces, disquiet stirring in his belly. He steps out of the niche. Sometimes it makes good sense not to mount a challenge – to be the one to back down, relinquish a nugget of power for free so you might charge for the next. 'All right, I'll leave you to it – you tell them whatever you like about the bog wifie. But promise me, loon – you winnae call me by that name again.'

LIZZIE

When Lizzie gets home, there is chatter from the parlour – tonight Jane is hosting the inaugural Women's League of Honour meeting, and Lizzie is both late and disinclined to attend. She will make her excuses, but supposes she ought to greet the visitors. She steps into the parlour, aware of the keen scent of pipe smoke and liquor she brings with her.

'Good evening.'

The women reply in chorus, reflexive – until they see Lizzie in her sodden clothes.

'Elizabeth, you were caught in the rain, I see.' Jane glances at her guests, a few women assembled round the fire with balls of wool in their laps. This was Jane's plan for the first meeting – women making themselves useful, knitting socks for the men at the front.

'Yes, it's still pouring, I'm afraid.'

Jane wrinkles her nose. 'There's a smell of whisky.'

It is pointless lying, for the husbands of these women will tell their wives of Lizzie's presence, drinking, amongst them. 'I've been up at the peats with the constabulary men, then I stopped at The Pheasant to see them off.'

'A bad influence, those officers.' Jane gives a little breathy laugh, clearly aware of Lizzie's breach of one of their honourable women's dictums.

'I suppose my Jock's up there too?' asks Anne Campbell – a sturdy woman with a bosom that could take a bullet and a gold chain that's tucked enough into her blouse that folks can see what her husband can afford, but no one can rightly accuse her of showing it off.

'Aye,' says Lizzie, 'and your husband too, Esther.'

Esther Sinclair's hands still at her needles. She is a woman of sharp edges, narrow hips. 'I dinnae resent him a drink, he works hard. I'd be careful being seen in there though, Mistress Calder. My husband tells me he's seen all sorts of rowdiness. I've heard him pray that the Lord might purge from his mind some of the lewd things he's had to listen to.'

Lewd things, Lizzie supposes, like the way they had spoken about the bog woman – though it was not the words themselves that had disgusted Lizzie but the way they reduced the woman to her crudest physicality. Johnny, at least, had called time on that line of talk.

'I'll pay heed.'

'Nae so much a worry with the likes of mine and Anne's good husbands, but I'll bet there were others there and all?'

'Oh, a few. Johnny Nicol was there.' Lizzie does not know why she mentions him specifically, given he is neither husband nor kin to these women, but he is in her head – it had been good of him, too, to question James's flippancy. It had irritated Lizzie, at the peats, when she had handed James the piece of twisted metal and asked if he'd get it looked at, and he'd just wrapped it in his handkerchief and told Lizzie to keep it for now. She had been indignant, complaining that a policeman should not be so uninterested in the evidence, but he had simply laughed and mimicked her with his hand on his hip.

Esther purses her lips. 'I rest my case. I hear it was Johnny you got tae carry that thing down from the bog?'

'That's right.'

'And has anyone found out what it is yet?'

The women have stopped knitting, wait patiently for whatever tidbit Lizzie might share to colour their theories. Word has spread as they've passed on the tracks, gathered at hearths to stitch and mend for the coming winter and impart truths – various – breathless as a grace before the meal gets cold.

'Well, that is what the constabulary men are trying to work out. Inspector Esslemont will have someone look through the records, see if there are any reports of missing women, murders, anything like that.'

Esther shudders. 'I dinnae like to think of it, some lassie abandoned up there.'

'I hear she's an ugly-looking thing as well,' says Anne, no better than the men.

'Stop,' says Esther, 'it's nae good for . . .' Her hand moves to her stomach, rounding over a curve that is scarcely there.

The women exclaim, and Esther gives a coy smile, softening her wind-bitten face. She lifts her knitting to show a chick-soft white sock hanging from the needle that would be barely large enough for a man's toe. 'I thought you might have noticed.'

Anne clears her throat, pats Esther's knee. 'Are you sure that's wise? Only . . . I dinnae think it's sensible tae get too attached.'

'This time it'll keep. I've never gone so far before. I feel it – and the Lord told me.' She dips her head as though thanking Him, eyes a touch too bright – tears, perhaps, or the gentle mania of someone who thinks they've heard a holy voice speaking to them through the kirk ceiling.

'Even so, you'll be all the more disappointed if . . .'

'I am used to disappointment, Anne. I have lost count. But this time, it'll be different.' Esther looks about her, a darting neediness, as though the other women's acknowledgement might be just the thing to make the pregnancy stick.

'Well, congratulations,' says Jane.

'It's wonderful news.' Lizzie smiles and Esther returns her gaze, a pale eye sliding over Lizzie's stomach – perhaps she thinks they share the same tragedies. Lizzie supposes the women are desperate to know. No doubt she is a favoured topic of claik, brought here nigh on a decade ago as William Calder's wife and no news yet. It is not a course she can see her life taking now – her husband has his appetites but presumably he sates them in town, for it was seldom, before he left, that he would visit her bedroom. Occasionally he would stand outside, the dark smudges of his feet showing under the door, as though to say: *I could if I wanted to*. Yet rarer still – and mercifully – he would open that door and come inside, and if the candle had been blown out she could at least pretend he was someone else. A certain shame, then, in making sounds akin to pleasure while her face ground into the pillow.

Lizzie excuses herself, blaming the fact that she is cold and damp, and lets Jane lightly scold her – *well, if you will go running around in this weather*. Upstairs, she loosens her hair and lets it drip down her back, flops on to her bed. She always finds it difficult, amongst these women who speak so highly of their good men – who love and cosset them, keep no secrets. Before she walked home, Lizzie had spoken to James outside the inn.

'You said you'd speak to your father about that money William was trying to get together.'

James had frowned. 'Ah, well . . .'

'Did you?'

'Yes, but . . .' James had glanced at his colleagues, beckoning through the car's fogged glass. 'There was a farm, up Nairn way. They were trying to get a great sum together, raiding their savings. My da counselled them against it, said the land wasn't worth that much. It fell through, as you said.'

'And?'

'And I was right, the money was drawn down anyway. A little over £500, I think.'

'What was it for, then?'

One of the constables had pressed on the horn, and James waved a hand. 'My da didn't want to say. Maybe I caught him on an off day, but he couldn't be persuaded. Look, Lizzie, I've got to get back. I'll have a go at him again another time. Your husband's probably got a record of it somewhere, in any case.' And James had withdrawn from her and ducked into the driver's seat, off back to his life.

William surely would have kept a record – vigilant man, and all that. And Lizzie ought to know what the money was spent on – ought to have known when they married, or been able to ask him. Yet he would never speak of that time, the rift with his father that had seen him turfed out to Blackwater. In the early days of their marriage, he had treated Lizzie like a child or an irritant – William twenty-five and she eighteen, asking foolish questions on how to run a household, what he liked and disliked, whether they ought to hire more servants: how to navigate her new life. She had tried, also, to ask William about his business; he had regarded her with amusement and said there was little of it she would understand. Still, those days were better than what came later – the silence, the closed doors, his bitter tempers that would smoke the house until Lizzie left it, went to walk miles through the Cabrach mizzle.

She is seized now by a feeling she can name: anger. It is anger that gets her up off her bed, lurching towards the door and out into the hallway. She can deal with a bit of anger. Lizzie moves swiftly up the stairs to the top floor of the house, where William has his study. There is only a little light, an oval window at one end of the landing that throws a white egg of light across the floor. It is a mundane thrill, going somewhere she has not been welcome. William's study was where he spent most of his time when he was not in town. A cold press of his lips to hers on arriving home, for the benefit of any watching housekeepers, and then he would go up and close the door behind him. Lizzie would sit alone in the parlour, imagining company in the other wingback chair, conversation, a kiss that deepened. She'd think about a life where she could lie in bed and look a man in the eyes and whisper: tell me all the things you have done wrong, all the ways you are imperfect. She would imagine being asked likewise, and forgiven.

When she reaches the study door, Lizzie slips her palm round the knob and it gives, slightly, but then rattles and goes no further. Lizzie tries to force it, but then she hears a tread on the floorboards below.

'Elizabeth?' Jane's head appears in the stairwell. She calls Lizzie's name again and there is little to be done except wait, her mind scrabbling for an explanation. 'What are you doing up here?'

'Why is the door locked?' Lizzie asks.

'Personal effects, chequebooks, hard cash – all of interest to thieves. Was there something you needed?'

'I was just . . . having a look.'

'For what?'

'Nothing in particular. Do you have the key?'

'For safekeeping, yes.'

The women regard each other in the dim passage. Jane's serene expression, face contoured by the moonlight so that she looks as though she's made of stone.

Lizzie relents. 'I'll be off to bed, then. Goodnight.'

Jane smiles – obedience a simple pleasure. 'Goodnight, sister. Oh, and we ought to make sure that body is buried. Mistress Sinclair has gone home quite upset by it all.'

There is an urge in Lizzie, then, to defend the bog woman against their suppositions that she is fearsome, horrific – she wishes they could instead wonder at the smoothness of the woman's cheek, the bumps of her spine like beads on a necklace.

Lizzie wishes they could have seen her small head cupped in Johnny's palm.

'James is looking into it – I'll decide what to do after that.'

'Aye, well,' says Jane. 'Let's hope he comes good.'

October 1905

JACK

Jack shuffled across the yard, the haar damp on his skin, reducing his vision to a few feet ahead. He never got to see Windyhillock properly – he'd been told the farm was five hundred acres, but there was no way of telling if that was true, for the grieve probably lied as freely as he cursed. It sat on the flat top of a hill, surrounded by fields that dropped away from the summit. It was strange, not being able to see the outer reaches of the pastures, as if Jack could walk out and suddenly find he'd gone too far, reached the edge of something. When he got to the chaumer he lifted the latch, ducked into their dismal lodgings where the lamp was already lit – that one oil lamp that could barely contend with the draught that swept in under the door.

Henry was on his bed reading. His brow was always furrowed when he did so, mouth moving unconsciously over the words. 'All right?' he said, looking up.

'I thought you were heading off home today?' Jack asked.

'Decided against it – I need the rest. I dinnae think I realized how much this work takes it out of you.'

'You'll get used to it soon enough. It's only your first fee.'

'Aye, I suppose.'

The loon was just fifteen, round in the face, with a boy's soft white arms and belly. His Bible lay open on the bed – a cheap one, curling at the edges – and Jack moved it out of the way so he could sit. He quite liked these Sabbath afternoons, the few free hours when he could exhale, talk of idle things.

'Would you have liked to have done something else?'

Henry shrugged. 'I didnae have the choice. Nae like you.'

'Who told you that?'

'Everyone knows – you could have kept on with your schooling, stayed off the farms. Your da goes to work in a suit and tie, or so I've heard.'

'Aye,' said Jack, tugging his boots off and chucking them on to the floor, 'but I dinnae want tae be like my da.'

'You're clever, though.' Henry looked at him, the bashful admiration lads of that age always have for those a few years older. 'You could have done anything.'

'Well, there was a romance about all this, in my mind.'

'A romance?'

Jack examined the muck under his fingernails. It sounded stupid, girlish, to use a word like romance – and preposterous, at Windyhillock.

'Och, you know . . . a man and the land. Chasing the lassies. Packing up and going somewhere new every six months. Like freedom, I suppose.'

'So you'll nae bide if Slora asks you to?'

In a couple of months, the farmer would confer with the grieve, decide which of the farm gang were worth keeping on. Jack hadn't decided yet whether he'd accept – if they found him worthy. Windyhillock was a dump, but still, he'd heard of worse. Better the devil you know, sometimes.

'Maybe. You're right, maybe I should do something else.'

'Like what?'

Jack pretended to muse on this, though in truth he'd often thought of it – a different life. You had to, when you were worked 'til your fingers split, out in the biting cold, shovelling the same pappy porridge down your throat day after day. 'I'll go wandering. I'll sing for my supper round every inn in Nairn and Elgin, then I'll go tae Aberdeen, then Edinburgh and London.' He grinned, getting into his stride. 'I'll sail the high seas and marry a mermaid, dance a jig on the crest of a wave.'

Henry giggled. 'But really?'

Really, Jack would try to make enough money to get a house somewhere, take his ma and his brother with him – but that wasn't the sort of fantasy folks wanted to hear about.

'That's what I'll do! Come on, man – you must have bigger dreams than working your way up to first horseman and wedding a kitchen maid and toiling in the mud for the rest of your days?'

'I wouldnae mind making it tae first.' Henry said it shyly, like he'd be laughed at for even entertaining the notion.

'But you're nae bothered by the maid?' Jack winked at his friend. 'You'd rather a farmer's daughter, is that it? Now, there's your ambition.'

The loon looked away, embarrassed. 'I'm nae bothered by all that.'

'Och, come on, is it Violet you like?'

'No!'

Jack went quiet, hoping it might elicit a confession. He himself was well aware of the virtues of the farmer's daughter, a bonny thing nearly his age. She had a head of golden curls like from a love song, offering something pretty in that place of shit and labour. He had looked out for her, just then, as he'd crossed the yard, directing a casual glance through the farmhouse window to where the family was sitting down to their roast beef – Slora and his wife and the twins, for Violet had a brother, Isaac, a lad who went about in scrubbed boots, kept well away from the gang.

'All right then, so it's first horseman you want, and you'll take or leave the wife?'

'I suppose so,' said Henry, 'but it's unlikely. I'm nae strong enough – or I dinnae look it. I can graft just as much as the bigger men, but when folks look at me they dinnae see it.' He plucked at the loose cotton of his shirt, the way it tented off his chest.

'You'll lay on muscle soon enough, you're still young. I was the same at your age.' Jack lifted an arm and clenched his fist to harden the bicep, a tight ball under his sleeve. 'Feel that now.'

'What?'

'Go on.'

Henry was hesitant, cupping his hand over Jack's arm, then pressing his fingers into the muscle. 'Right. Aye.'

'You'll be like this soon. And if nae? Well, just show folks what you can do anyway. They always say it's the quiet ones.'

'What do you mean?'

'You know, the ones folks think won't amount tae much, they turn out tae do the most damage. A splinter in the paw of a lion, and all that. There'll be no stopping you. You'll make first and then you'll be a grieve somewhere, even have your own farm. No, you'll own the land the farm's on!'

Henry scoffed, though he looked pleased. 'Now you're going too far.'

'Nah, I've faith in you.' Jack was exaggerating, but it seemed a good deed to encourage the loon. They sat for a moment on the bed, shoulder to shoulder as they'd been on the day they'd arrived, dragging their kists up the hill.

'Well,' Henry said eventually, 'I hope you'll bide.'

The other two were back by seven. Tam came first, whistling his way across the yard, and when Jack heard him coming he moved over to his own bed and lay there, nonchalantly turning his ma's hagstone between his fingers. Donald, the first horseman, arrived not long after, mighty pleased with himself at having spent the afternoon with one of the maids.

'I thought I was getting blue baws, it's been so long.' Donald was splayed across his bed with his boots still on, and took a demonstrative clutch of his crotch. 'Always the worst bit about the hairst, there's no time for . . . other activities.'

Tam chuckled at that and passed a bottle around.

'What have we got here, then?' Donald held the bottle up to the lamp: no label, a crumbling cork. He hoiked it out and took a swig. 'Nae bad.'

When the hooch reached Jack, it made his nostrils burn. He took a pinched mouthful and swallowed before he could taste it, then passed the bottle to Henry. There was a hierarchy at the farms – the first and second horsemen, the halflin, the orra-loon – and the orra-loon was watched by the rest of them, tentative as a calf still damp from the caul as he took a swig that was too big for him.

'That's, ah . . . strong.'

Donald smirked. 'Now then, Jack, I'm in a fine mood, and I could do with a wee bit of music. As good fortune would have it, I'm told that's your speciality.'

'Who told you that?'

Donald reached a long finger up, tapped the tip of his nose. 'None of your fucking business.'

Not like it was much of a secret anyway. Despite the miles between Windyhillock and the other farms, claik would travel. The gangs crossed paths at the feeing markets and meal-and-ales, chucking around descriptions of their colleagues' talents and temperaments that would stick like burs. With the whisky fuddling him, Jack supposed it'd do no harm to sing them a song – he was chuffed, if he was honest, at the chance to impress Donald and Tam. Those two were proper men with scars and tales; they seemed so much older than Jack and his eighteen years. He whistled a wee tune, teasing them.

'Ah,' said Tam, 'I think you're right, Don.'

The first horseman gave a shrug, as though it were a given. 'It's nae just the tune he does, supposedly. He'll sing a whole ballad if you ask him nicely.'

'Oooh.' Tam wiggled his unkempt eyebrows. 'Go on then.'

This felt to Jack like a bigger hurdle. Not that he couldn't sing, only it was the first time in front of these two. He'd been at Windyhillock a few months, and the men seemed to like him well enough, but still, he knew he'd scupper something if he cocked it up. Tam took his hesitancy for a game, the second horseman dropping to his knees and crawling across the boards. He looked up at Jack with giant eyes and affected a stupid toffee tone.

'Oh, sing us a wee ditty, Jacky boy.'

This was typical Tam – silly, unpredictable, so you never knew if he was messing around or off his rocker. Donald started a beat on his thigh, calling out for Jack to sing; the pair of them demanding it – go on, go on – voices a thump like a fist beating a chest.

Jack's mouth was dry. Words came, dissolved, returned – a clamour of those that would make them laugh, clever ones, utter filth and curses. He thought of the grieve, his self-important wee strut, the oily strands of hair arranged to cover his bald spot. The words formed, and then the first line, then the rhyme. There was the tempo, there was the song spilling from him –

O –
He's a face like an arse that's had a slap
All glowering out fae under his cap
A lash-tongued wife like you wouldnae believe
That's the lot o' Windyhillock's grieve.

A tight moment, then Donald smiled. 'We've got ourselves an entertainer.'

Tam had permission to laugh then – a roar with his mouth

open, showing the black craters in his gums. 'Nice one, Jacky boy! Do you do bawdy ones and all?'

Jack shrugged, tried to tamp down the relief before it surfaced as a ludicrous grin. 'I can do.'

'I daresay you could make up one about wee Violet.'

'Another time.' Jack had thought of a few nice lines about her, as it happened – even written them down in a notebook as if he fancied himself as Rabbie Burns. But they weren't what the gang wanted – those words would be scoffed at, get him called a jessie.

'You shy now?'

'No. Just . . . another time.'

'Aye well,' said Donald, 'you'd do well tae keep wee Violet out of your head anyway.'

'And her brother,' said Tam.

Jack snorted. 'I'm nae bent.'

'I just mean, those two look nigh on identical fae behind. Be careful you dinnae sneak up on the wrong one.' Tam was right – the twins did look similar from a distance, the same floppy blonde curls.

'Really though, leave her well alone, unless you want Slora tae have your baws off with a sickle. There's plenty of other lassies for the taking.' Donald appraised him for a moment. 'You been with a quine, Jack?'

Jack reached for the near-empty bottle and took some more, stalling by holding it in his mouth until it felt as if his skin was peeling off. 'No one you'd know.'

The horsemen sniggered. 'He's discreet, Tam. Good man.'

'And you?' Tam looked at Henry. The loon with his blanket pulled over his knees, nigh senseless from the hooch. He must have understood, though, because he flushed ruddy and the two horsemen laughed, their question answered.

Still Tam needled: 'Well?'

Jack felt sorry for the orra-loon; his simple look and the downy hair at his lip. 'Och, leave him be. He's only a boy.'

Donald got up, arrived at Henry's bedside in one long stride – the chaumer was small, though they always were. The lads slept close enough they could practically taste each other's breath in their mouths. Donald crouched in the dark, his limbs folded like a spider edging in on some witless beastie.

'Do you nae want tae talk about quines?'

But the orra-loon was spared. The chaumer door flew open, a figure emerging through the haar like some two-bit villain. He brought the stink of Sunday meat, the fat of a cheap cut. 'You'll put that rotgut away else you'll be good for nothing in the morn.' The glower of a stumpy pipe lit the top half of the grieve's face: his ludicrous moustache, ratty little eyes. 'And we're tae have guests.'

'Oh aye,' said Donald, the only one of them who'd speak to the grieve as someone approaching an equal. 'Who's that then?'

'Prospective buyers.'

'Eh?'

'Dinnae get your knickers in a twist, boys – Slora's nae going anywhere. It's just the land. Good productive land, this. And these men will want tae see that those who work it are good hard workers and all.' The grieve eyed them, a vague shimmer of disgust at the way they'd shed their boots, stretched out their aching muscles; at their idleness. When he reached Jack, the grieve stopped. It reminded Jack of the feeing market, when he'd been looked over, his worth assessed. The grieve had got right up in his face then, searching for any signs of weakness – bad skin, crossed eyes; any reasons to pay less. Jack had half expected to be ordered to open his mouth and have his teeth inspected like a mare, so he'd done it willingly, broken into a shit-eating grin while looking the grieve straight in the eye.

'We'd look better if we had another horseman.' The grieve nodded towards Jack. 'Is he ready?'

Donald narrowed his eyes. 'I daresay.'

'Good – do it at the next full moon then.'

Jack's heart flipped. He'd heard whispers of these things – strange ceremonies, rituals hinted at by a nudge and a wink; lads becoming horsemen.

'Right you are,' Donald said.

The grieve tipped back his head and blew out their pitiful flame. 'But for God's sake, dinnae go too far this time.'

LIZZIE

Lizzie stood with an elbow resting on the dining-room mantelpiece. She had been cooed over by the ladies and kissed by the men, their fingers slippery at her satin waist. Now, she was listening to her father holding court. He gestured at the wallpaper round the fireplace – wisteria bursting forth from the confines of a trellis, a cascade of unfurling ribbon. 'My wife was unhappy with how it was done originally – the colour looked wrong with the tiling, she felt.' George Brodie shrugged, as though to say he could not help but indulge her whims, despite it being true that the house had only just been decorated; indeed it had only just been built, the Brodies its first owners. A year or so earlier, he had come home to their old terrace and unfurled the plans on the dining table, pointing with a thick finger to the extra rooms they would have, their grand proportions. One of the best houses in Elgin, he'd said, and Lizzie's mother had squealed and summoned champagne.

'The new paper looks very fine,' said Helen Calder. She was dressed in burgundy, which Lizzie considered unfortunate given her complexion.

'Yes, that's what we thought – it brings out the veining in the marble. Italian, it is.'

Helen murmured in admiration, touched her daughter at the elbow. 'Jane, what do you think of the new scheme?'

'Well, I hope Mr Brodie got a good price for the decorators – their rates have become obscene.' Jane sighed at the stern look her mother gave her. 'It's nice,' she added.

'A shame William isn't here to see.'

'I can't imagine him appreciating it, Mother.'

Lizzie had only met Jane's brother a couple of times – and even then, briefly. He was always hurrying off, attending to business or seeking out other men to discuss it with. Old at twenty-five, he existed on the periphery of Lizzie's world – a figure in a corner, switch of dark jacket, large hand clutched round the neck of a bottle.

'A shame to miss young William tonight,' George turned to the Calder patriarch. 'Where's he off to, Hugh?'

'Business.' Hugh took a sip of brandy, swirled it around his mouth so the slack skin of his cheeks puffed out. 'Bit of a bind to sort out . . .'

Hugh turned away from the group, inviting George to join him with an incline of his head. Helen Calder immediately crouched to admire the carved fruit and flowers on the fireplace surround, and Lizzie copied her feigned nonchalance, eavesdropping as she studied the pattern in the rug.

'It's some nonsense at one of the hotels – silly woman. She's known to be a bit . . . anyway, we managed to calm her down.'

Lizzie glanced at her father, his face grave but pinked with pride at being invited into Hugh's confidence.

'I told William to give her enough cash to make her eyes light up and then let it lie, but he took it upon himself to find the lad who was supposedly to blame and . . .' From the corner of her eye Lizzie saw Hugh Calder mocking a slice across his throat. 'Anyway. Good job with the decor, Brodie.'

The men turned back to the room at the same time Bridget entered. 'The Esslemonts are here.' The maid flung the doors open, ready for their entrance. Lizzie watched her father smooth the scant fluff of his hair over his crown – Mr Esslemont was George's manager at the bank, or a few rungs up the ladder, if George were to be honest.

Jane tilted her head towards Lizzie. 'They are bringing their son.' Her voice was edged with something unpleasant.

'So I've heard.' Lizzie could barely remember the son – he'd been away at university. As a child she had played in the garden of the big Esslemont house a few times, remembered being led in silent awe down the hallway with its high ceilings and ornate coving. Outside, the young James had taken little persuasion to join in with the games. He had played merrily, leaping over the patio wall to the lawn, until suddenly he decided not to and had run off inside, leaving Lizzie and the other children calling after him.

'Doubtless we'll hear all about his great achievements,' said Jane, 'him being a promising young man et cetera.'

'You two were in the same year at school, weren't you?'

'Aye,' said Jane, 'same class and all, though the head teacher was more inclined to write a letter of recommendation to the university for him.'

The son walked in, his step an elegant arc as he held his mother's hand lightly in his own. A reverent dip to his head, cheeks flushed – there was cold in the air, the year pivoting towards winter. He lifted a drink from the tray held before him, nodded his thanks to the maid before sipping. James Esslemont seemed entirely at ease in his body, standing sedately while all around was a blur of handshakes and exclamations, until his gaze fell on the two young ladies by the fireplace.

'Lizzie Brodie!' He strode over, took her by the elbows. 'How wonderful—' a kiss on each cheek, '—to see you.'

'And you, what a pleasant surprise.'

'It's been years! You were a child when I last saw you.'

And now I am not, thought Lizzie, as James surveyed the

exposed skin across her collarbones, the curve of waist to hip – not quite practised enough in subtlety.

'And what pleasure is this? Miss Jane Calder – or, at least, I still presume?'

Jane offered her hand. 'Are you well, James?'

'I am. And you? What do you make of the decor? I hear the paint has barely finished drying.'

'Jane seems unmoved,' said Lizzie.

'I thought it was perfectly pleasant before. Though really, it's not something that concerns me.'

'Well, I like it,' said James. 'Better than my parents' house. I thought when I came back from university it might have changed, but everything's still maroon, and we still have that dusty old furniture of my grandfather's, and his grandfather's before him.' He chuckled, surely imagining the lacquered generations of chests and chairs, their fine old money.

Lizzie glanced at her mother, who was holding a silver candelabra to the light of the window, urging other women to admire it. 'My mother grows bored easily.'

'I empathize,' said James, 'though I also hope to know contentment in the way Jane does.'

'It is simply that I do not admire things that are frivolous.'

'Hear! Hear! Though,' James drained his brandy, 'where's the fun in that?'

There was a pattern to the dinners. The first course was for talk of mutual friends and airy town gossip, polite. Soup was sipped and lips dabbed gently with napkins, and women would pat Lizzie's forearm and tell her how bonny she'd become.

That evening, Lizzie's mother had seated her next to James, and she let him tell of his time at university, all the while taking sideways glances at how his hair flowed back from his temples, his deft gestures, the elegant way he buttered his bread. James told her of the offer his father had made of a position at the bank, which he was unsure whether to accept. 'I may do something completely different. I can't do everything expected of me, a man has to make his own way.'

'What might you do?'

James shrugged and sat back a moment, seemingly content at all the possibilities spread before him. 'I was thinking perhaps medicine, or the police force.'

'A fine thing to have so many options.' Jane was sitting across from them, clearly eavesdropping.

'Quite. What my father is offering is an excellent opportunity, but while it is easily offered, that does not make it easy, or appealing, to accept. And what of you?' James tilted his body, an angling of the shoulder that seemed to close Jane out of the conversation. Lizzie became aware of his closeness – James's legs spread beyond the width of his own chair, the hand that held his knife resting not so very far from hers. She had experienced this before; audacious men who encroached on her space, making her lean away, though she didn't have that compulsion with James.

'Well, my father will surely be hoping to marry me off soon.'

He lifted an eyebrow. 'And what do you make of that?'

Lizzie regarded him over the rim of her glass. 'Well, if he's fabulously rich and will allow me to organize parties every week, I suppose I might feel inclined to accept.'

James lifted his glass to hers. 'To a woman who knows what she wants.' And then, beneath the table, a touch at her knee. Lizzie waited a moment for him to right himself, but James's leg stayed where it was. She weighed her options – she could feign innocence, or snatch herself away and glare at him, askance. But it seemed the most exciting moment of her life so far – the wine and fluttering candles, the twitch of surprise at the corner of James's mouth when he realized she was game.

*

The main course, and talk turning to more serious matters. Jane perked up at the discussion of the latest Calder acquisitions – how satisfied she seemed with her family's relentless pursuit of property, of land; something she considered loftier than the wasteful replacement of mauve Lincrusta with hand-painted wallpaper. Hugh Calder speared a piece of beef with his fork. 'We've nearly secured the Richmond Hotel in Huntly. They've run us in circles over the price.'

'And William will oversee it, will he?' asked Mr Webster, a businessman who had made his money in textiles.

'Well.' Hugh chewed slowly while the room waited – that was his way, to take his time answering, confident his audience would wait. 'Perhaps. But we've other irons in the fire.'

'Have you another option?'

Hugh glanced at his daughter. 'Aye, we'll see.'

There was a murmur around the table. 'Well now,' said Webster, 'why would a young lady want to get herself embroiled in business?'

'It is not a foregone conclusion.'

'If anyone could do it, it'd be Miss Calder,' said George.

'Fair enough, she's a bright girl, but . . . come on then, Jane, tell us what you'd do with the place.' There was a teasing edge to Webster's voice.

Jane looked at Hugh, who shrugged. 'Well, a complete refurbishment, to start with. That place hasn't been touched since before I was born.'

Webster chuckled. 'Which is not so very long ago.'

'The lobby needs a complete overhaul, and the dining room, if we want to attract a different sort of clientele.'

'Oh aye?' Mr Esslemont set down his fork, his interest encouraging Jane. She raised her voice to be heard over Webster's scraping cutlery.

'Yes. At the moment the place barely breaks even. They rely on passing trade, folks in town for the feeing markets and so on – folks who don't have much money to spend. But I think we could attract guests from further afield for dinner and dances.'

Mistress Webster clapped her hands. 'We could help with the soft furnishings, we've some lovely damasks just come in.'

'Ah, very kind of you. Yes, we'll be sure to look into such things when—'

'They're divine. We've paisley or fleur-de-lis, in several shades. Excellent quality, just right for a place like that.'

'Yes, all in good time.'

'Mistress Webster is right,' Lizzie said. 'It's the little touches that attract the better sort of people. And you'd do well to consider such things from the outset – it'll affect the colours you use on the walls, the flooring, all of it.'

'I – I suppose so,' said Jane. 'Thank you, Lizzie. I'll be sure to consult you.'

From the head of the table, George beamed. 'My girl has always had excellent taste.'

'Sounds like you ought to hire Miss Brodie to advise,' said Mr Esslemont.

'Oh, I've no aspirations like that.' Lizzie was conscious of those round the table looking at her, sure that they could see the great effort she was making to appear poised, to not tremble as she was pressed knee to knee with James.

'Well, do consider us – both of you,' said Mistress Webster. 'We've some lovely tulles, too, for dresses. Come and have a look one day, Lizzie – you could make yourself something beautiful for the next dance.'

'And will you give me a keen price,' said Lizzie, 'given we are friends?'

A man slapped his thigh. 'She's a shrewd one!'

'Aye, she'll be giving us the odds on the by-election next,' said Jane, her smile tight.

Lizzie waved her hand, airy as a queen. 'Oh, Sutherland's a sure thing, no doubt about that.'

The men roared.

'Your girl's a political pundit and all, Brodie!'

George laughed along with them, but then his face grew serious. 'Really though – there is no need for my daughter to make her own dresses. Fine as your tulles are, Mistress Webster.'

'Surely not, but it is industrious.' James had not spoken much until then, had just sipped his wine and listened, the natural arrangement of his face seeming evidence to Lizzie of profound intelligence. 'What colour would you choose?'

One of the men snorted. 'All that schooling's made you soft, boy.'

'You'd look very well in green, Lizzie, I'd say. Or black.'

The wives tittered at that, said a girl of eighteen ought to wear gayer shades. Lizzie smiled as they chattered about what would best become her, absorbed more by the dawning realization that to know what might suit, James must have been looking at her, taking in the tone of her skin and her dark hair. Lizzie never wore green – but was open to suggestion.

'I'll consider both.'

'Do.'

And under the table, a fingertip stroke. Soft hands and heat and the line on a palm. They did not look at each other; it seemed the meeting of their eyes would dash something, send them jerking apart – and that was not what Lizzie wanted.

Later, the party moved to the parlour. By then the air was heady with liquor and the perfume of the flowers, the scent dabbed on the wrists and throats of the women who gathered to impart less salubrious town gossip. Lizzie stood a little apart from them, watching the men through the open door. They followed George on his grandly named art tour, cigars wedged between their lips as they regarded the paintings in their great curlicued frames. As they had passed the parlour, Lizzie stuck her head round the door and found that James had fallen back from the others. She watched him, anxious to commit to memory the way he looked, stood, moved. Eventually, he noticed her. A purse of his lips, eyes darting down the hall, and Lizzie realized with a swoop in her chest that he was looking for a place for them to go. She was about to leave the parlour when someone called her name.

Jane seemed hesitant, cowed in a way that was unlike her. 'I'd be keen to hear your ideas for the Richmond. I suspect you may have more of an eye for these things than me. Shall we take a seat?' Words quick, as though they were hot.

Lizzie took a sip of her brandy. It was strong, made her vision soft and gauzy; the long, cream satin of Jane's glove, the pattern in the carpet that seemed to shift beneath her. She knew James was still looking at her.

Jane waited for an answer. And Lizzie tried a sympathetic smile and said, 'Another time.'

October 1915

LIZZIE

This Sabbath, a thick frost. The moss on the kirk dyke is bristling with it, like hairs raised on an arm. The toll of the bell has summoned folks from warm beds – a test of faith on mornings like this. Still, the rain has ceased and the ground is solid, the footprints of the pious who traipsed through September's mud frozen now, a record of those who faithfully attended last Sabbath day. Lizzie looks for someone to strike up a conversation with; the Brawlands lot are near but occupied – Maggie smoothing her bairn's tenacious cowlick, the red-bearded ploughman leaning to whisper in the ear of Jock Campbell's eldest daughter. Beyond them, the drear congregation. There is usually more theatre, the clattery voices of the maids and the gangs posturing over lichened gravestones, old folks for whom the weekly trip to kirk is as much social event as Christian obligation. But it seems the cold has put paid to people's good humour, the most God-fearing in a tight huddle by the door: there is Jane and the pinched face of Esther Sinclair, her hand clawed round her belly.

'Winter's coming in,' Lizzie says to Rab's lad Henry, who is standing a little apart from the others, his neck and hands bare.

He looks over his shoulder, as if he thinks she is speaking to someone else. 'Aye.'

'Seems colder than normal this year too.'

'I'm used tae the cold.'

'That'll stand you in good stead.'

'It was bitter up there, where I'm from. The wind coming in off the Firth.' He shudders at the memory.

'You're from Inverness way?'

'Nairn.'

'Ah – my husband's family owned farms up Nairn way, once upon a time.'

They are disturbed by the creak of the gate. A murmur through the crowd, and some lad lets up a hoot. Lizzie looks over Henry's shoulder at the figure entering the kirkyard, lush indigo at his neck. He strolls, shakes hands, though one or two men are stony and will not offer theirs. Folks mutter their incredulity that Johnny Nicol is up and smart for Sunday service. Jock says something as he passes and Johnny throws his hands up in mock penance. 'I've come tae ask forgiveness for my sins.' And Jock manages a laugh at that.

Lizzie has not seen Johnny since the night at The Pheasant, when he'd stood next to James, defending the bog woman. She watches the farm lads as he stops to talk to them – hands taken from pockets, faces from collars, as if the sun has come out. Then Johnny starts up a song, voice low and furtive as he glances at the true believers by the door. Lizzie grasps a few words and understands that it is a hymn he has changed, made the tempo quick and rousing.

'He should hope the Reverend disnae hear him,' says Henry.

'Oh, it's only a bit of fun.' The song has made her smile. Lizzie lifts an arm and waves and then Johnny is striding through the assembly, not seeming to notice the way folks gawk at him.

'Blasphemy is what it is,' Henry says.

As he reaches them, Johnny removes his hat, pushes his fingers through hair that is soft and tousled – dry, for once. A slight agitation over the crown of his head that is either the wind or the collective movement of a hundred mouths, twitching to speculate on his presence.

'It's unusual to see you here,' Lizzie says.

'Well, I ought tae cleanse my soul at least once a year.'

Lizzie looks up at the flat grey sky. 'There couldn't be a finer day for it.'

'Well, is that nae the way – to suffer a little? It seems no good only tae trot down when the weather's fine.'

'Ah, is that it? It's not forgiveness unless you've lain down and been flogged.'

They look at each other. Heat in her cheeks, something in the words she used. Then Johnny laughs, and Lizzie joins him, a breach in the hush of the kirkyard. From the corner of her eye Lizzie sees Jane leaning in to hear something whispered by Esther, and drops her smile.

'It's better tae come regularly,' says Henry.

Johnny looks the lad up and down. 'Eh?'

'It's better tae come regularly tae kirk – if you let your list of sins get too long it's awful difficult tae manage.'

'You've nae a long list, then?'

'One or two is enough.' Henry nods towards the kirk doors. 'We should go in.'

It is an austere chapel: stone and wood, with sharp-angled patches of light that cut across the floor from the high-set windows. There is no stained glass to diffuse the glare, and even the hassocks are unyielding, patched with old tweed and stuffed solid with horsehair. Some diligent Cabrach wives have embroidered them with flora and virtuous advice: do ill to no man; pride cometh before a fall.

Lizzie takes the Calder pew up at the front, next to Jane, who stares straight ahead. As the congregation quietens down, it becomes evident that something is amiss. The air seems weighted, shot through with tension. Reverend Bruce steps out of the vestry and makes his way down the dim of the chancel, lit by white candles. He ascends to the pulpit and pauses there, brows knitted. Fractious in the strange atmosphere of the kirk, someone's babby gives a shrill cry, but the Reverend waits, glancing towards the arched ceiling as though the Lord regards him from a pine beam. 'We gather on this Sabbath, as we do every other. Yet today is a sombre day. Today, I must make an announcement that pains me, and will pain this community.'

There is a shifting in the pews, a whimper that Lizzie cannot be sure was just the bairn.

'I must tell you that our noble son, Jimmy Weir, who so courageously left these hills for battle, has been harmed.' He pauses, all the sensibility of a storyteller. 'He has returned, praise God, but he has been severely wounded.'

A wail goes up. It spreads and thickens down the nave, along the pews and into their laps, and there is surely no one clad sturdily enough to stop it reaching through their woollens, to grab at the hearts of them. Lizzie turns to look just as Mistress Weir slumps forward and the hands of women slide over pew and man to reach her. She convulses in three deep sobs, then stops and raises her head, as though bewildered by the attention. Folks turn away then – men slipping arms round their wives, maids laying their cheeks together. Henry with his hands clasped in prayer.

Lizzie could barely pick out Wee Jimmy from the other farm lads, though she knows he is young – the gangling redhead in the back seat on the day they left for war. Still, she recoils at it all – the waste, the awful cry from his mother and the way she coloured after, the eyes that flicked away from her. Perhaps it will be Lizzie one day, sticky with their cloying sympathy; her husband one-legged, eyeless or dead. But probably William will remain unscathed. He had said as much the night before he left: *I'll be back, Elizabeth. I'll certainly be back.*

The Reverend allows them a moment more, observing from on high their tears, the bitter headshakes. 'It is a terrible tragedy. A young man who could have given so much. And it comes at a time when we are tried by other misfortunes – not least the harsh weather, the ruin of so much of the crop. It is easy, at times such as these, to doubt in the Lord's goodness, but we must not turn our hearts from Him. For it is also at these times that the enemy thrives. When we are weakened, when we despair. It is at these times that the devil spreads darkness through our community.' Reverend Bruce's voice has risen, his grip on the pulpit drawing the blood from his fingertips. 'So stand by one another. Care for one another. And be vigilant for any presence that is unwelcome to people of faith.'

After the service, folks hasten away – it is awkward, troublesome, to speak to a woman as wretched as Mistress Weir, with a maimed son and simple daughter, a husband barely cold in the ground. In the kirkyard she rushes towards Lizzie, her bare hands outstretched. 'Mistress Calder.'

'I'm sorry for Jimmy, and for you.'

'Bless your husband. I dinnae know what I'd do without it, with Jimmy unable to work and me as well.' Mistress Weir spreads her fingers to show the huge knuckles, crooked fingers splaying in every direction. Lizzie looks at her blankly. 'His gift, Mistress Calder. The fund.'

Lizzie searches for someone who might rescue her, but they scurry from the kirkyard, collars turned up. Johnny has put on his cap and is heading off, absorbed into a group of men.

'William does not speak about his charity.' Lizzie tries to smile. 'Even to me.'

Mistress Weir claps a hand to her mouth. 'Oh. Well, I think it might gratify you to hear of it. Your husband has left a fund in the Reverend's care to provide for those whose men dinnae return, or who come back... damaged.' Her hand moves to take Lizzie's, squeezes. 'He is a good man, your husband. A good man.'

'I'm glad it has helped you.' Lizzie takes her hand away, chilled even in its glove. 'Please – send your son my best wishes. And if you need anything...' She tails off, alarmed by the proximity to misery, the woman's working mouth.

'If you need anything, be sure to let us know.' Jane has arrived beside them. 'We're having our Women's League meetings each week now – you'd be more than welcome.'

'Oh, thank you, thank you.' Tears brim again in Mistress Weir's eyes. 'Anyway, I'll let you go. I must get back to Jimmy.'

'God bless you,' says Jane.

The two Calder women turn towards Blackwater. The wind has got up, shudders over the braes and through the flattened grasses. Lizzie does not want to ask Jane about the fund, but the further they go, the sharper the curiosity nips at her heels. 'You knew about it, then?'

Jane a pace or two ahead. 'Of course. I know about all of William's financial affairs.'

'And you didn't think to tell me?'

'He is a modest man. It is right to use your good fortune to help others, without being proud of your benevolence.'

'And how much has he put in this fund?'

Jane looks round. 'Don't worry, sister, there is plenty left. He has seen to it that you will not go without while he is gone. And if – God forbid – he doesn't return, he has entrusted me to make provision for you.'

Lizzie resents the way Jane speaks – so like William. She resents the hurry behind, hair in her eyes, and the way her throat is dry, but eventually she manages to put shape to her agitation. 'I looked foolish.'

Jane stops.

'Just then, in front of Mistress Weir – I looked foolish when I didn't know what she was speaking of.'

'I wasn't aware you cared about looking foolish.'

'Sorry?'

'It is a terrible loss to Mistress Weir.' Jane sighs. 'I wasn't going to say anything but . . . you looked rather insensitive, laughing and joking with that man before the service.'

'Well, how could I have known?'

Jane gives a look of disappointment – as though ignorance is no excuse. 'Many are suffering at this time, Elizabeth. Perhaps it is better to be humble before them, instead of drawing attention to yourself.'

'I was only enjoying some company.' Lizzie means it as defiance, but instead only realizes how small her words sound.

JOHNNY

It is Jock Campbell's turn to host the men's prayers, though Johnny has it on good authority that they'll do nothing of the sort, so he goes along. In the kitchen, the men avail themselves of the spread Anne has left out; picking at cold cuts and grey hard-boiled eggs, chewing without tasting. They rock on their feet, adrift without the cosy bustle of a woman at the range. Men steal furtive glances at the clock and Johnny knows what they want because he feels it too – the yearning for comfort. Dougie, naturally, is the one to voice their thoughts. 'Shall we take a dram? In honour of the wee one.'

The men mumble their agreement, no one wishing to seem too keen – it is the Sabbath, and despite Jesus's own talent for turning water into wine, Johnny imagines the Lord might take a dim view of them getting fuddled straight after kirk. Jock pours out generous measures, fine enough stuff, but in the cold of the kitchen all you can smell is the alcohol, astringent in the nose. He pushes the drams across the table, the bottle nearly empty by the time he has supplied them all – Dougie and Sinclair, Johnny and Rab, Henry, Stephen. Alex hurried away after the service, but he was friendly with Jimmy, so perhaps only wanted to go and dab his eyes away from their blundering sympathy.

'To Jimmy.' They drink, each man lost in thought until Rab

manages to ask the question they've surely all been working up to. 'So, ah . . . what's the damage?'

Jock looks grim. 'A leg gone, clean off at the knee. That, and a chestful of shell. He'd nae even been out on the battlefield long – got stuck at the training camp with measles for weeks.'

'Christ, what a waste.' Johnny had assumed it was something like a limb, but still, it hurts to hear it. Jimmy was always a sensitive soul – he would weep when a lamb sickened and he couldn't hold his drink; one Hogmanay he spewed his guts up over the floor of The Pheasant and had to be packed off to an upstairs room to sleep it off. He'd been a pain that night, slopping from arm to arm, but Johnny remembers it fondly now – better that than holding on to past grievances, letting them ferment like a bellyache.

'Tragic.' Rab droops at the shoulders and Johnny gets the sense that he is talking about all of it – Wee Jimmy, the rain, the lost crop.

'Jimmy was a hard worker and all. You'd never find him sitting idle.' Sinclair casts a look at Johnny. 'Not like some.'

Jock shakes his head. 'Aye, and it's all the worse for a lad like that. Can send a man mad, sitting around with too much time tae think. He's been in strange temper, his ma told Anne.'

'Oh aye?'

'Just . . . saying queer things. Having nightmares.'

'We should say a prayer for him,' says Sinclair.

'Aye, well – later.' Jock glances about the group. 'While you're all here, there's something I want tae show you. In the barn.'

There is a general grumble of reluctance to step outside again. 'Och, man, what is it?'

But Jock is having none of their disagreement while they drink his whisky and pick at his wife's hospitality. 'No, come on, you have tae see this.'

*

Although the cold is fair expected in a Cabrach autumn, it seems to have come earlier, harsher than usual. Through the valley, women rush to darn moth-chewed pullovers, air long johns for the men who toil outside. Lines are weighted by damp Arrans that stink like a ewe's backside and folks survey their stocks like misers, calculating how long they'll last in peat, paraffin, treacle, oats. Johnny finds it harder, each morning, to rise.

Now, he and the others hurry across the windswept yard and file into the barn, Jock coming last and closing the door. He points to a spot above his head and the men squint in the low light.

'What are we supposed tae be looking at?'

Jock looks up. 'That.'

'What?'

'For God's sake – that.' Jock takes a book of matches from his pocket and strikes one, holds the flame high to illuminate the hook driven into the loft's ledge. As Johnny's eyes adjust, he can make out something dark hanging from it.

'I saw it the other day.' Jock hauls himself up the ladder, snatches the thing down. The men step closer; even Johnny is intrigued, despite himself, until he sees that what Jock is holding is nothing but a piece of old leather. Johnny takes it from him, turns it over in his hand. It is shined across the centre though the edges are cracked and brittle.

'What's your point, man?'

There is a low chuckle amongst the others, and Jock huffs.

'How did it get up there, then? I use that hook tae set a lamp on, if I've cause tae be in here once the light's gone. And I didnae put that thing up there. That's not all, either.' He beckons the men closer still, looks about as though someone unseen might be listening in. His face is pale, a few flecks of grey poking from his chin, missed in his morning shave. It is not like Jock to be careless. 'I was out the other night looking in on the mare – she's old, and she likes a wee bit of attention – and maybe I'm a soft auld thing but . . .'

'Get on with it, Jock.'

'I heard a lassie,' Jock hisses. 'I was patting the mare and I heard a noise like a lassie's laughter. At first I thought it must be one of my girls, come out to surprise me. So I walked down to the stables, but all the way it was like the hairs on my neck were standing up. I was spooked, I suppose. The dog was too – clinging tae my side. I locked up and went around the yard with a lamp, checked in here and in the byre, but there was nothing there. But I tell you, I heard it plain as day, this lassie's laughter. And it sounded . . . odd. Wicked, I suppose.' Jock runs his tongue over his lips. 'I went in and Anne called to me from the kitchen, so it cannae have been her, and I went upstairs and knocked on the girls' door and my youngest poked her head out and said all of them were in there.'

'And lassies have never been known tae lie,' says Stephen, smirking.

Jock looks askance. 'Not my daughters.'

'It is the most logical explanation,' says Johnny, 'that one of them was outside.'

Rab agrees. 'Aye, probably one of them playing a trick on their auld da.'

Jock's voice rises above its half-whisper. 'They are good girls, all of them. They said they were upstairs and I believe them. Anyway, the next day I came out here and that's when I saw this thing on the hook. It's fair shaken me, because I cannae explain how it got there.'

There is quiet, and the prickle at the back of Johnny's neck is nearly delicious because, despite his irritation, he never can resist a good tale. When he was wee he'd curl up in bed and wait for his ma to come and sit with him, talking low so his da wouldn't hear. His ma was from the coast, her voice slippery and lyrical, tongue able to contort in ways his couldn't. She knew strange stories – fairy folk who snatched babbies and left imps in their place, stones that turned to eggs that hatched great black wolves. Johnny would curl his toes, bright-eyed with fear, asking for more. Now, he expects someone to crack the silence with a laugh, to nudge the farmer's elbow and tell him what a good yarn he's spun. But no one moves; only the odd twitch of a lip, like they've come up with an explanation then found a hole in it. It is a tension Johnny doesn't like. He bursts out laughing. 'Good one Jock – very nice.'

The others gawk at him. Johnny carries on, the laughter hollow, but he hopes it'll hook one of them in the armpit, set them off too. Then Dougie clips him hard round the back of the head. 'Haud yer wheesht.'

Johnny's hand leaps up to clasp his skull.

'Come on man, nae need for that,' says Rab.

'Aye, well, he ought nae to laugh. There's been all sorts like this. Sinclair, tell them.'

'Tell us inside, man. It's fucking freezing out here.' And Johnny marches off, the rest of them following in silent procession to the four o'clock dim of the farmhouse.

In the parlour, coats left on. They drag chairs into a circle, Henry securing a position by the hearth. Johnny sits far away from him, rubs at the place where Dougie cracked him. It is a half-hearted search for blood, because what smarts most is the shock of it: Dougie, who he'd always got on with. Dougie, who might get blue-mouthed and lairy when he'd a drink in him but was otherwise harmless.

As soon as everyone's seated, Jock urges Sinclair to speak.

Sinclair thumbs his moustache, ruminating. 'Och, it's probably nothing, just . . . the other morn when I woke, Esther was already up – she's got the morning sickness, you see, gets her running tae the pail at the crack of dawn. Well I rolled over, about to rise myself, and there was . . . something on my pillow.'

'Was it an auld piece of leather?' Johnny asks, winking at Jock.

'No, it was – a tooth.'

Johnny is scunnered with all this – these men and their narrow wee lives, looking for magic where there is none. 'And you've checked your gob, aye?'

Sinclair tuts. 'I'm nae losing my teeth. But aye, of course I checked.'

'And did Esther?'

'I've nae mentioned it to her, nae in her condition. She came back fae the big house a week or so past, said Mistress Calder had been going on about that thing fae the bog, how she wouldnae allow it tae be buried. My wife was fair shaken. I dinnae want tae worry her with anything else.'

None of them clamour for an explanation – the men seem to accept Sinclair's tale, absorb it unquestioningly like one of the Reverend's sermons. They sit in silence for a time, the wind tickling the throat of the flue, and the conversation might have moved on if Henry hadn't suddenly sat upright. 'I've noticed it too.'

'Noticed what?'

The loon bites his lip, something swollen there like the bloom of a cold sore. 'How it's felt . . . strange. I've nae been sleeping. And when I do, I have odd dreams.'

'Oh aye?' Jock draws his chair a little nearer, then they all do, scraping them across the floor until the circle is so tight their shoulders nearly meet.

'Aye,' Henry says, 'I dream I'm trying tae speak, but I cannae. There's always something in my mouth, or stuck in my throat. I was thinking on it, and . . . the dreams started when the rain came on.'

'Just troubled by that,' says Johnny, 'that's all.'

But he goes unheeded, Jock rubbing his chin. 'Funny you should say that – it was the day after the rain came that I had all that business with the hook.'

Henry sits with a strange calm to him, the contentment of a mystery solved. 'And of course – what else happened that day?'

Murmuring amongst them, the cogs of their minds grinding in the cold of the parlour. Jock's mouth drops open. 'It's the thing out the bog.'

Henry nods, grave. 'Aye, that's what I think. That wifie Johnny hauled up is the cause of all this.'

Johnny should laugh, probably – dissolve their ridiculous ideas, the hard crust that has formed in the room – but he sees that the men are in no mood to be scoffed at, that it'll only make them double down, band up. There's a knack to challenging a foolish belief – you have to show it a deference it's entirely unworthy of.

'So how does that work then, loon?'

'She's got a mark on her,' Henry says, 'just like Jock said.'

Sinclair is pale as bone, his hand moving to cross himself. 'Wherever the devil rests his filthy paw always leaves a mark.'

'What did it look like?' asks Dougie.

'It's on her hand. It's all creased, deformed. As a matter of fact, it looks an awful lot like that scar of Johnny's.'

They stare at him. 'What, this?' Johnny holds up his hand to show the old wound, puckered skin in a sickle curve they've all seen plenty before. He has seen theirs likewise – scars from scrapes and scraps, pocks from the measles; no man here is unmarked.

Rab, sensible Rab, gives a low chuckle. 'That's nothing but the scar from an accident – caught in a binder, eh, Johnny?'

Jock frowns. 'He told me he'd been hooked by a bull's horn.'

'Well,' says Henry, 'it's neither of those.'

'Has he told you something different and all?' Jock asks.

The men look between Johnny and Henry, waiting for one of them to explain. Henry gets up, comes and folds himself into a squat in front of Johnny, all knees and elbows. 'Will I tell them?' he whispers.

'What are you doing? Get up.'

But Henry's got a fool's grin on him, and Johnny can't tell what he's trying to do – some cheeky attempt at conspiracy that Henry thinks will be reciprocated with a wink, then an evening down the inn reminiscing about Windyhillock? Or is Johnny being taunted? He sees, then, that the smile's false, and there's something spiteful in the way the loon is looking at him.

'Get the fuck up.' Johnny stands, suddenly enough that Henry is taken unawares and topples backwards to the floor in the middle of their circle. Undeterred, he scrabbles up, flushed as he comes face to face with Johnny.

'Well? Will I tell them?'

'Hang on,' says Rab, 'how's Henry tae know?'

This is the bit that Johnny doesn't like. It hardly matters if they find out how he came to have his scar – any farming man has heard or suffered similar – kickings, lashings, tar and feathers, notches snipped from ears. But it's how Henry knows – because he was there, at least for some of it, and won't it look right strange that he washed up in the Cabrach a good five months ago and yet only now will folks find out he's already acquainted with Johnny Nicol? He looks down at the floor – cowardly, he knows, but he can't bear Henry's goading expression, and he doesn't want to see Rab's face when he's shown to be a liar. 'We worked together. Years back.'

'Huh, is that right?'

Johnny glances at his friend. Rab's put out, he can tell; the farmer's not a proud man, but he's looking around at the others, embarrassed to have been caught so unawares. His confusion shames Johnny, and he hardens his face, makes himself look at Henry. 'Happy now, loon?'

'Oh.' The ploughman bites his lip. 'I wisnae going tae tell them that bit, I thought you didnae want anyone tae know about that.'

Johnny could fucking smack him. The way Henry looks at the group with an 'oops' expression on his face, as if it's all some cheerful misunderstanding. The men must sense something brittle in the air because they shift in their seats, alert for drama; and it's true that Johnny's drawn himself taller, could swear he feels the blood dropping into his fists and feet as though he might need them. But then there is a hand on his shoulder, and he knows it's Rab's – that broad, warm hand, gentle even now. 'I think I'll take the gang away back tae Brawlands – Maggie'll have the supper on the table soon enough.'

Johnny twists round to look at his friend. A pitying look on Rab's face like he's putting a lame beast out of its misery. 'But I'll have a word with you outside first, Johnny, if you dinnae mind.'

Outside, Rab pulls Johnny into the relative shelter of the barn, stands watching as Johnny paces between the tarpaulined equipment.

'I told Henry, dinnae feed that sort of talk. Makes the lot of them start spouting rubbish.'

'Why didn't you tell me you knew him?'

Johnny considers. He had thought about it, after he'd fled the kitchen on the day he met Henry at Brawlands. He could have made some throwaway comment, got it out in the open, but he didn't want the questions. 'It was a long time ago. I was only there a season.'

'Look, I'll have a word with him.' Rab who, in his enduring decency, doesn't probe any further. 'I was meaning tae, anyway.'

'Is everything all right?'

'Well, see when he says he's nae been sleeping? It's every night, he has these bad dreams, and then he winnae settle. Alex has been complaining about it, says the loon keeps tossing and turning, disturbing the other two.' Rab hunches his shoulders against the cold. 'And that's nae all. Alex woke up the other night and saw Henry leaving the chaumer. Thought he was off for a piss, but he didnae come back. When Alex went tae look for him, he found Henry wandering about the yard in his nightclothes. Below freezing that night, I daresay. Anyway, I'll speak tae him.'

Johnny touches Rab's arm. 'Thank you. You're a good pal.'

'I do think you ought tae get that body back in the ground, though. Something tells me they're only going tae get worse the longer she's unburied. Men like tae have something tae blame.'

'Aye, I'll think on it.' There is some natural curiosity that makes Johnny want to know the truth of the woman, but mostly he remembers the way Lizzie Calder had looked at her, her face all soft with wonder. He'll let Lizzie decide what to do.

Rab takes his leave and when he opens the barn door, Henry and Stephen are waiting for him in the yard. Johnny stays in the barn a few minutes longer – he'll let the Brawlands lot get a few minutes on him, keep his distance from Henry. He decides to take another look at where Jock found the leather. From the ground there is nothing untoward, just the rusted hook stuck into the beam. But then Johnny notices something else caught on the wood. He goes up a couple of ladder rungs, gets himself close enough to see. Caught on a splinter at the shelf's edge there is a tuft of hair, the vivid colour of copper wire.

An unctuous flip in his belly. Johnny snatches the hair, and it's coarse and wiry and brings a wet feeling to his mouth, but still, there is sense enough in him not to leave it there. He pockets it, will discard it along the road – and hope that it doesn't turn up somewhere else.

LIZZIE

Mysie turns the metal in her hand. 'And you say the other piece was sitting round her neck?'

'Aye. It must have formed nearly a complete circle when it was whole.' Lizzie has taken the metal from the bog for Mysie to assess, and has enjoyed watching the old woman peer at it through a magnifying glass. There is a wisdom to Mysie, earned by time and the life she's led – three daughters, two dead husbands, a hundred-acre plot and a house of her own, with numerous lodgers who've stayed until they've moved on or been thrown out. Johnny is her longest-standing; has earned his keep, because along with chopping firewood and ripping kail from the beds, he keeps Mysie entertained, and if there's one thing you need in the dark slog of a Cabrach winter, it's a good story. Lizzie can picture the pair of them in the front room, like it is now – stuffy, the fire kept going. She enjoys the generosity of it, the difference to Blackwater's cold. Jane leans towards austerity in the use of their peat supplies, says a cool home facilitates a sturdy disposition. She cracks the parlour window open when the fire's too high, eyes Lizzie when she skulks into the room wearing one of William's pullovers.

'I've a horrible feeling . . .' Mysie lifts the metal band and places it first over her wrist and then at her neck. 'I think it's a restraint of some sort. Or a shackle.'

'You think she was a prisoner?'

'Could have been. Or she might have been tortured.'

Lizzie hadn't thought of that. She'd imagined sorrow, yes – a smocked procession, torches aloft, laying a loved one to rest. Or men with their noses and mouths smothered with sackcloth, lavender choking the air, placing the body in the ground and rushing home to strip the shirts from their backs and check for lesions, purge their hands in steaming basins. She had considered murder, too. Always, though, she had imagined a quick dispatch – a fall, a blunt object, a knife through the heart.

'I've heard about all that business, way back when,' says Mysie. 'Women who were healers or midwives or poor, or couldnae have children. Women who spoke their minds or had a man they werenae married to. Women who just so happened tae be in the room when a pail of milk turned sour.' She gives a grim laugh. 'I daresay they'd have called me a witch, back then.'

'You think she was a witch?'

'There's nae such thing. Only women who rubbed folks up the wrong way.'

They sit quietly for a time, watching the fire. Lizzie thinks about the bog woman, wonders what those last few moments of her life were like – whether she faced them with terror or defiance. Her expression doesn't give anything away.

Lizzie's thoughts are interrupted by the sound of galloping feet on the stairs. Johnny at the door, leaning on the frame. Mysie looks him up and down. 'You going somewhere, loon?'

'No.'

'You're finely dressed tae sit around the house.'

His shirt is clean and hair combed back – one of his modes of appearance, the flop of ribbon at his throat. 'We've an esteemed guest.'

'I'm not so high and mighty as you might think,' says Lizzie.

'No?'

'The daughter of a clerk done good.'

'He'll have to give my da some tips then – he's a clerk who stayed a clerk.'

'Still, we're not so very different.'

'If you say so.' Johnny picks up the metal. 'What're you doing with this?' He turns it delicately, the same way he had tied the bog woman's wrapping, smoothed her hair away from her face before shrouding it. Another of his contradictions, perhaps, when he surely turns the soil with the force of any labouring man, stamps his feet hard on the boards when he sings his songs. Johnny wets a fingertip in his mouth and rubs at the rounded bead on the end of the metal, then frowns. He reaches into his pocket for a handkerchief and spits into it. 'Sorry, but . . .' As he buffs vigorously, Lizzie watches the metal transform, the dirt and peat sloughing off. Underneath, it is gleaming.

'Now, I'm no expert, but I think this is gold. Have a look.' Johnny perches on the footstool before Lizzie and hands her the metal. She holds it in front of the fire, lets its light show her what she had not seen before. It is gold – unmistakably.

'My goodness!' A relief, then, that the thing round the woman's neck seems not to have been an instrument of pain but something kinder, more precious. 'I suppose it's some sort of jewellery, though it still doesn't tell us who she was. If anything, I'm even more confused.'

'Nothing more from your policeman, then?'

Lizzie had expected – hoped – that James might write with an update, or that she'd hear from the man at the university, asking when it would be convenient to visit. But perhaps she shouldn't be surprised at James's silence – should have known from his demeanour at the peats, his haste to leave her outside the inn, that he would not follow through. 'He tends to lose interest in things, after the initial enthusiasm.'

'Well, we'll have tae work her out without him, then.'

Lizzie is glad that someone other than her still wants to know this woman. 'What do you think, Johnny – who was she?'

'Och, I dinnae know. I understand all this least of anyone.'

'But don't you have a theory, or a feeling? Something in your heart of hearts?'

Johnny rubs the back of his neck. 'I have learned tae pay greater heed tae my head than my heart.'

Their eyes meet for a moment and Lizzie holds his gaze, because he does not speak truthfully. She knows when she sees it – a person whose sleeve is easily tugged by emotion – for she was once that way too.

Johnny looks away. 'Well, I try tae, anyway. I wish I knew. If I had a good theory I could put paid tae all the nonsense being spouted about her.'

'Oh, what's that then?'

'Och, you know – she's got strange marks on her, she's a demon, she's a witch.'

Mysie rolls her eyes. 'That is just what I was saying tae Lizzie. Hundreds of years later and we're still hearing the same rubbish. Folks never change, eh.'

'It gets worse. Jock seems to have some notion she's got up and walked.'

Lizzie cannot help but laugh at that. She can imagine their tales, as twisted as the burns off the Deveron. Men at the inn with their lewd and limitless imagination, conjuring the type of woman who might disgust and tempt them, both; some sweet-breathed nymph who would uncross her legs to reveal the fires of Hell between them. Their wives, hunched over their stitching, adding embellishment here and there.

'They're giving you a run for your money with their tales, Johnny. Go on, what's Jock been saying?'

'Just . . . noises in the yard and that. And Sinclair found a tooth in his bed.'

'His wife's knocked up, isn't she?' says Mysie. 'I swear half my teeth came loose in my skull when I was pregnant with my youngest.'

'Aye, it's surely that.' But Johnny looks unconvinced.

'Don't tell me you believe them?' Lizzie nudges his knee – this a new intimacy, she realizes – and he acknowledges it with a glance, then moves away, not quick enough to be instinct.

'Of course nae. That's impossible.'

'It is,' Lizzie agrees. 'Though I'd like to get a look at her again, just to see if there's anything I've missed. What do you say, Johnny, shall we go and check she's still there?'

'I've nae wish tae bump into Henry the day. He's the one poisoning their minds.'

'Then we'll avoid him.'

Johnny glances at Mysie. The old woman is sitting back in her chair, regarding them wryly.

'When?' he asks.

'Now?'

JOHNNY

In the hayloft, Johnny blows on his hands to warm them to their task. His breath is noisy in the deserted barn and he's aware they should have found Maggie or Rab, probably, and told them they were here, but at the time it had seemed easier just to follow Lizzie. He fingers the twine around the body, quite sure he'd intended not to look at the woman again – sure, really, that he'd rather not. But Lizzie is watching and so Johnny starts on the first knot. It is tied differently to the way he'd done it. After James's inspection Johnny had wrapped the body tightly, securing the twine with strangle knots. But the ones she is tied with now are sloppy, the type of thing you'd be chastised for on the farms. Each knot is the same – slack and easy to undo – and when Johnny has finished he sits back on his heels, invites Lizzie to draw back the wrapping.

They see straight away that the bog woman has changed. She is powdered with mildew, blooming over her skin like a hoar-frost. It is thicker between her fingers, collects in the thread-thin lines on the soles of her feet. Johnny pulls the shroud from the woman's head and finds her face too is snowy – mould in eye creases, her nostrils.

'She's rotting.'

Johnny blanches to see how dauntlessly Lizzie touches her,

stroking the woman's forearm and inspecting her palm to see what has come away. She takes the woman's hand in her own. Apart from the mould, it is perfect – every line and crease and whorl, five fingernails that are hard and brown as nuts. Lizzie runs her thumb over the ruck of skin on the back of the bog woman's hand – it is not unlike Johnny's scar, that is true.

'This must be an injury of some sort.' Lizzie leans closer to inspect the thickened cords of flesh. 'Or a burn, maybe.' She looks up at Johnny. 'Isn't your brother a doctor?'

'A surgeon.'

'He'd be able to tell, wouldn't he?'

Johnny supposes he would – certainly he's seen a battered woman, their ma with a burst black lip, ghoulish with bruises. 'I . . . he wouldn't come, Lizzie. He's all the way over in Aberdeen. Always busy.'

'Couldn't you ask him?'

'He'll be busy, believe me.' Johnny hasn't seen Charlie for years. The last time, a February, the haar so thick they could barely see their feet in front of them as they carried the coffin out of the kirk, stink of lilies up their noses. Charlie at the front with their da, even though Johnny's the eldest. He resented that; he had loved his ma the most. 'Anyway, will I wrap her back up?'

'Wait.' Lizzie reaches into her bag, takes out a notebook and pencil. Johnny watches as she sketches the body, the deft movement of her hand.

'It's a good likeness, you've talent.'

'Thank you.'

'I'll have tae ask you tae do my portrait.' He imagines sitting still, having her look carefully at him.

'Ah, no, I just do still lives really. The odd landscape if the day is fine. With portraiture there's too much . . . interpretation. To be good, you have to try and work out who the person is, capture something of that. It's not my skill.'

Lizzie completes her sketch, then Johnny positions the wrapping back over the woman. 'I'll secure her better this time.' When he has finished, the woman is parcelled up tight, the sackcloth pulled neatly round the gentle undulations of her body.

'She won't escape from that,' says Lizzie. 'You can put the minds of those farmers at rest.'

When Johnny looks, her eyes are bright. She has always struck him as the sort of person who does not cry – stoic to the point of exhaustion. He hesitates; probably she doesn't need him to comfort her. 'Are you all right?'

'Aye, it's just . . . I don't like seeing her like that. I was probably stupid to think she'd stay the same, but . . . I don't know. I'm being ridiculous.'

'You're not.'

'I am. I don't know why I care so much.'

'Well it's . . . compassion, I suppose. We'll work her out. You'll hear from your policeman soon enough.'

'You don't have to call him that.'

'What?'

'*My* policeman. He's not mine.'

Johnny finds himself glad to hear it.

They are still there, crouching by the body, when the door to the barn opens beneath them. Better to announce their presence than be caught alone in the hayloft with Lizzie – Johnny doesn't want whoever it is to get the wrong idea. He stands, smacking his head against the low ceiling. Whoever has come in is quick, light-footed. The one person Johnny had wanted to avoid. 'All right, loon?'

Henry jumps. He looks up, and Johnny blanches to see how young he looks, how startled. An expression he's always felt stupidly tender towards because he's known that feeling, living right on the edge of your nerves. It troubles Johnny, then, his seething urge in Jock's parlour, the desire to hurt the loon. He had pondered it in bed that night, reminded himself that he is not that kind of man.

'What are you doing here?' Henry asks.

'We just wanted to check on the body. Lizzie thought something else might come to her about who she was.'

'And what did you find?'

'Nothing,' Lizzie says, 'nothing I'd missed, anyway.'

Henry watches as they come down the ladder, waits until they are close to speak again. 'She's falling to bits.'

'What?'

The loon looks knackered – pale and moony, with a skittish energy like he's a sheep with a dog going after him. 'I said she's falling apart – there's pieces of her everywhere.'

'Don't worry, she's wrapped up tight now.' Lizzie pats Henry's arm.

'Did Rab see you come in?'

'I didnae think we ought tae disturb him,' says Johnny.

'Odd nae to say hello though, given how good a friend he is. Rab's done a lot for you.'

'I should hardly think it matters just the once.'

'I can easy fetch him.'

'Really, it's fine.'

'He's secretive, eh, Mistress Calder?'

Lizzie glances between the two men. 'We wanted to be quick. Rab's so busy. We'll be off now.'

'All right, well, I'll see you Friday then,' says Henry.

Johnny hasn't forgotten, only he is not as enthusiastic as he might usually be. 'Aye, see you Friday.'

'And you too, Mistress Calder, I suppose?'

But Johnny is already ushering Lizzie out, steering her by the elbow. 'I'll explain as we walk. See you later, loon.'

Henry watches them go. 'I'll tell Rab you said hello.'

*

As soon as they hit the road, Lizzie asks: 'Friday?'

'The Stuarts have a do each year for Hallowe'en. I daresay I could wangle you an invitation.'

'Ah, the ceilidhs – every year I hear bits and pieces and think they sound like good fun.'

'Has no one invited you before?'

'Not that I know of. William wasn't one for socializing. Didn't like me to either.'

'Ah.'

'And because they never see me out, people think I don't want to be friends with the likes of them. They must think I'm – I don't know, some sort of snob.'

'Well, I understand. Folks make the best of it, but it's still just another night in the croft with the same ropey whisky. And no one is on their best behaviour on Hallowe'en night.' Johnny will leave the explanation at that – she'll see for herself the bairns with treacled fingers, the flushed maids perched on their ploughman's laps. There is no need to mention any of his own misdeeds in shadowed corners. 'I'm sorry no one's asked you before.'

'So am I. It's . . .' She inhales, tips her head back to look up at the dusky sky. 'It's lonely.' She says it baldly, without emotion, and yet Johnny feels the words alter something between them.

'I know that feeling.'

'But you're always surrounded by friends – everyone knows Johnny Nicol.'

'Aye, everyone knows Johnny Nicol.' Or some approximation of him. 'Anyway, you'll come, won't you?'

'I'd be delighted to. I'll just have to square it with Jane somehow, tell her I'm going to comfort Mistress Weir, or spoon broth into some sick old wifie's mouth.'

He laughs, and it feels good to. 'You've a gift for excuses.'

'Is there a dress code? Costumes? Do I have to look very wicked?'

Johnny glances at her; looks for the glint in her eye that Dougie swore he saw. But probably Johnny is deceiving himself, knocked half-senseless by the sudden image in his mind of Mistress Calder looking very wicked. 'Not really. Something a little dark will do.'

Halfway to Blackwater, two figures appear up ahead. They are pushing wheelbarrows that squeal down the track, disturbing the stillness of the evening. Johnny squints but can't work out who it is, just that they trudge in solemn step with each other. It is not unusual to meet someone coming the other way, but still, he'd rather have got home without it.

As the couple draw closer, Johnny makes out the heavy droop of an auburn moustache. 'Evening,' Sinclair calls. Esther is next to him, her weight tipping forward, leaning on the handles of the wheelbarrow.

'What brings you out?' Johnny makes his voice clear and bright, shoving out anything that could be construed as furtiveness.

Sinclair gestures at the barrows piled high with peat. 'Stocks are running low – the one group willing tae go up and gather in could name their price.'

'And demand you collect it and all.' Esther tuts her displeasure.

But this makes no sense to Johnny – they know scarcity in the Cabrach, but never of peat. Not here, where it's the very flesh of the place. 'What do you mean, stocks are running low?'

'Most of the men are feart tae go up tae the peats after . . . you know.' Sinclair glances at his wife. 'We'd little choice but tae go ourselves and take our share from what has been brought down. Even with Esther in her condition.'

'Can I help you home with it?' asks Lizzie.

'Aye,' says Johnny, 'let me take it.'

Esther releases her grip on the wheelbarrow, holds up a palm.

'I'll be all right.' She draws her shawl round her. There is little sign that she is expecting a child, no softening around the edges. 'What are you two doing out together, anyway?'

Lizzie looks to Johnny, and he sees her weigh it up like he does: their reluctance to mention the bog woman.

'We just bumped into each other,' Lizzie says. 'I was taking a walk, Johnny was coming back from Brawlands.'

'Coincidence.' Something shifts in Sinclair's countenance, and Johnny might not have noticed if it had not been a look he was used to – that of expectation, a demand he account for himself. But he owes the farmer nothing – will let him get his wife home to rest her feet, warm herself with a claik by the fireside.

'Anyway, we'll get on before the dark comes.' The couple move off. A little way down the track before Johnny catches the sound of Sinclair's lowered voice.

At the turning to Blackwater, Lizzie stops. 'You needn't come down the track with me.'

Johnny looks over her shoulder at the big house. He's never been inside – tried once, newly in the Cabrach and all bravado. He'd gone to see if there was any work he could pick up, curious at the man he'd seen passing in his motor car, but no one had answered his knock on the door.

'Are you sure?'

'Aye. It'll spare me the questions from Jane.'

'As you like.'

They stand a moment. A mackerel sky, pink-streaked. 'Thank you, Johnny, for looking at the woman again.' Lizzie touches his arm – a quick pat, unsure.

'That's . . . you're welcome. I want tae know who she is and all. Anyway, enjoy your evening, aye?' Johnny glances back down the road, and when he sees that the Sinclairs are long gone he presses a kiss to her cheek. Nothing untoward, same as he'd do with Maggie or Mysie – to say goodbye. But Lizzie is taken aback, steps abruptly away.

'Aye, Johnny, and you.'

They go their separate ways. With any luck, Johnny will get home to supper on the stove, and maybe he'll take a dram, think on the day and this, the moment just passed. She had touched him first; he had only responded in kind, but maybe it was too much. He reminds himself that she's good and married and he, well, surely he has just gone too long without a woman. It's easy, then, to mistake a kind word or glance – an innocent touch – for something else. Easy, and foolish, to be offered an inch and try to take a mile.

October 1905

LIZZIE

The caller's bow stretched over his fiddle. 'We'll begin in the traditional fashion with . . .' a few teasing notes on the strings, 'the Gay Gordons.'

Lizzie took her partner's hand, the heat of a certain palm she had come to know very well over the few weeks past. The accordion started, and the second fiddle, the music rising all at once.

'I haven't done one of these in a while,' said James, 'you must forgive me if I make a mess of it.'

'You will remember in a moment.'

'I'm sure. Only I must be careful to temper the expectations of someone who I sense is rather fond of dancing.' James was falsely modest. He knew the routine as well as Lizzie did – muscle memory, a circling round to the walk, the pivot, the polka. The dancers ringed round the town-hall ballroom knew it too, moved fluid in half-shadow with the gas lamps mercurial above them. Lizzie watched the other dancers: there was Webster's son, and the gingery girls from the house down the road; girls she had gone to school with, now in a strange interlude, waiting for their lives to start. These events were a chance to be seen, to try and catch the eye of a young man from one of the families that were making Elgin prosperous.

As the music wound down, James moved a little closer. 'Another dance?'

'Of course.' Lizzie was seldom coy with him – there seemed little need. In the past few weeks their relationship had progressed along certain lines: knees pressed together beneath dinner tables, eyes held, his hand on her waist for just a gleaningly improper amount of time. It seemed as if she barely needed to posture for his attention. And perhaps it was vanity, or pride, the way his admiration had made her see herself anew, but Lizzie did not mind – those had always seemed like lesser sins.

The compère called out his instructions: 'And now, ladies and gents, it's time for the Dashing White Sergeant. Three couples in a set, and we start in a circle.' Folks formed hasty groups with whoever was nearest. Lizzie and James paired with Webster's son and his fiancée, and then, casting about for another couple, ended up in a ring with a girl from Lizzie's year at school and the man accompanying her – the elusive William Calder. He had not been seen on the dinner-party circuit for some time, and Lizzie watched as he craned his neck to whisper in his partner's ear, the hand that spanned the width of her slender back.

Lizzie was in the middle of James and William as the group began to spin, eight counts, then another eight, laughing as they tried to keep the formation. Then split off into threes, Lizzie facing James, and set, and spin, and James watching her, James the nimble dancer with his good height, his fine clothes, his skin that she wanted to touch. And turn – to face William Calder. There was something off-time in his movements, a wrongness it was difficult to define. Large feet in heavy shoes that could crush her toes if she took a step too near. She had never been this close to him and found him to be a bulk of a man – not squat as such, but with a lack of definition. Lizzie was glad to pull away and catch James's eye again as the group began the snaky business of the reel. Webster's fiancée tutted as Lizzie, engrossed in her partner, careered into her path. But Lizzie refused to be touched by her admonishment as she took James's hand again, close enough to smell her perfume on his lapel.

The next dance required her to leave him. The way of it at these things was to swap partners – to cast off and meet someone new, with a stamped foot as greeting. Usually, Lizzie liked the swapping; it meant she could throw off men who were too old or young, too leering or slow-footed, or unable to tell left from right. That night, she rued having to separate from James.

'Shall we have a break?'

'Oh no, this is one of my favourites.'

'Then can we cheat? So we don't have to part?'

He laughed. 'That is not the dance.'

'But we can make it the dance – when it comes to swap, we just stay.'

James looked her in the eye. 'I will be back with you before you know it.'

The song seemed endless, the band toying with the crowd, firing the melody back up just as it seemed to be slowing. A glee in the room, folks sick with laughter, Lizzie being spun and spun but always searching through the crowd for James. When the fiddles finally slowed some fool hollered out for more, and the band glanced at each other – a consensus to improvise. Lizzie nodded to the lad she had danced the last set with and moved to the side of the hall to wait for James.

'Things are getting pacy,' someone said, next to her.

Lizzie turned to Jane Calder. 'Sorry?'

'The dancers.' Jane looked around the hall with the air of a headmistress observing a raucous playground. 'There is rather a debauched atmosphere forming.'

'Oh Jane, it's just a bit of fun.'

'Your James is enjoying it, certainly.'

Lizzie had taken her eyes away from him momentarily, but

easily found him again in the crowd, his pull on her magnetic. He was with a girl. This girl, she had her hand on his forearm, and James was leaning in close, listening. Lips in smiles, the girl passing her amusement to him like a Chinese whisper, then pulling back and James laughing, careless. The girl turned under his arm, the hem of her dress flicking above her ankles. Jane inclined her head towards Lizzie. 'He did say, didn't he, that he grows bored easily.'

'He is allowed to dance with other girls.'

'Of course.'

They watched. The last notes of the song, James dipping the girl to the floor, her back arching like a cat's.

'He certainly revelled in that,' said Jane.

Lizzie turned to face her. 'Are you enjoying yourself, Jane?'

'Ah, well. As much as I ever enjoy these things.'

'That is not what I meant.'

'No?' Jane's expression softened. 'I meant no offence.'

'Has he wronged you?'

'No. Only in that he is a man like a magpie whose eye is always drawn to pretty things. And you could do differently with your life, Lizzie, than merely be one of those.'

Lizzie almost laughed. Jane, so serious! Jane bound up in wool, thick-ankled, too stiff to dance. But Lizzie could spare a drop of pity for her, too – easier to disdain what you do not have rather than lament your lack of it. 'I will bear it in mind. Now, if you'll excuse me—'

James was moving through the crowd towards them, people parting to let him pass. 'There you are. And Miss Calder, good to see you.'

'Good evening.'

'Come on then,' James said to Lizzie, 'I've missed you. Shall we head off?'

'Oh, but we have to stay for Strip the Willow.' It was Lizzie's favourite – all the dancers lining the length of the hall, the bubbling anticipation in moving up the line. She wanted to dance with James and for everyone to see it.

'There will be other dances,' James said. A hand to her elbow that was sure, decisive.

'All right. Good evening, Jane.'

James took Lizzie's hand and began to lead her through the crowd. Lizzie followed, high off him – high so the room appeared in fragments – glittering points of light, girls watching from under their lashes; eyes and eyes. Envy as green as Lizzie's gown – green that suited her if he said so. James led her through the hall with certainty in his footsteps as the band began their melody – almost as though the music was made by him. Folks stared, and Lizzie thought: let them.

The foyer was crowded, a flurry of embraces and shrill goodbyes. 'Wait here,' said James, 'I'll go and get our coats.'

Lizzie stood amongst the throng: young men with dark jackets and hair stiff with pomade, but none as handsome as James; girls flushed and trussed and coiffured, standing waiting on the chequered floor that was black and white like a chessboard, with Lizzie surely the queen. Then, an interruption – a girl rushing through the crowd, half turning, looking over her shoulder. Lizzie recognized her as the girl who had been dancing with William Calder for most of the evening – and indeed, it was William who followed her. He shoved through, knocking into a woman who jolted forward and had to grab the arm of a companion to steady herself. The girl squealed something unintelligible, her voice clotted with alarm. She was crying.

'Stop, for God's sake.' William spoke as a command, but the girl went hurrying on, face contorted, her hair pulled loose from its plait on one side. By now, William had given up his pursuit and stood in the foyer with the air of a red-rag-riled bull, his coat clutched in his fist. He was not very far from Lizzie, so she could see that his tie was loosened and his neck marked with livid streaks. She approached him carefully, conscious of the hush in the room, folks waiting to see what might happen next.

'Mr Calder, is everything all right?'

William wheeled round to look at her. His eyes were dark, betrayed no indication of his conflict with his dancing partner – betrayed nothing at all.

'Miss Brodie. Fine. A comment taken the wrong way.' He nodded towards the girl, who was still weeping some distance away. 'Oversensitive.'

'Would you like me to check she's all right?'

'No. I've to go.'

Lizzie watched him put his coat on. Hands that were large and pale against the black wool, coarse hair growing on the backs of his fingers. Closer up, the streaks on his neck were more defined – three raw red marks reaching from the underside of his jaw down to his shirt, a fine line where one scratch went deeper, beads of blood glistening on the skin.

William Calder turned his collar up to conceal his injury, looked Lizzie straight in the eye before leaving. The doors were opened for him, and he stormed through.

JACK

Dawn at Windyhillock, a band of light on the stone wall. Jack rolled over, trying to snatch a few more minutes of sleep before the grieve came snapping in, pulling their blankets off to rouse their aching bodies. He pushed his knees up to his chest, settled a cheek to the warm indentation in his pillow – and found something there. Jack reared back, nearly cried out as his fingers grazed something sharp and dry. He groped for his matches and struck one as quietly as he could – Donald would be livid if deprived of his last moments of sleep.

When he looked down, Jack almost laughed at what was on his pillow: just an envelope, plain white and unmarked. It was sealed, and he grappled with it one-handed, racing with the match as it chased for his fingers. What was inside was apparent straight away. Coarse, vaguely oily: horsehair. It was tied in a knot, a complicated one Jack didn't recognize. And there was something else too – a square of paper with words in an unfamiliar hand:

Tonight, midnight, the stables. Bring these: candle, bread, whisky.

Jack blew out the match and folded the paper, tucked it under his pillow, then lay back down, though he'd get no more sleep. This was what he'd been waiting for.

The evening passed as normal: untacking and feeding the horses, setting out fresh hay, bedding in. Then supper in the farmhouse, the kail and brose, the gang wolfing the porridge down with barely a breath between mouthfuls. It did that to you, the labour – made you ravenous, undignified. When they had finished, they sat for a bit as they usually did, and no one could rightly put a finger on anything being different to normal, but Jack could feel it – was conscious of Donald's glances at the clock, the agitation in his own limbs as he crossed and uncrossed his legs, finding no comfortable position.

'That fire's nice,' said Henry, 'it's getting awfully cold now.' He was in the seat furthest from it, for Donald got to be closest, then Tam, then Jack – the farm hierarchy, strict as dogma.

'Nah,' said Donald, 'this isnae cold.'

Tam agreed. 'Aye, wait 'til January comes, loon, then you'll know what cold is.'

Henry looked at Jack, but he just shrugged. In truth, every man knew the pleasure of it – unclenching your fists, letting the heat from the range ease the rope burn and puffing knuckles. But you'd be a jessie to admit how you needed it, how sometimes the warmth felt almost like pain.

Henry tried again. 'Don't you think it's cold, Jack?'

Jack saw the loon, the eagerness in him. And he could have said aye, let Henry have his agreement, but suddenly he was scunnered with the small talk. 'No. This isnae cold.'

When nine o'clock came round, Donald sprang up. 'Bedtime then, let's be off, lads. Tam, I want tae check on the mare before we turn in – I noticed she was, ah . . . limping a little. You'll come with me to the stables. Henry, tae bed with you. And you, Jack.'

The first spoke in earnest, but there was Tam, unable to resist a wink. They filed out of the kitchen, Henry trotting behind the horsemen, and he was halfway across the yard before he realized Jack had stopped. He looked back, puzzled, but Jack waved him on. 'I'll be there in a minute.'

Jack waited in the cold, listening to the movement of the housekeeper inside, the door closing to the little room off the kitchen where the maids slept. It was a clear night, the sky lushly black and scattered with a million stars, probably. He stood and admired it for a time, felt the hitching in his throat that came, sometimes, when he regarded beauty. When all was quiet, Jack tried the kitchen door and found it unlocked. He would be quick, light-footed: in, snatch a bannock from the bread bin, and none of the maids would be any the wiser. But when Jack stepped into the kitchen he found someone standing by the range. A lone candle lit, enough that he could see a bonny young face.

'I didnae expect tae see you here, Violet.'

If the lassie was startled, she didn't show it. Her hair was loose and she was wearing her nightgown, her ankles bare and white.

'I just . . . I need a favour. Is there a bannock going spare?'

'How am I tae know?' Violet looked amused, and it did seem absurd that she would even need to eat, to go through the drear human motions the rest of them did.

'All right, I'll look myself.'

But Violet stepped in front of him, blocking his path. 'Jack Nicol, are you thieving from my father's kitchen?'

'It's only one bannock, miss. I'll take an oatcake, if you'd prefer.'

Jack saw then that the girl was teasing him, a smile playing at her lips. 'What's it for?'

'I cannae tell you that.'

Violet turned and took out a floury roll, the pad of her thumb pressing into the soft of it. 'This will have tae do. And I'm off tae bed now, but you should come and see me again sometime, just to tell me what it was for, like.'

Jack took the bread from the girl. She had long, rounded fingernails, pearly at the tips, and he hoped she did not notice the muck ground under his own. 'Thank you.'

Violet nodded. 'Goodnight then – horseman.'

Jack squinted at his pocket watch. The hand moved steadily towards midnight, its tick matching his heartbeat. He'd lain in his bed for the past couple of hours, fully clothed and feigning sleep, smoothing a thumb over the brushed-cotton patches on the quilt his ma had stitched. When it was nearly time, Jack inched his legs out of bed, feet into boots. He moved as quietly as he could, trying to avoid waking Henry. The loon was a light sleeper; sometimes it seemed as if he never slept at all, for you could clear your throat in the night and he'd start awake, scrabbling at the bedclothes.

'Jack? What's happening?' Henry, bleary with slumber.

'Nothing, loon. Go back off.'

Henry's sheets rustled and he lifted his head. 'Where are you going?'

'Dinnae worry, I'll be back soon enough.'

'But where are you going? Jack, it's late.' Henry sat up. 'Where are the others?'

Time was marching on – surely the hand had touched midnight. In truth, Jack did not know where he was going, but he had a younger brother, so he knew how to placate. He went to Henry's bedside and crouched down. 'Go back to sleep, my friend. I'll be back before you know it.' Jack reached out and smoothed the hair over Henry's brow, then stood up, resolving to ignore any further questions.

Outside, it was icy in the yard. The damp had settled in the ruts and mud-churn and petrified quickly to frost under the clear, open sky. Dead quiet too, just the sound of Jack's footsteps and his breath, his nerves showing in the quick of it. He could turn round, go back to bed, claim a misunderstanding, dodgy stomach. But no – this was what he wanted. He'd thought of it while at his tasks, attempting to prepare by recalling the bare scraps he'd heard: an initiation, acceptance into something. It would be fine – he was ready to be a man.

In the sack over his shoulder Jack had what had been asked of him: the roll from Violet and a sly bottle of whisky. The candle was in his hand and he hesitated, not knowing if he was to turn up with it lit. But he needed a light to guide him across the yard – just so he didn't trip. Up ahead he could make out something in the stables, a murky luminescence through the dirty window. Jack focused on that, used it as a beacon, so intent that he didn't realize for a moment that his own light had been snuffed out. The smell of smoke ribboning off the wick at the same time the hands clasped tight round his wrists; a palm slapped over his open mouth. A scruffy yelp escaped Jack's throat and he knew it must only be the lads, but he could not hold it back, not in that dark with his jumping heart and their hands on him. Instinctively, he struggled. Jack's limbs thrashed; quick, desperate jerks that did nothing but hurt. 'Don't panic,' someone said. They yanked Jack's arms back, the toe of a boot digging into the soft flesh behind his knee, forcing him to the ground. Coarse fabric tugged over his face and someone leaning in to whisper: 'It'll be easier if you stop struggling.'

They stripped him of his shirt, hard fingers at his chest, then something rough was chucked over Jack's head – a long and coiling thing, heavy across his shoulders.

'Come on, up.' Tam's voice, and relief spread through Jack – not from trust, as such, but familiarity. 'You've proven yourself fit.'

'Fit for what?'

'For the Society of the Horseman's Word.' Tam said it slowly, grandly. 'If you choose tae join us, you will be given a word of great power. It brings total harmony between man and beast. It is capable of rendering—' Jack could hear him smile, 'utter compliance. But I must tell you one thing about this word. It is the devil's word, and in return for it you must make him a vow and shake his hand. With this knowledge, you are tae answer me now: Jack Nicol, will you join us?'

The night thick around them. Cold needling Jack's bare skin, his belly churning. He wasn't sure if he believed any of it, the supposed power of a word, but was certain he wanted it anyway. So Jack whispered back, 'Aye.'

'And you have come tae this decision of your own free will?'

Jack nodded, the movement agitating whatever was looped round his neck; it felt like rope in its weight and roughness. He said again, aye.

'Well then, you must knock at the door and see if the High Horseman will admit you.'

Someone hauled Jack up and shoved him between the shoulder blades so that he staggered forward, hands reaching out for something to grasp on to and meeting wood – the stable door. He balled his fist and knocked.

'Enter,' said a voice from within.

The door was opened and Jack stepped over the threshold. The men took hold of him again and he was dragged further inside, then forced back down to his knees.

In front: 'Who comes? In the name of the word, speak your name.' It was a voice Jack didn't recognize – low and deep, not from around there. Something moved beside him and Jack jumped, suddenly aware of his vulnerability – down on all fours, face at kicking height. Someone laid a palm on his back, crouched down beside him. 'I will tell you what you are tae say,' Tam said. 'Go on, High Horseman. He's ready.'

'Speak your name.'

Tam's low voice: 'A brother.'

Jack split his dry lips. 'A . . . a brother.'

'A brother of what?'

He waited for Tam's instruction. 'Of horsemanry.'

'Who bade ye come here?'

'The devil.'

A pause. The figure before them shifted, leaned in close enough for the stink of his breath to seep through Jack's shroud. 'What way did you come? The crooked way, or the way of the straight path?'

'By the hooks and crooks of the road.'

'In what light did you come?'

'By the stars and the light of the moon.' Jack didn't know what any of this meant. The strange, lyrical words reminded him of the stories his ma used to tell, of devils and harpies, witches, soft-throated sirens who would lure men to a death by song. *Stupid men*, she'd say.

'And what is the tender of the oath?'

Tam's tongue was slippery on the words. They snaked out in what seemed like one breath, an incantation, and when Jack came to repeat them he found, somehow, that they came easily from him too. 'Hele, conceal, never reveal; neither write nor dite, nor recite; nor cut nor carve nor write in sand.'

A shifting in the air, like the twitch of lips or toes moving in boots, the flick of a horse's ear. The figure in front came closer still. 'Then I shall tell you the Horseman's Word.'

As soon as it had been whispered in Jack's ear, a roar went up. Jack was lifted off the ground by large hands, slapped between the shoulder blades so hard he knew there'd be evidence. 'To seal the oath!' someone cried, and Jack was being dragged out again, the rope round his shoulders heavy, what felt like a knot bouncing against his spine. Outside, the men pulled him along with such vigour that Jack barely had to lift his feet. In the chaos he grabbed at his blindfold, managed to loosen it enough to see a bit through the weave.

The men stopped and Jack felt them gathering round him. Then a light appeared up ahead, a lamp held by someone tall and wiry: Donald. Behind him was another figure. This one moved oddly, somehow slow yet covering the distance between them stealthily, making no sound. Jack tried to pick through the mess of hessian in front of his eyes but could grasp only the dark form, black on black, before he was grabbed roughly and pushed. The figure drew nearer as they spun him, their gnarling and twisting hands shoving Jack so he couldn't stop, feet crossing over. A distorted shape, face stretched, something grotesque – a blur of white, redness of mouth. Jack could hardly breathe, couldn't form words or thoughts other than repeating to himself: I want this, I want this.

Someone took Jack's shoulders and steadied him. 'Now it's time tae shake hands with Auld Hornie.'

Silence fell and the lamp was extinguished. Jack's fingers fluttered through the still night air and he stepped forward, heart so massive it might have choked him. The devil is not real, he told himself. His ma would have disagreed.

Jack knew it was in front of him. Body heat, a sense of mass. It was too late to stop. His fingers brushed something, and Jack forced himself to open his hand to it. What met his palm was furred, a clod of misshapen bone like a hoof. He couldn't tell what it was, only that it didn't belong to a man.

As his knees went, he said it to himself again: the devil is not real. But his da, even his da with his reason, would have said aye, son – sure he is.

LIZZIE

Lizzie stood on the town-hall steps, looking back into the foyer. 'I shouldn't, really. If someone saw us out here, just the two of us, alone...'

But James had already cantered down the steps, turned at the bottom. 'Come now then, while they're distracted.' He was right – the folks inside had gathered round the crying girl, whose tears had grown hysterical after William Calder left. Lizzie thought briefly to go back and check on the girl's welfare, but she was already surrounded, and Lizzie wanted only to be with James. She followed him down the steps, treacherous with ice, to where he awaited her. James pulled off his coat and draped it over Lizzie's shoulders. The smell of his cologne there, the sense of stepping into the very skin of him.

'Won't you be cold?'

'No.' And of course; it seemed ludicrous that something as mundane as cold might trouble him. James darted off ahead, flitting across the puddled gold of a street light. 'Come on!'

Lizzie could do nothing but follow. Down the streets of the town she knew so well, the shuttered shops on the high street, the fountain in the square with its surface gently freezing. Beyond, the houses – cottages pressed up close, great stone villas with thrusting gable ends, their inhabitants surely in bed at this hour.

It was with a certain sense of proprietorship that Lizzie caught up and strode along beside James – as though it all belonged to her.

'James, why did you ask me?'

'Sorry?'

'To the dance. Why did you ask me?'

'Well, I have come back to Elgin and I know very few young women.'

'And . . . ?'

'And? Well, I knew you'd say yes.'

Lizzie raised her eyebrows, decided coyness might in fact serve her. 'I had to think long and hard, actually.'

'I don't think that is true. Anyway, I had to ask you if I had any hope of being invited to another of your father's excellent parties.' He grinned, and Lizzie swatted at his arm. They carried on, turning on to one of the narrow lanes that branched away from the high street – not the direction of home. Down that quieter thoroughfare, away from watching eyes, James pulled Lizzie closer. And Lizzie felt then that she might be the happiest she could ever be. Though – 'James?'

'Yes?'

'That girl you danced with . . .'

'Lizzie.' James stepped in front of her and slipped his hands inside the coat, round her waist.

'Do you know her?'

'No.' James pressed his forehead to hers.

'You looked like you were enjoying yourself a great deal.'

James told her to stop. Edging forward, the graze of his lips against hers. 'It meant nothing. Whatever you think you saw – it's all imagination.'

Lizzie could taste his sincerity. It weakened her, a sense that her legs might buckle, her heart simply slide out of her chest and swoon to its death. But then James pulled back and started to run, then spun around laughing, beckoning for Lizzie to chase him. And she did, hurtling past some slack-mouthed old man, then round a corner, sending a cat leaping from her path. Lizzie called out James's name, but he was still ahead, slowing his pace just enough to taunt her. For a moment, Lizzie saw him as he once had been, when they were children playing in the garden at the Esslemont house. Young James giving chase or darting off, tongue out. Lizzie had run after him, pushing grass-stained knees higher and higher, gaining speed, until she had nearly reached him, reached out to grab a handful of his cardigan – victory, for a moment. But then James had writhed and twisted, shed the garment and dived away once more, eluding her.

Some other dark street, spent, they collapsed into each other. He kissed her with his thumb pressed to her jaw. I am being kissed in the starlight, Lizzie thought; oh wonder, perfection, all my girlish fancies. But underneath, something was growing in her: a dark and rushing feeling that insisted she must press herself against him. She had thought her first kiss would be more chaste than this hot hurry – the ribboning breath, the need. When James pulled away, Lizzie sank back against the wall.

'Have you done this before, Lizzie?'

'No.' She tugged at his shirt collar, brought his face to meet hers. 'Have you?'

Breathless. But he only brought his lips to hers again. Kissed and kissed.

There was a lamp burning in the window of the Brodie house. Lizzie saw it from the street, the yellow glow in the snug where the curtain had not been drawn. She walked carefully up the path, her toes numb, letting an explanation form and solidify in her mind. Lizzie inched her key into the lock, then opened the door. Only the benign tick of the grandfather clock in the hall, its face showing long past midnight.

'Lizzie?' Her father in the snug, then. She paused, considered whether to pretend not to have heard him. She could slip past and go upstairs, into her bedroom, pull the quilt over her head and feign sleep. It was a game she had played as a child, lying rigid in sham slumber, but she was always given away by her flickering eyelashes.

'Yes, it's me.'

'Come in here.'

George was sitting in his armchair with his feet on a velvet pouffe. He liked that room best of all. Lizzie's mother had insisted on the latest style for the others – pale and uncluttered, furniture with straight lines – but the snug was George's room, painted a dark red at his instruction and stuffed with things from the old house. There were tasselled tie-backs on the curtains, thick as ponies' tails, and two leather armchairs with kicking cabriole legs. The walls were cluttered with more of his art collection – George had insisted on hanging the paintings himself, pacing the house looking for picture hooks and cursing loudly when a hammer-blow knocked a chunk of plaster from the wall. *This room will be the undoing of me*, he'd said.

'Had you a nice time?' George removed his feet from the pouffe and patted it for his daughter to sit.

'Oh, yes, it was a very fine evening. And I'm sorry about the time. It got away from me.'

'You're old enough now, my girl. Tell me then, who was there?'

Lizzie reeled off names, the various offspring of his colleagues and associates. 'And William Calder was there.'

'Ah, he's not just about business then.'

'No, he did some dancing. But there was some incident, with the girl he was with. She was crying. I don't know if they had an argument.'

'Well, he seems quite an . . . intense young man.'

'He seems to have an anger in him.'

'Well now, I wouldn't speak ill of someone so important to the bank. Anyway, my darling, I hope you made a fine impression this evening?'

'I hope so.'

'And how was James?'

It was not a secret that she had gone to the dance with him, quite the opposite: George had beamed when Lizzie received the handwritten note on Esslemont-headed paper. But all the same, Lizzie felt herself blush, searched the tone of her father's enquiry for any indication that he might know she was different – a girl who had been kissed. 'Aye, Da, he is well.'

'I was pleased when he asked you, though not surprised. It's hardly escaped my attention, all those longing looks across the dinner table.'

Had they not been subtle? Lizzie supposed not, saw how easy it would have been for others to notice. It must have been no coincidence that her mother had continued to position her next to James at dinner – though perhaps she did not realize quite how her seating plan lent itself to the tumbling of their feet together, the skim of James's fingers over her thigh.

George turned his thick gold wedding band between thumb and forefinger, considering. 'He makes a very fine match. Just think, my girl an Esslemont . . .' He seemed momentarily caught in the astonishment of it. 'It would be good for all of us.'

'I will try to keep him sweet on me, Da.'

'You're a good girl. Now, best be off to your bed.' He gestured to the candle in its holder. 'Take that up with you.'

Lizzie took it, was halfway across the room when her father said her name again, and she turned to look at him.

'Well done.'

An odd remark. But it was late, and she was tired, and perhaps George had replenished his whisky a good few times. Lizzie nodded and said goodnight, holding the candle in front of her and letting him, for a moment, bask in her light.

JACK

He came to on the hard floor of the barn.

'He's awake! Congratulations, Jack, you're nae dead.' The men laughed as Jack rolled on to his side, wincing at the sharp pain in his ribs. Someone had thrown his shirt on top of him like a blanket, but somehow the gesture didn't seem kindly.

'Can take that off now.' Donald gestured to Jack's neck.

Jack looked down at the thing. A loop of rope knotted at the back, the tail of it chucked over his shoulder. With a sick feeling he realized what it was.

'Dinnae worry, it's nae tied right to – you know.' Donald clutched his own neck in his hand, squeezed. 'Well, I dinnae think so, anyway.'

Jack dipped his head and slipped off the noose, savouring for a moment the sudden lightness. He buttoned his shirt back on with unsteady fingers, conscious of being watched. Sitting around were lads he'd never seen before. Some were grown men, older than Tam or Donald – a band of crunched faces, leathery brows, a man with a nose like a boot had stamped it down. They supped at pipes, making the barn hazy with smoke.

'Right then, horseman, you've earned yoursel' a nip.' Donald produced a flask from his jacket pocket. Jack took it and gulped down three or four big mouthfuls, hoping the hooch would soften the throbbing in his knees. Donald watched with amusement, and Jack remembered – not just blacking out and falling, but the noise he'd made as he went, a high shriek like a quine. Fucking jessie. He blinked hard, furious at the prickling in his eyes. It was a stupid trick – must have been a trick – whatever they'd done to make him think he was taking the devil's hand in his. It would have been an old strip of hide wrapped round something, or even a hoof hacked from a dead ewe. With Donald, it could have been anything.

'Now Jack, the Society of the Horseman's Word is a brotherhood, and the word is what binds us. It is a word of great power, and that is vital for a horseman. Use it on your beasts to have them follow your every command. Compliance, Jack, is a wonderful thing.'

There was a murmur of agreement before Donald carried on. 'Of course, such a powerful word . . . well, some say it works not only on beasts.'

A collective smirk. Tam's throaty chuckle, which must have dislodged something, because he spat lustily on the dirt floor. Donald was watching Jack closely – pleased, when he saw that the new horseman had grasped his meaning. 'Now, with all that fainting, I cannae be sure you'll have remembered the word. And I need tae make sure you know it, otherwise you cannae be in the Society. But of course, you cannae say it out loud, in case someone's sneaking about in the shadows who isnae meant tae hear it. So—' Donald took a scrap of paper and a pencil from his breeks. A laugh from somewhere with an edge to it, almost uneasy.

'Aw, Don, dinnae,' said Tam, but was silenced with a sharp look.

'So, to make sure you know it, you'll need to write the word down and show me. And then we'll burn the paper.'

It was a strange word. Jack had never heard it before – not slipped into a story or book, not called out by another horseman to a chancy mare or whispered as he brushed down her flank.

But Jack had not forgotten it; when the word was whispered to him he'd taken it tight in his palm and held it close, heavy and dark and precious as his ma's hagstone.

Jack took the paper and pencil from Donald, considering the vows he'd made: neither write nor dite . . . but when he hesitated, the first crouched to his level. 'Go on,' Donald came closer, pressed his forehead to Jack's. It was warm, felt good. 'This is the last part.'

Jack rested the paper against his leg and set the point of the pencil to it. Hush all round as the lead pressed down and he formed a curve, wrist tilted to close a circle –

'Well, well, well.' A taunting thickness in Donald's voice as he snatched the paper away. He seized Jack's hand and pressed it hard to the floor so the fingers splayed. 'Here, Murdo.'

A man stood. He had been sat in shadow, other men at his feet, and Jack had not seen him, but hearing the name took his breath away. Murdo from Cauldbraes, the next farm along. Tam had told tales of the man, one night not long past when Jack had sat up with the horsemen, whispering so Henry wouldn't wake. Murdo, who could drink two bottles of rotgut and stay standing, who had strangled a lame ram with his bare hands, pressing and pressing until the beast went slack. Murdo, who strode out to the centre of them now, a giant of a man. It seemed the ballads Jack had heard were right, but then, that was their point. Their songs spoke of their world as it was: here is the gang, here is the grieve. Here is the tack-sharp wind and the work and the cruelty.

Murdo held a cart chain. He let it hang loose, swinging it through the air so the links clacked together. Fear moved in Jack like a tide, lapping the sides of him, then all at once, a great surge that he felt in his knees, his hands, heart, clenching every muscle because, in that moment, he couldn't be sure he wouldn't piss himself. Behind Murdo, Tam scrabbled to his feet. 'Stop! Slora will lose his mind if Jack cannae work.'

Tam went ignored. And before Jack could comprehend what those words might have meant, Donald had crawled on top of him, driven a knee into his back to hold him down. When it became clear what was going to happen, there was a choice: fight or submit. Jack bucked his back. The first pushed harder, knee crunching into spine, so Jack tried again, scraping at the floor so hard his thumbnail split and he paused, long enough for Donald to get him tight again, press his left hand rigid to the ground. The first horseman crouched over Jack, his face only an inch away. That close, the blue-white bulge of his eyes, he hardly looked like a man at all. 'You swore, Jack. Hele, conceal, never reveal; neither write nor dite, nor recite; not cut nor carve nor write in sand.'

A final clench of the hand around Jack's wrist. The sound of the chain as it lashed through the air. The hot red pain as the back of his hand split wide.

This time, Jack did not cry out. Everything in his body seemed to stiffen and he jerked, boots scuttering against the floor, realizing in despair that he had not fainted. Disbelief in the laughter of the men.

Jack could not move his hand. A liquid sensation, so he knew it was bleeding. Someone crouched next to him and whispered his name, the sound of Tam's voice making the tears come to Jack's eyes and he almost wanted to spit, tell Tam not to be soft with him now. Of all things, he could not take that. When Jack opened his eyes, the other men had crowded round him, pale and wide-eyed, even Donald. 'Christ, Murdo. You didnae need tae do it so hard.'

Murdo had paced a way off and would not look at the lad folded on the floor. 'He'll be fine. Chuck some whisky on it and wrap it and he'll be fine.'

Jack needed to see what they had done. He reached the hand out in front of him, lifted it to catch the light – that mess of flesh, a cave of black blood. Jack closed his eyes and longed for his brother; Charlie would look at it, clean the wound with something other than stinking rotgut. Jack wished he'd listened when Charlie had begged him not to leave, when he'd said he needed him – that their ma needed him. Their ma. Jack would have had it all done to him again if, afterwards, he could open his eyes and find her there. She'd kiss the top of his head and take him home. And he'd go, leave Windyhillock without a backward glance, and find some other way to be a man.

Instead, Jack got up: this was what he wanted. He accepted the back slaps and the ruffling of his hair and gritted his teeth when they shoved his hand under freezing water, chucked hooch on the wound and wrapped it in a strip of old linen. Then he drank enough that it didn't hurt any more, so that when he saw the blood seeping through the bandage he almost wondered where it was coming from. Jack thought, even, that at least there would be a good story in it later. It crossed his mind what the grieve might say – there was no way Jack would be working in the morn – but the grieve had wanted this too. A show of prowess and productivity, brute strength; another horseman inducted. When Murdo got up, he thumped Jack's shoulder and set the pain coursing through him again, and Jack nodded and tasted once more the Horseman's Word on his tongue, and knew it had all been worth it.

In the chaumer, the lads stripped for bed. With no one watching him, Jack suddenly found it hard to stay upright. With great effort he shrugged himself out of his shirt, trying to angle the sleeve over the wound without touching it. He struggled to pull off his boots with his one good hand, grew so frustrated that the tears threatened to come again. When he was down to his underpants, he slipped under the quilt and tried to settle. Everything hurt. He realized he was holding his breath and let it go, in one long, shuddering exhalation.

When Tam had set to snoring and Donald was breathing heavily, Jack finally let the tears come. So easy, the way they filled his eyes and spilled over, washed the sweat and the dirt from his cheeks. He had not cried in a long time. When he stopped, Jack became aware that someone was watching him. The room was lit with the lightening sky, weak yellow, turning away from the night. And there was Henry and his frown of concern, getting up.

Jack was drunk, so he let the orra-loon come silently to his bed, lie down, reach a slender arm round his body. Found that, once it was there, Henry had strength in him after all, the press of his palm at Jack's chest firm enough to be a comfort. He let Henry wipe his cheek, soak up the salt-wash of his tears. And by his ear, the loon's small voice, working round a prayer. But this was too risky; the others might wake and hear them, might see them. Jack turned on to his back. He reached to put his good hand over Henry's mouth, quiet him. Fingers to the softness of his lips, and for a moment Jack just let them be there, felt the flutter of the lad's breath. Henry opened his mouth a little. Fingertip somewhere wet and glossy. A tooth. A tongue.

Donald, shifting in his bed. Jack snatched his hand back and turned away.

'What the fuck have you lot done?' The grieve was crimson, his hands bunched into fists as he strode in circles in the smallness of the chaumer. Donald and Tam were up, wearing only their underpants and shirts, and even the first looked contrite.

'Things got out of hand.'

'Out of shitting hand! You're telling me. When Slora sees this . . .' The grieve narrowed his eyes. 'Out in the yard, you two. And you,' he nodded at Jack, 'into the house.'

Jack managed to peel back the quilt, averting his eyes from the mess the blood had made on it – something shaming in the rusted spots mixed with the sprays of flowers and polka dots, the squares his ma had stitched together. He pulled his breeks on one-handed, went without a shirt. Jack headed out across the yard with Henry scurrying behind him, past the other horsemen who stood waiting for their punishment.

The kitchen was strangely quiet. Perhaps a certain arrogance in expecting a calamity, that the maids might come running with panic and antiseptic. Jack sat heavily at the table, Henry standing over him like a fretful mother. 'Jack? You all right?'

'Never been better.'

'What happened last night? What did they do to you?'

'Nothing. Don't worry about it.'

'But . . .' Henry eyed Jack's hand, the sopping bandage.

'It's nothing.' It came out cutting, and Jack glanced up at the loon. 'Just leave it.'

'You can tell me, Jack. We're friends and that.'

The orra-loon was right, Jack could tell him. Part of him wanted to speak of it, just to put word and shape to what he thought he had seen in the yard, what he had taken in his hand. He almost wanted to say the Horseman's Word out loud, instead of turning it over and over in his mouth like a lozenge, too big to swallow. But Jack had found trouble enough by breaking his oath, and, besides, this was not a matter for wee boys like Henry.

'Just leave it, will you?'

'It's just, I saw what you did. The devil—'

'I told you, it's nae your business.'

'Please, Jack, I'm worried about you. In bed last night—'

'Dinnae talk of that.'

They were interrupted by the sound of the door opening. The twins were there, and when Isaac saw the sorry scene at the kitchen table he glanced back at his sister and stood in her way.

'He's hurt,' Henry blurted out, as though the seeping hand set on the tabletop were not evidence enough.

Jack pulled it away. 'I'm fine.'

'It's bleeding.' Henry was sheet-white, crusts of sleep at his eyes. He tipped forward suddenly, groping for the back of a chair, and Isaac rushed to steady him. The loon slumped against him, transgressing whatever boundary of manners and cleanliness usually kept the gang well away from the farmer's son.

'Come on, let's go outside,' said Isaac, 'get some fresh air.'

The orra-loon let himself be led out, Isaac still supporting him with an arm while opening the kitchen door. From out in the yard, there came a sharp crack and then the sound of someone dropping to their knees. A cry of pain that was ragged, wild: Tam's. Nothing like that from Donald; he would take his punishment silently.

When the door closed again, Violet stepped into the kitchen.

'Come on then – let me see.'

'What? No. It's nothing.'

Violet went to the range and poured hot water into a basin, the rising steam moistening her cheeks. She took a clean cloth from the cupboard and set all of this down on the table. 'Take the bandage off.'

'I . . . no. You dinnae want to see this.' In truth, nor did Jack. He didn't know what he might find under the bandage, how dirty and ruined his hand would be. But Violet took it in one of hers and began to unfurl the rag. She was frowning, tongue edging out in concentration.

'We'll need tae be quick, the buyers are coming again this morning.'

Once Jack's hand was unwrapped, Violet took it in her lap. If she was alarmed, she didn't show it, though Jack could see from the corner of his eye the bright blood, the flesh. He focused instead on the crown of her head as it bobbed forward, the pink line of her parting.

'So it's decided then, the sale?'

Violet shrugged. 'I dinnae think so, not yet. The pair of them are coming tae look round again.'

'I'd better make myself scarce then.'

'You can go back tae your chaumer – they winnae look in there. They're gentlemen.'

Violet began to bathe Jack's hand, dampening the cloth and dabbing gently. The warm water on the wound made him wince but then, as the basin turned red, it began to feel nice. Violet glanced up at him. 'So you're a horseman now?'

That expansion in his chest again, and he remembered he was shirtless. 'Aye, I am.' And Jack thought he saw the farmer's lass smile as she tended to his hand, hot and wet on her knee.

PART THREE

THE FALL OF THE YEAR

October–November 1915

LIZZIE

Lizzie's bedroom floor is strewn with clothes. She had been halfway down the stairs in her usual blouse and wool skirt when she decided to go back and try on something else. It is an occasion, the ceilidh, and she ought to make more effort for it – probably Maggie will be wearing at least the dress she wears for kirk, and Johnny will be trussed and smart with a ribbon round his neck. Lizzie wonders how he chooses the colour – at random, fingers slipping through a heap of silk and moire and grosgrain, or in some more considered way, an expression of his mood. Probably he is not as indecisive as she is now, a dozen dresses discarded on the bed. All that's left hanging in her wardrobe are summer things, unsuitable for the Cabrach's late October, but then Lizzie sees the box lying on the shelf above the rail.

She takes it down, kneels to open it. Still the smell of perfume – her mother's, jasmine and white flowers, still heady enough to taste. Lizzie unfolds the gown and strokes the black velvet with a fingertip, tentatively, because its soft nap and the scent are enough to flood her with memory, mostly of a feeling; how it had felt to wear the dress, to be looked at in it.

Downstairs, Jane emerges from the parlour. 'You'll not be late back, I hope.'

'I shouldn't have thought so, but no need to stay up for me.'

'I expect I'll be long in my bed by the time you get home.' Jane turns in early. A cup of warm milk by the fireside, then up to read her scriptures and sleep, surely, the unruffled slumber of the blessed. Her gaze moves down to Lizzie's dress. 'I'm surprised it still fits.'

'It's true it is a little tighter.'

'And I'm surprised you want to wear it again.'

'I have little else suitable for the occasion.'

Jane watches as Lizzie takes her coat from the hook and puts it on, rummages in its pockets for her gloves.

'I must make it known – again – that I do not approve. It is not becoming for a woman of your standing to go to a party like this, especially without her husband.'

When it had come to it, Lizzie had not lied to Jane about her plans for the evening. She was a bad liar, she knew – could always hear her voice growing distorted, expression overcome by guilt. And so she had appealed to Jane's sense of duty, gushing over how kind it was of the Stuarts to invite her, how they'd be affronted if she declined.

'It'll just be some stories and songs, I expect. Maggie and Rab are decent people.'

'It's not the Stuarts who concern me. Who else will be there?'

'Well, the Brawlands gang and their kin from other farms.'

'And that awful man, the singer?' Jane looks closely at Lizzie's face.

Again, Lizzie thinks of Johnny – perhaps running a comb through his hair, or gassing with Mysie before saying goodbye, rubbing two fingers over the cat's plush head. He might be whistling down the track right now, halfway to Brawlands. Lizzie had always liked it, back in town, before a party. She imagined all those parallel lives: Webster taking a preparatory dram, patting his wife's bottom as she placed it on the table beside him.

Mistress Esslemont folding a clutch of grey hairs into a chignon, frowning, her son in the doorway, smirking at her vanity in the way of people who cannot imagine ageing.

'I expect Johnny will be there, yes.'

Jane's arms are now crossed over her chest. 'I rest my case.'

Is it the judgement itself that irks her? That Jane should assume she knows anyone based only on claik and hearsay? Or is it that it's focused on Johnny in particular? Lizzie's own judgement tells her to look away, to let the comment slide. Such things have become easy, over the years – imagining she is but a cloud floating above William's dark tempers, that she has become hardened enough for every barbed word to bounce straight off her. But her eyes fix on Jane's and she lifts her chin. 'What do you mean?'

'You know exactly what I mean.'

The women regard each other. Jane has recently washed her face; it is scrubbed and tight from the hot water, as though she's been blanched. Only her light-blue eyes stand out, fixed on Lizzie. Jane Calder could outstare the dead. She waits until Lizzie drops her gaze, then allows herself a smile. 'Goodnight, sister. I'll see you in the morn.'

They fall to a hush when the knock comes. Maggie claps her hands. 'A visitor!' She presses a finger to her lips as her bairns clamber up, abandoning the apples in their basins. They crowd round the door with their loud whispers, the eldest boy height enough to peer through the keyhole.

'Who is it, Ma?'

'Well, we'll have tae go and see, won't we?' As she opens the door, a slice of night air cuts into the kitchen's sultry heat, crisp and welcome, for the room is close, sticky with the resinous scent of the bog myrtle draped from the rafters. 'Entrance only in exchange for a song.'

Their visitor is a dark silhouette in the doorway. Then he is the toe of a boot crossing the threshold, a sweep of dark coat, a startling flash of red silk that catches the eye as danger might. And it is silly, really, the quivery ripple in Lizzie's chest as he begins to sing:

O I'll lay ye doon, love, I'll treat ye decent
I'll lay ye doon, love, I'll fill your can
O I'll lay ye doon, love, I'll treat ye decent
For surely he is an honest man.

The visitor whips off his hat and bows with a flourish – ever the performer. Johnny lets Maggie pinch his cheeks with both hands, drawing his blood to the surface. 'Come in then, oh dark stranger.' She plants a fat kiss on Johnny's lips and for a moment he tips her backwards, as though they might waltz. She swats him away, giggling, and Johnny looks around the room expectantly – is met by the scowling guests round the table, the most enthusiastic of them managing only a jerk of the head as welcome. They had been like this, too, when Lizzie had arrived, straightening their backs and greeting her with exaggerated politeness.

Maggie has attempted gaiety – turnips with carved faces, hollowed-out to use as lanterns; best china dishes filled with sweets and marzipan. But the youngsters have sipped their cups of ale and fretted: a farm where things go missing, a speckled red rash that started on one maid and now afflicts the lot. They've spoken of someone's cousin from over the glens, a soldier of seventeen dead with a bullet in his brain. And Lizzie has sat alone, worrying it is her presence that has tightened the atmosphere. She has been waiting for Johnny to come and pick the night up, but now she sees his expression drop. It tugs something in Lizzie, his unmet need, so she calls out bravo. He looks over; colour in his cheek, a thanking dip of the head. Lizzie's appreciation galvanizes something in the others, too. Stephen the orra-man slaps his thigh and says, 'Nice one, Johnny.'

Alex drags his attention away from Jock's daughter, Jemima, who is sitting close enough to him on the bench that she may as well be on his knee. 'Aye, nae bad. You well?'

'He looks well,' one of the others says. 'Here, Johnny, how is it that we're all freezing our baws off and white as your grunny's moustache and you look like you've been in the sun all day?'

'Pact with the devil,' someone mutters.

They are right that Johnny looks well, still bearing a swarthy flush from the clement summer. Lizzie sees him for a moment as she had the day she found the body, hurrying up to Brawlands and passing him at work in the field. High noon, his shirt open to the waist.

'A fine outfit too, Mr Nicol,' says Maggie. 'You match with Lizzie and all.'

Johnny looks over, takes in her dress – the same black velvet as his lapels. His eyes rest on Lizzie a moment and his lips part, as if she's startled him.

'It's nae much of a costume though,' says Alex. 'What are you meant tae be?'

Johnny shrugs. 'Nothing really.'

'Sounds about right.' They are the first words from Henry all evening. He has sat at the table with a tetchy energy, eyes darting towards the door, taking frequent, tiny sips of his ale.

'What's that, loon? Speak up.'

Henry raises his glass to his mouth and drains it. A watery trail of foam clings to his top lip.

Johnny is impatient. 'I said I didnae hear you.'

But Maggie steps in front of Johnny and plants a drink in his hand. 'Right, now you've arrived, it's time for some dancing.' She crosses the kitchen and opens the door, calls out into the night for Rab, who is building the bonfire in the yard. While they wait for him Maggie tops up glasses, begins to hum a jig with all the forced brightness of small talk at a wake.

Rab comes in, trailing the scent of the bonfire. He digs in the sideboard and brings out a scuffed leather case. The fiddle he takes from it is a little battered, smudged with a dark patina where his chin has been. The farmer stretches his neck from side to side, taps his fingers on his thigh to bring the rhythm to them, then looks at the party, askance. 'Come on then! If I'm playing, you lot need tae dance.'

None of them move until Lizzie takes it upon herself to stand. 'Come on, let's have some cheer.'

Alex follows, pulling Jemima up with him. Then the rest of them rise, girls coy in taking their ploughmen's hands, a swoop of levity surging through the kitchen; the evening's first. Lizzie waits. She has waited many years to dance again, instead sustaining herself with the type of three-in-the-morning fantasies that leave her feeling desperate. She's imagined a life of showy town balls or rowdy ceilidhs, being spun so fast that the world becomes nothing but a streak of candlelight and tartan. She waits, too, because she wants to be asked. And Johnny is looking at her, moving across the room. He straightens the knot at his throat and draws himself tall. At the last moment, Maggie steps into his path.

'The first dance, with your hostess?'

'I . . . of course, I'd be delighted.' He removes his coat and stretches himself out, arms above his head. A gap where the tails of his shirt, tucked into his breeks, split open to reveal a soft triangle of stomach. Lizzie allows herself to look; to covet, she'll admit. A desire she has only fingered the edges of before, when she touched his knee in Mysie's parlour, felt his mouth on her cheek by the Blackwater track. It is fine to look – looking is all she will do. She fans her face with her hand because it is awkward, then, to stand alone at the side of the room. But a lad sidles up to her, plucks up the courage to offer his hand, and Lizzie takes it.

Rab's bow pulls its first note from the fiddle. 'Ready?'

'Hang on!' Stephen casts about for a dancing partner, but there are no lassies left. He takes a hefty swig of his ale, and with a belch and a slap of his knee lunges for Henry. The ploughman takes a moment to realize what is happening, is manipulated into the lady's position before he can protest. 'No, I dinnae want—'

'Wheesht, darling,' says Stephen, and laughter splits the room. Henry draws himself tall, but his body is slack so that he leans too much on Stephen's shoulder, earning a fruity whistle as the orra-man pushes him back. 'You're enjoying this too much!'

The music starts up and they march forward, Lizzie's partner good-natured in his dancing, accepting her first unpractised steps, guiding her with his rough hands. On the other side of the kitchen, Johnny turns Maggie effortlessly, letting her spool away from him then pulling her back, his step never faltering. He sees Lizzie watching, and probably she should look away, but he is compelling – there is a rightness to his body in motion, something of the same quality as how his clothes always fit him, the attentive way he listens. Grace, she supposes.

The music builds. Johnny's legs kick higher, as though under Lizzie's gaze he strives to improve himself. To their left, Henry struggles to keep his footing as Stephen swings him wildly round. Then, the tempo slows and Johnny pulls Maggie into his chest, his arms across her. There is a final drawn-out note and Stephen slows with it, dips Henry to the floor, but the loon is wrong-footed and skitters for purchase until Stephen hauls him back up, just in time to save him a crack to the skull.

'Whoa, whoa!' cries Rab. 'I dinnae need a ploughman with a broken neck. Take a rest, calm down.' He sets down his fiddle on the sideboard. 'Let's have some stories instead.'

They refresh themselves with topped-up ales, take positions round the table, Henry slumping down heavily and upsetting a brimming tankard so that it sloshes beer on to Johnny's breeks. 'For God's sake, loon.' He mops up the drink with a tea towel.

Henry seems exhausted, his face white and sheened like lard.

'You dinnae look well, my boy.' Maggie presses the back of her hand to his brow. 'Now, Johnny – your creepiest tale, if you please.'

Johnny dabs pointedly at the foam soaking his thighs, eyeing Henry. 'What do you want, then? The black dog of Glenrinnes?'

A lad rolls his eyes. 'Naw, you do that one every year.'

'How about the one about the tall dark stranger at the Glacks o' Balloch?'

'That's nae even scary.'

'I'd like to hear it,' Lizzie says, but the others carp and moan until Johnny folds his arms across his chest and says someone else can tell a story, if they think they can do better.

Eventually, one of the ploughmen leans in. 'I'll give you a chilling one, and it's all true. See, I called on wee Jimmy Weir the other day.'

Rab shakes his head. 'No, we dinnae want claik about wee Jimmy.'

'It's nae claik. It's all true, as I said.' And they want to hear about him, of course – their one-legged soldier who hasn't been seen at inn nor kirk, who has stayed shut away in his ma's croft at the bottom of the valley.

'See, I went down tae check how he was doing – we were pals before he joined up. He looks a mess, right enough, but he's getting around all right with his crutch. Makes a strange noise as he goes, mind – the tap of the crutch, then he heaves his body forward. Tap, heave, tap, heave.'

Discomfort seeps through them. Some of the girls have gone pale, the ploughmen studying their ales. Johnny is frowning, hands gripping the edge of the table. Next to him, Henry is listening carefully.

'As I sat with him, I started tae realize something wisnae right. He wisnae talkative but he'd manage a few words, remembering the auld times and that, but then he'd suddenly stop and stare straight ahead of him – it was like I wisnae there. And then he'd start trembling, just a bit at first, but then his teeth were knocking together and I had tae put my hand on his knee to try and stop him. But it was like . . . something stronger than him . . .' The ploughman's own hands are quivering in his lap. 'So then I said I'd go, let him get some rest, but when I went tae pat his shoulder he grabbed hold of me.'

'Stop,' says one of the maids, 'I dinnae like this.' She goes to stand up, but her friend takes her wrist, holds her back.

The ploughman looks up. 'Let her go, if she's feart. This next bit is worse.' He drinks deeply from his cup and looks, finally, at each of them. 'He grabbed hold of me and he came close to my ear and started tae whisper. Said it began with a smell, and it was a smell he knew straight away – burnt hair. It got stronger and stronger, as the nights went on. And then he started to feel a dampness on his arms, and he got it in mind that there was something under his bed.'

'You know,' says Stephen, 'I've heard it said it was as soon as he got back tae the Cabrach that his temper took a turn.'

'Aye, soon as he came up the auld droving road.'

'He was never prone tae flights of fancy before—'

'Let him finish,' snaps Henry. There is a hardness in him that Lizzie has not seen before.

Wee Jimmy's friend closes his eyes and winces, as though picturing the scene. 'Well, when he looked under the bed he thought he saw something . . . someone. Curled up small.'

They are quiet a moment and it seems, briefly, as though the whole of the Cabrach is silent too. As though the wind that flays the backs of the braes recedes to nothing, and the Deveron stills, and in the crofts and cottars the laughter dies. This hush until Henry sits back and says, 'He's seen her too.'

Johnny in an instant: 'Loon, dinnae start.'

'Maybe he's got a point,' says Stephen. 'Though that's assuming the creature from the bog is something worse than just a lassie. Haven't you found out yet, Mistress Calder?'

They watch Lizzie as she chooses her words, conscious they will be pocketed, passed on, repeated until they warp under their own weight. 'Not yet. The constabulary is still looking back through the records. Inspector Esslemont is writing to a man at the university, some scientist. We're hoping he can come out and see her.' Lizzie neglects to mention her other line of enquiry – that after looking at the bog woman again with Johnny, she had gone home and written a letter to his brother the surgeon, addressed audaciously to Dr Nicol of Aberdeen Royal Infirmary, in the hope that it would find its way to him.

'I reckon she was murdered,' says one lad, 'dumped in the bog so no one would find her.'

'No. That look on her face that everyone says she has? She was a filthy whore.'

Henry regards them with his chin cupped in his long fingers. 'I dinnae think she's a woman at all.'

Johnny stands. 'Enough.'

'Do you nae want tae speak of her?'

'No.'

'There's a lot of things you dinnae want tae speak of, Jack,' says Henry.

Lizzie frowns. 'Who's Jack?'

'The loon's nae slept in days, he's barely coherent.' Johnny shoots a glance at Henry then spreads his arms to the group. 'Come on, let's nae have this tonight. Let's do another dance, something calmer.' He looks at Lizzie; is seen looking.

'Ah, his intention all along,' says Stephen. The maids titter and Henry leans over to mutter something in Stephen's ear that widens the orra-man's eyes. 'The hayloft, eh? You kept that one quiet.'

Johnny's body tenses. 'You keep speaking, loon, but never loud enough for me tae hear.'

'None of your business,' Henry says.

'It sounds like it might be.'

'Does it? Not everyone's thinking about you all the time.'

Maggie claps her hands. 'Come on now, another dance.'

But Johnny has not finished. 'Aye, loon, you're right. I was up in the hayloft with Lizzie. We went to see if the body was still there, and guess what? She was, right where we left her. So you can shut your mouth.' He strides out into the centre of the room. 'Lizzie, will you come for a dance?'

She hesitates. The group is watching her, Henry flushed and intent, his eyes flicking between Lizzie and Johnny, who is standing adrift in the middle of the kitchen floor.

'Lizzie?' A thread of pleading in his tone. Lizzie wants to give him what he's asked for. She takes a step forward, but then there is the scrape of a chair across the flagstones, the sound as it smacks against the wall.

Henry is standing too. 'I really wouldnae, if I were you—'

Johnny snaps at him once more to leave it, then claps his hands. 'Rab, will you play? Lizzie, come on.'

This is not how she wanted it – Johnny in ill-temper, the air choked with tension. But Lizzie goes, noticing the glance that passes between the Stuarts as she crosses the room. But here is Johnny and the undone top button of his shirt, his outstretched hand. She meets his eye; sees, then, the crash of confusion there when someone grasps her arm and pulls her hard away.

JOHNNY

Johnny does not know what is happening at first – Lizzie stepping towards him then staggering back, Henry's fingers digging into her arm.

Johnny springs forward. 'Get off her, what's wrong with you?' He makes a grab at the loon's pullover, gets a good handful. Henry scrabbles to free himself, but Johnny clamps his arm across the loon's chest, forcing him to still. Henry can hardly speak. He flops back against Johnny's chest, panting, his head lolling back so their cheeks touch. Something about this accidental tenderness that tempers Johnny's anger.

'Come on, we'll go out and get some air. Put your coat on,' he says. Henry looks bewildered, lets Maggie take his coat from the hook and stuff his arms into its sleeves.

Johnny goes to Lizzie. She appears unharmed, though her dress has torn under the arm. 'You all right?'

She nods; she is calm. Johnny realizes he wanted something else, for her to be shaking and appalled so that he might fold her into his arms – just as comfort, or, if he's honest, a consolation to himself for the moment that's been taken from him. He does it anyway, but he is awkward and she stiff, turning her head towards the youngsters at the table who are observing them still.

Over her shoulder, Johnny sees that Rab is watching too – but surely Rab, gentle Rab, will understand.

Johnny releases Lizzie. 'I winnae be long.' He slings an arm round Henry's shoulders and leads him outside.

In the yard, the bonfire is making steady progress. Rab's built it up with the splintered limbs of the Scots pines that rim his land, then heaped the mouldered crop on top – some use for it, at least, though the dank black sheaves give off a smell like something long dead. When Henry reaches the pyre he hesitates, stretches his hands out to feel the heat. Johnny gives him a second for this feeble grasp at pleasure and then gestures towards the barn. 'Come on, we'll go in there a minute.'

Henry sees where he is looking. 'No. Nae with her.'

'Who?'

'You know.'

'She's probably nae at home. You said she's taken tae getting up and wandering, these days.'

Johnny opens the barn door and takes a step inside. He sees nothing untoward there, of course – only the tarpaulined binder, Rab's waxed jacket hanging on the door to the storeroom. He glances up at the hayloft where the corner of the woman's sackcloth is visible near the edge of the shelf, same as it was the last time he'd been here.

'Is she still there?'

'Of course she's still there.'

But Henry doesn't move and Johnny sighs; he's damned if he's going to try and coax the loon in like he's a spooked beast digging its hooves into the mud. 'We'll go tae your chaumer then.' Johnny regrets the suggestion as soon as he's made it; he does not want the sad intimacy of the place where the loon sleeps, curling his body as tight as a fist, the way he did at Windyhillock.

'All right.'

They move across the yard. It is dark, away from the bonfire. A timeless thing, darkness, so that it could be today or they could have fallen back through the years. Dark, so there's no way of seeing that they are men now, and changed, because it feels as it did a decade past when they used to leave the kitchen and head to their beds. Henry would walk close enough that Johnny could feel his breath on the back of his neck.

Now, when they reach the chaumer, there is a candle lit inside.

'You shouldnae be leaving candles burning, you'll have the whole place up in smoke.'

'I didnae leave it burning. We never do.'

And they hear, then, a noise from inside. A rustling, something turning over. The heave of a body.

'What is it?' Henry whispers.

Johnny doesn't know. Cannot say, truthfully, that it's just the cold raising the hairs on his arms. 'It'll just be—'

'She's got out.'

'I'll have a look.' Johnny edges forward, presses his ear to the door. From inside there is a breath, a snarl from the wetness of a throat. He will not show any fear, because fear is contagious. Instead Johnny thinks only of the motions he must make – clasping the latch, pushing the door open wide enough to get a foot inside. He sticks his head into the chaumer. Catches a dash of red hair and a body, limbs slipping, a gasp –

'Can you see her?'

The body rolls through the gloom and there, in the leery shine of the moon and a half-spent candle, is a bobbing white arse.

'Hey! Piss off!' Alex hisses.

Two flustered faces: the ploughman and Jock's good daughter Jemima. Johnny shoves Henry back and slams the door but the loon has seen too, gone beaming red. 'We should tell Jock.'

'Tell him what? Let her have her romance.'

'It's a sin.'

'Leave it, loon.'

'But this is what I meant.' Something of the Reverend Bruce in Henry, the hard-done-by frustration. 'The badness is spreading.'

A defiant response, then, from the chaumer – a ragged groan that slips under the door so that Johnny and Henry freeze a moment, their eyes not meeting. Another memory: Johnny's own dank bed, a quine who liked him, quine he couldn't care less about as soon as he'd rolled off her. Another one, different quine, who he'd lied to and said he loved her so she might offer herself up without him having to ask. And repeat, for years – Cullen girls with the reek of skink in their petticoats, maids from Towie or Tarland who'd come back from a country dance having lost more than just their wages. Lassies from the Broch – easy to persuade, for they were sick of sailors; barmaids he'd flatter in exchange for a drop of good Dufftown whisky. A hundred hearts toyed with in pursuit of one that might love him.

'Look, Henry, you're knackered. When those two are finished you should go and lie down, get some sleep.'

'No, I cannae. She's getting worse. I checked on her the other night.' This must have been when Alex found Henry wandering about the yard – Johnny can imagine the loon climbing shakily up the ladder to the hayloft, numb blue fingers trying to undo the body's knots, then tying them again – badly. And to think Johnny doubted himself.

'It's nothing but a dead body, loon.'

'No, it's more than that. Everything gets worse the more she rots. Sinclair was right – she's of the devil. Wherever he's been, he leaves a mark.'

Johnny sighs. 'Loon, the devil's nae real.'

'He's here, I can feel him. Don't you remember what it's like?'

If Johnny is honest, maybe he does. Has felt it in the driving rain and its uncanny timing, the cold that aches his bones though it's not yet November. The unearthing of things in him – the anger and the lust – things he thought he'd got a grip on.

But he says again, through gritted teeth, 'The devil's nae real.'

Henry doesn't seem to hear him. He steps close, so that Johnny can smell his sour breath and his unwashed skin, the stink of the unslept. 'Don't you remember? When he comes and it makes you different, makes you think things you're ashamed of? Makes you act on them?'

'Look, loon, you're tired. When those two are done, go and lie down.'

Henry looks, for a moment, like he might take Johnny's advice. Calmly, he lifts a finger and places it on Johnny's lapel. Delicate, stroking the soft of it. 'Will you come in with me?'

'What?'

'Like you used to.'

Another regret. A night at Windyhillock when Henry had taken too much drink and had to be packed off to his bed. A kindness, on Johnny's part, before the loon got picked on by the other men, made to mount the mare stark naked or drink a snifter of Donald's brown piss. Johnny had taken Henry to the chaumer, stripped off his shirt and breeks, then turned away as the loon fumbled into his pyjamas and got into bed. He'd let Johnny tuck him in, then started crying – a confused sorrow, weeping until he retched, so Johnny had lifted the quilt and got in with him, put an arm round in comfort. They had lain there, quiet save the odd cackle from Tam in the stables, and for some reason Johnny couldn't explain – can't now – he had pressed a kiss to the back of Henry's neck.

'Please, Jack?'

But Johnny has had enough. Scunnered with being called that name again, with listening to Henry talking in riddles. He realizes he's been frightened of the loon – the way Henry has been at Jock's, loose-lipped and hostile. Johnny had been worried Henry would let it all slip, but he sees now that the loon was donning a cloak of bravado too heavy for his shoulders. He wouldn't dare talk about Windyhillock, would have done it by now if he'd had the balls to tell tales on Johnny Nicol. It's an act, all of it, same as when he talks like the great I-am about the bog woman, as though he knows something the rest of them don't.

'No.' Johnny turns and walks away, realizing as he does so that he hasn't asked the loon what all the fuss in the kitchen was about, pulling Lizzie away from him. Probably he already knows.

Johnny has gone a few more paces when Henry calls out. 'I haven't forgotten, you know. Not any of it.'

Johnny stops in his tracks. He could turn round, look the loon in the eye and ask him to repeat himself, but he knows, somehow, that he would not like the Henry he would find. Another version, this one hardened by grievance. And Henry is not alone in his long memory – Johnny remembers it too, indelible as his ma's old tales, though at least those are ones he's had the freedom to tell differently.

He walks on towards the bonfire, only realizing Henry has stopped watching him when he hears the squeal of the barn door.

LIZZIE

Lizzie has watched Johnny and Henry's conversation from the window, their dark figures stepping together, then apart; Johnny walking away with the brisk pace of anger.

'I wonder what they were talking about,' she says to Maggie, who peers over Lizzie's shoulder.

'I dinnae know, but I hope Johnny's got his temper under control. Henry tends tae take things tae heart.'

Johnny paces by the bonfire with his shoulders wrung up, body locked with tension. 'I'll take him a drink,' says Lizzie.

Maggie looks at her carefully, then goes to the dresser and takes down a whisky bottle and two tumblers. 'And one for you and all?'

'I . . . yes, please.'

She pours the drams and passes them wordlessly, and Lizzie goes out.

In fact, Johnny's expression is not vengeful. Lizzie observes him through the smoke, his eyes cast down. He shakes his head when he notices her. 'A nonsense. He's knackered. Had too much tae drink.'

Lizzie hands Johnny a glass. 'Perhaps you haven't had enough.'

'You—' he tips half of it back in one, 'say things I wouldnae expect.'

'What was Henry on about?'

Johnny waves a hand: it doesn't matter.

'I feel sorry for him.'

'Don't.'

They stand for a moment and watch the sparks spitting off the fire. The night is clear and Lizzie looks up at the sky, washed with stars, little flecks like spilled sugar. She thinks to remark on its beauty, but Johnny is still frowning.

'I told you, didn't I, that they're getting strange ideas about that body?'

And Lizzie wants to say don't talk, not now. 'They're just making up stories.'

'Folks keep telling me we should bury her.'

'My sister-in-law is of the same opinion.'

Johnny turns to her. 'And what do you think?'

When did someone last ask for her opinion? 'I think . . . not yet. She hasn't given up her secrets yet.'

'All right, as you like.'

And when did someone last heed it?

Lizzie glances back towards the farmhouse – curtains drawn, just the flicker of the neepie lanterns on the sills. The yard is empty and it is good to be alone, watched only by the night's large moon. And it is for comfort, Lizzie thinks, as she steps in front of Johnny, that she places her hand carefully on his chest. He glances down, a brief confusion clouding his face, but then he stills and lets her rest there, and she cannot tell whose heart it is that beats harder.

They are disturbed by Henry, darting across the yard and back to the house. 'Boys! Come out!'

Nothing happens for a moment, until Stephen appears on the front step and then stomps reluctantly behind Henry and into the barn. Inside, he lets up a whistle. It summons the others, has the lads spilling from the house with their tankards. They file into the barn, scoffing and hollering, something in there rousing their excitement.

Lizzie glances at Johnny. 'I hope they're not . . .'

'Aye,' Johnny's voice is tight. 'I hope they're not either.'

They watch as a man parades from the barn. 'Come forth, ladies and gentleman, for the highlight of the evening!'

The farmhouse door has been left open, and Maggie sticks her head out. 'What's all this? Rab?' She steps outside, followed by the maids and the wide-eyed bairns and then Rab, frowning.

With everyone assembled, the ploughman compère throws his arms wide. 'Lads!'

Behind him the others march out, whooping and shouting. Henry at the back with a tooth-bearing grin and a heap of something in his arms. 'Here she is!'

Darkness rings Lizzie's vision. Henry is coming towards them, swinging the bundle high above his head. She blinks rapidly, smoke stinging her eyes, until Henry is close enough that she can discern what he is holding: a sack, drooping under one of the neepie lantern heads. It lolls back with a jagged sneer, smacks off the loon's shoulder as he breaks into a run.

'Burn her!'

Lizzie understands, then, that they have made an effigy: a crude likeness of the bog woman. They have warped her mystery into something horrifying, taken their fear and shaped that too – into revelry, malice – something they know what to do with. Someone snatches the figure from Henry but he runs along with them, his features suddenly ugly as his lips pull back to shout: 'Get her on the fire!'

'Let's have our fun with her first.' The men mass round the effigy, poking thumbs into her eye sockets, screeching names and accusations meant for the dead girl in the hayloft, though some are so absurd, so specific, that perhaps they are instead for all the women who have ever wronged them – talked back or embarrassed them, chosen someone with greater wit or better looks. They laugh at the slurs, pick the worst words they know, and Maggie clamps her hands over the ears of the bairns and ushers them back inside. Lizzie turns to Johnny; if he is laughing too she will –

But Johnny is scowling. And when he sees her face, appalled, he presses his glass into her hand. 'Stop! For God's sake, stop!'

Johnny pushes through the throng, tries to pull Stephen back but is shaken off. When the men see that Johnny seeks to spoil their game they surround him like he's carrion, one gripping a handful of his hair and shoving him back. 'Piss off, Johnny!'

The men outnumber him, one or two bouncing on their toes and sailing loose fists through the air. A puck of spit, hurled on to Johnny's velvet lapel. But it is Henry who finishes it. He's been lifted on to someone's shoulders, reels unsteadily with a dirty sneer plastered on his face. 'Come any closer, Jack, and you know what I'll do.'

A moment of hesitation. Johnny looks at the revellers and the chaos and then turns away from them, comes back to Lizzie. She slips a trembling hand in his.

'Let's go,' he says.

'Where?'

'I'll take you home.' Less certainty than when James had said it, Johnny's eyes on the ground by her feet.

'All right.'

They find the Stuarts standing by the house, blocking the door so that the bairns can't get out. Rab is chewing his lip; the night has got away from him, and his eyes track the movement of the effigy as she's chucked from man to man.

'I'll take Lizzie home,' says Johnny.

Maggie glances at her husband. 'I'm nae sure you ought tae be seen—'

'She can hardly walk all the way back alone.'

'All right, well. I'll get you a lamp. But I'll need it back tonight, Johnny. You'll need tae bring it back tonight.'

They are bobbing light on the road. Lizzie looks back in the direction of Brawlands, as though she might parse through the darkness what Henry and his friends are doing. 'What if they throw the bog woman on the fire too?'

'They wouldnae dare. Rab wouldnae let it go that far.'

'I don't know, they seemed so . . . wild.'

'They'll lose interest after they've burned the effigy, I promise you.'

Even if Lizzie is not sure she believes Johnny, his reassurance calms her. He asks her if she's all right, offers her his arm to link with hers.

'Aye, I was just . . . shaken. And it's got so cold.'

'Would you like my coat?'

It seems too intimate, both the level of his sacrifice and the wearing of his clothes. 'No. Don't let yourself get cold.'

'I won't be—'

'No. Thank you.'

'As you like.'

Lizzie looks at Johnny in profile. For all the good shape of it, his face is not perfect – a slight crookedness to his nose, perhaps accidental or the spoil from some laddish scuffle; a scar the length of a fingernail by his eye. It is a storied face; would be pleasing to draw, despite her usual aversion to portraiture.

'And are *you* all right?' she asks.

Johnny inhales deeply, lets it out as a sigh. 'I'm fine.'

'What did Henry mean, back there?'

'It's nothing, honestly. He's pished.'

'Then why are you still frowning?'

He is quiet a moment, and Lizzie can tell he is wrestling with something.

'I . . . do you think there could be some truth in it? That the bog woman has brought something . . . untoward?'

Lizzie has wondered this herself, of course. She hardly believes in ghosts or demons, but who is to say there aren't different mysteries, only a short leap beyond all the other little-understood things – dreams, hiccups, attraction, a mirage in the road. But Lizzie is sure the woman from the bog is merely that; not some totem of ill-fortune, a curse on all the Cabrach.

'No. I think it's a convenient way of finding something to blame for a run of hard luck.'

'But it's the look of her. How one minute she's smiling and the next she's . . . sneering.'

Lizzie runs her thumb over the worn-smooth fabric on the elbow of his coat. 'Maybe it's both, and folks don't like that. They'd rather be able to say she's all one thing, good or bad, saint or sinner. They don't know what to make of her, that's what they don't like.'

'Aye, you're surely right.'

Eventually, Blackwater emerges through the darkness. Johnny holds the lamp towards its dour face and dark windows – Jane will be in bed now.

'You can turn round, if you like,' says Lizzie. 'I'll manage the rest alone.'

'I cannae turn now, we've only one light.'

So they carry on, slower and closer, hips nudging, until they reach the point where the road meets the track to the house.

'Really, you go back. I'll be fine from here.'

Johnny does not break his stride. 'I'll see you to your door.'

At the house, Lizzie goes up the steps. Before her is the heavy black door and beyond it the cold flagstones, a house of murk and shadow. The lonely traipse upstairs to undress and slide her limbs between cold sheets, holding her feet in her hands to warm them and hoping that sleep will come quickly. But Lizzie is not tired. It is approaching midnight and she is wide awake, skin prickling with something, though it does not feel like fear any more. Behind her, Johnny stands on the gravel in his soft coat, lifting the lamp.

'Will you come in?' she asks. A sense, dim, that this is reckless. But something about the night, the unreality of it, makes it seem as if there will be no consequences.

Johnny glances about, as though someone might be loitering on the lawn with a keen ear for his answer. 'I better nae. If I get warm it'll make it harder tae go back out. And Maggie's keen to have her lamp back.'

'Of course.'

'Although, will you be all right?'

'Well, I . . . actually I wanted to ask you a favour. But you're right, it's a long way back for you.'

Johnny comes up a stair. 'No, I can help, but what if someone's seen us? I wouldnae like for folks to get the wrong idea.'

'No one's seen us. There are benefits to being so remote, Johnny.'

He is almost at the top now. 'But do they nae say the hills of the Cabrach have eyes?'

Lizzie slips the key into the lock. 'If they do, they're asleep now.' She opens the door and steps inside; Johnny remains on the threshold, biting his lip.

'What about your sister-in-law?'

'Don't worry about her.'

Jane had told Lizzie to be careful – she will be.

JOHNNY

In the hall they shed their coats and shoes. When a candle is lit, Johnny can get a sense of the space – it is unremarkable, large enough, but the floor is plain buffed wood and the walls bare white. There is a coat rack slung heavily with Lizzie's summer jacket and a man's things – a blazer, a scarf, a coat of good wool. Johnny looks away. It is better, in these circumstances, not to think too much; instead to be as furtive as an animal, instincts tightly strung. He's done such things before, of course – knows how to diminish his breath to a flicker, how to train his ears like a dog's for footsteps. He knows how to hold his limbs ready to break into a run and how to find a warm body in the dark – though he won't, he won't. But as Lizzie leads him upstairs, a memory makes itself known – of wanting, of following that want upstairs, of who he found there and how she welcomed him, at first.

They go to the top floor, where Lizzie stops outside a closed door. He can see her only by moonshine; doesn't know what she's doing, at first, when she raises a hand to her head. She tugs, and a section of her hair tumbles from its style.

Lizzie holds out a pin. 'Do you know how to pick a lock?'

He is down on his knees. The hairpin slips into the keyhole without resistance, that is the easy part. Johnny twists the pick as quietly as he can, trying to hook something in the lock's mechanism that will allow him to turn it. Lizzie stands over him, the candle held in front of her to illuminate his work, but instead all Johnny sees is the way it throws light over her body. But he is here to do this favour, only this, and he bites his lip as he drives the metal harder into the lock, worrying the pin will snap. 'I'm nae sure I can do this.'

'You can, please.'

Johnny twists more forcefully still, and is almost shocked when something clicks and the mechanism releases. He eases the catch round, a hand on the doorknob, turning with painful slowness. Lizzie gasps as the door opens. 'You did it!'

The pride that swells in Johnny's chest as they enter the room is absurd, really, but he lets himself have it because he's pleased her, and now she's looking around the room as if it's been a good long time since she last saw it. This is her husband's domain, Johnny supposes, though he's blown why the man would keep it under lock and key – if Johnny had a wife, he likes to think he'd give up all of his secrets. The shelves in the room are lined with thick books, and a huge stag's head is mounted on the wall, its antlers grey and desiccated. Johnny sits on the edge of the desk and runs his thumb over the polished wood, the sharp line where it meets the inlaid leather. He thinks of his brother sitting somewhere like this, with his medical notes and prescriptions; or his da, though he wouldn't have had the luxury. Only a scrubbed and splintered table for a man who was a clerk at twenty, a clerk still at fifty-five.

After a moment, Lizzie steps in front of Johnny. 'Thank you,' she whispers, 'for the favour.'

'I'm glad tae be of help.'

They regard each other for a moment. Now is the time he should nod curtly and take his leave and he will, of course, but as he considers it they hear a noise – quick steps, voices, not beneath them but outside. Lizzie has frozen. 'Did you hear that?'

'It'll be guisers.'

Lizzie rushes to the window. 'There's a light.'

'It's Hallowe'en night, it'll just be guisers.'

Johnny slips into the dormer. It is a small space and it takes him a great deal of effort to manoeuvre himself without touching Lizzie. Through the window, filmy with condensation, he can see little but the crag of the treeline, the disc of moon above it. 'There's nothing here.'

Lizzie's velvet sleeve brushes unbearably against the skin of his forearm. 'There, look, a lamp.' She is right – beyond the yews, smudges of light along the road. Then a man's voice, distant, but Johnny still catches an edge of panic in it.

'What if they've got her?'

'It'll just be folks hurrying home out of the cold.'

Lizzie drops back against the wall. 'Sorry, I'm being silly. I just hated what they were saying about her tonight.'

'So did I.' He is standing close enough to Lizzie that not touching her would be the stranger thing – forced and improbable, a resistance of simple human nature. But no, that is a fine scapegoat, and he is a man who believes in free will.

Below them a floorboard groans. They listen to the slap of bare feet crossing a room.

'She'll just be checking—'

But Lizzie finds Johnny's lips in the dark and silences them with her fingers. He forgets, briefly, how to breathe. The footsteps beneath them move back the way they came and Lizzie drops her hand.

'I need a drink,' she says. 'To calm me.'

'Are you sure it's wise tae take more?'

He can see her mouth move around the words. 'I don't care.'

Down in the parlour, the embers in the hearth are still glowing. Lizzie tells Johnny to put another slab of peat on and so he crouches there, building up the fire. By the light of a match it is difficult to take in how large the room is, only that the ceiling is high but it is not as grand as Johnny had imagined. He gets the peat to catch and then turns to watch Lizzie. She is at the drinks cabinet, and when she lifts her arm to pour a dram Johnny sees again where her dress has torn. He makes himself look away; he's acting like a boy, some orra-loon who has never seen the flesh of a woman before – though, not for some time, despite what folks might suppose. His last trip wandering there had been a quine behind the bar at the inn he sang in. She had given him a glinting look and then come to his room when he was half sunk to sleep, addled by the cheap bottle he'd bartered off a loon outside. He had let her come in, unbutton his shirt, start to kiss him with lips that tasted of ash and curses. He blamed the rotgut for how, when she had gone, he had rolled over and pressed his face into the pillow, cheeks wet with tears he could not explain.

'Here you are.' Lizzie kneels next to him and passes him the whisky. 'Slainte.'

'It's good stuff.'

'William's finest bottle.'

'Will he nae notice it's been drunk?'

Lizzie shrugs, seems disinclined to ponder it. Maybe she thinks the chances are her husband won't return, or, if he does, will have more to worry about than two filched glasses of thirty-year malt.

'You dinnae speak much of him,' Johnny says. He has noticed the wedding photo on the side table, finds he doesn't want to examine it too closely.

'There is not much to say. His family own hotels, inns – The Pheasant being one of them. They have land and farms, mostly up Nairn way. Anything else you want to know?'

He tries to sound breezy. 'Which farms?'

'Round Nairn?'

'Aye, it's just, I met a Calder once up there. Nasty piece of work.' Common name, of course, though when Johnny had arrived in the Cabrach and heard it, he'd come up to Blackwater House to try to get a look at its owner.

'Henry said he'd worked up there too. Did you two know each other?'

Johnny could tell Lizzie, he supposes – but he has seen how curious she is, the way she'll keep digging once she's struck a vein. The tenacity with which she's pursued the story of the bog woman, though she surely realizes there's no way of knowing it. He could tell her, but then she might mention it to Henry, and that might encourage the loon. Then it might all come cascading out – might even do now, if he's not careful. He knows how the liquor slackens him. 'No. I never knew him.'

'It's a small world, though, isn't it, on the farms?'

'Nae that small.' Before she can probe further, Johnny changes the subject – blurts out a question he's been wondering about but probably shouldn't ask: 'And are you happy?'

She pauses, the drink at her lips. 'With what?'

'Well, as I said, you dinnae speak much of your husband.'

Lizzie looks away. 'What a question.'

He declines to take it back, finding, suddenly, that it is vital that he knows. He tells himself that, if she is unhappy, he will do everything in his power to alleviate her sadness; yet some other part of him scoffs at this earnest attempt at virtue, for couldn't it be said that a woman in such circumstances might be in search of affection elsewhere, and that if someone were to provide it they would be justified in doing so?

'Tell me,' he says.

Johnny thinks he knows what she will say – probably in the same dispassionate way she told him she was lonely. He watches as she gathers herself, takes a sip of whisky and holds it in her mouth a moment before swallowing. 'No, I'm not happy. Are you?'

'Not especially.' He is lost on how to proceed, scrabbles for something else to say. 'Will I tell you a story?'

Surprise flickers in her expression but Lizzie nods. 'I'd like that.'

It gratifies him – comes natural, the spinning of a yarn, one of the few good things he's nurtured in himself. And the occasion is fine too, with the moan of the wind, the firelight turning the silverware in the locked cabinets to mirrors.

'Are you sitting comfortably?' It was what his ma always asked him.

Lizzie smiles as if she too remembers this childhood line, and she pushes her legs out from underneath her, stretches them towards the fire. Johnny watches the hem of her dress lift a little to expose her ankles, a lovely sweep of calf.

'Are you all right?' Lizzie touches his arm. 'You don't have to, if you don't want to.'

'I do. What sort of story do you want?'

Lizzie drops back on to her elbows. Doesn't look at him as she slides her foot across the rug to meet his. Her toes nudge up into the high curve of his arch. Johnny knows he shouldn't allow it – this woman whose wedding photograph is on the table behind him – but he lets her foot stay.

'Tell me a story about you,' she replies.

This alarms Johnny, vaguely. The stories he tells are of giants and harpies, mermaids posing on slick Firth rocks, or else anecdotes from his travels – all of the comedic, tragic, stupid things that other people do. He hesitates and Lizzie nods towards his hand, the ugly pucker of his scar. 'Tell me how you got that.'

'Och, just a caper with a bunch of lads. Messing about, went too far.'

'Did it hurt?'

'Like hell. I couldnae work properly for weeks – couldnae get a firm grip on anything. But I had to pretend I was fine.' Johnny remembers those weeks, shrivelled in his bed in the freezing chaumer or doing the few jobs he was capable of – picking the earth for stones, polishing tack with his one good hand. It had its consolations, though – the respect he earned from the others, how his injury elicited special concern from Violet.

'Tell me what happened.'

'Just an accident. Nothing much to it.'

They are quiet a moment. Lizzie is still touching him but Johnny has relaxed now, sure that this is enough, that he can stop it going any further. But then she readjusts herself so that she is lying on her side, balanced on an elbow. 'Fine, then tell me something else. Has there ... been a Mistress Nicol? Or nearly?'

Johnny cannot deny that it is fair for her to ask, rues his own lines of questioning that have emboldened her to this. He takes a large mouthful of his dram. 'No. Folks say I'm nae the sort of man you'd take home tae meet your ma.'

She laughs softly. 'Ah, but isn't there always a difference between what folks say and the truth? You'd have liked to, though, get married?'

Johnny shrugs. 'I dinnae think much of it. Havenae met the right person – or at least, not one who's available.'

'I've heard that hasn't stopped you in the past.'

Johnny looks down at her, expecting chastisement but finding something else in her eyes – that glint Dougie had mentioned. 'I'm nae like that.'

'So it's just that the women can't resist you, is that it?'

'I suppose.'

She senses his discomfort, surely. Laughs as she gets up and goes to fetch the whisky bottle. Johnny shouldn't have any more but he lets Lizzie pour it, touches his glass to hers. She drinks and then she is kneeling before him. Johnny looks at her – eyes black, hair loose. Her dress is too tight. He suddenly feels something like irritation – all his attempts at restraint being undone like knots. Lizzie places a hand on his leg and Johnny almost jumps, heart so huge he thinks he can taste it in the back of his throat. So it is a relief, then, when she leans closer and puts her fingers to the scarlet ribbon round his neck and unties it, letting the silk glide over his skin. He watches it slip through her fingers and drop to the floor and thinks – is it my fault, that this is the effect I have? Johnny gives up. He puts down his glass and takes her into his arms.

Lips meeting. Whisky taste, hers and his, and who is the first to edge a tongue into a mouth? Doesn't matter, either or both, both as bad as each other. God, he thinks, as he twists his hand though her hair, what is the point in restraint, and what – her fingers, hurrying at the buttons of his shirt – what is the point in seeing what you want, what you could have, and not taking it? He kisses her jaw, her neck. I am a bad man, he wants to whisper – because it is true, probably, that he is, or once was, or will be forever; or maybe that he isn't at all because now her palm is on his stomach, touching him as if he's something holy.

Lizzie says his name – *John* – in a breath. Her pressure on his chest, pushing at the same time as he pulls her down and they both fall backwards. Johnny's shoulder smacks hard against something solid and he swears as the side table teeters, struck with enough force to knock over what is on top. It comes crashing to the carpet, a gilded picture frame, landing so the wedding photo is face up, inches from his eyes.

October 1905

LIZZIE

The house was alive with preparation. The pressing of napkins and aprons and a white damask tablecloth, wine glasses polished, bedazzling rows of knives. The housekeeper frowned as she arranged the centrepiece, plucking leaves and stems and releasing the coy sweetness of the lilies.

'Bridget, will we do the kail?' asked Lizzie.

'Soon, quine – be patient.'

Lizzie tutted and turned. Down the hallway, the snug door was ajar, and she could see her father's shadow moving over the wall as he paced the room. She slipped quietly along to linger outside the door, listen to his low voice. 'I just thought they would come. Not so much William – chance would be a fine thing – but Hugh, he's always seemed to enjoy himself here.'

George's wife placated him. 'They'd probably already made the commitment before you invited them, darling.'

'Aye, maybe. I don't know, I just keep wondering if I've done something to rile them.'

'I'm sure it's not that.'

'No.' George let go of a heavy sigh. 'I just had high hopes. Do you know what tonight is costing me?'

'The Esslemonts are coming – surely they matter more? And next year the Calders will come too; I'm sure by then they'll be like family.'

'You're right, darling.'

'Now,' said Lizzie's mother, 'I'd better finish getting ready.'

'Aye, and send my daughter in on your way out.'

George tutted fondly as Lizzie entered the snug. 'You're not so discreet in your eavesdropping, my girl. If you're going to go sneaking around, you'll need to be more careful. Now, let me see you.'

Lizzie turned in front of him. She was wearing a dress she had made herself, despite her father's insistence she could choose anything she wanted from the boutiques in town. Instead, Lizzie had bought the fabric from the Websters', slipped the scissors through its smooth nap, stitched together the pieces of black velvet to fit her perfectly.

'Well now, you look very bonny – and grown up, my goodness!'

'Thank you, Da.'

'I knew you wouldn't show your old man up. We have many people to impress tonight, eh?' George himself was resplendent, his waistcoat a fine cream silk, complimenting the gold braid of a pocket watch. As George dabbed a handkerchief to his brow, Lizzie touched his arm.

'Da – all will be well.'

George softened. 'It will, we'll have a grand evening. Now, I was meaning to ask: will you play for us tonight? Bridget had the tuner round specially.'

In truth, Lizzie had not laid her hands on the piano for some time, finding herself too distracted, lacking patience. But it seemed a fine idea to sit later with the attention of the room upon her, and so she agreed she would play.

'Marvellous!' George cried, clapping his hands together – he would not have to impress all by himself.

The bell went. It was not yet time for the guests to arrive, so Lizzie went out into the hall to see who had come so early. Bridget opened the front door, then called out. 'Miss Elizabeth, it's Jane Calder come tae see you.'

Jane was dressed for the party in her usual grey dress, but was quite alone.

'Oh, Jane. You're rather early . . .'

'I was hoping to talk to you, Elizabeth.'

Lizzie assumed Jane wanted to solicit her advice on furnishings for the Richmond – her father had said something earlier about the deal having gone through. She supposed she could impart some wisdom on pattern and colour, but was impatient first to carry out her plans with Bridget – their annual tradition. 'All right, but come and join us first, Jane. There's a wee game we play every year on Hallowe'en.'

'A game?'

'Yes, come and I'll show you.'

The late-October air nipped at Lizzie's collarbones in the dark garden. A frost lay on the lawn, moisture gleaming on the path and the backs of the stone lions.

'Go on then, Miss Elizabeth. You go first.' Bridget watched with her hands on her hips as Lizzie crouched down and, with great gallantry, stuck a hand in the kail bed.

'It's soaking!' Lizzie grimaced as her fingers clambered over the earth, soil wadding beneath her fingernails. She felt each of the kail stalks in turn, assessing for length and musculature, the firmness of leaves when pressed between two fingers.

'No choosing, just pick one at random,' said Bridget.

Seized by adventure, Lizzie plunged into the centre of the bed, up to her elbows in the frilly leaves. She closed her fist around a stem and took a firm grasp, standing quickly so that she tore it from the soil. 'I think it's a good one!' Lizzie held it up, found the stem to be strong and hefty, nearly as thick as her wrist. 'Jane, it's your turn.'

Jane, who had until now stood a way back, watching with something like bemusement, bent down at the kail bed. She got a sure grip – no choosiness, no fingers tickling leaves – and as her kail came free she let out a little giggle, then clapped her hand to her mouth. 'Goodness, I've got one.'

'Quick then, in with you both,' Bridget said.

In the kitchen, Jane set her kail carefully on the table while Lizzie slapped hers down, spraying the surface with loose earth. 'Bridget, do the readings!'

The housekeeper rolled up her sleeves. Lizzie watched with reverence as she picked up Jane's stalk first. Bridget pursed her lips at the size of the plant – it was hearty and huge, the leaves a deep green. 'You've plucked my prize stem, Miss Jane.'

'And what does that mean?' Jane leaned forward, looking girlish, even a little eager.

'Well, apart from you being awfully strong—'

'It means,' said Lizzie, 'that you'll have a prize husband: tall and strapping and youthful.'

Jane raised her eyebrows.

'And poor,' added Bridget, tossing down the kail. 'Roots as clean as though I'd scrubbed them myself.'

'Well, then,' said Jane, 'it is fortunate I do not intend to rely on a man for my prosperity. And what of Elizabeth's fortune?'

Bridget picked up Lizzie's stalk, appraising it with a shrewd eye. 'Well, it is of middling length, so your fellow will be neither tall nor short.'

Lizzie supposed that James was not that tall, in the grand scheme of things. 'What else?'

The housekeeper took a leaf between thumb and forefinger, rubbed it. 'It is nae the youngest plant, nor is it withered. And you have hauled up half the bed with it.'

'What does that mean?' Lizzie wanted Bridget to say it, though she knew all the interpretations by heart – they performed their divination every year, reading stalk and leaf and root for their romantic prospects.

Bridget fixed her with a knowing look. 'It means he'll be rich. But before you look so smug, madam, you've to taste it.' She tore off a strip of leaf and had barely held it out before Lizzie grabbed it and stuffed it in her mouth. She cringed as her teeth ground through its toughness, the gritty flakes of soil. The stalk's fibres twisted round her tongue and made her gag. Worse, the kail was horribly bitter. Lizzie spat the green clod into her hand and Bridget burst out laughing. 'Miss Jane's husband may be poor, but yours will be of vile temperament, I'm sorry tae say.'

Lizzie tossed the soggy kail into the bin. 'Let me pick again.'

'One pick only,' said Bridget. 'Besides which, I've a dinner tae make. Away with you, ladies.'

As they left the kitchen, Jane slipped an arm through Lizzie's – a sisterliness that was new and unlike her.

'I've never done such a thing,' said Jane. 'I'm glad my supposed suitor is to be youthful, rather than my father pawning me off to one of his business associates.' She grimaced and began taking the stairs in a hammy imitation of an old man – hunched forward, a hand on the small of her back.

Lizzie laughed. 'Aye, it's a bit of fun, though this year's was wrong. I should have chosen my stalk more carefully.'

'Never mind, it's only a game.'

It was only a game, but it irked Lizzie not to have it go in her favour – she rather expected things to turn out the way she wanted them. 'You're right. I hardly need assurances from vegetables as to James's intentions.' She looked for Jane's reaction. Lizzie longed to tell someone about the silken things James had whispered in her ear, the strength in his arms and the lovely fulsome lustre of his hair, but Jane's expression had returned to its usual seriousness. How quick she was to shrug off gaiety, as though it were a sin she had to atone for.

'Actually, Elizabeth, that is what I wanted to speak to you about. I suspect the kail may be right.'

'What?'

'I . . . I'm not sure James will give you what you expect of him.'

Lizzie, softened by the fun they'd had, decided to be charitable – Jane never had liked James. 'Oh, don't worry. I am confident in his feelings for me.'

'Elizabeth—'

'Jane. You are as clever as they say at business, but this is a matter of the heart. Now—' The bell rang again, their first guests arriving, 'let us enjoy ourselves tonight.'

JACK

'I hear the buyers are coming tonight.' Donald released a gust of pipe smoke that hovered in the dank air of the chaumer. 'Father and son, apparently. Posh fuckers.'

'Rich fuckers,' added Tam. 'Mind your manners with them, if you still want tae have your baws in the morn.'

Jack rolled his eyes; there was always a generalized threat of castration at Windyhillock, but as far as he knew they'd all kept the pair. This despite their exuberant sinning, all the things the grieve and housekeeper forbade – havering in the yard, skipping kirk, calling on the maids once the candles were out. Threats were doled out as freely as curses at Windyhillock, though seldom followed through.

The gang were getting ready. The horsemen, having had their turn with the cracked shard of mirror, passed it to the orra-loon, then ignored Henry as he crouched on his bed scraping a razor over the few downy hairs that had finally sprung on his top lip. Donald, rummaging in his kist, took out a small glass bottle. 'Here, Jack, come over.' Jack did as he was asked, sure it was some rotgut he'd have to swallow down, but Donald unscrewed the cap and put the neck of the bottle to his throat, then jerked it back. He handed it to Jack. 'Put a drop of this on.'

Jack copied him. The scent was heady, cloying; made Jack

think of some faraway land, somewhere warm, far from the reek of horse shit that never left the chaumer. Only the Lord knew where Donald had got it, and probably it was cheap, but still Jack liked it. 'Any of you lot want some?'

Tam took the bottle and splashed himself liberally until the first snapped at him not to use it all. When it came to Henry he seemed unsure, shook his head. 'He disnae care about the lasses,' said Donald. 'And mark my words, this will impress them. Though . . .' He dug again in his kist, pulling out something jet-black and fluttering, a ribbon that shone under the lamp's feeble flame. 'Let's have a go with this.' Donald positioned himself on the edge of his bed and beckoned for Jack to stand between his legs. Long fingers slipped the ribbon round, cool against Jack's skin. When he had tied it, Donald drew back and barked at Henry to give him the mirror.

'Proper smart.' Donald showed Jack what he looked like. It had changed him. He looked older and better, distinguished from the rest of them.

Tam let out a fruity whistle. 'Very nice indeed!'

Jack couldn't help but smile, his fingers running over his silky throat. With this, he could be someone different.

'Here.' Donald nodded at Henry, on his bed by the door. 'Doesn't our Jack look handsome?'

The orra-loon murmured something.

'What was that?'

'Aye.'

'Aye what?'

Henry looked down at his lap. 'Aye, he looks handsome.'

'Ooh Jack, Henry thinks you're handsome,' said Tam, and the three horsemen laughed.

'Aye,' said Donald, 'you look smart enough for Slora's girl and all. I know you've got eyes for her.'

Jack shrugged. He'd brought Violet up a couple of times with the gang, casual, watching for signs that they liked her too – or knew he did. That, and he liked to say her name – a relief in the freedom to speak aloud one of the words that filled his mouth when the other one, its two syllables, lodged sticky and forbidden in his gums.

'Come on,' said Donald, 'admit it.'

'Aye, she's bonny.'

'Well, I reckon she likes you too.'

Jack checked to see if Donald was serious. He'd thought it himself, in the way Violet stole glances at him as they walked out to kirk, or contrived to forget something so she could run back to the house, have him hold the gate open for her. But he liked knowing that someone else had noted all this too.

'And,' said the first, 'you're nae a proper horseman if you've nae been with a quine.'

'Who says I havenae been with a quine?' said Jack.

Donald lifted an eyebrow. 'She'd make an impressive first go.'

'I wouldnae bother,' said Henry.

Jack looked over at the orra-loon; he'd made an effort for the evening, but his shaving was bad and his Sabbath-best jacket baggy, giving him the look of a wee boy wearing his da's suit. 'Eh?'

'She's got someone else interested in her.'

Jack laughed; of course Violet was replete with admirers, lads from the other farms who'd trail round her outside kirk as if she were an angel dropped from heaven. None of them seemed like competition.

'Who's that then?'

'The prospective buyers – the younger one.'

Jack remembered Violet's words in the kitchen as she'd bathed his hand, what she had called the purchasers: gentlemen. He touched the ribbon round his neck. 'Shut up. Why'd a rich fucker like that be interested in a farmer's daughter?' He knew why, though – for all the same reasons he'd lie shuddering under his quilt with his cock in his hand. 'Who told you that, anyway?'

'Isaac said.'

'Since when do you speak to Isaac?'

Donald smirked. 'Now, now, boys, the night is young – save your scrapping for later.'

'Aye,' said Tam, 'I reckon it's time for Jack tae do us a song, and since we're on the subject of Violet . . .'

Jack was hardly in the mood, riled by what Henry had said, but the other horsemen were watching him expectantly.

'You'll have tae say please.'

Donald snickered. 'Fuck off.'

Jack started tapping his foot – softly, slowly, a lack of commitment. 'Want it about her tits or her—'

'Och, don't,' said Henry.

Jack echoed his protest in a stupid falsetto. It seemed ridiculous he'd been so close to that sanctimonious wee loon a couple of months back – the pair of them sharing stories after kirk or walking the length of the pasture as the sun dropped away, trying to glimpse the iridescent wings of the peewits as they soared overhead. That all felt like a lifetime ago now; Henry wasn't his idea of fun any more.

'We want it all!' cried Tam.

It was easy to think of a song – all the worst words Jack knew, the things he'd heard about. He started off quite subtle, pairing his innuendoes with leery great winks, progressing on to words that would shock even his ma – that coarse woman from the coast whose mother was a fishwife, who'd learned to mind her manners on marrying a man who considered himself decent. As the horsemen goaded and the song picked up, Henry seemed to shrink further away from them. 'You need tae stop.'

'What was that?' asked Jack.

The orra-loon was practically shaking. 'I said, stop. It's disgusting.'

'Is this not what you think about, Henry, in your bed? Imagine Violet climbing in next to you? Have you got eyes for her and all?'

Tam sniggered.

'No.'

'Lack of imagination, eh? Well, let me give you some more ideas.' Jack picked up where he'd left off; made it worse, said things that made even Tam's mouth drop open. He didn't really know where they came from, the words to describe things he'd never done – only that the thoughts lived within him, like he was born with the knowledge. Jack realized then that the girl he was singing about was not Violet, not really. She was someone else, some quine with no face and no name. Not the type in the sentimental songs he used to sing – pretty lasses, winsome glances – no one liked those songs any more.

Henry started to protest again, but Donald waved him away. 'Carry on, Jack.' But the orra-loon was insistent.

Jack stopped. 'What are you whingeing about now?'

'I said, there's someone at the door.'

'Well fucking open it, then.'

Henry obeyed. Isaac was standing in the doorway, and as he stepped into the chaumer he looked from side to side at its squalor – the filthy floor, their yellowed undergarments slung over the rafters. Probably he'd never been inside before, the cosseted wee boy who slept in the warmth of his da's big farmhouse. Isaac looked straight at Jack and it was obvious he'd heard – Slora's boy was blushing. 'My da asked me to put you on notice. Folks will be here soon, so . . . be ready, I suppose.'

Donald gestured at himself. 'What do you think we've been doing, loon?'

'Enjoying yourselves, by the sounds of it.'

'Listening in, were you?' said Jack.

Isaac took a step back. 'I havenae been loitering outside the door, if that's what you mean. But I'd suggest you be more discreet, if you dinnae want folks tae hear. Anyway, glad to see you're all dressed.' He looked to the orra-loon. 'Henry, could you give me a hand with something?'

The loon looked mildly panicked, but nodded vigorously. 'Aye, I'll be with you in a minute.'

Isaac ducked back out, leaving Henry to smooth down his hair, put his boots on. He licked his chapped lips, then hesitated. 'Ah, Donald? Could I get some of that cologne, actually?'

The first laughed. 'Who've you got tae impress?' But he chucked the bottle over anyway, and the three horseman watched as Henry dabbed the scent uncertainly on his neck.

October–November 1915

JOHNNY

There is nothing for it but to look – the only thing Johnny can do in the taut, silent moment, waiting to see if they will be discovered. In the photo, Lizzie is wearing silk, off-white, a man to her left who is surely her father, the resemblance striking. Then her groom. At first he is just a man, same as any other from town with that haughty countenance. But then Johnny realizes this William Calder is different to the one he has glimpsed, squinting through sunshine, the dust rising from a car as it sped away from the Cabrach. This man has hair on his head and not his chin, is younger. His eyes are blue under a heavy brow and, despite the occasion, are not lit with any happiness – not lit with anything.

Johnny lowers himself down, presses his face to the carpet, waits for the momentary dizziness to pass. It's fair possible that he's wrong, because he's half pished and senseless from pleasure, and he only saw the man once at Windyhillock, is blown if he can really remember his face. But he can't bear to look again, instead scrabbles to his feet, grabbing for his coat.

'Wait,' Lizzie says, 'I don't think she's heard.'

But Johnny is doing up his shirt, fingers fumbling with the buttons. 'I cannae.'

'Please . . . come back to me.' She is still on the floor, grabs at his leg to stop him, but Johnny tugs it away with enough force to knock her backwards. 'I have to go.'

And that is how he leaves her, dishevelled on the hearth rug, the mouth he'd kissed left open, aghast.

It is dawn when Johnny arrives at Brawlands. The lamp was spent halfway between Blackwater and the farm and he lost his bearings in the darkness, the sky a black burden as he groped forward, tripped over his own feet, his good coat snagging on a fence. He'd lain on the verge reeking of chilled sweat and seeping drink, and raged at the God he doesn't really believe in. The closest Johnny's come to feeling like there might be something more than his lonely, pathetic life was right there, that moment, before it all went wrong.

At Brawlands, all that's left of the bonfire is a charred ring on the ground and a few blackened branches, curls of ash that flick spectral past his vision as Johnny glances about the yard. There's no one around, the gingham farmhouse curtains still closed. He thinks to set the borrowed lamp down on the step and head off, but as he does the door opens and Rab sticks his head out.

'Johnny?'

'Wind got up last night. Had to wait it out.'

The farmer grabs his sleeve. 'Get in here.'

The first thing Johnny notices is the range. Rab and Maggie are both early risers, but this is a fire that's been kept going for hours. The room is sweltering and there's a stench that turns Johnny's stomach – something fatty and unclean that brings to mind the branding of cattle, the bubbled flesh and terrible noise the beasts make.

Maggie looks knackered – grey and drawn – and there's a tinge in the room, the skittish remnants of some past panic. The kitchen is a mess, table cluttered with cloudy glasses, apples in their buckets gone shrivelled. 'Morning, my dear.' Johnny summons all the levity he can muster. 'Are you worse for wear today?'

She ignores him, and Johnny looks for the source of the room's strange feeling – sees, then, in a chair by the range, a figure humped under a heap of blankets. Liquid eyes that look up at him, unreadable but with an intensity that is enough to frighten him, make his mouth go dry. 'Morning, loon. You all right?'

Henry shrugs his shoulders and the blankets tumble down. Underneath he's wearing just his vest, his breeks held up with a length of old rope. He lifts his arms out, palms face up.

'Go on,' says Rab, 'take a look.' He and Maggie watch as Johnny crouches before the ploughman. Henry's hands are wrapped in thick, seeping bandages. The loon is pale as milk and it dislodges something in Johnny's memory, turning of a stone, and underneath is another lad, eyes rolling back, purpling skin awful against his golden hair.

'Burnt.' Rab's voice is too loud in the small room. 'Our Henry thought he'd be the one to throw that . . . that dummy on the fire. Only he fair cocked it up. Fell clean in.'

The loon mutters something, so quiet that Johnny has to lean closer. 'What's that?'

Henry struggles to get the words out, winces in pain as he tries to get his hands back under the blanket. 'I said, it's your fault.'

Johnny glances at Rab. 'It was an accident, loon. Just an accident.'

'No, Jack, it was your fault.'

Johnny stands. 'Stop calling me that.' He sighs. 'I wasn't there, loon. How could it be my fault?'

'What he means,' says Maggie, tucking the blankets back round Henry, 'is that you upset him. You could see he wisnae himself last night but still you were sharp with him.'

Johnny can't help it – he rolls his eyes. Anywhere in the world he'd rather be than in this stinking kitchen, being blamed for

Henry's own stupidity when all he'd done was defend himself against the loon's nonsense. Same nonsense he continues with now, pretending he's some innocent wee lamb when Johnny's seen the other side of him, the goading and threats that no one else seems to pay attention to.

'You're talking shite, Henry.'

'Leave the loon alone,' Maggie says. 'You sound like a bully.'

Words that hurt. Johnny steps away, his hands open in surrender. 'All right, fine. It's just . . . it has nothing tae do with me. It was just hard luck.'

Rab gives a sharp laugh. 'Aye, hard luck. Endless fucking hard luck.' He heads for the door. 'Johnny, come on. The fence in the top pasture has come down again and if I lose my sheep and all I might as well just . . .'

Johnny is quite sure he can't work – body aching, spew plotting in his throat. But he follows Rab outside, all the same – hoping, in some small way, that it might redeem him.

At least no wit needed for it. Johnny rights the fallen posts and holds them steady while Rab hammers them in. His hands are tight round the mallet, snarling as it sails through the air, and Johnny closes his eyes, waiting for it to clip him – wonders, even, if he might deserve it. When the worst of the damage is repaired, the two men stand with hands on hips, looking over their work. They have not exchanged a word.

'Rab? Do you want tae talk about it?'

The farmer frowns. Then his shoulders cave and Johnny turns away, allows Rab the dignity of spending his frustration unwatched. He lets Rab heave and sob, kick at the clods of dislodged earth. Johnny looks anywhere else – out over the land, bonny maybe in the clear few weeks of summer but bleak as purgatory for most of the long, wretched year. He surveys the ugly brown fields, the few trees that are bent like crones come hobbling over the braes. Why anyone ever thought to come here, to stay, is beyond him. Stupid Johnny Nicol and all, who rolled up with his polka-dot cravat and a few years' worth of gossip, really fucking pleased with himself at finding a place so remote the Lord would surely have forgotten it. And here he is now, the fall after the pride, back with the two men he hoped he'd never see again. Johnny turns to find Rab beside him, sniffing. He lays a hand on his friend's shoulder, for all the good of it.

'So what happened?'

The farmer pulls himself loose – but talks. 'Henry was . . . agitated, after you'd gone. The lads were all shouting, burn her, burn her. A bloody frenzy in them, and Maggie was terrified, the bairns crying fae the house. But the lads wouldnae stop. Henry got a hold of the thing, started all this talk about how the woman out the bog has the mark of the devil on her. He said . . . he said she's just like you.'

'Rab—'

'He said something dark was here, kept ranting and raving about how he disnae sleep, how his head gets filled with things that disgust him but he cannae stop. He kept saying your name. Christ, Johnny, what did you say tae him in the yard?'

'Nothing, I swear. He's just . . . I dinnae know what's wrong with him. But it's nae my fault.'

Rab's expression darkens. 'Then he lost his mind. Snatched that effigy up and went running tae the fire. I think I knew what was going tae happen before it did, but I couldnae stop him. The skin was coming off him in strips.' The farmer spits hard on the ground. 'So I'll ask you once more, Johnny – what did you say tae him in the yard?'

A clench in Johnny's bowels – the drink or these last awful hours, or the humiliation at the way Rab asks it, the realization his friend considers him to be liable to dishonesty.

'I didnae say anything.'

Rab sighs. 'All right.' He walks away, scanning the pasture for any more damage.

'Wait. How bad are they? The burns?'

'He'll nae be working for a while.'

'I'm sorry, Rab.'

'He might even lose some of the feeling in his hands, the doctor said. I sent Alex and Stephen out tae get him, didnae know what else to do.'

'That must have been what we heard on the road. Thought it was just guisers.'

Rab looks at him then – Johnny in last night's shirt and the breeks he saves for best, his bare neck because, Johnny realizes, sickened, his red ribbon must be lying on the floor of Lizzie's parlour.

'Aye, must have been them. They'll have gone past Blackwater.'

'It was the time. Lizzie was frightened, after all that, and she asked a favour of me. Her husband's away, Rab, I couldnae say no. Bloody wind and all.'

'Aye, filthy weather.' Rab takes up his mallet again, starts hammering on a post that's already set well into the ground.

'It wisnae like that.'

The farmer holds up his hand. 'It's nae my business.'

Johnny could ask his friend to believe him, but then, that is not how belief works, especially in the face of other evidence. Do something once and it may be considered an aberration. Twice, careless. Three times, a habit. Any more than that and it's a reputation and Johnny – lady's man, philanderer, flirt – has lost a grip on his. He doesn't have the energy left in him so he walks away as the bile rises in his throat, building so quickly that all he can do is set his hands on a post and brace himself. He has always hated this part – the loss of control, whole body strained and retching. The spew spatters his boots, pools on the hard ground. When it stops, Johnny gulps in the cold air and wipes a hand across his trembling lips. He doesn't want to face his friend again – thinks to head back down the field without a glance, go home, curl in his bed and beg no one in particular for the succour of sleep. But Johnny finds himself going back to the farmer's side.

'Rab, they didnae burn the bog woman, did they?'

'No. Henry's fall put an end to all that.'

'You still think it's a nonsense, aye? That she's getting up and walking. That she's of the devil?'

Rab looks out over the Cabrach, avoiding Johnny's eye. 'Away home with you. I'll see you at kirk in the morn.'

LIZZIE

Lizzie is late for kirk. Jane had already set off alone, and when Lizzie opens the doors to the chapel she finds it full, akin to the Sabbaths after Whitsun and Martinmas when the farm lads would drag themselves in to atone for their transgressions at the feeing markets. The front-row pew is taken by Jane and the Sinclairs: Esther crying, her husband stroking her back. The Sinclairs are never happier, closer in their marriage, than when lamenting some bad lot.

As Lizzie moves down the aisle folks look at her, some turning their heads to openly stare, but she tries not to think about it – in a place like the Cabrach, people stare for something to do. It is not because they know anything of Hallowe'en night – if they did, then Jane would too, and Jane has said nothing in the day since then. After Johnny left, Lizzie had stayed on the parlour floor for some time, stunned by the manner of his departure and her own curdled desire. But she had steadied herself enough, eventually, to clear away the used glasses, put William's whisky back in the cabinet and the wedding photograph back on the table. She had gone to bed and lain bitter and despairing at how the night had slipped from her grasp, but was relieved at least that Jane had not discovered them.

Lizzie spots Rab's head above the seated others and stops at the end of his pew. 'Can I squeeze in with you?'

The farmer looks at her, then turns to his wife. 'Maggie – shove the bairns up.'

'There's nae room.'

'Maggie.'

His wife tuts and nudges their children along as though it is a great imposition, though there is space enough – Henry is not with them. Lizzie thinks to ask where he is, but there is something in the Stuarts' demeanour that stops her. In fact, the whole kirk seems as weighted and joyless as it was on the day Jimmy Weir's return was announced. Perhaps there is more news from the front – certainly folks are praying already, huddled in their coats.

The Reverend emerges. He takes a sip of water and his lips are still damp when he speaks. '1 Corinthians 6:10.' A pause, as though inviting those well versed in the scriptures to test themselves. 'Know ye not that the unrighteous shall not inherit the kingdom of God? Be not deceived: neither fornicators, nor idolaters, nor adulterers . . .' Reverend Bruce looks over his flock – who cannot meet his eye?

'Wickedness is in this place. And I will tell you what will become of the sinners amongst us.' He looks directly at Lizzie as he exercises his vivid imagination – the boiling rivers of Hell, lascivious demons swinging pitchforks. Lizzie tries to sit firm under the heat of his gaze, to take on something of William's air of guiltlessness, but eventually it unnerves her and she looks down at the dirtied floor beneath the pew in front of her, and the foot of the man who is sitting there. The space where the other foot should be.

'We all must be vigilant,' says the Reverend. 'Surely all in this congregation consider themselves good and pious folk, but wickedness soon spreads. Think of your pastures. When there is a blight in one crop, does it fell that crop only? If one plant is struck down by pestilence, do others not follow? And so you will understand better than anyone how we must root wickedness out. We must wrench from the land the foul crop of sin that is advancing beneath our noses.' He slaps his hand on the pulpit. 'When you see wickedness, cast it out!'

From in front of Lizzie, a whispered amen. Wee Jimmy Weir grapples for his crutches, heaves himself up. He is wearing a shirt and jacket, but she can see the scarred flesh emerging from under his collar. 'Lord help us.' The lad looks about. Barely a hair on his chin, this young soldier. 'Lord help us.'

Others rise to join him, opening their calloused palms to the ceiling. They begin to call out, voices that start discordant, then shape themselves into something like a chant. Rab with eyes closed and prayers ardent: heal him, Lord, heal him. His words get lost amongst other pleas – for protection, forgiveness, grace; the entreaties of a pale and grasping crowd, hoping God might see fit to listen to them: Lord, the binder was left out in the damp and now it rusts. Lord, I picked the scabbed skin on my arm and now it won't stop bleeding. Heavenly Father, my head throbs and I know I succumbed to the temptation of liquor, but can you blame me for taking something to chase the cold away? Father, she kept on in my ear and I did not plan to strike her, but she brought me to the limit of what a man can endure when the bairns keep crying and the stores run low, and what can I say, Lord, only that it is not – none of it – my fault.

Jimmy begins to tremble. It starts in his hands, a rattle of fingers on thighs, but then he cannot seem to control it, his arms jerking in spasms, joints twisting like there's something inside him. Lizzie catches sight of his bulging eyes and the lips that move over senseless words, lost in the roar of the crowd. She reaches for him, just a hand of comfort, but it startles Jimmy and he rears forward, one of his crutches clattering to the floor. The noise silences the congregation and they turn, fix their eyes on Lizzie as though she is to blame when Jimmy folds himself over and sinks to the ground.

*

Later, in the kirkyard, women crowd round their wretched soldier. They cluck and stroke at Jimmy, press kisses to his cheeks as he stands, glassy-eyed, letting them deliver their ministrations. As Lizzie passes, she hears their offers – of prayer from most, though one or two promise tinctures and poultices, herbs for calming the nerves. She wants to offer her own compassion, but gets the sense she'll only make things worse. Instead, Lizzie hurries on, and has almost reached the kirk gate when someone calls her name. She turns and finds Esther there.

'Course, we've someone tae blame for all this, if anyone had the courage to say it.' Esther is standing wide-legged, rooted in the surety of her grievance. 'Perhaps we've allowed the devil to walk amongst us, but someone must have opened the door and ushered him in.'

Her accusation silences the crowd. They watch, for a moment, until some knock-kneed lad made bold by hardship calls out too. 'Aye – it all started with you. Hauling that thing up fae the bog – if you'd an ounce of sense you'd know that some things are meant tae stay buried.'

'Nothing but trouble ever since.'

Lizzie does not know the man who is speaking, but they are all poised now, ready to cast their allegations like stones.

'And now there's Henry Boyle too.'

'Who?'

'Rab's lad.'

'What about him?'

'Accident on Hallowe'en night.'

'Speaking of which,' the farmer Sinclair steps forward. 'Tell us what happened on Hallowe'en night? With you and Johnny Nicol.'

'Aye, he's tae blame for all this as well.'

Lizzie envies Johnny then – elsewhere, nestled under a quilt with an arm thrown over his head, oblivious to the scorn. She'd thought he might have troubled himself to come to kirk, come and taken her aside and explained why he'd fled.

A lad beside her leers. 'Of course, wouldnae forget about Johnny, would we Mistress Calder?'

'Aye, *Mistress* Calder.'

A loon by the gate sniggers. 'She's nae the first tae be lured by Johnny Nicol, and I'm sure she'll nae be the last.'

How can they know? Johnny had left in the dark, was surely not foolish enough to dawdle on the Blackwater track. Only a day between, though isn't it true that a day is all they need in this place – folks who preach of loving thy neighbour in one breath, then spend the next on their devout commitment to claik. Lizzie can find no words to satisfy them; is never sure if they want her, the wifie from the big house, to be held up as an exemplar of virtue, or if they'd gladly have her revealed to be as depraved and duplicitous as the next person.

'Disgraceful,' says Sinclair. 'Her husband off fighting for king and country and she's . . . well. Why don't you tell us?'

Lizzie casts about for someone who might put a stop to all this. But Maggie looks away. Rab, his hands on the backs of the bairns, turning to go.

'Come on, confess!'

There is a tingle at the top of Lizzie's nose – not from the cold but a feeling she remembers, though she's not indulged in it for a long time. She'd wanted to cry on Hallowe'en night but the tears hadn't come, and Lizzie had wondered if she'd lost the ability, all those years of restraint damaging the part of her that would allow such a release. But now it will happen here, in front of everyone, and they will be gratified – taking her tears as a fine show of guilt. She hears a man mutter an insult, the same word they'd hurled at the effigy on Hallowe'en night, and wonders if they'd dare call Johnny the same. That is the way, with shame – men will take it on themselves eventually, if they've the conscience, but women will readily be handed theirs.

And then there is someone by her side. 'Sister, come.' Jane has her coat fastened, hair pinned back so the wind cannot disturb it. She shoots a look at the crowd. 'That's enough, leave her alone.' Her tone has the young men slinking back behind the headstones, the women pausing then closing their mouths, unwilling to defy the instruction of William Calder's sister.

Lizzie lets herself be steered away. 'Thank you, Jane.'

'What's that?'

It diminishes Lizzie to say it again, but she does, loud enough for Jane to nod, satisfied.

'Now, the Reverend would like to see you. He's asked that you attend the manse.'

'Why?'

'How could I possibly say?' An edge to Jane's voice that could be sarcasm, were such hurtful intention not a sin.

'Nothing happened, Jane, I promise. Johnny walked me home, that's all.'

Jane's countenance belies nothing. 'If you ask me to believe you, sister, I will take you at your word. Now, off you go.' She leaves Lizzie to hurry to the rear of the kirkyard, where a gate in the dyke wall leads to the path to the manse. Lizzie has almost reached it when there is a wail behind her, someone tugging the sleeve of her coat. Lizzie turns. This close, she can see the broken veins in Esther's cheeks, the eyelids swollen from weeping. 'My babby,' she says, 'my babby.' A shaking hand that goes to her belly, to round a curve that is not there.

The offer of tea does not sound like a question, but Lizzie says yes and thanks him. The Reverend pours efficiently, hand bloodless round the ebony handle of his teapot.

'Thank you for coming,' he says.

Lizzie waits for him to continue, looking around the parlour, which has changed little since the last time she was there – in the days before her wedding, receiving marital counsel from a man never married, as if such things were academic. The furniture is outdated, walls hung with painted agricultural scenes, though the Reverend can surely stand at an upstairs window and see cattle in all their animate glory.

Reverend Bruce pours milk into a cup and stirs. There is no sugar laid out. 'You know, Mistress Calder, I pray for you every day.' He looks at Lizzie as though he is bestowing a great honour upon her, though in truth Lizzie suspects that the care of his flock comes less from righteous benevolence than a certain pride in his own goodness. 'I pray you that you might be guided. He is a good and courageous man, your husband, is he not? He has sacrificed a great deal for his country. You know all this, don't you?'

'Yes, Reverend.'

'He keeps you well and in fine surroundings, and he cares for his community. He is honourable and he fears the Lord.'

Lizzie nods – she could tell him differently, but there is an image of William lodged in the Reverend's mind, soldered like a saint in a stained-glass window.

'Yet . . . I fear it is insufficient for you.' Reverend Bruce frowns, perplexed, an expression Bridget used to wear when young Miss Elizabeth would not eat her kail, or refused to go out in the sunshine. The man settles back, lowers his voice and asks, 'Is there anything you would like to confess?'

He is no different to the mob in the kirkyard. His mouth ajar, brightness in his eyes as though the prospect of hearing her roster of sins might excite him. Perhaps this is all any of them want: an admission of guilt, and all the better if it is filthy and salacious, thereby reminding them of the great moral shortcomings of everybody else.

'It's just that, in your loneliness, with your husband away, I worry that you have . . . sought companionship elsewhere.'

'I am sorry, Reverend, you do not speak plainly.'

'Johnny Nicol.' Beads of spittle speckle the tea set. 'I fear you have been rather taken in by him.'

Hearing his name is still a pleasure. Lizzie wishes Johnny were sitting next to her on the settee. He would be grave, apply his sincerest attention to the Reverend's speech, apologize for the misunderstanding that had arisen from his attempts at chivalry. And when the holy man's back was turned, Johnny would wink his rogue's wink, and they would leave together. But again, she notes, he isn't here, because he doesn't care to attend kirk – and perhaps Johnny is good at shucking off the things he doesn't care about.

'He is very charming,' the Reverend goes on. 'It is easy not to realize you are being taken advantage of and, well, perhaps you are not the greatest judge of character.'

'No advantage has been taken.'

The Reverend searches her face as though trying to work out what Lizzie means. Perhaps he could accept with ease that nothing needed to be taken: it was given freely. And perhaps such weakness is one of the greater sins in the Lord's logbook – knowing the good and righteous path but choosing instead the old, familiar one. People don't change; they carry on making the same mistakes – blindly, or worse: with purpose, certain that they are right.

'What I mean is – men like him – they show you kindness and know the right words to say to get what they want, but all the while they are leading you on. I noticed the way he encouraged your wilfulness at Brawlands, when you didn't want the body to be buried.'

'That was my decision.'

'You need not take the blame. I know what he is like.'

'No, Reverend, it was me. But Johnny is akin in wanting to find out who the woman was.'

Reverend Bruce gives a bark of laughter. 'I suspect, Elizabeth, that he couldn't care less. His supposed empathy is only for his own ends.'

'No, he has tried to help me.' But then Lizzie remembers asking Johnny if he might write to his brother; how he had dismissed the idea out of hand, simply said that they would work the woman out somehow. Reassurance, but only words. Perhaps her demeanour alters, because the Reverend reaches out and pats Lizzie's hand with his cool fingers.

'The time has come to bury her, dear.'

'Reverend—'

'It is for the best. Can't you see that no good has come from that thing being uncovered?'

'But Inspector Esslemont has written to a man at the university. We should at least wait and see if—'

'Do you think of nothing but your own desires?' he snaps, roused to sudden anger. 'Inspector Esslemont wrote to me a couple of weeks ago. This academic, he's joined up. There is nothing more that James can do, and he has instructed me to bury her.'

Lizzie is silenced by the shock of it – two conniving men. Two men in their staunch black uniforms, exchanging letters. Unless the Reverend is lying – Lizzie can imagine him on his knees, justifying it to the Lord: Father, I did it for her own good.

'Can I see the letter?'

'Elizabeth.' Soft, as though she has wounded him. 'I can get it for you, if you really feel you must see it.'

But Lizzie shakes her head. Can imagine too a fine morning on Fore Street, James signing his name with a flourish and licking the envelope, placing it on the hall table for a servant to post. Going about his day afterwards, no qualms at all in abandoning the matter. To him the bog woman was never more than a curio, an anecdote to share at dinner parties. Lizzie wonders if he had ever truly been interested, or whether his arrival in the Cabrach had been only to satisfy the same gnawing curiosity she had felt – to see what her life was like without him in it.

'I believe you. But it is not for James to decide what happens to the woman.'

The Reverend sighs and rises. Lizzie thinks he will dismiss her. Instead, he goes over to the window and looks out at the sky that holds weight in its even whiteness, as if carrying a fist of coal in a silk handkerchief.

'I hoped not to have to tell you this.' His expression is pained. 'It cannot have escaped your notice that Jimmy Weir was at kirk this morning. I'd encouraged him to come, thought it might do him good to be amongst the fellowship of his community. He has been struggling, and . . .' Reverend Bruce shakes his head, steels himself. 'He came to see me a couple of days ago. He was deeply troubled, had been up all night. He told me that he thought the root of his distress was an image he kept seeing in his head, one he couldn't dislodge. Said he saw it when he closed his eyes to rest, but that it came to him in daylight too. I asked him what this image was and what he described to me was, well – can you guess?'

Lizzie thinks of the things she has heard from the front – shattered bones and spongy feet, gangrene's black appetite, lads with melted faces gulping blue morphine tablets that barely touched the pain.

'I don't know, Reverend.'

'He told me it was a body, lying curled in a ditch – intact, as though it had only lain down to sleep, but dead. Does that remind you of anything?'

'Well, yes, but—'

'I cannot help but worry his fears were encouraged by the talk he's heard since returning home.' The Reverend looks at Lizzie with his man's sure logic and his eyebrows raised. For a moment he succeeds in seeding guilt in her, but Lizzie still feels she owes something to the bog woman, another attempt at understanding. 'I am sorry for him, Reverend, truly I am, but if we bury the woman now, without knowing who she was, we'll never put paid to all the superstition. Is that what you want? All this magical talk, the devil living amongst us?'

The Reverend glances out of the window again, as though beyond the mossed dyke Auld Hornie might walk abroad, be carousing in sables by the kirk gate. 'The devil *is* always amongst us.'

'I'm not sure he'd be so blatant as to appear as a strange dead woman?'

'I didn't say she was him. Just that he's here.' This with the surety of one who has seen a dark figure move out of the corner of an eye, or started at an invisible tap on his shoulder when knelt in prayer.

Lizzie is exhausted, suddenly – all ability at persuasion spent, the will for it too. Imagine a life where you might be listened to, where your opinion matters. And perhaps this shows, for the Reverend Bruce gestures to her then. 'Come here, Elizabeth.' He stands back to allow her space at the window. 'Look into the kirkyard – what do you see?'

She does as he asks, sees the mournful huddles of headstones, the few ancient trees that tilt in supplication towards the kirk. The kirk itself, low and steadfast, with its gable to the braes.

'Over in the corner,' the Reverend says.

Lizzie leans closer to the glass. Mounded by the dyke is a heap of earth, spotted through with pebbles. Next to it, a narrow rectangle of open ground, a hole like a patchwork piece cut neatly from cloth.

'We will do it before the next Sunday service. It is all arranged.' The Reverend turns and goes back to the table, begins to tidy away the tea things.

JOHNNY

Frost crusts the windows of The Pheasant, away from the wary reach of the lamps that burn low and blue, for the paraffin supply is scant and the roads from town too treacherous to convince many to deliver a replenishment. Sleet falls daily, the worst of weathers – cold as snow, with none of its prettiness. The men at the inn seek warmth from their whisky, but the good stuff's double the price so it's a dingy bottle from under the counter for most. Lord knows what's in it, but if it knocks them half blind to their beds then so much the better, for no man wants to wake in the night and feel the worry creep over. Johnny sets his meagre coin on the bar in the expectation that Agnes will give him a wink and a slosh of her better stuff, but out comes the illicit bottle for him too.

'Och, Agnes, you're breaking my heart.' It is an effort to keep his voice light, colour it with the cheekiness he reserves for the barmaid. 'What have I done?'

She slides his dram over without ceremony. 'You know fine well.'

When he plays dumb, Agnes folds her arms over her bosom and looks down her nose at him – a look usually cast at men like Dougie when he's had too much and starts spitting and roaring. 'Look, loon, it's nae my business who's tupping who, but—'

'But you'll claik about it anyway?'

'I've a right to an opinion. William Calder is a good man – this place wouldnae be open without him.' She gestures around the establishment, as though it's anything other than a dingy country drinking-hole for ploughmen and pissed-up farmers. 'So I dinnae think folks ought tae be disrespecting him. Not when he's gone off tae fight for us and all. As I said, he's a good man.'

'Aye, a good man or a rich man, or are they one and the same?'

'Jealousy disnae become you, loon.'

'I'm nae fucking jealous.' But it doesn't seem worth arguing about, so Johnny takes the glass and winces as the liquor burns going down. He had thought he'd left this sort of rotgut behind, come up in the world – but supposes he's not too good to drink it down like the rest of them.

He joins the men round the hearth, welcomed by a few mistrustful looks and the odd mutter of greeting. Dougie is splayed out, his lips quivering at his dram, but Jock's nowhere to be seen, nor Sinclair – not since Esther's latest trouble. And no Rab. Johnny hasn't been up to Brawlands since he puked his guts up in the top pasture – he should go, probably, to offer a pair of hands to replace Henry's. But the look on Rab's face, the way Maggie had been with him – avoidance seems easier. Alex is here, at least, and he's shaved his chin clean, a pruned moustache all that's left. 'Where's it gone?' asks Johnny. The lustrous red beard had always been a source of pride for the ploughman, who'd sit and twist wiry strands round a finger as he spoke.

'They'd take a dim view of it at the drill hall.'

'You mean . . .?'

'Aye, well, I havenae decided yet, but I'm seriously considering it.'

'What about Rab?'

'Supposedly there's four thousand men in the borough who havenae joined up. I'm sure he'll be able to replace me.'

Johnny has seen this coming, if he's honest. Still, there's a feeling in him like when he's out drinking and everyone's merry until lads start peeling off, taking themselves to their beds. And then the last dregs of a bottle and no one left to share them with, just Johnny alone in the middle of the floor, wondering how he got there.

'Come on then,' Alex says. 'Fill me in before I go.'

'On what?'

'You know. What happened at Blackwater.'

A couple of others shift in their chairs, clearly eavesdropping. Johnny nearly rolls his eyes but stops himself – he needs to keep some friends. 'Nothing happened.'

'Och, come on. You mean tae say you stayed the night at the house of a quine you've eyes for and your breeks stayed firmly on?'

'They would have if he's any sense,' someone mutters.

'Fat chance,' says another.

'I didnae stay the night.'

Alex smirks. 'She didnae want a cuddle after, then?'

This prompts a laugh from a few of them – but then they want more, of course. It's always been like this, the way they'll sit slack-jawed and green while he tells them of some lass he's dallied with, then come Sunday he's expected to be straight and sober for kirk. Go on Johnny, have your fun, bring us back the spoils. No, stay and help on the farms, else we'll call you idle. Go, get your boots on, soldier. And wouldn't it be easier to appease them? To bedeck the night with bawdy embellishment, ingratiate himself once more? But Johnny doesn't want to talk about Lizzie in that way. He could tell them it was only a kiss, but perhaps that doesn't matter – to confess to kissing another man's wife might as well be confessing to taking her to bed. Lust lacks the nuance of other sins – violence, for instance. No man could say that landing a fist in someone's face is the same as killing him.

'I'm sorry, lads, but there's nothing tae tell.'

A few of them tut, turn back to their ruminations, but Dougie sits up straight. 'You're a disgrace.'

'I just said, man – nothing happened.'

Dougie lifts an eyebrow. He seems to have aged a decade in a matter of weeks – his cheeks cross-hatched with broken capillaries, nose mushrooming between them. When he opens his mouth to take another sip, Johnny notices the cracked front tooth. 'What'd you do tae yourself? You've a mouth like a neepie lantern.'

The farmer looks bewildered, tongues the sharp edge of the tooth as if it's new to him. 'I fell.'

'On the ice?'

'No. It was the other night. I woke up and . . . that was it, I'd dropped off in my chair. I like tae take a drink after the last rounds outside, but I dropped off and when I woke there was . . . wetness, all over the floor.'

Alex leans to murmur in Johnny's ear. 'Pissed himself.'

The old man tuts. 'I heard that. No. I checked the pail hadnae been upset and I checked under the door in case some rain had got in, but that wisnae it either . . .' He settles back into his chair as if he's forgotten he was speaking.

'So what was the liquid on the floor, then?' Alex asks.

Dougie's head snaps up. 'I dinnae know, but it smelled . . . peaty.'

Another dram down. Usually Johnny tells himself he will have a couple then call it a night, but he's on his third and there's a relief in knowing he'll likely have another and then stagger home, three sheets to the wind, then drop into his bed and dream of absolutely sweet fuck-all. He sits at the bar now, away from Dougie's ramblings and the sassy way the men look at him, and he is placid enough until the door opens and there is Henry, in his loose coat, two hoofs of bandage emerging from the cuffs. He greets the men at the hearth, and someone must ask about his hands because he holds them before him, shrugs as if it's nothing.

'You'll have some stories tae tell with those,' says one man, his tone almost admiring.

When Henry comes to the bar, he seems not to notice Johnny at first, sitting alone in the corner. He fumbles in his pocket for coin and manages to shake out a few silvers that roll across the bar. The urge to help stirs in Johnny, but passes soon enough. 'All right, loon?'

Henry winces as he tries to catch a rolling penny. 'Never been better.'

Agnes catches the coin and gives it back to him. The whisky she pours for the loon is a different colour to Johnny's – honeyed and clear, and it smells like something fit for drinking instead of sluicing a stable with.

'You want another?' Henry asks, nodding to Johnny's half-empty glass.

'No. Ta.'

'Suit yourself.'

The men drink in silence, Johnny occasionally glancing at Henry out of the corner of his eye. He's still incredulous that the loon's shown up here at all, with his colourless lashes and his serious face, and the hands Johnny is sure he can smell through the gauze. He can imagine the loon biting his lip while Maggie washed them, closing his eyes rather than seeing the mess. And he can't stand it, gets up to go, but it's like it has always been, Henry finding the gumption to speak only when he sees that his opportunity might disappear.

'It was a shame I couldnae go tae kirk on Sunday, I'd like tae have seen.'

Johnny sits back down on the stool. 'Seen what?'

'Have you nae heard?'

A lurch in Johnny; there are things that will make him sweat, and one is being the last with the news. 'Heard what?'

The loon waves a cumbersome hand. 'Och, nothing. Just a wee scene.'

Johnny looks at Agnes, but the barmaid won't meet his eye. 'What is it, loon?'

'You can ask Lizzie Calder, next time you see her.'

'Is she all right?' Johnny's words rush out before he considers that maybe the loon is just provoking him, chuffed at a chance to gain the upper hand.

'You can ask next time you pay her a visit. I'm sure she'll have you back tae Blackwater.'

Johnny is not sure that is true – can still see the look on Lizzie's face as he left. 'I'll nae be troubling her again.'

Henry turns his head to look at Johnny, a brief brightness clearing his face. 'She'll be disappointed.'

Johnny sighs. 'I'm nae up for discussing this, loon, truth be told.'

But Henry won't let it go. 'I'm sure she's hoping you'll come back, mind. We all know what sort of woman she is.'

Johnny should leave it well alone. Should get up, put his cap on, go without another word. But he finds he doesn't want to. So he asks the loon, takes on a high tone of curiosity. 'And what sort is that?'

Henry's reply is lost as Johnny wrenches him up from the stool, gets the lad skittering on tiptoes, his fine golden dram gone flying across the floor. A shout goes up. Agnes is out from behind the bar, slapping a forearm across Johnny's chest. She hauls him back far enough that Henry can wriggle free, but Johnny is all strength, goes back at him, makes another grab for the loon's neck.

'Get off!' Agnes wrenches Johnny away again, aided by a man

come bounding from the hearthside. 'You think you're the big man, eh, Johnny? Attacking someone who cannae fight back?'

'Fucking bully,' shouts Dougie.

'Get him out!'

Agnes and the farmer drag Johnny towards the door, shove him out into the night. And out there, in the biting cold, Johnny walks away, spitting obscenities meant for the ploughman. Every bad word he knows, whether it makes sense or not, the release all that matters. Only when he's finished does he realize Henry has followed him.

Above them, a full moon spotlights the shameful scene: the loon, bent double, his raggy breath billowing into the frozen air; Johnny Nicol pacing like an animal, horrified at how easily it came to him to use his body instead of his words. Supposedly he is not that kind of man. He's not like his da – bony, stiff waistcoat, shined shoes his wife had sweated over. The pinched lips when folks ruffled wee Johnny's hair and said things like, *Och, John, he disnae look a thing like you.* The taste in the air not just of the salt and the fish and the smoke but of some unsaid thing, until Charlie would toddle up behind them, cracking a smile, the very spit of his father. Later, the clock on the mantelpiece ticking as John senior took his dram, and his wife washing the dishes as quietly as she could. Later still, her hair – her lovely mermaid's hair – twisted in his grip. No, Johnny is not like his da.

'I'm sorry, aye?' he calls. Henry doesn't look up; he's still crouched over, mucus slugging from his nostrils. Johnny goes to him.

'What is it you want?'

The loon sniffs, straightens up. 'I want tae stop the darkness here. It's spreading, Johnny. It comes for me too.'

'You dinnae need tae worry, a good lad like you.'

'But so much has gone wrong. First the rain and the ruined crop, then Wee Jimmy coming back like he is. And Jock's thing in the barn and Sinclair's wife, and my hands. And how I cannae sleep for the thoughts that come over me. So much ill-fortune. And . . . and it all seems to come from you.'

'What do you mean, for God's sake . . .' Johnny sighs. 'Look, maybe I'm soft in the head, but you'll need tae be more specific.'

'It all happened after you and Mistress Calder took that thing out the bog. You and Mistress Calder – she is married, Johnny.'

That she is. And Johnny wonders if this is what really grieves the loon, grieves the whole lot of them – envy. The feeling of inadequacy when they see a man who's the hero of the story when they themselves have nothing but bit parts.

'You ought tae do the decent thing and leave her well alone,' Henry says.

It chastens Johnny. This was a word his da liked to use; they were decent folks living in a decent house, and every morn John Nicol senior would walk out to his decent job – looking, to all intents and purposes, like a decent man. Johnny dips his head. 'It's nae so easy as that.'

'To be decent?'

He winces. 'I . . . no. Not when I feel like this.' Johnny doesn't quite dare say it, put form and language to the feeling that sometimes seems big enough to panic him. Because it demands certain things – a nagging sense that he ought to be better, to make himself worthy. He forces himself to look at Henry, whose expression curdles like a drop of vinegar in milk. It disturbs Johnny, how the loon is one thing one minute, something else entirely the next – like the horses he'd worked with who were calm and still and would let you stroke their pretty manes, until you did something they didn't like and you had to leap to avoid a hoof in the groin. Still, he presses on, anxious to justify himself, hoping that his vulnerability might tug some old thread of understanding between them.

'Don't you get it, my friend? Have you never . . . have you never loved anyone?'

Henry spits on the ground. 'It's nae love you want, just approval. Same as it ever fucking was.' And then it is like a thought has slotted into place. 'I suppose you've nae told her about Windyhillock?'

It is chilly, here, in the midnight courtyard of a rural inn, where the water in the well-trodden ruts has turned to ice and the sleet has begun to drop, but this has little to do with the blood running cold in Johnny Nicol's veins. 'What – what about it?'

'You know full well.'

For a moment Johnny is not sure he does. There are memories he's let slip, eroded by time and whisky, others that have been pushed down for so long they've petrified deep inside him.

'Once we washed the blood away, we could tell he wisnae the same.'

Johnny starts like he's been struck. 'Stop. I dinnae want tae hear of it.'

'That's too bad, Jack. You've hidden from it long enough – I really ought tae tell you.'

'Please . . .' But there is nothing to do but let him.

Henry sees this and takes his time, savouring the moment. He is standing close, and Johnny can see every detail of his face: a man's face, now, squared out and sharpened on the whetstone of a cruel life.

'His eyes were rolled back and his mouth was hanging open, two or three teeth gone. It was a shame; Isaac had a lovely face.'

It sickens Johnny, but he cannot leave now, has to hear the rest. He's always hated that at the farms, being forced to look at things he'd rather not – lambs pulled blue from their mothers, dead and gurning beasts with their eye sockets pecked clean.

'But it wisnae the beating that did it – any man can withstand a bit of blood. Less so the rest of it.'

When Johnny speaks, he can manage no more than a whisper. 'I never knew if he lived or died.'

'Aye, well. You ran off too quick for that.'

'Which was it?'

The loon raises his eyebrows, then smirks. 'You just said you didnae want tae hear of it.'

'Please, just this bit.'

'Here's an idea. I'll go and tell Mistress Calder what happened, and then you can ask her.'

'Henry—'

'We can make it a game – you won't know when I'm going tae tell her and then you'll find, one time when you go sniffing round her door, that she knows what happened to Isaac. And you can beg it out of her, if she'll even let you in.'

He's been an idiot, of course, to drop his guard. Johnny had not considered that Henry would clype to Lizzie, wouldn't have thought he'd have the gall. But now he understands how loons like this – bullied and belittled and wronged – will do more than simply store up their resentments. They will nurture them, clasp them like precious things close to their heart. And they will know when they see it – the softest thing to lob them at, as though splitting a new wound will do anything to heal their own.

'Listen, it didnae happen as you think.' Johnny flails in his memory, trying to get straight what did happen, sift out the lies he gladly took on when he was eighteen and stupid and driven by his cock and his big mouth.

'Oh, I know exactly what happened. It's a good story, Jack – I'd be glad tae tell it. I'll see you around, aye?'

Henry heads back towards the inn and Johnny looks on, dumbed for a moment by the cold and his own terror. Through the windows he sees good men who'd sooner side with a poor injured lad than the man who dangled him by the scruff of the neck, and fair enough. Fair enough.

Johnny turns away from the lamplight and the fellowship, sets off down the track that's so black he can't see his own feet in front of him. It usually never troubles him – usually he'll get into his stride, eyes adjusting to the dark, warmed by the alcohol. It's different tonight. The hooch hasn't touched the sides, and he's conscious of his breath and his heartbeat and the hairs raising on his arms – the feeling of eyes on him. Johnny digs in his pocket for his ma's hagstone, runs his thumb over its smooth surface just as she did – her good luck charm, protection from the devil. But Johnny doesn't believe in the devil. He could come sashaying down the road now, twirling his cane, and still Johnny would be resolute. Auld Hornie was only ever a good excuse, a scapegoat: I did it because he sat on my shoulder, prodding and goading. I did it because the devil's inside me – he's the pride and the vanity, the lust, the need to be someone. The excuse no longer satisfies him, and maybe that's what shame is – being forced to accept what you have done, for you've good and run out of things to blame.

LIZZIE

Wednesday. The air is damp and there is white on the higher ground; it will not be long until the snow falls elsewhere. Lizzie crouches by the fire in her bedroom, clinging to the semicircle of warmth it throws out, studying books. She had crept to the study the night before, while Jane slept, and taken from William's shelves the encyclopaedias and history books, dusty tomes with mildewed endpapers that she hopes will supply a reason not to put the bog woman back in the ground. So far she has been largely disappointed, thumped the *Encyclopaedia Britannica* on to her lap and found within its pages only a short, useless entry on peat and its formation.

She returns instead to her sketchbook, where a half-finished impression of the bog woman looks up at her. Lizzie has tried to capture the woman, but has struggled with the angles of her joints and the great rowdy lick of hair, the childlike hands. Worst of all is the woman's face – it slips from her mind's eye, or changes, the face Lizzie remembers now dropped in on itself, one side collapsing so that the cheek is concave, and where there was the unbearably frail skin of her eyelid there is just – nothing.

All of this is a distraction, of course, from Johnny. In more generous moments, Lizzie frets that he has fallen ill, or else was so shaken at the potential for discovery that he is too fearful to come. But that type of cowardice seems at odds with the man she had seen on Hallowe'en night, demanding she dance with him in the middle of the kitchen, drinking gladly of her husband's whisky and kissing her with the surety of a god or a king. But a king is only a man, after all.

Mid-morning, the doorbell goes, and Lizzie leaps up. An absurd delight swells in her chest: here he is, arrived to stand brazen on the doorstep, to make everything right.

Instead Lizzie finds Jane in the hallway, the front door just closing.

'Who was that?' Lizzie asks.

Jane holds up two envelopes. 'Just the postman.'

'Ah.'

'Were you expecting someone else?'

'No,' says Lizzie, honestly, for it strikes her then that Johnny is always disinclined to explain himself.

Later, having returned to her bedroom for more fruitless study, Lizzie is summoned. Jane calls out her name as she comes along the hallway, and again, insistently, as she knocks on Lizzie's door and opens it simultaneously.

'Elizabeth—' Jane stops when she sees her brother's books stacked on the carpet. She is agitated, straining against her practised serenity as she demands Lizzie follow her upstairs.

The door to the study is ajar, and Jane gestures at the lock. 'Would you like to tell me how this happened?'

'Perhaps . . . it broke?'

Jane snorts. 'I'm no fool.'

Inside the room, despite its position in the roof and its long-empty hearth, it feels warmer than it ought to. Elsewhere, Blackwater is prone to impudent bloomings of mould, splits in the sills from the condensation weeping off the windows, but in William Calder's study all remains well.

'I must say, I was quite surprised to come up here just now and find the door open,' Jane says. 'Was there something you wanted in here, sister? Some sort of mystery you were trying to solve?'

'No.'

'No? Come now, you must have been looking for something?'

It had been Lizzie's intention to open drawers and rifle through papers, read the words in her husband's ledgers like tea leaves. But later, because after Hallowe'en night she had been distracted by other things; with a grave cut in the kirkyard, the mystery of the bog woman had seemed more pressing. Probably she had been foolish to expect her tampering would go undetected in the meantime.

'Those books I was reading just then . . . I only wanted to get them.'

Jane appears to soften. 'Ah. Then why didn't you ask me for the key? Do you think me joyless enough to deprive you of a little reading?'

'I don't know.'

'You've damaged the lock, is the thing. Rather a lot of force went into breaking it – I'm surprised you had the strength. Or did you have help?'

Lizzie shakes her head, then watches as Jane's hand goes to the pocket of her skirt and withdraws something. The scarlet ribbon is neatly folded, and Jane lays it on her palm. 'What happened? I suppose he dropped it outside and you brought it in?'

'He came inside.'

'Ah. And?'

'And I asked him to help me break into the study.'

Jane stands before Lizzie with her unlined face, her breath that smells of air. Her silence demands more.

'We kissed.' Pleasure in the speaking aloud of it, and Lizzie looks at Jane to see if this admission moves her – to jealousy, or anger, or desire – anything.

'Go on,' Jane says, but the impulse to speak of it has passed, and Lizzie realizes it had only been for herself. What had she wanted? For Jane to smile and delight in the tale as if they were two young girls, whispering secrets? How could Jane understand when it seems entirely possible that she's never loved a man, nor anyone?

Lizzie has no sense of how to continue – in innuendo and deflection, or matter-of-factly like she gives evidence: then he ran his finger along my collarbone. He put his arms round me. He began to undo my buttons. Or would she buckle under scrutiny, instead say – I touched him, I undressed him. All Lizzie is sure of is that they did as was done to them – who is to say who started it?

Jane waits for Lizzie to flounder, then holds up a hand. 'Fear not, sister – I have no interest in the details. I could ask someone else if I wanted to know. I daresay your singer's been down at the inn telling all who'll listen. Quite a score for him, I'd imagine.'

Doubt again. Doubt whose ears prick up, who strides cleanly into the room to breathe at Lizzie's neck. 'He . . . he wouldn't.'

'Then how did everyone know?' Jane must see the way Lizzie's face drops, because her fingers go to her cheek, tuck her hair tenderly behind her ear. 'Oh, sister. Have you fallen in love?'

Lizzie instantly denies it. But perhaps that's what this is – the pathetic, shameful need for his apology, the rage that grows as he continues to withhold it. The way that, if Johnny walked into the room right now, Lizzie would drop to her knees and press her head into his hands. 'I don't know.'

'My brother has proved to be a disappointment to you, is that right?'

Again, the desire for confession. Their wedding night, Lizzie in front of William with nothing covering herself. Her groom in his black suit, shoes not yet removed. He had appraised her impassively, risen from the bed to loosen his belt, gone through the motions. No love in it. Those first years of marriage, Lizzie had ventured forth in good faith, only to be met with silence. She dreamed it might get better, that one day she would show him love and he'd take a liking to it, muster some to give back to her. And when those dreams came to naught, she came up with others – unrealistic, but flames to warm her hands on, all the same. She imagined some other man, who'd take her to town and to dances, for strolls by the burn. She would tell him all her bashful fantasies, the regrets that clutched her throat in the thickest part of the night. Then, when these fruitless imaginings hurt more than they soothed, she ceased them, too. A relief, really, the relinquishment: my husband will never love me, I will never love him, and it is pointless to cry over it.

'The thing is,' Jane goes on, 'you and William seemed well suited. Both impulsive, undisciplined, always going after something you'd have done well to leave alone. You rather deserved each other. So it was a kindness, really, for my father to arrange things.'

'And you encouraged him.'

'You're clever, sister. Yes, I may have made a few suggestions. You might think I sought only to feather my own nest, but my intentions were nobler than that – I only wanted to protect my family. And that desire, you see, has never diminished. So when I see a threat to us, I am forced to act. Have a look at that letter there, the one on the left.'

Lizzie looks at the desk – sees for a moment only the magnifying glass and the pen stand, polished to a high shine as though William rubbed a chamois over them just yesterday. Then she notices the two letters, their wax seals cleanly split. She turns the left-hand envelope and finds the address written in a hand she knows so well.

'You opened my post?'

'Aye,' Jane says, 'I did.'

16 Fore Street
Elgin
Moray

25th October, 1915

Dear Lizzie,

I hope you are well. I have heard the Cabrach has been much afflicted by ice and cold weather, and hope this note reaches you before the snow does.

I'm afraid progress has halted on the bog discovery – we've a shortage of men and are having to prioritize other things. But I'll look into it again, personally.

With regards to your other enquiry, I did as you asked and spoke again to my father. He wouldn't budge, I'm afraid – old men and their loyalties – but when I asked what William Calder had used the money they'd drawn down for, he said: 'He insulted Thomas Slora gravely, and that is all I will say on it.'

I hope this is of some use to you.

Yours,

James

'The thing is, sister, I've no interest in whatever men you choose to lose your head over – it is yours to lose. But if you're going to start digging around in the past, trying to destroy William and the Calders . . . well, I'm most certainly interested in that. So I'll be leaving you shortly, and Miss Gow will be coming with me.'

'What? Why?'

'The snow will smother us by morn.'

'No, but... why? It is winter, Jane. And Miss Gow arranges all the food, orders the fuel in—' It ought to please her, to be rid of Jane, but Lizzie only sees how empty the house will become. All these years there has at least been Miss Gow's brisk foot on the stair, or the closing of William's door. She cannot bear silence, the gaping space it makes for thought.

'Please...'

But Jane hauls a briefcase on to the desk and begins sweeping in the correspondence from William's letter rack, taking deeds and certificates from the tray.

'I'm sure you will find company enough.' Jane takes a small key from her pocket and opens the desk drawers, scooping up chequebooks and cash. In the deep bottom drawer is a stack of old ledgers, the labels on the spines curling with age. She heaves these out, before kicking the drawer closed and locking it again.

'Your singer will come to see you, won't he?'

'I don't know.'

'Ah, he's turned out to be a disappointment already, has he? Not quite the decent man you thought?' Jane picks up the second letter and hands it to Lizzie. 'Read this later, when I've gone. My case is packed, so I won't be keeping you much longer. We must get away before the weather gets too bad.'

Lizzie looks out of the window, where the snow is falling steadily. It will cover everything, block paths, bear down on the roofs of crofts and of Blackwater. Already it casts the study in a strident light, passing on a quality of blankness to the emptied desk and carefully arranged books, the dead eyes of the mounted stag, regarding them as Jane strides from the room.

After Jane and Miss Gow have left, Lizzie holds the second envelope in her hand. Its postmark is from Aberdeen and the writing unfamiliar – untidy, written in haste. It has been opened already, of course, but it takes Lizzie some time to find the nerve to slip the paper out.

23rd October, 1915
c/o Aberdeen Royal Infirmary

Dear M. Calder,
Your discovery sounds intriguing indeed, but I have no desire to find myself in the vicinity of my brother again. I am sorry to disappoint you.
Sincerely,
Dr Charles Nicol

Lizzie reads the missive again, six or seven times, searching for whatever story there is in its terse brevity. Little wonder Johnny would not write to his busy brother – clearly there is some rift, too wide and impassable. But why hadn't he told her so? If he had, Lizzie could have reassured him that she knows what it is like to find yourself so adrift from your family that it seems easier not to try to swim home. If Johnny had said it, she could have empathized. It dawns on her then, anger flooding her body, that he did not explain himself because he knew that empathy to be undeserved. Because somewhere, Johnny Nicol has done something very wrong.

October–November 1905

LIZZIE

Lizzie was aware of James across the room. She sipped from a crystal glass, conscious of every movement, although she pretended to be absorbed in the discussion: the Calders' acquisition of the Richmond Hotel.

'Deeds are all signed, Hugh tells me,' said Helen Calder, 'though I don't really get involved in business.'

'Leave that to your bairns, eh?' Webster turned to Jane. 'Has your da said you can run it yet?'

Helen rolled her eyes. 'Sore subject.'

'Ah, William's the favourite, is he?'

'He won't have the time, with all these farms he wants to buy,' said Jane. 'They take a great deal of management.'

Webster patted her on the arm. 'It would be a lot to take on anyway, dearie. You find yourself a husband and then you'll soon forget about trying to be in business.'

'That is not my intention.'

'Och, you'll meet a nice young man and then you'll change your tune.'

Jane forced a tight smile and Lizzie felt a stroke of pity for her – a strange creature, trapped between what she was and what she wanted to be. She could never have the freedom of her brother or a man like James.

Jane's dignified rebuttal of Webster's probing encouraged the talk to move on, while some guests excused themselves to fetch drinks and Lizzie took the opportunity to step a little way back from the group. She threw a glance over her shoulder and James caught it, sauntered towards her across the Turkey rug. He touched her back; not really her back but her waist, a little outside of what might be considered proper.

'Ah, Miss Brodie.' His voice was low. 'May I say you look exceptionally fine in that dress. I knew black would suit you, but I didn't know it would make you look so—'

He was interrupted by Jane, practically stepping between him and Lizzie. 'I hear you've news, James?'

'News? Do I?' He glanced at Lizzie and then looked down at his drink, as if something helpful might be found floating in the martini. 'Oh . . . of course, you must mean my decision to join the police force.'

Lizzie tried not to look wounded at Jane knowing something about James that she didn't. They had little appetite for talking of serious things, anyway, when their time alone was short and furtive and charged with kisses. 'I thought your father was setting up a role for you at the bank?'

'I can't let my old man make all my decisions for me.' James tipped back the rest of his drink, catching the delicate gilded rim on his tooth with a sharp crack. He looked, for a moment, uncharacteristically bashful, then waved the glass before him. 'Another, I should think.'

The meal was achingly long. Endless courses – the soup, the fish, the lamb, meat cleaved apart with reverent slowness. Under the table, Lizzie tapped her foot in impatience, inches from James's – she wanted her time with him. Then Webster's tedious jokes and moving to the parlour with the women, the after-dinner port and gossip and the clock ticking round. Finally, the men came through – noisy and relaxed from cigars and time spent without their wives. The room was hot and Webster, who had already dispensed with his jacket, threw open the French doors to let in the night air. For Lizzie it was an opportunity. She caught James's gaze from across the room and tilted her head towards the dark garden. Was most gratified when she heard him make his excuses and slip from the parlour.

When Lizzie stepped out, the cold shocked her. The frost was already thick on the lawn, gleaming on the waxy black leaves of the rhododendrons. She walked a little way on to the patio – pure treachery, a sheet of ice that invited a fall. Out here, her home seemed beautiful: grand and symmetrical as a doll's house, windows spilling light. She waited for James to emerge – he was probably playing, hiding from her, and would make a grab at her waist when she least expected it. Her skin prickled with anticipation, and she turned sharply when she heard a noise. But it was Jane Calder who appeared through the doors.

'Elizabeth, I need to speak with you.'

'Later, Jane.' Lizzie was in no mood for further delay, and certainly not one created by Jane, already guilty of one interruption.

'It's important.'

But nothing could be as important as the man Lizzie saw then, leaning against the garden wall. 'It will have to wait.'

'Lizzie. If you go to him now, you will humiliate yourself.'

Jane was just jealous – Lizzie had worked that out. And so she felt rather grand as she ignored her and headed off down the steps, paying no heed as Jane called after her again. As soon as Lizzie reached James his arms were round her, pleasure so huge she could have split open with it.

'This is brazen, even for you,' James whispered.

'For us.'

'Your idea, though, wasn't it? Come with me.' James took Lizzie's hand and they walked the perimeter of the garden, staying close to the wall. 'What have you been doing today?' An innocent question, as though they were promenading in broad daylight, he a husband making enquiries of his wife.

'Well, I have read a little, and taken a walk. And agitated the cat and got dressed. And – oh – I divined my fortune.'

'And what's it to be?'

'If I speak of it, it won't come true.'

'A hint, then.'

Lizzie tapped her nose with an index finger. 'No.'

'Tell me, please.' James stopped, pulled Lizzie close.

'Well, it is only a silly game, so you must take it with a pinch of salt.'

'Go on,' he murmured.

'According to the kail, I am to marry a rich and prosperous man.'

James pulled back abruptly, as though he'd been pinched. 'Not many of those going begging around here.'

In Lizzie, a barb of fear that she had laid the hint on too thickly. Or perhaps she had uncovered some intention, like talking of a much-desired gift with someone who has already bought it for you.

'We should probably go back in,' said James.

'Oh, but—' Lizzie moved closer to him, hoping he would not be able to resist her. And he could not – one sharp kiss in the silent garden.

'Come on, people will be wondering where we are.'

Indeed, the party turned to look as they entered the parlour. 'Errant children,' Webster said, giving George a wink.

'James! There you are.' Mistress Esslemont marched across the room and took her son by the wrist. 'Come on, we've decided we'll do it now.'

James groaned. 'Mother, I think now is not the time—'

'Nonsense.' Mr Esslemont rapped his sovereign ring against the edge of his glass, drawing the room's attention. The couple stood, sharing surreptitious smiles, James wedged between them. By the fireplace, Jane watched intently.

'We have some news,' said Mr Esslemont. 'We were going to keep it quiet a little longer, but we're all friends here!'

'And too excited!'

'My wife and I, we're delighted to announce that our James is engaged.'

Lizzie was confused – did they think he had already asked her, out there on the lawn? She looked to James to explain, but he was gazing vaguely ahead of him, attention not catching on anything.

'Who is she?' someone asked.

'Aye, you've kept this discreet, my boy!'

At the nudge of his mother, James spoke. 'Miss Charlotte Kellas.'

The ladies gasped and the squeals rang out, and James was given a hollow slap between the shoulders by his father so that he jerked forward in surprise. Mercy, perhaps, that in the excitement they didn't notice Lizzie groping for a chair to steady herself, sure her knees were about to give way.

'The Kellases are a very old Forres family. We've known them since James and Charlotte were children.' Mistress Esslemont was breathless, drinking in the attention. 'She's a delight, isn't she, darling?'

James's hard swallow, a bob in the neck that Lizzie had kissed. 'Yes. We're very pleased.'

'Och, but a crying shame you're off the market,' said Webster, saliva gathering at the edges of his mouth. 'I'm sure you've many lady admirers.'

This was when they looked at Lizzie: pity. Folks who had seen it play out – all those longing looks across the table. Webster, drunk at the last dinner party so he got lost in the Esslemont house and discovered them fumbling in a spare bedroom; Jane, who was shaking her head as though to say – I tried to tell you. Lizzie looked for her father, seeking his comfort. When she caught George's eye, he pressed his lips into a thin line. A moment, that was all, to toss a whiff of sympathy, and then he raised his glass and called out clear and hearty: 'A toast to James and Charlotte!'

'To James and Charlotte!' echoed the party.

'We should have some music,' said Webster.

Jane clapped her hands. 'Mr Brodie, didn't you say that Elizabeth had volunteered on the piano?'

'I'm very out of practice—'

'Aye,' said Webster, 'and we've all had enough to drink that we won't notice a bad note.'

The wives called out, men stamping their feet. George said to his daughter, 'Lizzie, please – play for us.' A chivvying nod: go on, don't let me down.

Lizzie had no choice but to sit at the piano. The room arranged itself – women perched on the chaises and chairs with their little sips of sherry, James at the back, pinned in place by Webster's arm slung across his shoulder. He stared studiously at the carpet as Lizzie placed her fingers on the keys. Her mind was blank, the usual tunes not coming to her – the guests wanted bombast, the triumphant fanfare of a wedding march, but what came from her fingers was mournful. A song in a minor key, notes seeping like tears. Lizzie would not let her own come, not here, blinking hard when the white and black began to blur.

After a few bars, Webster began tapping his foot, swaying absurdly with his arm still clamped round James. 'Come on, pick up the pace – this is a party!'

Folks laughed. George was amongst them, putting on a brave face, slapping his friend on the back. Lizzie played a few more notes, an angry staccato, then she stopped mid-bar and closed the lid of the piano. She had reached the doorway before anyone noticed, her father coming to take her by the elbow and twist her away from the room. 'Are you all right?'

She wanted to fall weeping into his arms, but George would not forgive his daughter for making such a scene. So she forced a smile and released herself from his grip. 'Aye, Da. Just going for some air.'

Lizzie slumped in a chair in her father's snug, livid at James's audacity. The way he had pressed his knee to hers for the length of dinner, whispered all the easy compliments of a charming man. She had been changed by the way he'd looked at her. At first that admiration had taken her aback, and she would turn in the mirror and wonder what it was, specifically, that had earned it. But as the months had passed and he'd kept looking, she had begun to feel it was deserved.

She knew he would come, and this gratified her; she wanted to hurt him. She sat in wait until the doorknob turned and an elegant figure appeared, pausing before stepping in. Lizzie wanted to be dignified, to sit in silence like Hugh Calder would, until James had to fill the space with his apologies. But the words shot off her tongue. 'So was this a planned arrangement, or did you suddenly see her anew, having had your appetite whetted elsewhere?'

'Lizzie.' He said her name with a calmness that infuriated her.

'I thought . . . I thought it would be me.'

He did not laugh, though might as well have done. 'You and me, it was just fun, Lizzie – a romance. I'm sure you'll have others.'

'And what if I don't want others? What if I only wanted this one?' Her voice sounded girlish, and she hated it, and hated James as he came towards her.

'Listen, it was always expected of me.'

'You said their expectations didn't matter to you.'

'It's not as simple as that. All this stuff about fine old families, preserving our good name – it matters to them.'

'And do you love her?' A desperation in her tone, Lizzie knew, and she couldn't breathe as she waited for his answer.

'Well, I'm sure I could. I am fortunate that she's very bonny, at least, though delicate as a china doll and fair-haired, so not my favourite. I rather feel like I might break her.' Despite the dark room, Lizzie could tell he was smiling, enchanted by his own wit. 'She is very refined and not at all spirited – not like you.' His hand went to her hip, and he took a step closer. She stiffened at first, because how dare he, and then as he gripped her waist it was as if she lost any ability to decline, any will to do so – though there was little of that anyway. James pressed his forehead to hers and then he did not move, only stood with his mouth ajar, waiting until she kissed him first.

'You're heaven,' he whispered, his voice tight. James bunched the velvet skirt in his hand as if he meant to lift it but then let it drop, let his arms fall to his sides so that his body was an invitation. He let her tug the tails of his shirt loose, work her hands up under the cotton so she could dig her fingernails into his back until he winced and she was satisfied. They stood, then, with their arms clamped round each other, his leg between hers so that he could have tipped her over easily. They teetered a moment, and when they finally collapsed on to the chaise it felt like melting, or imploding, or being reduced to nothing at all.

JACK

The grieve had them line up in the cold outside the chaumer before they were allowed into the party. He held a lamp aloft and inspected them – collars to be straightened, an extra button done up on Donald's shirt to cover the straggle of black chest hair. When he reached Jack he pinched the ribbon between thumb and forefinger and smirked. 'Poncey, but you'll do. And the orra-loon . . .' Henry was at the end of the line, having run up, breathless, to the grieve's whistle. 'What's that on your head?' The grieve plucked something from Henry's hair – a stalk of hay that he turned in his fingers then tossed to the ground. 'Christ, this one cannae even wash properly. Right, we'll go in. And dinnae think I'll nae be keeping an eye on you. It may be Hallowe'en, but that's nae excuse for bad behaviour – I've a rusted scythe I'll be using to hack your baws off if I see any.'

On the way across the yard, Henry fell into step with Jack. 'Isaac heard that song.'

'And? Did he realize who it was about?'

'No, well, he asked, and—'

'You told him?'

'It was obvious.'

Jack rolled his eyes. 'I'll make another one up and all – I'll call it Henry the Clype.' He sped up, eager to catch up with Donald and Tam and leave the orra-loon behind – he had his own friend now.

When Jack got into the farmhouse parlour, he gave himself a moment to take it all in. The room was large and clean, with good thick curtains that kept the cold at bay. Slora's wife had loaded the place with fripperies – rugs and plump cushions, ornaments on the mantelpiece. Jack looked greedily at them all, remembering what it was like to have things beyond the bare essentials. His ma had liked her trinkets: seashells, little china bells, dried flowers that would flake and flutter to the ground as the thuds came from upstairs. Jack touched the ribbon at his neck again – that was his embellishment.

A spread was laid out on the sideboard, the heaps of sliced meat somehow sickening. Jack took a dram and tipped it back, finding with pleasure that it didn't burn on the way down. The other guests were mostly farmers, men like Slora who had done well for themselves working a patch of someone else's land. They cast cursory glances at Jack, pausing at the ribbon. Then, realizing he was one of the workers, the men turned away – no advantage in idle tattle with a horseman. They mainly seemed to orbit one man, older, dressed expensively and talking at length – one of the purchasers, Jack assumed. He was unremarkable, and Jack nearly laughed. How easy it was to assume that the wealthy would somehow gleam, be carved from solid gold.

In the corner, Henry and Isaac stood together. They were laughing, and the orra-loon reached to brush something from Isaac's shoulder. Emboldened by their overt friendship – Slora's clear tolerance of it – Jack decided to find Violet. Downing his drink and taking another, he moved to the centre of the room and caught sight of her blonde curls in the alcove by the hearth. Her arms were wrapped round herself as though she was cold, and she was speaking to a man with his back to the room. Jack hesitated – he could tell this visitor was also moneyed, with his stiff collar and spotless worsted, the ring studding his smallest finger. He was most likely the other buyer, come sniffing around the farm to see what he wanted from it. Slora wouldn't like Jack speaking to him, probably, but maybe this man was not so high and mighty, given his obvious taste for the farmer's daughter. Jack could see the man was standing too close, cornering her into the alcove, so he took a hefty gulp of whisky and decided he'd intervene.

'Good evening, Violet.'

'Oh, Jack.' She gave a careful smile that suited her, turned her cheeks to peaches that Jack wanted to stroke, or else take a bite from. He found he wasn't afraid to step forward and grasp her elbow, good drink like confidence in him so that he pressed a quick kiss to her cheek.

'I'd suggest you don't try that again in front of her father,' said the buyer, who Jack was surprised to find was only in his mid-twenties, though his hair was already retreating at the crown as though it couldn't bear to be too close to his face.

'Pleased to meet you, sir – I'm Jack Nicol.' He performed a small bow, so that no one could say he hadn't treated the visitor with reverence.

'One of the workers, are you?'

'Recently promoted to horseman.' Jack glanced at Violet, sure she knew but keen all the same to remind her.

'Filthy job, that.' The buyer perused Jack's outfit – the badly pressed shirt, breeks with one dropped hem. Jack drew himself tall and accepted the judgement – it hardly touched him, because he felt, then, his youth and his charm and his good looks, the ribbon round his neck. There was nothing at the other man's throat but three faint marks, as if someone had scratched him.

'Have you worked with horses much, sir?'

The man snorted. 'Worked? No, not in your sense. I've always ridden – got three pure-bred stallions at our country place. Flighty beasts; you can't be afraid to use the whip on them.'

'Oh, I've other methods.'

'Such as?'

Jack tapped his nose. 'Trade secret.'

The guest raised an eyebrow. 'I was just telling Miss Slora about our latest acquisition – the Richmond in Huntly. I suppose you wouldn't know it. You'll have to come to the grand opening, Miss Slora, as my guest of honour.'

'Oh, well . . .' said Violet, and Jack could see that she was unsettled by the visitor. He'd seen men act this way before – all that grandiose puffery that only really served to flatter themselves.

'When is it?' Jack asked. 'I'll do the entertainment – discounted rate and all that.'

It took a moment for the guest to comprehend. 'You?'

'He's known as a fine singer.' Violet glanced at Jack, then looked down to hide her smile.

'Aye – and a dancer.'

'I've no use for that,' said the buyer. 'Now, haven't you somewhere to be, boy?' He took a step closer to Violet, but Jack moved nearer too, hemming the girl in.

'I really suggest you go and take a walk somewhere.'

'An excellent idea.' Jack dipped his head, deferential. 'Violet, would you like to join me?' But Violet seemed alarmed – her back pressed to the wall, both men impeding any means of escape. It irritated Jack how the other man's unseemly interest was hindering his own, because he knew – *knew* – that Violet liked him. She was spared having to answer, anyway, as someone shouldered their way between the two men: Isaac, reaching for his sister.

'Vi – will you come here a minute?'

'Aye, of course.'

When she had left the parlour, Jack turned back to the guest. 'I didn't catch your name.'

A vein stood proud in the man's forehead. 'Calder.'

'It's been a pleasure, Mr Calder. Now, I'm off to take a walk as you suggested – Miss Slora will surely be waiting for me.'

'She'd not dirty herself with a horseman.'

Jack drank back his whisky – two glasses in him now, and he could feel it in the way his feet were warm for once, and he didn't care if Slora saw him giving cheek to the prospective buyer. He winked and said, 'I've got many charms.'

Mr Calder smiled, though really it was nothing more than a showing of teeth. 'And I have this.' He reached into his breast pocket and brought out a small square box, edged in gilt. It looked wrong in his large hands, an indelicacy, as he flipped the lid open with his thumb. 'Now this – this is how you convince a woman to give you what you want.'

Jack allowed himself a glance – a slender gold chain hung with a diamond pendant the size of a screw-head, or a split pea, or whatever other graceless comparison a lad like Jack could make. He looked away and Mr Calder snapped the box shut. 'No contest, eh?'

In the kitchen, Jack took Donald's chair, closest to the range. He'd filched a bottle of Slora's whisky on his way out of the parlour and nursed a glass of it in his lap, tipping it back and refilling in time with the anger that pulsed through him. Usually, drink would rally him, the whisky diluting all his petty worries, the things that hurt. But this time Jack couldn't let it go, kept seeing in the cut glass the beauty of Mr Calder's diamond necklace. Jack was an idiot to think that his pointless charm could be a match for the dazzle of money.

After a time, the door opened and Jack sprang up, hoping it would be Violet, but Henry came in and took his usual chair. He looked taller in his good clothes, somehow – was probably taller than Jack now. His ma would always joke about it, say he'd be short like her, and Jack's long, lanky da would say, tightly – *he'll grow*.

'What are you doing in here?' Jack asked.

'I've come tae warn you. You need tae be careful, Jack – Slora'll go mad if he sees you trying to get in with Violet.'

'I dinnae care about Slora. I'll do what I like.'

'He'll hae your baws if—'

'For God's sake, that's an empty threat if ever I heard one.'

'It upset Isaac and all. He wants you to stay away from her.'

'If I'm nae feart of Slora I'm certainly nae feart of his wee boy.' It felt good to say it – Jack was tired of being told what to do. Done with that: the instructions and orders, the duties constantly bearing down on him. His brother Charlie telling him he couldn't go away, that he needed him – that their ma needed him. His brother had pleaded, even as Jack told him it was for the money, that if he could get a few good fees and move up quickly he'd come back and get them, help them make a fresh start. What Jack couldn't say was that if he saw, once more, his ma with a black eye, or his ma in a heap at the bottom of the stairs, he was worried about what he'd do to his da.

Henry moved his chair next to Jack, nudged him on the knee. 'What's got into you?'

'Eh?'

'It's just . . . you've changed. After that night.'

Jack groaned. Henry had tried to bring up the night of the ceremony several times, until he was told in no uncertain terms to shut the fuck up about it.

'You messed about with something and now it's changed you. You took his hand in yours. Is he real, Jack – the devil?'

'Course he's nae real.'

'But it's left a mark on you. I don't know, we were friends before. Then after that night, you treated me like dirt.' So that was the loon's real woe – how Jack had grown up and left him behind, suddenly had less in common with a sleekit wee boy who wouldn't join in with the sparring and the smoking and chasing after quines.

'It's nae my responsibility tae look after you.'

'No. But I looked after you when you needed it—'

'I never needed it.' Jack got up and stalked across the kitchen. He had put from his mind the moment in bed with Henry's arms round him, not sure what kind of a man it made him to have found quite as much comfort in it as he had.

When Henry spoke, his voice was quiet. 'There's a darkness come here, I can feel it. I have . . . thoughts. Terrible thoughts. Things I'm ashamed of. I lie in my bed at night and I—'

'Think about Violet? You needn't be ashamed by those thoughts.'

'Not about Violet.'

Jack looked at the boy, his stained cheeks. And he thought for a moment that he understood, clarity moving like a shadow across the wall. Henry and Isaac standing close in the parlour, a fleck of hay on Isaac's shirt that Henry carefully picked off, one fingertip inside his collar. But with another mouthful of whisky his thoughts became hazy and all that came instead was anger; resentment at being detained by Henry's nonsense when Mr Calder might be climbing the stairs, sneaking after Violet. Jack couldn't let it happen – had resolved that Slora's girl would be his. He set down his glass and headed for the door.

'Where are you going?' asked Henry.

'None of your business.'

'It's too dangerous to go looking for— stay here with me, Jack.'

But no, he didn't want to be told what to do. He wanted the opposite – to articulate his desire and find it answered. He wanted to be fanned, fed grapes, to have each foot rubbed by a separate maid. He wanted people to leap at his command as if he were a king or a laird, or even just some rich fucker from town who didn't buy things but *acquired* them – the world, flopping into his lap. And Jack remembered, then, something the rich man didn't have; thought of the Horseman's Word, and what it might be like if its supposed abilities were real. He hadn't used it yet; instead he kept it latched in his throat, proud of himself for being the sort of man who might have power and choose not to use it. But what was the point in that? He ought to find out if the word really could subdue a frisky pony, make her trot behind him good as a dog. And what about using it on a person? What if he whispered it and then asked Henry to get on his knees on the floor and lick his boots – would the loon do it? Would he do it gladly? Because that was the other thing – Jack could not be sure whether the word inspired willingness with it.

'Please, Jack,' said Henry, 'let's go outside, go back tae the chaumer.'

But Jack had opened the door. 'No, loon – I've spent far too much time with you.'

LIZZIE

She heard something. Lizzie turned her head where it was pressed into the cushion of the chaise, and the sound came again; a noise distinct from the flustered rustle of her dress, or the tune being bashed out on the piano down the hall. 'What was that?'

'What,' James's voice through his quick breath, 'was what?'

It happened again as the door scudded over the carpet, and Lizzie watched as a narrow band of light cut into the floor. 'James!' Her hands stilled at his back and he lifted his face from her neck.

'Christ.' His tone was resigned rather than panicked. James rolled off her, leaving Lizzie with her velvet dress bunched above her waist as a long black shadow entered the snug. She struggled to get up, scrabbling like a toppled beastie to rise off her back and pull her dress over her thighs as her mind filled with hurried pleas: please not my father, not my mother, please let it be Bridget, only her. Their visitor stood a moment until Lizzie, hating the silence, finally spoke. 'It's not what it looks like.'

A sharp laugh. 'Do you think me a fool? Put a light on.'

'Happy to oblige, Miss Calder.' James took a lighter from his pocket, brought it to a candle. His expression seemed almost one of amusement: a boy being a boy, caught, expecting a gentle scolding and to be sent on his way. He reached into his trousers to tuck his shirt in and readjust himself. 'Any further requests?'

'You have taken advantage of her,' said Jane, looking at Lizzie in her rumpled velvet, hair pulled from its pins.

James threw up his hands in mock outrage. 'Slander, Jane! It was rather led by Miss Brodie, as it happens.'

'Oh, come on.'

'Women are capable of it, you know.'

Jane coloured. 'Certainly, but particularly when they have been led on.'

James finally looked irritated. He took up his discarded jacket, slinging it over a shoulder and heading for the door. 'It's none of your business.'

Jane blocked his exit. 'How could you? She's barely more than a girl. You've . . . well, I should think she's in love with you.'

James wouldn't meet Lizzie's eye. He stood in front of Jane, expecting that she would move for him. When she didn't, he pushed past her and opened the door, then paused for a moment. 'I am not responsible for anyone else's emotions.'

Lizzie thought she detected something in his even tone – a shadow of regret, perhaps, that was enough to make her get up, rush after him. 'James, wait.'

In the hall, he turned to face her. 'Are you, then?'

'What?'

He frowned. 'In love with me?'

Lizzie supposed she was, for what else was love if not the knowledge that she would do anything to keep him? She thought of ardent lovers in novels, who'd dig up graves and haunt moors, throw themselves under horses. Somehow, though, it felt like a far more pitiful devotion to clutch his wrist and whisper, 'Yes.'

As James stood looking at her, muffled laughter erupted from the parlour. 'Well, apologies for that.' He extracted himself with a jerk of the arm and walked away.

Lizzie couldn't face the party again. She retreated to the snug, and when Jane saw her it was as though she had seen it all – the breath hitching in Lizzie's throat when James kissed her, the notebook under her pillow where she'd practised signing new initials, the trickling of something, now, down her thigh.

'Silly girl.' But Jane also sighed, made herself soft. 'Didn't I try to tell you?'

'Why did you say that? That I love him?'

'Don't you?'

'You've humiliated me.' Lizzie's voice teetered.

'Don't be ashamed.' Jane lifted a hand and swiped a tear from Lizzie's cheek in her own, practical way. 'I knew as soon as I saw him that he'd be trouble.'

'You don't know him.'

'I know his ilk,' said Jane.

'This is not what he wants . . . I'm the one he wants.' Even then, Lizzie wanted to believe it. For hadn't James looked her in the eye, and smothered her with earnest compliments, and said, only half an hour before, that she was heaven?

'Did he tell you that?'

'No, but . . . he feels something, he must . . .'

'Men will lead you on, Elizabeth. That is the way of it.'

'How would you know?'

'There are not many women in the world of business. I am surrounded by men.'

'That is not the same thing. Perhaps they have thought you intelligent, but you do not know what it means to be desired.'

Isn't there always a silence after a blow has been thrown? Lizzie liked the feeling. It felt good to wound, the victim unimportant, but it just so happened that Jane was there, and Jane stood and took it, a gloss in her eyes that made her look, for once, quite pretty. She took the other words, barbed and bitter and atrocious, until eventually she cut Lizzie off.

'Why is it me you blame? For trying to warn you? I only

showed you what you were too proud to see.' Jane managed, in her enduring dignity, to keep her voice low. 'Why is it me you blame?' And she stepped away, withdrawing – finally – her hand of consolation.

JACK

It was quiet upstairs. Jack had clattered up as though his feet were too big for the treads, clumsy with drink and desire. He went down the dim passageway, trying doors. The bedrooms were dark and empty, containing only the boxy forms of dressers and drawers, beds with their sheets tucked tightly at the corners. One room was Slora's and it was strange to see his things – the mundane humanity of a dressing gown on a hook. A sampler hung above the bed that his wife had stitched with a Proverb: When pride cometh, then cometh shame: but with the lowly is wisdom. Jack nearly laughed at how little heed Slora seemed to pay to that. He carried on down the landing, drawn on by want, yes, but also how good it felt to turn his back on Henry and Mr Calder and even the gang, everyone who thought they had the measure of him. To walk on, instead, towards the door that was opening ahead of him.

'Jack?' A voice like honey, his Violet. She said his name again and there was such pleasure in the hearing of it that way – not barked across the yard but whispered carefully, as if it were worth something. He reached the end of the corridor and stepped over the threshold into Violet's bedroom. He couldn't see her, to start with, and Jack wondered for a moment if he had imagined it, her sing-song voice, until she lit a lamp and was haloed by its light. 'You look very well tonight, Jack. Different from the others.'

The air was thick between them. Jack didn't dare breathe as Violet reached out to adjust the ribbon round his neck. The softness of her fingertips made him step back, away. 'There,' she said, 'you're straightened up.'

'Thank you.'

'Are you all right?'

'Aye.'

'Then come here.'

Jack had thought about how this moment might be – playing out fantasies in his head, late-night imaginings of things in this room, in the larder, in the hayloft. Yet as Violet reached for him, again he felt the urge to move away. Some dingy sense that Mr Calder was right and touching him might sully her, leave a mark on her creamy skin. But that skin was so warm – and who would Jack Nicol be if he were offered something so readily and did not take it?

Her coy smile. 'Do you want to kiss me?'

He did want that. Jack put his hands round Violet's waist, and after a time, the notion that he could have refused her seemed ludicrous. She cupped his chin in her palm to bring him closer and it made him hungrier still but – somehow – made him want to cry. He blinked hard and nudged Violet to sit down on the edge of her bed, liking the way she dropped easily into his arms. He felt for the buttons on her dress, slipped a finger between two of them to touch her bare skin. She giggled, nervous, but carried on kissing him. Jack undid a button, two, pushed his whole hand under the cloth. He would be able to tell Don and Tam about this, that he'd touched Slora's girl, make them sick with envy. Jack's other hand began to creep up Violet's leg – under a hem, over the silky run of a stocking, then again the shock of bare skin. Violet froze. She pulled back, her face still close, but there was something like panic in her eyes – though who could tell in so dark a room?

'It's all right.' Jack kept his hand where it was and tried to kiss her again, but it was not the same, something in her taut now, stricken.

'Jack, I . . .'

He knew she was slipping away from him, and so Jack leaned in, nudged her hair away with the tip of his nose. The two insistent syllables of his heartbeat as he opened his mouth at her ear. When he spoke she stiffened again, a tension flooding her body that he could feel in his.

'Stop,' Violet said, at the same time as his whisper.

And Jack – Jack said the Horseman's Word again.

'What?' She pulled away, smearing him off her lips with the back of her hand. 'What does that mean?' Violet stood now, hands twisting round her back to do the buttons up. She opened the door and the scant light from the landing spilled in – just enough for him to see the wide white swivel of her eyes like he had seen in any number of spooked mares.

Jack stayed in the bedroom. He was drunk, tasted acid in the back of his mouth, wanting to spew though he hadn't eaten anything; just sick of himself, probably. For a long while he did nothing, and then he balled his unbandaged hand into a fist with a mind to slam his knuckles against the furniture, wreck a good part of himself too. He was sweating, his breeks tight round his groin, something in him that needed to get out, so he took his screwed fist and pounded it against his forehead. He did it a few times, then finished the whole brainless business with a blow that caught the bridge of his nose. He sat on the floor for a moment, stunned, until he heard a noise. Another of his ma's stories: a tread on the stair, a monster coming, keep very still. The footsteps grew closer, moving down the passage towards Violet's room. The door opened like a mouth.

'Don't you have work to do, boy?'

Only through pride did Jack get up. Any man can find himself on the floor, but what separates him from other, lesser men is that he'll get back on his feet. The room swayed. Jack peeled his tongue off the roof of his mouth. 'I was spending time with Violet.'

Calder let out a bark of laughter. 'And how did you fare? Did you manage to persuade her?'

Jack couldn't bear to admit that the Horseman's Word hadn't worked, and that he'd been stupid enough to think it might. Worse still, that he had tried it in the first place. Had it been his own decision, free will? Or had the devil told him what to do? An imp on his shoulder who parted his lips and made him whisper the word in Violet's ear. If Henry asked him again – *Jack, is the devil real?* – he'd say aye, sure he is. I'm sure he is.

Calder began to laugh. He laughed all the while as someone else came up the stairs, moved down the landing, someone light-footed. Light from a lamp and the waning moon, caught in golden curls.

LIZZIE

Lizzie was on her knees in her bedroom, packing away the velvet dress, when the summons came: a swift tap on the door and no waiting until she answered. Bridget stepped into the room. 'Miss Elizabeth, your da wants to see you. He's in the snug.' The housekeeper did not meet her eye.

Downstairs, the hallway was too quiet. George Brodie was usually a man of noise: tapping his foot, whistling. When he sneezed it was a great operatic performance. The silence unsettled Lizzie, a rising fear in each step, not sure what it might mean. After she had left the snug that night she had been hopeful the events contained within might remain a secret. She could surely rely on James's discretion – it seemed as if everything that had happened between them had mattered so little to him it wasn't worth recounting. The way he had turned his back on Lizzie as though their romance were already forgotten. It was Jane's silence that was not a given – how could it be? Lizzie had refused Jane's comfort, seeking only to lay blame somewhere else, because holding it was burning her hands. She had curled up in bed the morning after and remembered the way her voice has risen, her cruelty, the words she had used. But as Lizzie entered the snug now, she was careful to convey none of this. It could be that her father's summons was to console her on James's betrothal. Perhaps he had only needed, first, to spend his own time in disappointment – that he would not be having an Esslemont for a son after all.

'Da. Bridget said you wanted to see me?'

George was sitting in his armchair. Usually he would be luxuriant, legs up and crossed at the ankle, soft leather slippers. But this evening he was hunched and troubled, and had no smile for his daughter. 'Did he force you into it?' He was trembling a little, his face almost tender. Lizzie recognized this for what it was: an offering. He had formed the story and was inviting her to take it as her own. But despite her faults, Lizzie Brodie was not a liar.

'No.'

George ran a palm over his head. He poured himself a drink, took a mouthful and rattled it from one cheek to the other before swallowing. 'You did it quite willingly, then?'

'Yes.'

There was a long moment of silence, in which Lizzie hoped that whatever wrath her father held might crest quickly, then dissipate. Perhaps she even hoped that he might console her, might understand – how she'd seen what she wanted and done everything she could to secure it. Was she not, in that way, her father's daughter?

'I can only hope that the Esslemonts don't find out. It will be embarrassing for me – for my position – if this comes out.' And of course, that was it: his judgement on the basis of how it might stain the good name of George Brodie. Hadn't he always been at his most adoring when it was the opposite, and she was admired? Be charming, my girl. Be game and sprightly, play your piano and spend my money on silk dresses that become you, for in the currency of beauty I can make my investment back twice over.

'Are you going to chastise James too?' Lizzie asked.

George sat upright. An edge of something sharp in the soft contours of his face. 'Oh yes, I'll ruin his engagement too – that will stand me in good stead for promotion. Think, for God's sake!' He massaged his temples with his fingers. 'Why, Lizzie? I had thought you were a good girl.'

'I did not realize one ill-considered act would place such judgement on my whole person, Da.'

'Ill-considered? That's putting it mildly! It is not just a mistake, but a sin, too. Although that is for God to judge, not me.' This an afterthought, an ought-to-say – it was always the more earthly opinions that George performed for. Lizzie thought of James, going about his evening, oblivious to the great fat mark of damnation against his name. Perhaps it did not apply to him. Thinking about him crushed her insolence, and all she wanted was to be comforted. She sat on the pouffe by her father's feet, hoping he might fold her in his arms as he had when she was a child.

'I thought he might marry me . . .'

Her father did soften, his voice quiet. 'We are not good enough for the likes of them.' He shook his head, his anger spent. 'If people find out . . . there's things they'll call you, Lizzie.'

She knew this; had heard the names spat in parlours by women made crude by wine, or those in kirk, less vulgar, but the sentiment the same.

'Aye,' said George, standing, 'there will be consequences.'

It had been easy to forget the very notion of these. When she was with James, Lizzie had felt as if she held the world in her hand, untouched by anything as petty as the opinions of other people. She could imagine a life where all the things she wanted – love, wealth, pleasure – were ceaseless. But that was a fallacy, of course – she had been made stupid by James's admiration, so pinioned in the bright light of his gaze that she had become willingly blind to what was happening beyond it.

Lizzie watched her father leave the room, closing the door quietly behind him so that once again she was left in the snug, chastened and alone.

PART FOUR

ROUND MARTINMAS

November 1915

JOHNNY

It is past noon by the time he wakes. Johnny had got home from the inn the previous night and looked in the sideboard and his kist for the last dregs left in a few cloudy bottles, and then he had drunk until his brain could barely latch on to a thought, let alone worry about anything. He had got into bed with his hand wrapped round a final dram, sucking the whisky down his throat before closing his eyes. Sleep was oblivion. Sleep was oblivion, and even when he had woken in the early morning he was still too pished for fear, his ears ringing, and he had turned on his side and thought of Lizzie. Johnny had told himself a tale of Hallowe'en night: a narrative only of pleasure in how she had held his face in her hands and said his name – *John* – and it was like casting aside all the versions of him that had come before. He had made up his own story, after that. Lain stiff with concentration and taken himself in hand and brought his relief quickly, a vicious hunger. And he had allowed himself, after, body slack and sweating, to imagine rolling over and finding her there – the way she would bring her face close, and kiss him, and tell him she adored him. The way, in all his dreams and thoughts and fantasies, she would tell him he was worth something. That is what Johnny loves about stories – they needn't be true.

He sits up. Pain in his temples and the crown of his head,

heartburn throwing fire up his throat. The light is thin and white through the curtains and Johnny realizes it's the middle of the day, and he's still in bed, wasting time. He throws off the sheets and stands, then makes his way to the window and draws the curtains back. The land is changed – the dyke a formless hump, tree branches fattened. Insistent snow, the type he's seen before in all his Cabrach winters, that smothers and drifts, thwarts and stymies, drives men to despair. He will go while he still can.

Johnny dresses and splashes icy water on cold cheeks. In the mirror he is wan and blotchy, veins in his neck bulging as he scratches a razor down, quick of the blade at his throat and he nicks it, jerks forward to get the blood in the basin.

He goes, sure what he must do now: get to Lizzie before Henry can. He will tell her the truth, all of it, and he'll atone for Hallowe'en night, then he'll tell her – probably – that he loves her. It is as simple as that, and Johnny could nearly laugh as he crests the hill, on his way. The snow is falling heavily, and he didn't bring a scarf or hat, and his boots are more hole than leather, but somehow it feels more gallant to go like this, disregarding his physical comfort for the sake of love.

Johnny reaches the fork in the road – one way to Blackwater, the other to Brawlands. He stops and searches through the falling snow for any sign of Henry. The farm is indistinct, but he can tell the barn door's open and smoke is rising from the chimney, and there are figures trudging about the yard. He didn't check the time before he set out, but it's light enough to know that Henry will still be at work, detained for a while yet.

Johnny gives himself a moment's rest. He's at the crashing point of his hangover where the edges of the world have sharpened again and he realizes he's thirsty – can't remember the last time he had a glass of water. He tips his head back, opens his mouth and lets a few snowflakes fall in – but a drop of wet on the tongue isn't enough to sate a thirsty man. Johnny decides he'll go down to the burn; it'll be awful on his hands but he needs to drink. The snow is deeper on the river's banks and Johnny sinks up to his ankles, tottering forward, until he is close enough to crouch and cup his hands and plunge them into the water. He drinks like something desperate, the cold making him gasp and lose his balance, one foot plunging into the rush of the burn. Johnny collapses back on to the bank and it's as if his whole body has turned to stone, petrified with the shock of it, and all he can manage to do is draw up his knee to his chest and get the sopping boot and sock off, clasping his foot in his aching red hands. He has to concede, then, that what he'd thought was heroism is looking increasingly like debasement.

The blizzard comes like a dropped veil. Johnny can't see through it, and he supposes he'd be as well just staying there and letting the snow cover him. Maybe he'll be found in a few days with the tears on his face frozen to diamonds – the closest he'll ever get to one. The booze is leaving his blood, and without its cosseting he can't stop the thoughts creeping in. Last night, hauling Henry to his feet, the loon with flailing arms and bandaged hands. Hallowe'en, when he'd left Lizzie bewildered on the floor as he'd gathered his things and fled into the night. He has to justify his reaction to her – the abject fear at recognizing the man in the photograph. Calder, same hands and eyes; Calder, who'd smirked at him all those years ago when Johnny was nothing but cocksure and foolish, who'd thought he was entitled to take whatever he wanted.

Johnny gets up on his hands and knees, lets the dizziness wash over him. He's tempted to lie down again but doesn't, glad for once for the pride that makes him stand up, get his sock and boot back on. There is only so much time that a man will lie with the snow soaking through his breeks, romanticizing his misery. He tries to orient himself, finds the snow has thinned enough to show him the flat grey face of Blackwater, some way distant on the other side of the burn. It means the road is behind him, and he doesn't have too far to go. And then there will be Lizzie, and Johnny will explain himself, and then he won't have to be alone any more. Is that what he thinks? That somehow there might be something noble in the purity of his feelings that makes the fact of her husband inconsequential?

And Johnny finds, then, some impetus – maybe the same thing that's always kept him moving, traipsing from place to place to see if it's finally what he's been looking for. The possibility that, if she loves him too, it might be the same as redemption.

LIZZIE

Lizzie is huddled on the chaise in the parlour, the cold her only company. When William was here, the house was warmer – he liked to keep his study fuggy, would prod the dining-room fire with the blackened end of a poker before sitting down to his meal. He had instructed Miss Gow to ensure their peat supplies were replete, had coal delivered thrice-annually, was possessed of stout boots that he bought from town. Lizzie must concede to the Reverend that perhaps she has been ungrateful to her husband, refused to acknowledge the sensible qualities that others say he possesses in abundance.

Outside, the blizzard has diminished, and Lizzie can see as far as the yews, their boughs drooping under the weight of the snow. All is white, and so it is by simple contrast that she notices something dark moving through the trees. Lizzie will not deny the way hope flutters in her chest, and it is sweet and insistent enough that she forgets, for a moment, that she is angry with Johnny. She rushes to the window and tries to discern the figure through the confusion of snow and branch. Whoever is there is dressed in black and is narrow-shouldered, and for a moment she thinks of the foolish notions of the men – that the bog woman has clambered from her wrapping and is walking amongst them. Lizzie wonders how she'd move, how she'd got up the braes in the first place – whether she followed the procession that had condemned her, standing tall with jutted chin, or if she was shackled and rattling, or dead already. She's losing hope of ever knowing.

It is not the bog woman, of course. And it is not the man she wants it to be – no colour at the throat. Lizzie drops back from the window, suddenly keen not to be seen, because she is unsure, now, whether this is someone she wants in her house.

The doorbell tolls. A deep bellow through Blackwater, rattling the silverware in the cabinet and the framed men. Once more Lizzie hesitates – there is no one she wants to see but Johnny – but she goes. When she opens the door it takes her a moment to recognize the figure, wrapped in a dark coat – the lad from Brawlands. Henry removes his hat, stands on the doorstep with it held before him. 'I'm sorry tae disturb you.'

Lizzie sees his hands, then – bound in thick bandages, shaking with cold. 'What's happened, are you all right?'

'I'm fine. My apologies, Mistress Calder, I didnae mean any alarm.'

She opens the door a little wider. 'Whatever it is, I suppose you'd better come in.' She leads him into the parlour, where he declines tea, instead perching on the edge of the armchair nearest the hearth. He stretches his hands towards the warmth, saying nothing.

'I didn't imagine I'd find you at the door,' Lizzie says, to prompt him.

There is a chill, then, in the way he regards her. 'I'm sorry if I wisnae what you were hoping for.'

'It's just unexpected, that's all. What happened to your hands?'

'I fell on the bonfire at Hallowe'en and burnt them.' This without embellishment, a statement of fact, as though he were speaking to a policeman. Possibly he is only unsurprised at the inevitability of it all. Lizzie remembers that night, the running men and Henry's vicious glee as he threw the effigy around the yard, the sense in the air of hurtling towards something.

'And they're bad?'

'They're getting better, Maggie says. But the first couple of days were agony. I was sick with the pain, tossing and turning with a fever. I . . . someone spoke to me, in the night. I couldnae tell if it was real or not, or if it was a woman or a man, but then I . . . I think it was God, talking to me.' Henry flushes. 'He said I should always do what I think is right, and so, well, that's why I'm here.' He bites his lip, on some precipice. 'I thought it wisnae my business, you and Johnny Nicol. I watched you together and it made me angry. I told myself just to leave it, but the Reverend is right. When we see sin, it is our duty to root it out.'

He is quiet for a moment. Lizzie feels the chastisement but somehow without irritation, because the lad looks tormented.

'I remembered it all,' Henry goes on, 'when I came here and saw Johnny again. I thought I'd forgotten, but I cannae escape him. And then that thing came up fae the bog with its hand scarred like his . . .' He shakes his head. 'Och, maybe I shouldnae tell you. Maybe it's up to you tae work out who Johnny Nicol really is.'

Lizzie thinks of Johnny, and how to her he has shown kindness, care – sincere, or so she thought. But she also considers the brother who refuses to see him, the judgement of Jane and the Reverend, the cold way some had looked at him in the kirkyard these few weeks past; everything she has ignored because it has suited her to. 'Tell me,' she says.

'He tried tae kill a man.' Henry pauses, checking for Lizzie's reaction before hurrying on. 'He was angry because he liked a girl but so did another man, who was buying the farm. And Johnny thought he could still have her – he's the proudest person I've ever known.'

Lizzie's first inclination is to laugh at the absurdity of the tale – surely just another version of The Ballad of John Nicol, the man with his own folklore, who'd turned up in the Cabrach one summer's day with barely more than the ribbon round his neck. The man who goes wandering, comes back to tell you whatever you want to hear. An entirely dishonourable man, perhaps, but surely not a violent one?

'I don't know why you're telling me this, Henry, but I'd suggest you ought not to believe everything you hear.'

'It's true. This girl, her brother told Johnny tae stay away from her. But Johnny got him on the ground and he punched and punched until his hands were soaked in blood. He beat Isaac's face tae mince and then—'

'Oh, hush – what a tale.'

'Then he put his hands round his throat and pressed until Isaac stopped moving. Please, Mistress Calder, it's all true.'

'Who told you this?' Lizzie asks, trying to ignore the doubt that hooks a finger between her ribs.

'I was there. We worked together, ten years past. He was my best friend.'

'But—' The realization is like falling; the moment of the drop, the knowledge that the landing will hurt. 'He told me he didn't know you.'

'That man will say whatever he needs tae get what he wants.'

Lizzie gets up, unable to be still. 'Did you see it yourself? Who else was there?'

'Another man saw it – the one who liked the same girl. He was a businessman, a man of good standing. A good man.' Henry gets up and follows Lizzie across the parlour. 'He strangled Isaac with his bare hands. It was like something had taken hold of him, that night – it chilled me tae the bone. I'd never seen Jack like that before.'

'Jack?'

'That's who he was back then. He wants to hide it – that's why he's angry with me, because I remind him.'

'I wondered why he always seemed so short with you.'

'He wants me tae be scared so that I winnae talk. But I have tae.'

The next question buds on Lizzie's tongue. 'And did he . . . did he die, this Isaac?'

There is a shade of disgust in Henry's expression. 'That's nae the point. Jack wanted him tae.'

'But he didn't die?'

To tell her, Henry gathers himself up. 'No. But he wisnae the same when he woke up. Just this dumb look on his face, like he was looking straight through you. Had tae have his ma wash and toilet him. She wept over him every day, and sometimes I went and spoke tae him, too, though he couldnae answer me. Far as I know, Isaac never spoke again.'

Lizzie closes her eyes a moment. 'I don't know what to believe.'

'Why would I lie?' Henry is exasperated, but he comes to stand before her and asks the same question again, softly, something like pity in his voice. And Lizzie can think of no reason – this good and pious ploughman who only seeks, as the Reverend does, to save her from what she has been too blind to see. Who surely has nothing to gain from this revelation other than the simple satisfaction of honesty. He is not like Johnny and all his concealments – the jaunty satin at his throat that detracts from his lying mouth; the songs and stories – any but his own.

They jump as the bell goes again.

'Do you want me tae get it?' Henry asks, and Lizzie shakes her head because she knows who it will be, and sure enough when she opens the door he is there on the step, the snow melting on his skin: Johnny come too lately. Unkempt, as though he has tried to better himself but not quite managed – hair falling over one eye, the reek of whisky under cheap cologne. Still, for a moment Lizzie wants to pull him indoors. Wants to take off his wet clothes and lay him on the chaise, press her heat into his chest, swaddle him in blankets. She has imagined this moment, these past few nights – his apology would be simple and they would laugh at how frightened he'd been of being discovered with her. They would continue where they had stopped on Hallowe'en night, and afterwards she would lie in his arms and tell him how his fleeing had roused some old misery in her – of seeing a man she loved, back turned, leaving.

'Johnny.'

His smile is strained. 'What's wrong?'

Lizzie moves aside so that Henry, lingering behind her, can step into the doorway. Johnny presses his eyes closed.

'Has he told you?'

'Aye,' Henry says, 'I have.'

'What did he say?' Johnny's tone as it was on Hallowe'en night, simmering with something vengeful as he taunted Henry across the kitchen table. Lizzie searches his face in what little light is left, seeking some justification that is as much for herself as it is for Johnny, for all of this seems like her punishment, too, comeuppance for a woman who would not pay heed. She watches the clench of Johnny's neck, the stiffened tendons, a tension that travels up to his jaw. His eyes, admired before in soft and gorgeous firelight, are shaded now with a violence that comes and then goes, whip-quick. A second, no more – but she saw it.

'He said you tried to kill a man.'

'Do you believe him?' Johnny asks.

'He has never lied to me – not like you have. You said you didn't know Henry.'

Johnny dips his head.

'And you . . . you left me, with no explanation. Yet somehow everyone knew you'd been in my house, presumably because you went down to the inn and told them.'

He looks up at her. 'I didnae say a word.'

'Fine, but what about the rest?' Lizzie looks at Johnny's hands, held out in front of him. So cold, red across the palms. He raises one and she waits for it to crack Henry, finds herself surprised when it is not like that, instead just the uncaring swipe of air. Pitiful man – she can see the holes in his boots, and the way he's tied his neckerchief to try to conceal the razor nick in his throat. This last, out of everything, makes her want to cry – not for him but herself, and the shame of wanting someone who everyone else could see was a dud.

'What do you want me tae say?' Johnny asks. 'That I'm nae a bad man? Well I can do, if it helps, but I'm nae sure you'll believe me.' He laughs then, short and cruel. 'Look after yourself, aye?'

He is about to go when Lizzie asks him to stop. 'You will answer this,' she says. 'Did you ever care about the bog woman?'

His shoulders drop. 'Of course I cared.'

'Yet when I asked you to write to your brother, you refused.'

Johnny looks away, out over the braes to the thin sunset, even now acting like it's all a story to be told later, he the hero gazing wistfully at the horizon.

'I wrote to him myself, you know. Would you like to know what he said?'

His head snaps round. He is angry, Lizzie thinks, and she tips her chin in defiance, waiting to be admonished. But Johnny only turns again and canters down Blackwater's steps into the snow.

Lizzie calls out after him – ragged, deploring, the same question twice more. But Johnny doesn't turn; he isn't going to fight for her.

JOHNNY

On Johnny walks, the yews behind him folding over Blackwater. He goes with purpose, irritated at the way his squeaking boots make him ridiculous, thinking to stop at the fork in the road and wait for Henry there. He knows the loon is following behind, panting to catch up, but what Johnny doesn't know is exactly what Henry told Lizzie – how lurid and horrific he made it and whether, giddy off power, he was moved to exaggerate. It doesn't matter, probably – whatever he told her, it was enough.

In the end, Johnny is not long off the Blackwater track when he decides to stop. He turns and calls out through the dusk: 'You got an explanation, then, loon?' Johnny's voice seems too loud, and he can imagine everything in the Cabrach turning to look – a cat peeling an eye open, a spider pausing mid-scurry. It should stop him, this sense of being observed, but he can't find it in himself to care.

Henry stops. 'I'm sorry.'

'Sorry? Is that it?' Johnny lurches towards the loon and Henry stands rigid, eyes startling bright in the twilight. 'Well?'

'I can offer no more or less.'

Johnny rolls his eyes at the loon and his riddling words. No doubt he'll start up with his talk again – his darkness and his demons. They are a few paces apart, Henry's arms by his side, his lips trembling, but it's as if he thinks he's deserving of whatever comes next because he doesn't flinch as Johnny comes nearer.

'What did you tell her?'

'That you strangled him.'

'Loon, you werenae even there.'

'But that's what I was told.'

Johnny reaches Henry. He doesn't know how he'll do it; will instead give himself over to the rage, see what happens when he prods that old, neglected beast. Could he really? A simple vengeance, tale as old as time – knocking a man down, blood on snow, leaving him half dead in a ditch for the cold to pick at. There is always a way for men to justify these things – crimes of passion, the red mist. 'And you believe everything you're told, aye?'

'They stated it as fact – Slora and the grieve and the others. I was told nae tae ask questions, and I didnae.'

'Too scared tae?' Johnny flexes his fingers, tells himself to do it. Pauses when the look on Henry's face changes and the loon draws his body up, makes himself a match.

'There's many things I am, Johnny, but I'm nae a coward.' Henry meets his eye. 'I saw how you'd changed. Truth be told, it didnae seem such a stretch tae believe them.'

It wounds, this. Johnny roots his feet on the ground, bracing against the sense that a blow has already been thrown, square at his heart.

'And it felt like being betrayed,' says Henry. 'I felt so stupid.'

'Loon, it wisnae me.' Johnny is sure of it. That morning, as he'd shaved and dressed and set out, he'd dredged up the memories. He'd brought them out into the light and had a good look: Violet and her silky dress, Isaac's words that had scraped so close to the bone. Blood on Jack's knuckles and how it had felt to give himself over to something. Waking fully dressed, boozed, shot with dreadful clarity. The keening that came on the watery dawn – *my brother, my brother* – and a pooling mauve bruise on a soft young neck. He'd looked at them all and found them ugly, yes, but found, too, that he could just about be absolved.

'But you were there,' says Henry. 'And folks always say, don't they – there's nae smoke without fire.'

Johnny's ma used to say this, and a hundred other clichés he'd thought of as wisdom. She used to say you're a long time dead, and a good tale never tires in the telling, and the apple never falls far from the tree. He didn't like that one, the way it made him think of the father he refused to be like – and he wasn't, he isn't.

'Henry, I swear – it wisnae me.'

The other man looks up. And Johnny sees his gaping want – to be told a different story, to trust in it. 'Do you promise me?' he whispers.

'I promise you.'

Henry sighs, a great heavy thing, like it's been building in his chest for years. 'Maybe I always knew it wisnae – in my heart of hearts.'

'Did you? Really?'

'Aye, I think so.'

Johnny hesitates to ask why, a sense that it will pain him in a different way, but he does.

'Because I know who you really are, my friend,' Henry replies. 'You're gentle.'

Johnny finds, in his exhalation, a relinquishment of everything: the last crumbs of half-hearted fury, the need to defend himself. He is flayed – pink and soft and skinless – the way it is when someone sees you, calls you something you'd been too scared to claim.

'But I told Lizzie anyway, and I shouldn't have and I'm sorry – for what it's worth.'

'It's done now.' Johnny makes as if to turn and be on his way again, reluctant to let Henry see his face, the tears threatening to spill. But he can't help but look at the loon – still there, night settling behind him. Johnny will make his manner soft, summon all he has to ask without accusation or animosity, finds that when he tries, it is easy. 'So why did you tell her?'

Henry manages something like a smile. 'I just . . . I suppose I wanted you tae know what it feels like tae lose something that matters to you.'

Above them, a white sickle of moon has slipped out from behind the snow-clouds. Johnny is exhausted, soaked to the skin, but wants, finally, to speak of things. He takes Henry by the wrist and they stand with their faces close as they did back then – still the same loon with the soft hair on his lip and the eyes that might be blue or green, might change as the light does. 'Did you love him? Isaac?'

'Och,' says Henry, waving his free hand, 'it was never really him.'

The breath hurts in Johnny's lungs, the sharp clarity of the freezing air. He takes Henry's hand in his, such as he can with the palmful of bandage – because Johnny knows, and he understands: how it is to be so ashamed of what you are that you'll do anything – lie, run, break a few hearts – to conceal it.

'I thought you were long gone,' says Henry, 'and then I came here and found you again, and it was like everything I thought I'd buried came back. I tried nae tae think about it, but that didnae work. And then I tried tae blame someone else – it was easier tae think that someone was putting these feelings in me and it wisnae my fault. I did the same back then. I thought you'd let the devil in, because those thoughts that made me so ashamed, well, they came every time I saw you.'

'Henry—'

'No, let me say it. I thought if I put a stop tae one sin it might wipe my own slate clean, but it turns out it disnae work like that. So if I'm tae be honest, I told her because it hurts tae see you with her. Because I have loved someone, Johnny. I still do.'

When Johnny realizes, through the falling darkness, that Henry is crying too, he pulls the loon into his arms. It is strange to do it like this with a man – not like the hasty embraces with Rab, or the lads who'll bang a fist hard into his back – but instead to be still and tender, to feel it deep in his chest.

'Anyway,' says Henry, pulling away, 'I hope you can sort it.'

Johnny watches Henry walk off into the snow – past him, back home, where Johnny hopes he'll lie warm in his chaumer and feel at least the austere pleasure of setting down a burden. As for himself, Johnny doesn't think he can sort it – Lizzie won't believe him. She's heard too much of what he's done, who he is – rogue, rake, liar, ruffian – it hardly seems a stretch that she might believe him capable of more. God only knows what his brother wrote, Charlie who never forgave him for leaving that small house with its Firth damp in the walls, for not being there to protect their ma. Johnny would be furious that Lizzie wrote to him, if only he had the energy. Besides, all of it's his own fault – he has let the story of his life be written by too many hands, each constructing him differently. Here is the babby who came out to winks and nudges, so very different to his da. Here is the lad who wasn't clever like his brother. Here is Jack who went to toil, appeased men with his foul songs – the very same loon who never really had the stomach for all that. Here is Johnny, a glint in his eye and a hand round his dram, who folks crowd to listen to. Here is John, who no one hears. Other men, men like William Calder, can toss coin at a reputation – the money to conceal, to scrub clean, to crown them in glory. John Nicol has nothing but his quarterly traipse to kirk to pray for his soul, his half-arsed promises to try harder.

He looks over his shoulder – that great house, shutters closed now. He had walked away with grace at least, so she may yet think of him as dignified – and he'll take that, it'll do. Johnny straightens the knot at his throat and carries on down the road. The comfort in repetition, because all he's ever done is run.

LIZZIE

Raw out, but the air is dry and still as Lizzie turns off the Blackwater track. The Sabbath has passed and the bog woman remains in the hayloft, since her grave was filled with snow. But now it is receding, and Lizzie has found no other clue that might delay her burial. She wants to see the woman once more, just in case, and so Lizzie has risen from her bed and put her coat on – small things that have felt, these past days, almost insurmountable.

When she reaches the fork in the road, Lizzie pauses. She could take the other way, go off down the old droving road to Johnny's, to offer him forgiveness. It's true, she supposes, that no one here is unblemished by transgression and defect, the capacity for cruelty. But Johnny's sins are too great. Lizzie goes, as intended, to Brawlands.

In the hayloft, Lizzie kneels by the packaged body. It appears not to have been disturbed again – the hessian neat, knots tight. She undoes the cord that secures the shroud round the neck, just enough to show the woman's face. And here she is, asleep for now, with her mouth that might be smiling or sneering – that mutable expression that means whatever you want it to. Lizzie knows she is not wicked, despite what people say; that it is not this poor soul's fault that the weather was ill and good fortune scant, that things have been lost – crops and babbies and the wits of boy soldiers. She lays a hand on the place where the woman's heart would be, and wonders if, inside the darkened shell of her, it is still there, red and vital. Lizzie considers what her own is like, for isn't it true that things untended will degrade, as a house with no fire will rot? She had only wanted to know, on Hallowe'en night, what it might feel like to be held by someone who loved her. And perhaps it was pride that encouraged the certainty that he did – that same old swell, the pleasure of being admired – or else it was the look on Johnny's face, a look that spoke of goodness, or at least an attempt at it.

Later, Lizzie gets back on the road. The afternoon slips to gloaming and she should return home quickly, to light her lamps and sit alone. By the crossroads she sees someone up ahead on the track, coming towards her – the ploughman from the Stuarts' ceilidh, who'd told the tale of Jimmy Weir. When they meet, he makes to stride straight past her, but Lizzie calls out. 'Am I not even worthy of a hello?'

He stops. 'I didnae think you'd recognize me.'

'Hallowe'en was not so very long ago.'

The lad removes his hat. 'No, but you'd other people you were looking at that night.'

'Aye, well. I've been chastised enough for that.'

'None of my business, of course. Probably for the best you didnae stay tae see Henry's accident – the way the loon screamed, my God. But then, Alex says he's prone tae exaggeration.'

'They're getting better now, he said, his hands.'

'Glad tae hear it. Anyway, good evening tae you.' His cap back on, a move to go.

'Wait. Jimmy, how is he?' It has troubled Lizzie, their broken soldier – how he was brought back wide-eyed and gibbering in the deluge of September, when their nerves were already as frayed as old rope from the rain and the spreading talk of the devil's woman from the bog. The way he had been at kirk and the fear that sent him to the manse, surely stoked further by the Reverend's true belief that Hell burns just beneath the grassy pastures, indistinct from peat.

The lad sighs. 'They found him dead, couple of days back.'

For a moment, Lizzie tries to square it. This is a place of death – of scratching by on barren soil, of trees with no leaves, diseased beasts and old, old men – but boys of eighteen should not be lost. 'I'm sorry. How did he go?'

The lad's countenance shifts as he folds his arms over his chest, meets her eye. 'What I'll say, Mistress Calder, is it's a great travesty that he'll nae be buried in the kirkyard when that creature has a space cut for her there.'

'You mean—'

'Aye. Done himself in.' He lifts a hand and places it round his neck. 'A length of rope like this.' He presses down, knuckles whitening from the strength in them, needed as it is for his labours, for there is not much use in a lad without a good grip on scythe or reins. He raises the other hand, cheeks going red, an awful burble from his throat and this is when – only when – he presses with the strength of both his hands.

Lizzie sees it then. Clarity like a gift, so sudden it makes her gasp, makes her pick up her knees and break into a run. The wind propels her back to Blackwater, and above her the birds sing. A peewit's chaos call, at first like a girl's giggle, then the gleeful cackle of some garrulous old witch. And Lizzie herself could laugh at how obvious it is: Johnny with his wrecked hand, a poor young lad hardly capable of damaging another.

If not Johnny, then who? Lizzie picks over Henry's tale, trying to find some hole in it, its characters: Johnny and a pretty girl, a farmer with land to sell. And she remembers now another one, just offstage – a rich man who wanted it all.

It is without alarm, the coalescing of her theory. Henry and Johnny working up Nairn way, Johnny posturing for a girl's attention against a wealthy man who wanted to buy the farm. William's business before they married, raking funds together for a sale that fell through – hard cash that was paid anyway, to forgive a grave insult. Johnny in the parlour on Hallowe'en night: I knew a Calder once. Johnny later, fleeing shortly after the wedding photo had fallen and a Calder – the same one, surely – had looked straight back at him.

Lizzie goes up to William's study, stands a moment on the threshold. She did this in the days of new marriage, appearing in the doorway with a drink on a silver tray: something of an offering. William would suffer her to place her hands on his shoulders, knead with hard fingertips. It was an affront – she in a gauzy nightgown, the skim of it over her breasts, and he could have tipped back, succumbed. The last time she'd tried he'd wrenched himself away, sent the whisky flying – said something about what a fucking penance it was, being stuck out here with her. And it hurt, it did – it does. Her punishment, and his too: a house on barren braes, a wife he'd never love.

The study will be stripped of obvious evidence – Jane will have seen to that. The desk is already empty of correspondence, save the note from James. Lizzie picks it up and tears it cleanly down the middle, satisfied at least that her old friend had served a purpose. She paces the room, toeing for loose floorboards, sure that the Calder vigilance must have slipped somewhere. Delicacy won't do it – she will need to take the books from the shelves and the pictures off the walls, and lift the rugs, and split the seams of his housecoat. She does it all gladly, tearing the pictures from their frames only to find nothing behind but board and wood. Lizzie pauses, breathing heavily, her reflection captured in the shining blade of William's letter-opener. She digs in the chest of the grandfather clock, tears the cushions from her husband's armchair, and still there is nothing, and nowhere left to look.

Lizzie stops, exhausted by it all. Perhaps she is deluded, reaching for explanations to absolve Johnny. She sees, suddenly, how foolish she must look – standing in the middle of the wrecked study with broken glass and a library of splayed books at her feet. From above the hearth the mounted stag regards her, though if he forms any judgement, Lizzie cannot tell. The creature has been there since before the wedding, the spoil of a hunting trip when William was a younger man. She has heard him tell the story many times, in a familiar proud cadence – the beast felled by a single shot clean through the heart, then dragged back to Blackwater for some old cook to butcher. William, of course, would not have dirtied his hands. She imagines those hands slick with blood – not a stretch at all to picture it, or those same hands round a neck. She can see them afterwards, dipped in holy water and made clean. He has washed himself again and again – in cahoots with the Reverend, funds for poor widows, the bestowing of riches that dazzle brightly enough to restore a reputation.

There is one other place to look – in fact, Lizzie wonders why she hasn't done so already. The study has always seemed like the heart of him, William a spider in the centre of a web, surrounded by his books and papers, words and deeds. But beyond all that vigilance there is still a man who must sleep.

She goes to his bedroom. At first it seems like there is nothing the room can offer her – it is painfully tidy, the bed stripped back to a smooth white sheet. But on the dresser there is a tin of pomade, and the bed holds the indentation of his body on one side, the other half of the mattress flat and sprung. Lizzie sits there and wonders if William too had imagined a different life – had knelt on the carpet and asked God for it, then waited for slumber under the cold sheets. Idly, she opens the drawer of the bedside table. It is cluttered with handkerchiefs, tinctures for coughs and sleeping, a tiny vial of laudanum, unopened. There are unpaired socks and an old bow tie with a broken clasp, a tortoiseshell comb with half the teeth gone. Here is the William whose order has slipped. Lizzie rifles through it all and withdraws a small square box, edged in faded gilt. When she opens it, she gasps – cannot help but take it out and swing it like a pendulum before the light: a fine gold chain with a diamond pendant. Never has William given her anything like this – it is surely a gift for a woman who perhaps refused it, and for a moment Lizzie pities her husband and his thinning hair and slumping mattress and this one disordered drawer. She knows about rejection – can see how it might have left him wretched as a Cabrach January. But isn't the necklace also the sort of gift a wealthy man might present to a woman of slimmer means, so flashy and overwhelming that she would surely be obliged to offer something of her own in return?

Underneath the small items in the drawer, there is something larger – the burgundy leather of a ledger like the ones Lizzie had seen in his desk drawer. She takes it out, thumbs through the pages that are powdery with age, the top margin printed with the date '1905'. There are crowded columns of figures – money given, then taken; a great deal more lodged in the latter. William has listed his life in pounds and shillings – money expended on grand meals and bets on horses, a mighty sum as deposit for the Richmond Hotel. He has gathered the rents for his farms, the crofts stuffed with those who worked for him at places that sound like misery – Cauldbraes, Rainybanks, The Ends. Amongst this bountiful harvesting, at the bottom of the page he has listed a debit. The handwriting is slim, as though even William has been chastened into smallness:

£500 to T. Slora of Windyhillock Farm. A settlement.

Lizzie turns the paper over. A pause – like savouring the end of a storybook, taking a moment before reading the final lines, to be satisfied with who is the hero and who the villain. At the top of the page there is another payment. Lizzie reads it and closes her eyes – an expectation, fear, that when she looks again it will have been her imagination, seeing again only what she wants to see. But here it is, her vindication:

£50 to J. Nicol, formerly of Windyhillock Farm. For silence.

November 1905

JACK

Mr Calder stopped laughing as the figure entered Violet's bedroom. Not the girl but her brother, and he was seventeen but held himself like a man, with a composure Jack had never noticed before. 'What are you doing in here? You've terrified my sister.' Isaac's voice was quiet, yet he did not seem timid, and it struck Jack as possible that gentleness and weakness are not the same thing. 'I told her to stay away from you.'

'You heard him,' Mr Calder looked at Jack and inclined his head towards the door, 'off with you.'

But Jack couldn't let it go. 'She likes me, she told me.' It was all he wanted – all of it – this one good thing.

'Then why have you made her cry?' Isaac said. 'She doesn't like either of you, you're ... brutes.'

The word punched at Jack. Some part of him found it reasonable, if he was honest, but that was quickly pushed away. Mr Calder looked Isaac up and down. 'Who the hell are you to speak to me like that?' Something in the rich man's demeanour suggested consequences for the disrespect, and Jack saw the moment Isaac began to shrink away, his courage dissipating. And maybe Jack was always keen to align himself with the stronger side – hadn't he seen, in his few fees, what happened to the lads who didn't? He never wanted to be one of them, made a bucket for everyone's frustrations to be kicked around the yard. And so he let the anger come – the posturing anger of dented pride, sneering and strutting, filling him up. His body, animal, so that when the first person moved, he was ready.

Men's bodies pitched together in the dark of a girl's bedroom. They grappled, knocking heads and chests and knees, until they fell to the floor. Men rolling and grunting, a shot of spit landing squarely on Jack's chin, and without thinking he licked it up. Calder snarling. Isaac saying no, stop, no, his voice a squeal that flattened as the first fist landed in his face, and then the sound became thick and burbling as that face was caved in – nose at the wrong angle, teeth wedged in tongue.

In the chaos, Jack's wrecked hand was knocked. Pain surged, blackening his vision, and he had to take a moment. Wet on his palms, the taste of metal like the bits he forced between his horses' jaws. The spent body of a lad underneath him, spluttering blood. Jack had fought once before – some playground scrap with barely a graze at the end of it. His da, glibly unaware of his own hypocrisy, clipped him round the ear and said no son of his would be a bully. And Jack's ma, his ma – how her face had fallen. The shame had flayed him.

Jack brought himself back. Into this dark room, down on the floor. Was the devil there with him? Canny in a corner or folded in the curtains, or something bolder – sitting louche on the bed with his legs crossed, tickled by it all. Was he the pain in Jack's fingers, the rising bile, the stink in his breath, the awful clotted pleas that came from Isaac's throat? Was he the strength in the hands that pressed there, the great big hands themselves, or the man they belonged to?

No, probably not.

'Jack – a word.' The grieve strode across the yard, his finger hooked and beckoning, not stopping to check if he was being followed. Jack sloped behind him, conscious of the bald stares of the gang clustered outside the chaumer. The men were ashen, Henry standing in last night's clothes with his teeth chattering. The grieve threw open the door to his cottar and barked at his wife and bairns to get out. They filed out into the daylight, the wife tutting and griping, hoisting her shawl round her shoulders in pointed resentment at being thrown out into the cold before the sun had even finished rising. Inside, the grieve gestured for Jack to sit. 'You'll need tae get packed sharpish, boy. Slora's spitting feathers.'

'You know it wisnae me.'

'Was it nae.' The grieve's tone was flat, as if there was no question.

'No!' Jack held up his injured hand, the bandage wrapped round it separating his thumb and fingers. 'How could it have been, with this?'

The grieve loomed over him. His moustache was greasy and he smelled ripe with booze and catastrophe. 'Look, loon – it's your word against Mr Calder's.'

'Then ask Isaac who it was.'

The grieve barked a laugh. 'Aye, we'll do that if he wakes up.'

Words deserted Jack. He replayed Isaac's noises in his mind – a curdled wail that didn't sound like it could come from a man. It had turned his stomach then, still did the morning after with the sick taste of whisky repeating on his tongue. Jack knew he'd thrown a few punches himself, caught up in his own flashing rage, but that was it. That was it.

'Listen,' said the grieve, 'even if I stood up for you, who do you think Slora would believe? You sing your filthy songs and you scurry around his daughter and you think you're untouchable.'

Jack swallowed this – it was fair.

'Besides, the orra-loon said it was you.'

'He wisnae there!'

'Saw your hand round the boy's throat, he said.'

'As I said – he wisnae there.' And he hadn't been – Jack and Calder had been alone with the limp body, a thumbprint on its neck, until the door flew open and Henry came in. The loon had dropped to his knees, pressed himself to Isaac's chest, and wept. And perhaps now, if Jack had not been freezing and knackered and still half drunk, he'd have been angry. But betrayal seemed a double-sided thing – let you be furious if you wanted it, but left space to be the victim too. His da, trudging home with the damp of the Firth settling on his face, home to his wife and his eldest boy who looked nothing like him. Again Jack thought to defend himself, but suddenly it seemed easier to submit – to keep his mouth shut and take it.

The grieve shrugged – uninterested, in any case, in the truth. 'Aye, well. We all know what you are.'

'What am I?' asked Jack. In that moment, he hardly knew it himself.

'Eh?'

'You said just then you know what I am.'

The grieve smirked; he would enjoy this. 'You're an arrogant wee bastard, Jack.'

'But I'm nae a liar.'

'Right, and you expect me tae speak in your defence, do you? What's in it for me?'

Jack had no answer to that – nothing to offer in this world where you were only worth what someone else could gain from you. 'Have you spoken to Mr Calder about it? About what happened?'

'Aye.' The grieve reached into the pocket of his jacket and pulled out an envelope, slapped it on the table. 'He says to take this, take the blame, and keep your mouth shut.'

Jack picked up the envelope. The grieve watched as he

struggled, holding it down with his injured hand and easing the seal open with an index finger. Inside was a wad of notes.

'Now,' said the grieve, 'take that and go far, far away from here.'

Jack tossed it back on the table. 'Buying a scapegoat, is he?'

The grieve pushed the envelope back. 'More than that, loon – he's buying silence. Because if you mention this tae anyone, here or anywhere, he'll find you. He'll find your ma and all.' The grieve crouched down so his face was inches from Jack's. 'Now, you can have my advice for free, I'm good like that. You dinnae exist any more, Jack Nicol. Take a new name and run far enough away that Thomas Slora will never hear what it is.' The grieve pressed the envelope into Jack's hand and he opened it again, looked inside. Forty or fifty notes – more money than he'd ever seen. He wanted it. A pocketful of hard cash to bolster a feeble inventory: his ma's hagstone, the Horseman's Word. With that money he could go anywhere he liked – go wandering, drink good whisky, be someone else. He could get his ma and his wee brother Charlie away from the man he had to call his da.

In the chaumer, Jack threw his things into his kist. There was no time to fold his clothes, beat the mud from his spare pair of boots. Donald and Tam sat on their beds, watching. When Jack had packed, they got up and gave him a slap on the back. He felt they ought to have defended him, but then, they were not there. Would probably have kept their mouths closed even if they had been – he was just a horseman. There'd be another one along soon enough.

Jack dragged his kist out into the yard. It bumped over the ruts, the churned mud frozen to craggy hillscapes. The sky was grey, the suggestion of sun under cloud as if the thing couldn't move itself to come out and shine. And it was freezing, though Henry was out in just his shirtsleeves, a browning smear of blood on his cotton chest. Jack thought to go to him – thought to press his forehead to his friend's, tell him he'd see him in some other life. Tell him: good luck getting to first, getting your farmer's daughter. But the look Henry gave him made him stop cold – and Jack saw, too late, what he had exchanged for the grieve's deal.

LIZZIE

Lizzie spent her days in the snug, cheek resting on the velvety brocade of the chaise. She knew this made her desperate, lying for hours imagining she could still pick out the smell of James's cologne. Bridget would come in from time to time and push her hair back from her face, pat her hand. 'Come on,' she'd say, 'there's no good will come fae your moping.' But moping suited her – the drama of it, wearing her humiliation like a garment.

One afternoon Lizzie heard men's voices in the hall and she scrabbled upright and smoothed her skirt in case it was James come to apologize, to tell her he had changed his mind. It was a well-constructed fantasy – he would be breathless and aghast, would drop to his knees before her. He would take her hands in his and kiss them, over and over. But the snug door opened and it was only her father.

'Ah, Lizzie – away upstairs.'

She got up, avoiding George's eye as she crossed the room. Out in the hall, they had a guest. Hugh Calder seemed to appraise her for a moment, showing more interest than he ever had before. He had always been indifferent, lacking the charm to try to talk to a young lady or prise laughter from her. Men like Webster treated it as a game, jubilant in declaring, *Ah, I've got her smiling!* Mr Calder was still in his coat and gloves, two stiff leather hands holding his hat in front of him. 'Miss Brodie.' He gave an approximation of a smile.

'Mr Calder.' Lizzie nodded at him and moved off, conscious of his gaze before he stepped into the snug and closed the door behind him.

Lizzie loitered before tiptoeing back. An ear pressed to the door – the creak of armchairs, the languid groan of a man taking his ease.

'It's a pleasure to see you, Hugh. It's been some time.'

'Must have been not long before we took over the Richmond.'

'Going well?'

'Aye, very well. I've let Jane take it on.'

'Oh?' George's voice rose a little, curious. 'And she has proven herself?'

'I've no concerns yet, other than appeasing my son. William's furious, but it's his own doing. He nearly put the window of my study through when I told him. I dread to think what he'll do when I tell him I'm turfing him out to Blackwater – can't imagine he'll take kindly to that.'

'Is that your country place?'

'Something like that. It's out in the back of beyond and we've got inns and suchlike close by. I don't bother visiting much, but they could probably do with someone to take a bit of care over them – money to be made, hopefully. And there's less chance of trouble out there, or at least of trouble making its way back to me. He's a bloody liability.'

'Well, if it comforts you, whatever he's . . . done hasn't reached my ears yet. I don't think it could have got out too widely.' There was a silence, George's invitation unanswered. 'I don't want to pry, but . . .'

'A nonsense, too much drink. But it royally cocked up our latest purchase. We had nearly signed for another farm near Nairn, but we've had to walk away with nothing.'

'I'm sorry, Hugh.'

'I just need to get him settled. Find a wife, that'd sort him – they can live the quiet life out in the arse-end of nowhere.'

There was a noise that made Lizzie start, but it was only another drink being poured, the affable touching of glasses. 'Troublesome bairns, eh?' said her father.

'Aye – I hear you've one as well?'

George sounded weary. 'Christ.'

'Sounds like she ought to find herself a husband too – I'm sure it would give her a great deal of satisfaction.' Hugh's voice was greasy with suggestion.

'Are you proposing something?'

'Och no, not me, this was all Jane's idea. She's a clever girl. Though I suspect it's for her own benefit – she'll be worried that William will come and interfere with the hotel, without the new farm to occupy him.' A moment, the men leaning in. 'Well, George, what do you say? Could be advantageous for us both – the meeting of two good families.'

Lizzie waited. She could imagine her father frowning as he did when considering the terms of a business transaction, assessing if it would benefit him.

'Will he have her?' George asked.

'He'll have no choice. You get your girl on side and I'll tell William. Jane's already made me pitch it as my idea to put him out in the Cabrach, so I'll take the blame for this too.'

A glass placed down on a table, something settled, the ordinary power of men on an ordinary day, the grandfather clock in the hall ticking blithely round. Lizzie had known she would be handed her comeuppance eventually – was gratified, at least, that she was not the only one to have done wrong. She wondered what lapse of judgement had threatened the Calder empire, brought about William's punishment. She knew too little of him to guess – only a few stark impressions, his shouts in the townhall foyer and his empty eyes, the large hands round a wrist.

'Hugh, hang on . . .'

'What is it?'

'He'll . . . he will look after her, aye?'

A pause. 'Aye, rest assured.' This with a robust sort of confidence, the final flourish to seal the deal.

November 1915

JOHNNY

Journeys – he is good at those. At going, not knowing where he might stop off along the way, then turning up somewhere new and getting the lie of the land. At carrying all his worldly goods on his back, few as they might be. Johnny had packed a knapsack already this morning, folding his clothes and setting them in, his few books. He didn't know what he might need – just himself, probably. Mysie had watched from the doorway with the cat in her arms, stroking an idle thumb over the creature's head and chastising Johnny for the scratches his kist had left on her floor. And then he'd shut that kist up with all the things he was leaving behind inside, and combed his hair, put on a clean shirt. He'd paused with his hand in the box of ribbons, considering which one to tie round his neck – emerald, indigo, russet. Black, white. Johnny had let them slip through his fingers and eventually taken out his hand – settled, instead, on nothing.

Rab had had everything ready when he arrived at Brawlands. Johnny had stopped some distance off to watch his friend in the yard, Rab toiling with his sleeves up under the low winter sun. As he approached, Johnny doffed his cap to Maggie and she waved at him, and that seemed like enough. Rab he clapped on the back. 'Thanks for sorting everything out, my man.'

Rab had nodded. 'Come up for a dram, will you? Before you go?'

Johnny had agreed, then muttered something about the strength of that same marmalade sun getting in his eyes, and he turned away so his friend wouldn't see the pathetic gratitude Johnny felt for his forgiveness. Henry was up in the top pasture, his familiar frame casting a long shadow over the ground. Johnny went and had a few words, in private, pressed himself brow to brow with the loon and told him he'd see him in some other life.

His final stop was the chaumer. Only Alex was there, and he clapped Johnny on the back and told him he'd decided, and his kist was packed and all. He was ready to fight.

'What about Jemima?' Johnny asked. 'Won't it be hard tae leave her?'

'Och, she'll be here when I get back. I'll miss her, though, and the – you know. We'd a good system set up.'

Johnny humoured him. 'Oh aye, what's that?'

'I'd go up tae Jock's farm and in tae the barn. If she'd managed tae sneak out she'd leave an auld piece of leather hanging on a hook under the hayloft. If it was there I'd go up and – you know. If nae, I'd go away again.' He drew back, pleased with himself. 'Foolproof.'

Now, Johnny leaves the farm with his head up. The burden he carries is unwieldy – an awkward shape to it, nothing to get purchase on. But it is lighter than he remembered, and he is almost surprised at how easily his muscles bear the load. He looks at the land as he walks; there's a freedom to turning his head with nothing catching at his neck, as if his range of motion has expanded and he can finally see clearly. He thinks maybe he'll give up the adornments for good, find another way to distinguish himself, even knowing as he does that reinvention rarely works. You can style yourself as something else and flit off to where folks don't know you, but something of the past always lingers. The reek of the midden, a stain you can't wash out.

When he reaches the kirk, Johnny idles down the track as he always does, reluctant to enclose himself between the headstones and the house of the Lord. Over at the manse, he half expects to see the dark figure of Reverend Bruce standing by a window, but they are all empty. It was a kindness, Johnny supposes, for the Reverend to agree to this.

Johnny goes over to the corner of the kirkyard where he's been told everything has been made ready. The hole in the ground seems small, insufficient, though he finds when he sets his burden down next to it that it will fit quite easily. The shovel is waiting for him and he picks it up, tests his grip on the handle, the line of his scar facing up towards him. He is about to start when he hears the gate. Lizzie, wrapped in her coat and wearing William Calder's rubber boots. Her expression is sombre and she does not wave to Johnny, only comes to his side and asks, 'Will we start?'

'She's nae heavy. How about I go down and you pass her to me?'

Lizzie agrees and Johnny pitches himself over the side of the grave. The sky is a patch of limpid blue above him, but in the ground it smells damp and metallic and alive, and there is something good in that. Above him, Lizzie picks up the bundle, bracing just as Johnny did, in the expectation of a great weight, but the crease flattens from her brow and she kneels, passes it easily to him. And Johnny takes the bog woman and lays her back in the ground.

'Come on, come down.' He reaches a hand to help Lizzie but she doesn't take it, just swings her legs over and drops gently into the grave. There is space enough for both of them on either side of the woman. Rab had offered to make a new box, something sturdier, but Johnny likes the idea of letting the soil come to meet her limbs, and how she might then join the land, flow out through the burns and out to sea. He looks at Lizzie. 'Do you want tae see her?'

'No. I think it's best we just let her be.'

They stand a moment more, then Johnny digs in his pocket and takes out a small black stone, feels for a moment the weight of it in his palm. He crouches and sets his ma's hagstone on top of the shroud. It works, he thinks, as protection – look at what happened to his ma when she relinquished it to her eldest son.

Johnny clambers out, mud sticking to his knees. He reaches a hand again to Lizzie, but again she will not take it, and he finds it is all right – a certain grace in offering something and accepting when it is refused.

There is only one shovel. Lizzie insists on helping and so Johnny lets her have it, uses his hands instead to take fistfuls of cool earth and cover the bog woman over. It is labour like that at the hairst – the bend and ache, the sense of having so far to go, but Johnny doesn't mind. He glances at Lizzie from time to time – the wilful expression on her, how absurd she looks in those boots. And then he averts his eyes and they pour over the last bit of soil. Johnny wipes his blackened hands on his breeks. 'Right, then.'

'Thank you – for inviting me.'

'I wisnae sure you'd come,' Johnny says, and leaves it at that.

They leave the kirkyard and head down the track, and it is not really the right direction for Johnny but he goes anyway, will stay quiet and carry on for as long as she'll let him accompany her. They walk until the kirk is a shadow in the valley behind them, the grave a dark speck like a mole on an arm. 'Did you decide who she was, then?' Johnny asks.

A dozen paces more before Lizzie replies. 'Sometimes I thought I knew, but then I'd change my mind. I could never quite tell if she was the sinner or the sinned against.'

'Maybe she was both.'

'Aye, maybe. I think I've made my peace with it now – there

are things you have to know for sure and others that remain mysteries, and maybe that's all right.' Lizzie's tone doesn't invite further speculation so Johnny remains silent, grateful in simple terms to walk beside her, and for the beauty of the morning. The sun is bright and new, casts a liquid light over the land, the loveliness of frost melting to clear water. It is like this, though, when you're about to leave a place.

Eventually, Blackwater is in front of them. They stop at the point where the road joins the track, Johnny squinting through the sunlight. 'I'll probably nae see you again for a while,' he says.

'Oh? Why's that?'

Johnny looks down, scuffs the track with his toe. 'I'm joining up.'

Lizzie cocks her head at him as though she doesn't understand. 'You don't have to do that.'

'No, but I'll be called up soon enough.'

'Ah, and you want it to have been your own decision?'

She knows him – more than anyone, she knows him. How he'd sooner march off with honour than be dragged, that old sin of pride coming in useful after all. Only pride that was enough to smother the reason he'd never wanted to go to war – because he'd come close enough to a wrecked young man that he never wanted to see another.

It is hard for John Nicol to meet Lizzie's eye. The way she looks at him, and here, in the wavering sunlight, doesn't look away. 'I know who you are,' she says.

At first it alarms him – this thing Johnny has always been frightened of, in case, without his stories and songs, embellishments, appeasements, he is uncovered and found wanting. But it is only with gentleness that she looks at him. 'I didn't know what to do after Henry told me. I knew deep down that it couldn't be true, but then . . . I have been deceived before, only seeing what I wanted to see. But I've worked it all out, I think.' Lizzie takes a step nearer to him, closes a hand round Johnny's wrist. 'Why didn't you tell me the truth? You didn't even try to defend yourself.'

'I was told never tae speak of it, so I didnae. Tried nae tae think of it either. It's like, there are some stories you can never find the words tae tell.'

'But didn't you think you deserved to?' Lizzie is frowning slightly, a look of such deep care that Johnny's lungs seem to crumple inside him. It hurts, as the tears come, and Lizzie pulls him into her, his face at her neck. She cradles his head in her arms and it is like when spring comes, and the sun deigns to rise again, when you have forgotten what it feels like to be warm. Where has softness been, these years?

They are cheek to cheek. Johnny presses into her hair, and its smell of all things: soap, earth, whisky. Her mouth is at his ear and she moves her lips to whisper. 'You'll stay awhile longer, won't you?'

If he pulls back to look at her, some enchantment might be broken – she might slip into the ground, a pile of ash and peat, a dream. Johnny would part oceans he has never seen, dance a jig on the crest of a wave, to have it all be true. He opens his eyes. And she is still here, on this road, cosseted by curving hills, a faint sigh in the wind that seems to urge them forward. Lizzie takes his hand first – not that it matters – and begins to lead him in the direction of home. And this, Johnny thinks, is romance. This is what I have wanted to sing of.

THE END

ACKNOWLEDGEMENTS

Putting a book out into the world involves being indebted, in the best possible way, to so many people – I will attempt to thank them all here.

Thank you to my agent, Daisy Parente, for having such faith in this novel (and by extension, me) and always being a voice of wisdom. To my editor, Kirsty Dunseath, for so sensitively drawing out the book's potential without denying me my freedom with it – I have learned so much from your advice. I am immensely grateful to the whole team at Doubleday and Transworld for their vision and expertise – Sara Roberts, Izzie Ghaffari-Parker, Beci Kelly, Vivien Thompson, Barbara Thompson, Georgie Bewes and everyone else who has been involved behind the scenes.

I have been incredibly fortunate, amongst the solitary days of writing, to have met and befriended so many talented and perceptive writers. Thank you to all those from my CBC class, the MM mentorship and the 2025 debuts group for their advice, celebrations and encouragement – I wonder how many books have got over the line thanks to a writers' group chat. I am especially grateful to Harry Godfrey for his generous feedback on an earlier draft, and to Joe Gardiner for the walks and thoughtful conversations. A very large thanks is due to Amy Twigg (and

Steve), whose support has been constant – your friendship is a happy consequence of my ever deciding to write this book.

Writing a novel set in the past necessitates a fair amount of research, and learning about early-twentieth-century farming was made fascinating by the accounts of writers who not only captured so sensitively the hardships of the time but also, vitally, the joy and fellowship (and Aberdonian humour). Particular to this was the work of David Kerr Cameron, which informed a huge amount of my writing.

Thank you to all my colleagues at the day job for the camaraderie and friendship, especially Sarah (peas) for granting me the flexibility to write. Thank you to Jack for all the writing chat and for being the most energetic hype man. To my dear friends – Padraic, Mike, Abi, Jacob, Bertie, Heather, Tanya, Pierrick, Kay – you're all wonderful. Thank you to Hayley for always listening – it means more than you know.

I am blessed to have had the support of my family throughout the writing of this novel. I couldn't have done it (or much of anything I've achieved in my life) without my mum, whose love and care is unwavering, and my dad, who would have been prouder than anyone. Thank you to Andrew and Jenni and the boys, and all the Rowes. Finally, and most expansively, thank you to Ben for very kindly telling me to get on with it, for your pragmatism, and for everything, really. You make nothing seem insurmountable.

Gabrielle Griffiths grew up in Aberdeenshire and now lives in Brighton. She was a Madeleine Milburn Agency mentee in 2021 and is a graduate of the Curtis Brown creative writing course. Her short fiction has been shortlisted for the Bridport Prize.